A MEMORY
BETWEEN US

Also by Sarah Sundin

WINGS OF GLORY SERIES

A Distant Melody

WINGS *of* GLORY
BOOK TWO

A MEMORY BETWEEN US

A Novel

SARAH SUNDIN

Revell

a division of Baker Publishing Group
Grand Rapids, Michigan

© 2010 by Sarah Sundin

Published by Revell
a division of Baker Publishing Group
P.O. Box 6287, Grand Rapids, MI 49516-6287
www.revellbooks.com

Printed in the United States of America

Library of Congress Cataloging-in-Publication Data
Sundin, Sarah.
    A memory between us : a novel / Sarah Sundin.
        p. cm. — (Wings of glory ; bk. 2)
    ISBN 978-0-8007-3422-0 (pbk.)
    1. World War, 1939–1945—Aerial operations, American—Fiction. 2. Air pilots, Military—Fiction. 3. Americans—Great Britain—Fiction. 4. B–17 bomber—Fiction. I. Title.
PS3619.U5626M46 2010
813'.6—dc22   2010012836

Published in association with the literary agency Books & Such, 52 Mission Circle #122 PMB 170, Santa Rosa, California 95409.

10   11   12   13   14   15   16   7   6   5   4   3   2   1

In loving memory of Roderick M. Stewart, my great-uncle, who served in the squadron of B-17s flying into Pearl Harbor during the attack, commanded a squadron with the 94th Bombardment Group, and piloted a Flying Fortress under the Golden Gate Bridge.

1

2nd Evacuation Hospital; Diddington, Huntingdonshire, England

March 3, 1943

Lt. Penelope Ruth Doherty braced open the window and drank in cool air to settle her stomach. "There, gentlemen. Isn't it nice to have fresh air in here?"

In the bed next to the window, Lieutenant Lumley snorted. "Ma'am, I'm from Arizona. To me, this soggy English air is more lethal than Nazi bullets."

Ruth smiled at her patient, who had broken an ankle when his P-38 Lightning crashed on landing. "Good air circulation is important for wound healing." And for clearing the nauseating smell of breakfast sausage from the tin can of a ward.

"Say, Red, you know what would heal my wounds?" The new patient, Lieutenant Holmes, pointed to his lips and dropped Ruth a wink.

Ruth gave him a sweet smile. "You'd like another dose of castor oil?"

"And it's Lieutenant Doherty to you." Ruth's medic, Technical Sergeant Giovanni, set his supply tray next to Lieutenant

Holmes's bed. "Now, time to swab your wounds." A German shell had filled the navigator's back with shrapnel.

"Besides, her hair is more auburn than red." Lieutenant Lumley's gaze had a softer cast than usual. Thank goodness, he was due to be discharged.

"I'll be back with the morning meds." Ruth passed one of the potbellied coal stoves in the aisle.

"Ouch!" Lieutenant Holmes cried out.

"Whatza matter? Does it sting the widdle baby?" Sergeant Giovanni's voice oozed fake sympathy.

"Better not be iodine. Makes my throat swell up something fierce."

Ruth's feet stopped along with her heart, and she slowly turned to her medic. Sergeant Giovanni's burly face stretched long in horror. Of course he was using iodine.

Anaphylaxis. She needed to act quickly without alerting her patient, keep a level head, and control her emotions as she had been trained. Panic would make his condition worse.

She returned to Lieutenant Holmes's bed and put on her cheeriest smile and voice. "What would feel good on those wounds would be a nice rinse with cool water. Sergeant, would you please fetch Dr. Sinclair? I'd like to discuss Lieutenant Lumley's discharge with him." She locked her gaze on her medic. "Now," she mouthed.

"Sure thing, boss." The sergeant strode for the door.

Ruth grabbed towels from the drawer in the bedside table and braced them on either side of her patient's torso, and then gently poured water over the brown stains and dabbed them with another towel. Too late, but she wanted to reduce the amount of iodine in the poor man's system. "Now, doesn't that feel nice?"

"I'd rather have a kiss."

"And I'd rather have a million dollars, but neither is going to happen."

"I don't know about that. I can feel that kiss already. My lips are all tingly."

Ruth's hand tightened on the towel. He was going into anaphylaxis, but where was Dr. Sinclair? Only he could give the adrenaline needed to save this man's life. "Excuse me. I'll be right back."

At a fast clip, Ruth went to the medication room, where Lt. Harriet Marshall was completing her narcotic count from the end of her night shift. "Excuse me. I need to get some adrenaline and morphine. Lieutenant Holmes is going into anaphylaxis."

Harriet's elfin face blanched. "Oh no. Thank goodness Dr. Sinclair is on the ward."

"Not yet." Ruth grabbed a tray and put two sterilized syringes on top.

"So—so why are you already getting the meds?"

"I want to be ready when he comes. I can't waste any time." One vial of adrenaline.

"But he hasn't ordered them yet."

Ruth leveled a look at the girl. "I know the treatment for anaphylaxis."

"That—that's presumptuous of you. You'll make the doctor angry."

Ruth pulled a vial of morphine. "I don't care about the doctor's feelings; I care about my patient's life." She ignored Harriet's gasp and returned to Lieutenant Holmes's bedside.

He stared up at her with wild eyes. "My throat—it itches, it's swelling up. Was that iodine?"

"Yes, sir, it was, but Dr. Sinclair is on his way." She gave him her most soothing smile. "Now, let's get you in a more comfortable position." Ruth patted his back dry and helped him roll over.

Lieutenant Holmes clawed at his throat. "I can't—I can't breathe." Red hives dotted his fair skin.

"Sure, you can breathe. Stay very calm. Very calm, and think about something else. Where are you from, Lieutenant?"

"New—Hampshire." His chest heaved out the words.

Ruth filled a syringe with adrenaline. "So you're used to this cold weather, unlike Arizona over there. Me too. I'm from Chicago. In fact, this must feel warm and balmy to you."

The patient's only response was a series of raspy, labored breaths. Where on earth was that doctor? "Lord, help me," she whispered.

Ruth pulled up a dose of morphine and chattered about the way the snow filled the streets of her slum and made them look clean for a change, until the thaw made them look worse than ever. But as Lieutenant Holmes gasped for air, all she could see were Pa's last breaths as the blood clot settled in his lungs and Ma's wheezes as she wasted away with pneumonia.

As a nursing student, she couldn't help her parents, and now as a nurse, she couldn't help this young man. She glanced at the clock on the wall. If Dr. Sinclair didn't come in the next sixty seconds, she'd give the adrenaline herself.

And lose her position? As the oldest of seven, she had a responsibility to her brothers and sisters. How could they get by without her support?

Images of those beloved faces swam before her—her purpose, her joy. Why did it always have to be this way? Why did she have to choose between doing the right thing and protecting her family?

Dr. Sinclair burst through the door, his white lab coat flying, and Ruth let out a deep sigh.

"Lieutenant Doherty, get me some adrenaline."

"Right here, sir." She handed him the syringe.

He stared at it. "Three two-hundredths of a grain?"

"Yes, sir."

His jaw jutted forward, but he administered the dose and followed it with morphine.

Within the course of an hour, they had stabilized Lieutenant Holmes. Ruth cleansed his wounds, replaced his dressings, and changed the wet bedding. Then she took the empty syringes and vials back to the medication room, where she dropped the syringes into a pan filled with blue green bichloride of mercury solution.

"I suppose I should be mad at you." Dr. Sinclair leaned his tall frame against the open door.

Ruth shook the pan until the syringes were submerged. "My job is to care for the patient."

"And to anticipate my needs. I'm flattered."

"Don't be. I know proper treatment."

"You should have been a physician."

Ruth shook her head. If he only knew what she had to do to scrape up money for nursing school. "Too smart for that."

His chuckles drew nearer, and Ruth stiffened. She didn't feel like fending off another pass from this man.

"I know this great restaurant—"

Ruth turned and glared at him. "How would your wife feel if she heard you talk like this?"

Dr. Sinclair lifted one salt-and-pepper eyebrow. "Come on, Ruth. There's a war on. All the rules have changed. Besides, you talk one way, but I see it in your eyes. You're just like me."

Ruth clamped her teeth together. "No, sir. I'm not."

"Heart of iron." He thumped his fist on his chest. "You have one too."

She stared into his chilly blue eyes, and the cold seeped down to her toes. How did he get so close to the truth? Long ago she'd clamped an iron shell around her heart and nothing and no one could pry it loose, but deep inside, the tender flesh still beat.

"Come on, Ruth." His gaze settled on her mouth. "Just one kiss. I can't resist those lips one day longer. You must be a great kisser."

Her insides shrank into a squirming mass. She had listened to Eddie Reynolds when he told her she was the best kisser in the whole eighth grade, with that great boyish grin and that sheet of brown hair flopping over one eye, but she would not listen to this poor excuse for a physician.

Dr. Sinclair put his hand on her waist.

Ruth's lungs collapsed under the weight of memories. She slapped away his arm. "Don't touch me. Don't ever touch me."

"Oh, come on—"

Ruth shouldered past him and out onto the ward. Her breath returned in little bursts, and white sparkles appeared before her eyes. She made her way down the long semicylinder of the ward. "Sergeant Giovanni, I need—I need a short break. I'll be right back."

"Good time to do it while the doc's here."

Ruth grabbed her blue cape from the hook by the front door and stepped outside. After she swung her cape around her shoulders, she braced her hands on her knees and forced slow, even breaths.

She couldn't work with Dr. Sinclair, but what could she do? Should she talk to the chief nurse? Would it do any good?

Ruth straightened up. Her vision was clear and so was her course of action. A discreet talk with the chief and a transfer to another ward. She just needed to get away.

She marched down the muddy road flanked by the corrugated tin Nissen huts that served as wards and into the administration building. Lt. Vera Benson's door stood open, and Ruth stepped inside.

The chief nurse held a phone to her ear. Ruth backed up to exit, but Lieutenant Benson motioned for her to sit down.

"I'm so sorry, Agnes. Already? Three nurses PWOP?" She arched a strawberry blonde eyebrow at Ruth.

Pregnant Without Permission—the easiest way for a nurse to be relieved from her commitment to the military.

"Yes, that does create a problem. I'll see what I can do. We don't have our full contingent of nurses here either, but I'll talk to the girls."

Lieutenant Benson hung up the phone. "Now, how can I help you, Lieutenant Doherty?"

"Was that another hos—I'm sorry. It's none of my business."

Lieutenant Benson tilted her head and smiled. "I invited you to eavesdrop, and yes, it's our business. The 12th Evac is setting up in Suffolk. Horribly short-staffed. Even more so than we are."

"I'll transfer, ma'am."

The chief tilted her head in the other direction. "Excuse me?"

A smile floated up Ruth's face. How often did a solution come so quickly, so neatly? If she didn't know better, she'd think God was on her side. "Please, ma'am. A transfer is just what I need."

2

Thurleigh Army Air Field, Bedfordshire

May 13, 1943

Maj. Jack Novak whipped his gaze like a lasso around his nine crewmembers to grab them, unite them, and jolt them with enthusiasm and confidence.

Beside him, his B-17 Flying Fortress waited in the early afternoon sun, a streamlined beauty bristling with machine guns. Jack knew Forts and he knew men, and under his guidance, this Fort and these men could handle anything the Nazis threw at them today on their first combat mission.

"Okay, boys," he said. "You heard what Colonel Moore said in briefing. Yesterday—just yesterday—the last German and Italian troops in North Africa surrendered to the Allies."

His crew whooped and cheered.

"My dad always said never hit a man when he's down, but in Hitler's case, I'll make an exception. Agreed?"

"Agreed!"

"Now let's drive them from Europe. Today we'll bomb just one airfield, but it's Hitler's airfield, where he sends up fighters to harass our planes and ships. Are we going to let him do that?"

"No!"

"Dead right, we're not." Jack's grin swept upward. "He's in for a surprise. Today we double the strength of the U.S. Eighth Air Force."

"Four new bomb groups, but we're the best." Lt. Bill Chambers looked as if he belonged on a rocking horse, not in the copilot's seat of a massive four-engined bomber. At least he'd stopped twisting his fingers together as he had during briefing. Maybe the kid could handle combat after all.

"Okay, boys, let's show what the 94th Bomb Group can do." The crew filed through the door in the waist section of the B-17. Jack clapped each man on the back—his radio operator and his flight engineer, his navigator and his copilot, two gunners to man the waist, one for the tail, and one for the ball turret bulging beneath the fuselage.

Last came his bombardier, Capt. Charlie de Groot, who pulled his flight helmet over a shock of yellow hair. "What'll it be, Skipper? 'Praise the Lord and Pass the Ammunition' or 'The Army Air Corps'?"

The first song memorialized Pearl Harbor. On December 6, 1941, Jack and Charlie had left Hamilton Field near San Francisco in a squadron of twelve Forts—at peace, unarmed. They arrived in Hawaii, surprised by war, by the zipping little Zeros with red meatballs on their wings, by Japanese bullets and American shells flashing past them. Jack could still see the roiling black smoke columns and flaming oil against tropical blues and greens, and still feel the confusion, helplessness, and rage.

Jack and Charlie had flown many missions in the Pacific, but now they were in England. Jack winked at his best friend. "'Nothing'll stop the Army Air Corps.'"

"Aye, aye, Skipper." Charlie took a drag on his cigarette and stepped up into the plane. "'Off we go into the wild blue yonder,'" he sang, his bass incongruous with his round baby face.

Jack sauntered down to the nose of the plane. He tugged the yellow Mae West life preserver into a more comfortable position under his parachute harness and reassured himself it was there. Yellow lettering on the nose of the olive drab plane read *Sunrise Serenade*, a great song and a fitting name for a daylight bomber.

He set hands on hips and surveyed the airfield, the coordinated rush of men and trucks, the smell of aviation fuel and nervous excitement—boy, was it swell. At Thurleigh Army Air Field, two squadrons from the 94th had been training with the veteran 306th Bomb Group, while the other two squadrons took lessons from the 91st Bomb Group at Bassingbourn. The 306th was Jack's younger brother, Walt's, group.

Former group.

"Poor kid." Jack couldn't wait to get back in combat and take a few shots at the Nazis who had put Walt in an Oxford hospital with his right arm amputated.

Jack scanned the thirty-six planes parked around the perimeter track, which circled three intersecting runways. As squadron commander, he was responsible for morale, and today it was pitch perfect. If his men performed as well in combat as they did in training, he'd be the next group executive officer. He couldn't wait. He thrived on command— the electric charge of getting the best out of both man and machine.

Jack reached his hands up into the nose hatch. With a jump and tuck, he launched himself inside. Most fellows used the door, but Jack preferred the challenge of the athletic maneuver.

He leaned forward into the nose compartment, where Charlie adjusted his Norden bombsight, and the navigator, Norman Findlay, fussed over his maps. Norman, not Norm.

Then Jack crawled back through the narrow passage that led up to the cockpit.

He forgot to pray. Jack paused on hands and knees. He was his father's namesake, his father's image, except Dad wouldn't forget to pray. Neither would Walt, and Walt was the only Novak man who wasn't a pastor. His older brother, Ray, probably prayed whole psalms from memory, translated them into Hebrew for fun, Greek and Latin if he was bored.

But Jack—fine pastor he was. He closed his eyes. *Lord, please direct this mission. Guide these bombs straight to the target. Please keep us safe and get all 169 planes back intact.* He opened one eye and glanced at his watch. Time to report to his station. *In Jesus's name, amen.*

✯

"This is a milk run." Bill Chambers's brown eyes glowed over the rim of his oxygen mask.

Jack smiled at his copilot. The kid had already picked up air base slang. "Ain't over yet, buddy."

But he had to admit it had the makings of the milkiest of runs—perfect weather, only thirty miles over enemy territory, no antiaircraft fire, and no sign of the Luftwaffe. Charlie had done a masterful job bombing the Longuenesse Airfield at St. Omer in Nazi-occupied France. The rest of the squadron made the rookie mistake of bombing short. Once at home, Jack would review procedures.

Technical Sergeant Harv Owens, the flight engineer, leaned over the back of Bill's chair. "Hey, Billy-boy. Novak ever tell you what happened to his last three copilots?"

"Harv . . ." Jack warned.

"Shot dead right in front of his eyes. All three of 'em. This is the jinx seat, I tell you."

Jack groaned. High morale was vital, not just for peace of mind but for teamwork, efficiency, and success. "Back in your turret, Harv."

The engineer grumbled, stepped onto the gun turret platform in the back of the cockpit, and stuck his head into the Plexiglas bubble in the top of the plane.

"Is—is that true?" Freckles stood out stark on Bill's ashen forehead.

Jack gave the instruments a quick check and set his hand on the boy's shoulder. "I'm not superstitious, and you shouldn't be either. If you have to be, remember bad things happen in threes."

"So I'm in the clear?"

No one was in the clear, but Jack patted Bill's chair. "Want to trade seats?"

"No, sir."

Jack smiled and looked out each window to keep the eight other B-17s in his squadron in sight. The coastline wiggled in front of him. Soon he'd exchange dangers, from flak and fighters to something worse—the English Channel. "The Army Air Corps Song" played in his head—"If you'd live to be a grey-haired wonder, keep your nose out of the blue." Jack kept his eyes off the blue as well.

An antiaircraft shell exploded in a black puff about a thousand feet above them.

"Oh no. Flak," Bill said.

"Inaccurate and meager—best kind."

Harv spun his turret with its twin .50 caliber machine guns. "Hey, Adolf, you call that shooting? Send some of your boys up here, I'll show you some shooting."

"Can the chatter," Jack said. "Keep the interphone free."

Twin black trails of smoke streamed up about fifty yards in front of him. Jack held his breath and urged the shell higher. Worst thing about flak—you couldn't fight back.

Flurry of noise, smoke, flame. He snapped his head to the left. Glass cracked. The nose dipped. Jack pulled the control wheel back until the flight indicator was level, then eyed the gauges for all four engines—looked good. Frigid air whistled through the right overhead window, now an open mouth with glistening clear teeth.

Jack jiggled shards of Plexiglas off his lap. "There, Bill, that wasn't so bad, was—" The words floated in his mouth and turned to bile.

Bill stared at him, eyes wide, glassy, unblinking. A jagged chunk of shrapnel jutted from his right temple. Jack's chest sank. *Dear Lord, not again. Poor kid. He thought he was safe.*

Bill's body slumped onto the control wheel and sent *Sunrise* into a dive.

Jack planted his feet, yanked on the controls. Futile. He had to get Bill's weight off the wheel.

He tore off his seat belt, scooted over, and pushed Bill against the seat. With his back firm against Bill's body, he put all his weight into the control wheel. "Harv," he called, his headset cord and oxygen hose stretched to maximum length. "Get Bill back to the waist section. And Charlie? You won't believe this."

"Coming, Skipper." Even through the interphone's scratchiness, Charlie's voice sounded heavy. Jack sympathized, but mourning had to wait for later.

Jack struggled with the wheel. He had to pull *Sunrise* up. The coastline was sneaking under the Fort's nose, and only 28 percent of airmen survived a dunking in the Channel. Jack wasn't going into the drink. Not today, not ever.

"Harv!" Where was that man?

Harv hunched over, oxygen mask to the side, and wiped his mouth with the back of his hand. How come the biggest, toughest-talking guys were the first to lose their lunch at the sight of blood?

Jack's ears rang, exploded. His body arched and pitched forward, as if someone had whacked his backside with a giant paddle.

He pushed himself off the instrument panel. The sting in his rear end changed to warmth, to heat, to scorching daggers. Jack groaned and sagged backward.

Someone grabbed him from behind. "You're hit, Novak." Harv's voice cracked.

"Figured as much." Jack got his balance and rolled back over the copilot's seat. His left leg drooped, his foot wet and warm. A scream escaped his guard, but he had no time for pain. He had a plane to fly, a squadron to lead. He hefted up his arms and forced rubbery fingers to coil around the wheel. "Bombardier? Still with us?"

"Shook up," Charlie said on the interphone. "No time to show off with loop-de-loops, Jack."

"Come 'ere." His tongue and brain felt thick, but he could do this. His kid brother, Walt, had landed a Fort with his right arm almost severed.

Jack clamped his mouth against the screams and blinked hard at the controls. Number two engine was losing manifold pressure, oil pressure—he needed to shut it down and feather the propellers, rotate them parallel to the slipstream to decrease drag. First he had to level the plane, but pain shook his body, his arms, the wheel.

Charlie crawled up into the cockpit. He wasn't great with the controls, but he'd managed as copilot three times before. Charlie looked at Jack and Bill, flashed alarm, and quenched it. He scrambled into the pilot's seat, plugged in his headphone, and grabbed the wheel. "We're at eight thousand feet, Skipper. What do you want to do?"

"Keep her there." Jack fumbled with his mask. "Okay, men, we're below ten thousand. You can go off . . ." What was it called? The stuff you breathed?

"Go off oxygen, men," Charlie said. "Norman, why don't you come up here?"

Oxygen. That was it. "Eight thousand. Gotta turn on the carburetor air filters." How come he could remember "carburetor air filters" but not "oxygen"? He reached for the switch on the panel to his right, but his hand wouldn't go in that direction.

"Harv," Charlie said. "You and Norman get the skipper some first aid."

"No." Jack shook his head. The controls blurred before him. "I can—I can do this." But his voice climbed, and his vision darkened.

"We'll get you some morphine, bandage you up, then you can come back and fly."

"As long as—as long as I can come . . ." His lips tingled. His body drooped back.

★

Pressure on his backside—red hot, ripping, digging. He lifted his head and cried out. Worse than Dad's spankings or Grandpa's whippings, and he'd had plenty.

"Sorry, Novak. Got to stop the bleeding." Joe Rosetti's Brooklyn accent.

Rosetti? The radio operator? Jack opened his eyes. He lay on his stomach in the radio room, the icy aluminum floor under his cheek. How had he gotten back there? He must have passed out.

That left Charlie at the controls. And Norman? Oh no.

How much flight training had Norman completed? "Engine two. Rosetti, they've got to feather engine two. Tell them."

"Radio to pilot. Novak wants you to feather engine two. Okay, I'll tell him." Rosetti kneeled beside Jack. "Already done."

Jack's breath came rapid and shallow, and he tasted sweat on his lips. "How's she look?"

"Not good. Engine one is losing oil. Charlie says we may have to ditch in the Channel."

"No!" Jack pushed himself up, screamed at the pain, and collapsed on his face. "Tell Charlie no. Don't ditch. That's an order."

Rosetti relayed the information. A long pause. "Understood."

No, Charlie didn't understand. How could he? Jack had never told him the story. Never would.

Jack's eyes closed, and he slipped under the waves, cold and gray and impersonal.

Fourteen years old. Just wanted to impress the girls, with their fresh young curves stretching their bathing suits in enticing new shapes. He could swim across the San Joaquin River. Sure he could. Couldn't be more than half a mile.

Nothing could stop Jack Novak when he put his mind to it.

Nothing but the current flowing from Stockton. Nothing but the tide sucking him toward San Francisco Bay. Nothing but the cold Sierra melt-off draining his strength.

He drifted past downtown Antioch, his shouts for help lost among noise from the shipyard, the canneries, and the paper plant.

Jack slipped under the waves, cold and gray and impersonal.

Don't ditch, Charlie. Whatever you do, don't ditch.

3

12th Evacuation Hospital, Botesdale, Suffolk

May 14, 1943

Ruth scraped mud from her shoes, entered Ward Seven, and hung up her cape. Whoever picked white for nurses' shoes while serving in England needed a psychiatric discharge.

The night nurse, Lt. Florence Oswald, sat at the nurses' station. "Well, Ruth, you look fetching as always." Venom colored Flo's voice green.

"Thank you," Ruth said with a forced smile. "How were the men last night?"

Flo picked up a clipboard. "Lieutenant Ryan was discharged, and Lieutenant Flanders spiked a fever. And we got a new admit." Her tiny brown eyes lit up. "Took a flak burst in his backside. Lucky us. He's a major and he's gorgeous. Of course, none of us stand a chance with you around."

Ruth took the clipboard and scanned it. "You know I don't date, Flo."

"Yeah, you're just waiting for the right one."

Ruth let the clipboard slap against her thigh. "Listen, I am a nurse. I'm here to care for the men, not flirt with them. Need I remind you, this is a hospital, not the USO."

"I'm aware of that." Flo's lip curled.

Ruth sighed, but it didn't matter if the women liked her. She joined the Army Nurse Corps to feed her family, not to make friends.

She opened the door to the officers' surgical ward, where only three beds were occupied.

Ruth offered up a prayer for the men's recovery, nothing more than a habit, but a precious habit because Ma taught her, and maybe if she prayed enough . . .

Lord, I know you're there. I'm not good enough for you, but Ma always said you loved everyone—everyone. So why don't I see it? I wish—I wish you'd give me some sign—

"Ah, Lieutenant Doherty, like a breath of fresh air."

Ruth snapped from her thoughts to Lieutenant Flanders's flushed face. She smiled. "Good morning, Lieutenant. Understand you have a little fever. How do you feel this morning?"

"Better." He glanced to the closed door. "Now that you're here, and Oswald's gone."

Ruth put a finger to her lips. "Lieutenant Oswald, and she's a fine nurse."

"No, you're a fine nurse. You care." He coughed, deep and liquid and rattling. "Got a letter from my girlfriend yesterday."

Ruth dipped a compress into a bin of cool water on the bedside table. "Doris? How is she?"

"Good. Busy with her Red Cross work. I'm so proud of her. But . . . well, she doesn't know about my pneumonia yet."

Ruth wrung out the compress and smoothed it over his forehead. "I can help you write a letter today. We'll tell her she has nothing to fear because these sulfa drugs work wonders. And she may actually be pleased. Your pneumonia kept you home from today's mission."

The man in the next bed raised himself on his elbows. "Another mission? Life isn't fair. The other fellows are flying, and I'm stuck here."

"Not fair?" She quirked an eyebrow at Lieutenant Jones, whose leg hung in traction.

Lieutenant Jones dropped back down to his pillow and groaned. "All right, I know. Pubs and jeeps don't mix." He cussed.

"Watchyer language." A voice rose from a bed across the aisle. "S'a lady present."

Ruth glanced at the long figure stretched on his belly on the cot. "It's all right. I can take care of myself. I've done it all my life."

"No 'scuse," he mumbled. "Rude, 'n a sign of a poor 'cabulary."

Ruth gave Lieutenant Jones a nod. "Work on that vocabulary."

"Yes, ma'am," he said with a grin.

She crossed the aisle to the newcomer and read his chart. "Maj. John Novak Jr.—welcome. It's nice to have a gentleman around here."

"Jack," he said. "Name's Jack."

She smiled down at him, but his eyes were shut. Flo was right—he appeared to be a handsome man, with broad shoulders, wavy black hair, and a trim mustache. But gorgeous faces had long since ceased to affect her.

Ruth pulled down the blanket and removed the major's dressings. According to the chart, he'd had extensive surgery the day before to remove steel from his backside and left thigh. She sighed at the sight of all the stitches. Combat produced the nastiest wounds.

Despite her gentle motions, Major Novak moaned a few times as she worked. "Won't sit down f'ra while."

"No, sir, you won't. You'll keep us company for a month or so."

"A month? Uh-uh." He shook his head on the pillow and pushed himself up with his hands. "Gotta go back. Gotta fly."

Ruth pressed on his shoulders, and he collapsed on the pillow. "No. You have to rest. You have to heal. You can't fly a plane if you can't sit."

He groaned in acknowledgment, his jaw slack.

Ruth checked the bottle of plasma flowing into his veins to replace the blood he'd lost. "How's the pain, Major?"

"Sore."

She scanned the chart. It had been four hours since his last pain shot. She went to the medication room for a vial of morphine and a sterilized syringe, and then returned to her patient. "You have morphine on order. Let's not wait until you're in agony. I'll give you another dose."

"I like you," he said.

Ruth popped the needle in the vial and flipped it upside down. "You do, do you?"

"Uh-huh. You're kind. I'm gonna marry you."

How many times had she heard that? Ruth laughed, injected air into the vial, and drew up the contents. "Really, this is all so sudden. Why, we just met. You haven't even seen my face."

"Doesn't matter. You're kind."

Ruth flicked air bubbles from the syringe. "Marriage is serious. You should go in with eyes wide open."

Major Novak opened one eye—cornflower blue—and he smiled. "Kind and pretty."

Oh yeah. He was gorgeous. Not that it mattered. "You're full of morphine."

His eye flopped shut, and his smile broadened. "I like morphine. Morphine's kind."

The other patients joined in Ruth's laughter. "You've got competition," Lieutenant Jones said.

Ruth moistened a cotton ball with rubbing alcohol and swabbed a spot on the major's right hip. "You like morphine, huh?"

"Mm-hmm."

"All right. Here comes the bride." She injected the medication and straightened up, chin high. "What God has joined together, let no man tear asunder."

Lieutenant Flanders broke into applause, Lieutenant Jones sang out the wedding march, and Ruth drew the blanket over her new patient's back. "Congratulations, Major. And thank you for providing our amusement for the day."

His lips bent in a little smile. "Know something? God loves you."

Ruth almost dropped the empty syringe. Her mind whipped back to her prayer at the start of her shift. "Excuse me?"

"He does," he said, voice slurred, eyes closed. "God really, really loves you."

How could this man know? He couldn't have heard her pray. She hadn't spoken out loud, had she? "Why—why did you say that?"

"S'true. Christ died for you. S'all you need to know."

★

Ruth tromped back to quarters at the end of the day, blind to the ever-present mud, blind to the rows of Nissen huts marring the manor grounds of Redgrave Park.

Christ died for her? It was all she needed to know?

So that's it, Lord? That's the answer to my prayer? About time you answered one. Ma said I could call on you in times of trouble, so why didn't you heal Pa after he fell? Why did you take both Pa and Ma from me? Why did you let—

Ruth clamped her jaws together. Major Novak was wrong. Christ died for the hospital chaplain with his pristine collar and serene smile, for Ma with her faith through the darkest days, for innocent little Penny Doherty—not for Ten-Penny, and not for Ruth.

A touch on her elbow made her jump.

May Jensen looked up at her. "I'm sorry. I didn't mean to startle you."

Why couldn't Ruth's roommate leave her alone? "That's okay. I, um—"

"Are you all right?" May's almost colorless eyes probed deep.

"Just a long day." Ruth feigned a tired smile.

"Looks like you need a good night's sleep. Going in?" May gestured to Redgrave Hall.

Ruth still couldn't believe they let a Chicago slum girl live in such a place. A grand, white Georgian façade had been tacked on the front of a Tudor home built in 1545. It had a courtyard and eleven bedrooms—eleven!—and she hadn't even counted all the rooms downstairs.

Ruth opened the door and hoped May didn't see the tremble in her hand.

"I'm here to *care* for the men, not *flirt* with them." Flo Oswald stood in the entry hall by a chipped marble statue, her hands on her square hips, her chest stuck out in a grotesque manner. Half a dozen nurses lounged on chairs nearby.

"Need I remind you, this is a hospital, not the U-S-O." Flo emphasized the letters with an exaggerated shoulder shimmy.

"That's just like her," one of the nurses said through her laughter.

"Someone should tell her to get off her high horse."

"You just did," Ruth said.

Half a dozen heads turned to her. Half a dozen jaws dropped. Flo's chest deflated.

Ruth fixed a cold stare on the group, raised a thin smile, and brushed past them through the door to the sweeping staircase.

May followed, oblivious to being ignored. "Did you really say that? About the hospital and the USO?"

Ruth turned on the stairs and looked down to May's bright eyes. "Yes, that's a direct quote."

May's face crumpled in laughter. "Good for you. I'm here to do the Lord's work, and it bothers me when girls treat this place like a matchmaking service. It makes all of us look bad."

Ruth allowed herself to smile. May was the only woman who still pursued a friendship with her, despite many rebuffs. Although May's persistence annoyed her, Ruth admired her work ethic.

Upstairs in the room they shared with four other nurses, Ruth reclined on her cot and pulled out pen and paper.

May sat on her cot next to Ruth's, took off her cap, and smoothed her pale hair. "What are you doing tonight?"

Ruth raised her pen. "Letters."

"Listen, I know you prefer to keep to yourself, but Kate and Rosa and I are going into Bury St. Edmunds tonight to catch a movie. It doesn't matter what's playing—anything to get away from the hospital for a while. Would you like to come along?"

Although May was plain, even homely, her smile had an engaging glow. How long had it been since Ruth had a friend? Ten years. Ten long years. A soft yearning pulled at her heart. Wouldn't it be nice to have someone to talk to and laugh with? Someone she could trust?

No. Every time she trusted someone she got burned. Besides, while the other nurses had money to play with, Ruth had a family to support. Her aunts and uncles had opened their homes for the orphaned Doherty children, but they couldn't afford to feed and clothe them.

Ruth looked down at the blank paper. "I'm sorry, but no. I'm behind in my correspondence."

"That's right. You have a large family, don't you? Well, maybe another time."

Ruth put pen to paper. "Maybe not," she whispered.

4

May 25, 1943

"Please, Lieutenant? I'll be a perfect gentleman."

"I'm sure you would, but as I've told you before, I don't date."

Jack blinked. The ward came into focus sideways until Jack righted it in his mind. Morning, and after seven if Lieutenant Doherty was there. It had to be Tuesday, since she took every other Sunday and Monday off. The days mushed together, but one way to keep track was by the nurses' shifts and how they changed the atmosphere. Lieutenant Oswald worked nights, and everyone pretended to sleep to avoid her flirting. When Lieutenant Jensen covered daytime breaks, she brought calm and hope. But Lieutenant Doherty's cheerful competence made her everyone's favorite.

"Then let's skip the dating and get married."

Jack grumbled. "Leave her alone, Jones."

"Ah, come on. I'm just having fun."

"Don't forget, I can handle myself." Lieutenant Doherty crossed the aisle and came to his side. "How are you feeling this morning, Major?"

"Much better." Jack rolled over, winced at the pain in his

rear end, and flopped back onto his stomach. "Except when I do something stupid like that."

She chuckled and pulled down the blanket. "Be patient. You'll be sitting up in no time. Now, let me take a look at those wounds."

Jack rested his chin on the pillow so he wouldn't have to watch her work. "Of all the foolish places to get shot. How am I supposed to tell my grandkids? My brother lost his arm, but at least that's honorable."

"Oh my. How'd that happen?"

"Shot by a Focke-Wulf 190 over Bremen. He flew a B-17 with the 306th."

"Really? We had patients from that group when I was stationed at Diddington."

"Come to think of it, he had pneumonia this winter. Maybe you met him—Walter Novak." Jack glanced over his shoulder, but the sight of the pretty nurse dressing his rump unnerved him. He turned back.

"Walter Novak. That sounds familiar. Does he look like you?"

Jack chuckled. "Not a bit, other than the black hair, the build. Nice fellow. He never would have made a pass at you."

"Hmm." The snip of scissors on tape told him she was almost done. "Yes, I remember him. Shy, but very pleasant. How's he doing?"

"Going home soon, but I'm worried about him. He's blue. Lost his arm, can't fly, and the girl he loves is marrying someone else."

"Oh dear." Lieutenant Doherty pulled the blanket back in place. "He didn't take my advice."

"Advice?"

She sat on the empty cot next to his. "To tell her how he felt. He had everything to gain and nothing to lose."

Jack rolled onto his right side and raised himself on one elbow, which was uncomfortable but not painful. "I told him the same thing, but he won't do it. Stubborn Novak pride."

"Hmm." She opened the drawer of the bedside table and rearranged supplies. Although her hands never idled, she always listened. "You have two brothers, right? Are all of you like that?"

"More or less. Ray's the least stubborn. He's got a true pastor's heart."

"Don't you also? You always make the men behave."

Jack fiddled with the brown wool blanket. "I don't know. I'm not a born pastor like Ray. He gets fired up writing sermons. I don't. I have to work at it. That's one reason I joined the Air Corps right out of seminary."

"One reason? What's the other?" She glanced at him through dark lashes.

Boy, she was swell. He grinned. "Had to fly."

Her gaze darted back to the drawer. "And after the war? What then?"

After the war? Jack didn't think much about it, didn't want to. Although the faces of four dead copilots flashed in his mind, he wouldn't trade his job with anyone. He'd flown antisubmarine missions with the 7th Bombardment Group from Pearl Harbor, then reconnaissance missions over New Guinea and the Solomons with the 19th Bomb Group in Townsville, Australia, but when his war-weary squadron returned stateside, he rejected a boring training job like Ray had and volunteered for combat again.

"After the war?" Jack sighed. "Maybe I'll be ready to settle in a cozy little parsonage and write scholarly yet stirring messages."

"I'm sure you'll do a fine job." Her brows drew together

as she lined up rolls of gauze. "Your brother Ray—he's a gentleman too, isn't he?"

"Yeah." He shifted his elbow so his arm wouldn't fall asleep.

"Imagine that—three in one family. I mean, you and your brother are two of a very small number of single men who haven't made a pass at me. I—well, I appreciate it." She still shifted things in the drawer although surely it was organized by now.

"You're welcome." Jack studied her changed demeanor—not her usual deft blend of friendliness and standoffishness, but rather, she looked small and vulnerable. "It's got to bother you. Seems as if someone asks you out every day."

"At least once a day." She slid the drawer and her confident smile back in place. "Not a week passes without some poor soul declaring his undying love, and my month isn't complete without a marriage proposal."

Jack laughed. "Glad I'm above that."

"Are you? You've already proposed."

"What?" His jaw dropped.

"It's all right." Lieutenant Doherty pulled a thermometer from her pocket and popped it in Jack's open mouth. "It was your first day, and you were heavily drugged."

"Shorry 'bout dat," he mumbled around the thermometer. What other stupid things had he said?

"All forgiven." The sparkle in her eyes told him she meant it.

Lieutenant Doherty wrote on the clipboard while the mercury rose, and Jack glanced around the Nissen hut, which was like a giant tin can sawed in half. Four coal stoves ran down the aisle, with ten beds on each side, only eight of which were occupied. Jack didn't mind the extra attention.

After Lieutenant Doherty removed the thermometer, Jack

took a sip of water to wash away the taste of rubbing alcohol. "Enough about the Novaks. What are the Dohertys like?"

She shook down the thermometer. "I don't think we have any unifying characteristic, except we all work hard."

"Your parents must have been exceptional." She always spoke of them in the past tense, so they must have passed away.

"They were." Lieutenant Doherty rubbed the edge of the clipboard with her thumb. "Pa worked real hard at the plant until he fell and broke his back in '32. He hated being an invalid, and it eventually killed him—blood clot in his lung. And Ma truly worked herself to death. She died two years after Pa, right before I graduated from nursing school."

Jack slid down to rest his cheek on the pillow. "And the kids?"

"Well, I'm the oldest. Three of us are on our own. Ellen's married with two little ones, and Harold's in the Navy. The other four are with aunts and uncles, split up, but I had no choice."

"Wow." Why had so much tragedy come to the Dohertys and so little to the Novaks?

"But Chuck graduates next year. Then I'll only have Bert, Anne, and Maggie to support."

Did they all have that gorgeous red brown hair? Jack studied the way she wore it pinned under her white nurse's cap. "Now I know the names of all the Doherty children except you. What's your first name?"

"To you?" She batted her eyelashes. "You can call me Lieutenant."

He laughed and gave her a heartfelt salute. She had to be the most attractive woman he'd ever met.

She stood and wrapped a blood pressure cuff around his

arm. "I know you flyboys are casual with each other, but I prefer military decorum."

"I can see why. Keeps a professional distance."

She paused and looked him in the eye. "Yes. That's important."

"I understand." With so many men attracted to her, she needed privacy. Jack kept quiet while she took his blood pressure and pulse. Unlike the other nurses, who checked their wristwatches, Lieutenant Doherty looked over her shoulder to the clock on the wall. When she turned, her white uniform sleeve rode up and revealed a crooked half-moon scar on her wrist where a watch should have been. Jack had a hunch her military decorum would prohibit discussion about that. Better stick with the family.

"So how old is the youngest Doherty?" he asked after she finished.

A warm smile made her even prettier. "Maggie turned eleven in April. I got a letter from her yesterday. I can't believe how grown-up she sounds. She writes a real nice letter, and her handwriting is lovely. Want to see?"

"Sure." He smiled at her sisterly pride.

Lieutenant Doherty pulled a letter from her uniform pocket and knelt next to the bed. Jack hoisted himself up on one elbow to see, and to be at her eye level for once.

"Read this paragraph." She pointed to the middle of the page. "She describes her teacher so well I can almost smell the chalk dust."

But Jack looked to the top of the page where it read, "Dear Penny." He tapped the name and gave her a smug smile.

She flinched as if the letter had slapped her across the face.

"Don't worry," he said in a low voice. "I won't tell anyone."

"I don't go by that name anymore. I hate it."

"Because of your hair?" It wasn't a copper shade at all, more like the cherry wood cabinet in the parlor at home in Antioch, but kids still teased.

"No, I just . . ."

Jack had never seen her flustered before, a trait he found sweet and appealing. He gave her an encouraging smile.

She closed her eyes and drew a deep breath. "All right." Her voice was barely above a whisper, and she leaned a bit closer. "My name's Penelope Ruth, but I've gone by Ruth since I left home. I much prefer it."

"Ruth." He savored the sound of her name and the presence of her face no more than a foot from his. "It fits you."

"It does?"

Jack nodded, careful to maintain visual contact. "When was the last time you read the book of Ruth in the Bible?"

Her gaze flitted to the letter in her hands. "Oh, a while, I guess."

"Read it again. She's fascinating—strong willed, loyal to family, hardworking, and kind. Like another Ruth I know."

The Ruth he knew met his gaze again, her eyebrows raised. A ring of gold surrounded the pupils in her blue eyes, and Jack suspected a ring of gold surrounded her heart. He wanted to be the man to find it.

5

June 5, 1943

Ruth slipped Aunt Pauline's letter into her cape pocket, passed precise military rows of the hospital's Nissen huts, and rubbed the heel of her hand against her forehead. How on earth would she manage?

Redgrave Hall stood to the west, but Ruth headed south across the road the ambulances used and entered a lightly wooded meadow and another world. How could one family own so much land? Two hundred acres? Stables, parks, lodges, kennels, even an orangery—imagine that—a greenhouse just for citrus.

If Ruth had resources like that, she wouldn't be in a fix.

When Congress doubled Army nurse salaries in December, she thought her troubles were over. Even Aunt Pauline couldn't complain about forty-two dollars a month. Surely that was plenty to feed and clothe eleven-year-old Maggie.

Aunt Pauline, however, never seemed to be satisfied.

Ruth sat on the grass by the lake that cut a stomach-shaped path across Redgrave Park. She hugged her knees to her chest, her dark blue cape tented around her against the gray chill.

Somehow in the past she'd always had a reprieve. Aunt Pauline had made noise in the spring of '41, but when Harold joined the Navy, Ruth was able to divide her salary in four instead of five. More noise in the spring of '42, then a small pay raise in June. More noise in the fall, then December's hefty raise.

But now? Where would the money come from now? Promotions were meager in the Army Nurse Corps. All the nurses were second lieutenants except the chief nurse, a first lieutenant. At twenty-three, Ruth was too young and inexperienced to become a chief nurse.

She'd always solved her own problems, but now she longed for advice, and she kept thinking about Major Novak.

What was it about that man? She thought about him too often. Thank goodness he'd be discharged by the end of the month, and she'd never have to see him again. In the meantime, she could share her problem with him. He might be a pastor, but he wouldn't say something hackneyed about waiting on the Lord. She couldn't afford to wait.

Her stomach twisted like the lake before her. How much time did she have? Today's letter complained about how costly things were nowadays. Aunt Pauline's grumblings would escalate—what sacrifices she made, she didn't know how much longer she could manage, could Ruth spare any more? Last would come a chilling statement—what a shame it would be to send Maggie to the orphanage.

Ruth had never tested her beyond the orphanage threat. Would her aunt follow through? How long did Ruth have?

She gripped the edges of her cape. No matter what—no matter what, she wouldn't let a Doherty go to an orphanage. Ever.

"Good evening, Ruth."

She looked over her shoulder. May Jensen stood silhouetted against the darkening sky.

"Hi," Ruth said in an unwelcoming voice.

"I love this spot. Isn't it beautiful?" May sat down about six feet from Ruth and leaned back against a tree.

"I come here when I want time alone."

"Don't mind me. I brought a magazine, the latest *Army Nurse*. Have you read it?"

"No." She turned to study the gray ripples on the lake, and to shut down conversation so she could consider her problem.

No one else had room for Maggie, so Aunt Pauline had to do. Where on earth could Ruth get the money? She had no product or service or inclination to start a business. Never again.

If only she could hold off Aunt Pauline for one year until Chuck graduated and Ruth could divide his allotment among the other three children.

If only Harold would contribute from his Navy pay. Ruth rested her chin on her knees. That wouldn't happen. Five dollars here, ten dollars there. And Ellen couldn't contribute, not with a shiftless husband who couldn't even support his own family. Besides, Ellen considered Ruth's financial responsibility a just burden.

"Hmm. That's interesting."

Ruth scrunched up her face. Why did some people assume everyone wanted to hear what they were reading?

"Make sure you read this article on flight nursing."

"Oh?" Ruth had to admit flight nursing fascinated her with its adventure, independence, and responsibility. Of course, air evacuation had more detractors than champions and had been used only on isolated occasions.

May held up the journal. "It tells about the graduation of the first class from the School of Air Evacuation at Bowman Field in Kentucky. Thirty-nine flight nurses. Brig. Gen. David Grant—you know, the Air Surgeon—he was there. He was incensed that no one planned to give them wings, so he pinned his own wings on the honor graduate, ordered wings for all flight nurses."

"Wow." Grant had already earned Ruth's admiration with his advocacy for nurses, from a physician, no less. "With him on board, maybe air evacuation will stand a chance."

"Wouldn't that be great? It's such an advance for nursing."

Ruth dropped her knees to the side so she could face May. "Can you imagine? A plane full of patients, one nurse, and one medic. If something goes wrong, the nurse gets to solve the problem. No physician to consult."

"No physician to boss her around."

"Sounds like a dream." Ruth and May laughed together, and Ruth's chest tightened. How had she let herself get drawn into a friendly conversation?

"That's not the only benefit. Look at this." May flipped a page and lifted the magazine. "They get to wear trousers and flight suits. Don't they look cute? All this and flight pay too."

"Flight pay?"

"Because it's hazardous duty. Sixty dollars a month."

"Sixty dollars?" Ruth reached for the magazine. "Could I—could I see that?"

"Sure." She handed it over. "They wouldn't take me. I'm too small. But doesn't it sound fun?"

"Yeah. Lots of fun." Sixty divided by four would mean fifteen extra dollars per month per child. That would keep Aunt Pauline quiet. Yes, it was hazardous, but she had her ten thousand dollar GI life insurance, which could see each child through high school.

She flipped forward—requirements, requirements. There: five foot two to six feet, 105 to 135 pounds, twenty-one to

A MEMORY BETWEEN US

thirty-six years old, graduate nurse commissioned in the Army
Nurse Corps, at least six months in an Army hospital. Yes,
she met all those. Next, she'd have to meet Class III requirements on the Form 64 physical exam. That would be tough,
but Ruth was healthy and strong. The next requirement was
a willingness to be close to combat. Why not? She'd survived
Chicago in the Depression. Then the last requirement—the
desire to fly.

Desire to fly? She'd never flown before. She was willing to
fly, but a desire was different, stronger. Major Novak had it.
His eyes lit up when he talked about planes and flying. He
made it sound exciting, alluring, and freeing.

Ruth glanced up. To the east, a deep purple tinted the
clouds, and on the western horizon orange flame burnt a
hole in the overcast. What would it be like to soar above the
clouds, among the colors, to be away from the earth with its
pressures and trials if only for a few hours?

She clutched the magazine, her hope, her solution. Yes,
she had the desire to fly.

42

6

June 23, 1943

The wheelchair clattered over the walkway. Jack leaned forward into the wind and shifted onto his right hip to reduce jolts to his wounds. "Faster, Charlie. I want to get airborne."

"Any faster and we'll knock those stitches out. I don't want to draw your nurse's fire."

"Lieutenant Doherty? I'll take her flak any day. She's something else."

Charlie huffed and pulled the wheelchair short to avoid hitting a medic. "You're something else. Poor woman."

"She can handle herself." As much as he enjoyed the fresh air and the visit with Charlie, he wanted to keep it short and get back to Ruth's company. Sure, he respected her wishes and called her Lieutenant Doherty, but he thought of her as Ruth.

"Want to hear about the new base?" Charlie steered the wheelchair past the last Nissen hut and up onto a grassy ridge.

"Sure do. Park here and let me get out of this thing." Jack ignored Charlie's offer of help and pushed himself to standing. A wave of dizziness and a jab of pain made him draw a sharp breath. He let it out slowly. The sooner he got moving, the sooner he'd be back in combat, and the sooner he could implement his plan with Ruth. "So how's Bury St. Edmunds?"

"Fine. I still can't believe they put us at Earls Colne at first. The runways aren't long enough for B-17s."

"Typical Army." Jack clamped his teeth together and took one step, then another.

Charlie hovered by his side. "Simple to fix. Earls Colne is fine for medium bombers, so we switched places with the B-26 Marauders at Bury. It's a good base, and the town has everything the men want—shops and pubs and atmosphere, even a ruined abbey."

"The hospital staff's favorite place." Jack grinned and shuffled forward. The town and air base lay about fifteen miles southwest of the hospital. Once he was discharged, he planned to visit his hospitalized men every week, and he might as well visit on Sundays, when he could worship at the hospital with a chaplain he knew. If he ran into Ruth, so be it.

"Got our new CO yesterday."

Jack whipped around too fast. He winced at the pain and at the mischief in Charlie's light blue eyes. "How long were you going to wait to tell me?"

"Till now. Col. Frederick Castle."

"Castle. Hmm. What's he like?" Jack turned to circle the wheelchair.

Charlie sat on the grass and stretched his stocky legs in front of him. "Shouldn't you make your own judgment, Skipper?"

"Yeah, but any information will help."

Charlie shook out a cigarette and stuck it between his lips. "Fairly young. Mid-thirties. Hap Arnold's godson."

"What?" Jack stared at his friend. "Hap Arnold? The commanding general of the whole U.S. Army Air Force?"

Charlie nodded. "His godson."

"Wow." Jack continued his trek. The colonel would be untouchable if he were a problem. On the other hand, if Jack got on Castle's good side, he'd get on Arnold's good side.

"West Pointer. Men are thrilled about that."

"I bet." Last thing flyboys wanted was spit and polish.

"What they really hate is he's HQ. Air Chief of Staff for Supply."

"Let me guess. No combat experience, better with logistics than people."

"Come on, Novak. Wait and form your own opinion."

"Don't worry. You know I'll give the man a chance." Jack circled the chair, relishing the feel of moving muscles. "Besides, I can work with anybody. Just have to figure out the best approach with my men." If Castle proved unpopular, Jack's job would be more challenging, to enforce policy yet maintain high morale.

Jack clasped his hands overhead and stretched his arms high. Felt good. "How's Babcock handling my squadron?"

Charlie laughed, and the cigarette wiggled in his mouth. "You can't stand having someone else in your position, can you?"

"As long as he knows it's temporary."

More laughter. "Temporary in our squadron, but Castle will give him another, guaranteed. Of the four squadron commanders, we've already lost two, plus you in the hospital. And Babcock's kept up morale even though the 94th has lost sixteen planes on nine missions."

Jack swung his arms behind him for a stretch. "He's that good?"

"Yeah." Amusement crinkled Charlie's round face. "He's a good pilot and a born leader. You know his dad's in the House of Representatives."

Jack grumbled and plodded around Charlie's feet. "No, I didn't know that."

"Ever hear of 'Baby-Face' Babcock?"

"Hothead from Indiana?"

"Illinois."

"'Baby-Face' Babcock? He looks nothing like him." How could a pastor from the California backwaters compete for a promotion with a Washington politician? "A politician. Oh boy."

"Don't worry. You'll get your squadron back. Besides, he's good but not as good as you."

Jack smiled. As always, the bombardier had perfect aim. "Taking lessons from the politician?"

"Got to survive this war somehow."

"And I've got to get back in." Jack lowered himself into the wheelchair. "And for that I need good nursing care. Get me home, Skipper."

"Hey, that's my line." Charlie nudged the chair over the crest of the ridge and let it pick up speed downhill. Jack whooped as they raced down the walkway to Ward Seven.

When they returned, Ruth and Lieutenant Jensen stood chatting over a clipboard at the far end of the hut. Ruth must have just gotten back from her break. Now he could introduce Charlie to Lieutenant Jensen. Jack eased himself to his feet, caught her eye, and waved her over. Her gaze bounced from him to Charlie and back, and she held up one hand. Later. That meant never.

"Boy, the nurses here are a skittish bunch," Jack said.

"I have that effect on women." Charlie shook Jack's hand in parting.

After Charlie left, Jack grunted his way into bed and leaned back against the tubular metal headboard. He gritted himself against the discomfort, but he liked to watch Ruth work. He chuckled. A patient falling for a nurse had to be the oldest cliché in the book.

Since he'd told her of his plan to visit on Sundays, her behavior had changed. Sure, she'd come by soon and perform her routine, but in a crisp manner. Then she'd chat with the other patients, everyone but him. Hours would pass until he could coax her into conversation.

Maybe she'd figured out he'd fallen for her. But why would that bother her? Crushes never fazed her. Or maybe she was falling for him.

Jack grinned and pulled a book from his bedside table to make himself look busy. Yeah, that would faze her, she who never dated.

"You're in a good mood, Major." Ruth stood at the foot of his bed, clipboard clutched to her chest.

Sure would be nice to hear her call him Jack. He put his book back on the table. "Had a nice visit with Charlie, and Dr. Hoffman says I'll be released next week."

"You must be glad."

"Wish it had been earlier so I could have seen Walt before he went home, but yeah, I'm glad. How about you? Gonna miss me?" He dropped her a wink.

"Immensely," she said with a roll of her eyes. "Over on your stomach, please. Time to change your dressings."

Ruth's silence during the exam intrigued Jack, but he wasn't about to let her ignore him. Soon the scissors snipped, and she was done.

Jack hitched himself up to sitting. "You won't have a chance to miss me. You go to church services here, so I'll see you on Sundays if I'm not flying."

"That's true." She stared at the clipboard, and her eyelids fluttered.

"What do you do on Sunday afternoons?"

Ruth's gaze pinned him to the wall. "I do not date, Major."

He laughed. "Whoa. I'm not asking you out. I know better." This woman called for an indirect, creative, strategic approach, and he'd found an accomplice in Lt. May Jensen.

"Good," Ruth said with a sigh. "I count on you to be more sensible than the others."

Not more sensible, just more subtle. "Sorry. My question came out wrong. I wanted to ask what you do for fun. You don't date and you never talk about friends."

"Fun?" Ruth tilted her head and shrugged. "I read. I go for walks. I run errands in town every other Monday. I see a movie if I have money left over."

Yeah, he had her flustered again. "Alone," he said.

She set her jaw. "Yes, alone. I see no need to defend myself."

If he wasn't careful, he'd crash on takeoff. He sighed, shifted his legs to the side, and motioned for her to sit down. "I don't mean to attack you. Nothing wrong with doing things alone. Now, come on. Sit down."

"I have work to do."

Jack looked at her from under his brows. She'd finished her rounds and had time to spare. He patted the side of the bed. "Come, my child. Sit and talk to Pastor Novak."

A smile squirmed about her lips. "Going to counsel me?"

Jack groaned. "If you saw my seminary grades, you wouldn't ask."

She sat, but on the empty cot to his right. "So you're an exceptional pilot but a mediocre pastor?"

"Uh-uh." He wagged a finger at her. "We're talking about you."

"About why I'm so odd?" Her eyes sparkled. "Haven't you

SARAH SUNDIN

figured it out? The men love me, the women hate me, and yes, I see the correlation."

He laughed. "Lieutenant Jensen doesn't hate you."

"She's odd herself."

"Sounds like a good friend for you, but you reject her." Jack laced his fingers behind his neck and leaned back against the cold metal bed frame. "And you're an attractive woman, but you don't date."

"Never have."

"Never? You've never had a boyfriend?"

She whisked a strand of hair behind her ear. "Well, I had boyfriends in junior high, but not—not since eighth grade."

Jack's jaw dangled, but he couldn't get himself to close it.

Ruth sat up taller. "I'm devoted to my work and my family. Dating would interfere. Besides, if I married, I couldn't take care of my family. So why bother dating?"

Jack considered several answers—how falling in love enriched your life, how a caring husband would support her family, how he could show her how wonderful it was—but her question was rhetorical. There had to be more, some jerk who'd broken her heart, but until she trusted him, he had to take her story as it stood.

"Your family's blessed to have you. I'm sure your hard work will be rewarded someday." Jack let his gaze linger until she looked away.

Yes, Lt. Ruth Doherty was a challenge, but Jack loved a challenge.

7

Sunday, July 4, 1943

Ruth sat on her cot in dress blues for Sunday services, and her little black leather Bible fell open to the book of Ruth. Again.

Since Major Novak suggested the book, she had read it daily. Something about the story touched her as nothing in the Bible ever had. This Ruth suffered loss, clung to family, and lived as an outsider, yet God provided Boaz to care for her, Boaz to keep the men in line.

Major Novak kept the men in line.

She shook the memory from her head and concentrated on verse 12 of chapter 2, where Boaz said to Ruth, "The Lord recompense thy work, and a full reward be given thee of the Lord God of Israel, under whose wings thou art come to trust."

The refuge of safety and comfort beckoned, but to enter that refuge required trust, and although Ma always said God was trustworthy, Ruth knew better. God hadn't helped Ma keep the Doherty money jar full or provided the tuition for nursing school. Ruth had.

"Ready for church?"

May Jensen's voice startled Ruth, and she flapped her Bible

shut. "Oh. Not yet." The invitation to walk together lurked in the air, and Ruth needed to swat it down. "Go on ahead."

"All right. I'll save you a seat."

Now how could Ruth avoid sitting with May? She sighed and opened her Bible again. Although she had memorized the verse, she felt compelled to see it in print, to see the promised reward for hard work.

"I'm sure your hard work will be rewarded some day," Major Novak had said.

Ruth groaned. He was not her Boaz. She didn't have a Boaz.

She stood to check the stockings on a line stretched between antique wall sconces. Nope, still damp, like everything in England. Like Ruth. She had to be damp in the head to let a patient get to her.

The major had been discharged a week before, but she kept glancing at his bed, now occupied by a whiny bombardier with a mild case of frostbite, and kept remembering Major Novak's humor and intelligence and chivalry. Today he was coming to church. Why couldn't he be a good little patient and disappear when discharged?

Ruth fingered her khaki rayon slip on the line, which also felt damp. What was wrong with her? Dashing pilots were as common in the area as mud, bicycles, and chipped beef on toast.

Why did she waste time thinking about him anyway? Even if he were an ordinary man, dating was impossible. But he was better than ordinary. He was a pastor, for crying out loud. A pastor with Ten-Penny Doherty?

A laugh ripped out. She clapped her hand over her mouth, but the room was empty.

Ruth grabbed her Bible and strode down the hallway. Major or no major, she would always attend Sunday services, as she'd promised Ma before her death. In church she heard the hymns Ma used to hum. In church she heard the Scriptures Ma used to quote. In church she could see Ma's face lit up even in the depths of adversity.

Ruth opened the grand front door, and the sunshine made her eyes water. Ma had peace and joy because she loved the Lord and the Lord loved her. Ma was good, but Ruth was—

"God commendeth his love toward us, in that, while we were yet sinners, Christ died for us."

Ma's favorite verse. Ruth huffed. Not her. No matter how many times she prayed for forgiveness, her sin and punishment hung thick and black over her. God didn't love her. He'd never shown—

"Christ died for you. S'all you need to know."

She groaned and quickened her pace down the walkway. Major Novak, May Jensen, the Lord God—why couldn't they leave her alone?

No such luck.

As soon as she entered the Nissen hut chapel, May pounced on her, took her arm, and dragged her down the aisle. "Jack saved seats for us."

"Jack?"

"Major Novak."

She knew that, but since when did May call him by his first name? May led her to the spot Ruth usually occupied, and Major Novak stood and flashed a grin. How did she get distracted from her goal of avoiding her roommate and her former patient? How, how, how?

The major was handsome enough in pajamas, but in full dress uniform—well, it just wasn't fair. The khaki shirt and tie, the olive drab jacket and trousers, the gold major's leaves on the shoulders, the silver wings and row of medals on the chest—they made any man look good, but this man didn't need any help.

Worse, she sensed a shift, a disturbing shift in position. In the hospital she'd stood over him, but here he stood over her, and the reversal of power cramped her throat.

She lifted her chin to open her airway. "Good morning, Major. Good to see you dressed."

He laughed and gestured to the row of chairs. "Ladies?"

Ruth darted in first. She'd sit next to May if she had to, but she would not sit next to that man.

He gave them a sheepish smile. "Pardon me if I avoid sitting as long as possible."

"Oh, Ruth, look at this." May patted a pale blue cushion on the seat beside her.

The major winced and nudged the cushion with his knee. "Grandma made it. Must have plucked every goose and duck on the farm. I can almost hear the squawking, see Grandpa stomping around yelling at Grandma, 'What in tarnation do you think you're doing, Nellie?'"

Ruth laughed, and the major's smile made her long for the talks they'd had on the ward. He begged for her stories of the dark and dirty Chicago slums, which he called exciting. She preferred his tales of three little boys in the grass and river and open sky.

May patted the cushion. "Service is starting."

Major Novak frowned and eased himself down. Then he whispered in May's ear, and Ruth noticed a sour twisting in her chest.

She put it out of her head and envisioned her parents to her left instead of a nurse and a pilot, placed her brothers and sisters in a line to her right, felt baby Maggie on her lap, and let the hymns and Scriptures and sermon transport her to when life was secure, people were whole, and God was kind.

For the closing hymn, the chaplain announced number 269.

"Under His Wings."

Jolted her back to the present, to reality, to a God who hounded her.

Ruth's voice came out thin and croaking. Few people seemed familiar with the tune, but Ruth knew she'd never be able to get it out of her mind.

> Under His wings I am safely abiding,
> Though the night deepens and tempests are wild,
> Still I can trust Him; I know He will keep me,
> He has redeemed me, and I am His child.
>
> Under His wings, under His wings,
> Who from His love can sever?
> Under His wings my soul shall abide,
> Safely abide forever.
>
> Under His wings, what a refuge in sorrow!
> How the heart yearningly turns to His rest!
> Often when earth has no balm for my healing,
> There I find comfort, and there I am blessed.

Why did God taunt her? He wouldn't give her that kind of love and security. She didn't deserve it. He'd made it very clear that day in the alley.

She clapped the hymnal shut and set it on the chair, but when she turned, Major Novak blocked her escape.

"Just a minute, Lieutenant. I have something to ask you."

Ruth struggled to focus. "Oh?"

"What are your plans this afternoon?"

Plans? Oh no, he'd caught her off guard. He knew she had every other Sunday off. What provided the best excuse? Letters? Laundry? What?

May slung her purse over her shoulder. "Jack, I warned you. She'll make an excuse."

"You wouldn't make an excuse, would you?" Major Novak dropped a wink.

Under the force of that wink, Ruth's knees crumpled, and so did her excuses. "No."

"Oh, good," May said. "You shouldn't be alone on Independence Day."

Ruth's grip on her Bible tightened. What was wrong with being alone?

"And I warned you, May." The major pointed at Ruth. "Look at her jaw. She's getting defensive."

She forced her jaw to soften. "I am not."

"Good," he said. "Let me explain. You took care of me for a month and a half. I'd like to thank you, take the two of you on a picnic."

The two of you? Ruth relaxed only to realize she couldn't get out now. "A picnic?"

"Yep. I got some ham and cheese in town. Swapped my cigarette ration. Amazing what people will do for a couple smokes."

"Ham? And cheese? Wow." British rationing was much stricter than American.

"Yep." He nodded in his usual way, without breaking his gaze. "You'll go?"

Without an excuse, she could only accept or be rude, and after all his kindness, she couldn't bear to be rude to him. She mustered a smile. "What's more patriotic than a Fourth of July picnic?"

Once outside, May mounted a bicycle with a bundle strapped to the back. "I'm serving as pack mule since our dear major can't ride yet. I thought we'd go to that spot we like by the lake, Ruth."

We like? May made it sound as if they were the coziest of friends who whispered and giggled together. Once. They'd had one good talk.

"Can't do much of anything yet." Major Novak frowned at the scattered clouds as they walked down the path. "My squadron's on a mission. Should be over the target about now."

Ruth studied his face. "Nothing sadder than a bird with clipped wings."

He raised half a smile. "This old bird's only temporarily grounded, and light duty isn't as bad as I thought. Get to watch the new CO at work, see how he runs things."

"How do you like him?"

He shrugged. "Castle's not a man you like. Too formal. But I respect him greatly. Hardest worker I've ever seen. Turns out he flew a bunch of missions before he came to the 94th to see what it's like. Never told the men, didn't want to draw attention to himself. Impressive. The men grouse, but he's whipping them into shape."

"You too?"

"Nah. Either he likes my work or he took pity on my torn-up backside."

"Must be pity, Major. I've seen that backside."

May's laughter rolled backward from the bicycle. "It's healed now. We'll send a report and clear you for whipping."

Major Novak glared at Ruth, upper lip curled. "Thank you so much."

"You're welcome." She felt lighter in her step, the nurse-patient relationship restored.

When they reached the lake, May leaned the bicycle against a tree. The ladies spread a brown Army blanket on the grass under the tree and sat down while the major stretched on his side.

"Ice." He set a bucket before him. "The men had a practice mission yesterday, so I put a bucket of water in the waist compartment. Gets mighty cold at twenty thousand feet."

May traced a squiggle in the condensation on the bucket. "What a clever idea."

"That's how the men get ice for parties." He opened a brown paper bundle, pulled out a pocketknife, and sliced off a golden curl of cheese. He held it out to Ruth with a mischievous grin. "You can have some if I can call you by your first name."

She gaped at him. "You know how I feel about military decorum."

"I also know how you feel about cheese. And there's ham if you call me Jack."

She rose to her knees. "Fine. I'll eat at the mess."

"Why? Real English cheddar and ham. And I've got biscuits and red currant jam, not orange marmalade."

"Red currant?" Ruth sat back on her heels. She was so tired of orange marmalade. And cheese? He knew a poor girl would do anything for food, didn't he?

"All right . . ." Her tongue stumbled. "Jack."

"That's better." A smile crept up his face. "Ruth."

Only a name, one short syllable, yet in his voice a caress. He knew it. She saw it in his eyes when he handed her the cheese. Ruth let it dissolve over her tongue, savory and sharp.

"Oh dear," May said. "There goes our sunshine."

Ruth looked up as a bank of clouds snuffed out the last sliver of sun. "It's so gray in England."

Major Novak—Jack—sawed his knife through the chunk of ham. "Down here it is, but not up there. You get high enough, and it's always blue."

"I wish I could see that." She tried to imagine soaring above the gray.

"You will." He pointed a slice of ham at her. "You'll make flight nurse. I know it."

Ruth took the ham and relaxed. If he wanted romance, he wouldn't want her to leave. Instead he encouraged her goal and made her feel as if she could be selected. She sandwiched the ham in a biscuit. "Wouldn't it be nice if we could fly above the gray days?"

"We can in prayer." Then May laughed. "Okay, I know it's trite, but it's true, isn't it? No matter how gray life seems, prayer takes you above it all, to clear blue hope."

The biscuit turned dry in Ruth's mouth. Hope? Her only hope was to push on and meet her goals. Nothing clear or blue about it.

Jack smeared jam on a biscuit. "Well, May, you sure know about gray days."

What did content, placid May Jensen know about gray days? But as May lowered her reddening face, Ruth realized she knew nothing about the woman except she came from Minneapolis.

"You ever hear her story, Ruth?" Jack asked.

A pang of embarrassment. "Well, no."

"There's nothing to tell." May made great work of layering ham and cheese in a biscuit.

"Sure, there is," Jack said. "You have a lot in common. You're both orphans."

Ruth stared at her. Come to think of it, May never mentioned family, but May didn't talk about herself. She asked questions and listened, and Ruth had never asked. "You—you lost your parents too?"

May squirmed. "My mother died in childbirth, and my father died in the flu epidemic when I was a baby."

At least Ruth had the privilege of knowing her parents. "Your family raised you?"

"No. It's a long story." May's cheek twitched, a flicker of hurt, and suddenly Ruth understood why May still pursued friendship with her.

"Who . . . who . . . ?"

May met her gaze. "I was raised in an orphanage."

"An orphanage?" Cold fear gripped her heart as it had when Ma died, the fear of her brothers and sisters in the loathsome place. "Was it—was it awful?"

"I never knew otherwise." May lifted one shoulder. "We were always cold and hungry, but wasn't everyone in those days? And . . . well, I wasn't the type to be adopted, but it helped to know Jesus was rejected. I think he has a special place in his heart for those of us who are alone, don't you?"

Ruth nodded because it was expected, but she hadn't thought about it. Jesus had friends—but his friends betrayed him, denied him, and fled. Ruth's throat constricted. Could he understand?

"It wasn't all bad." May leaned forward, her eyebrows tented. "Please don't misunderstand me. I was blessed. The couple who ran the home had deep faith in God and taught me likewise, and I loved the children who came and went. I was able to comfort them. Even as a little girl, I had a ministry, and that led me to nursing and to Thomas." Then she clamped her lips together.

Ruth sensed May's reluctance, but for some reason she pressed on. "Thomas?"

"He was—he was a seminary student who volunteered at the home. We shared a heart for orphans. We were engaged."

Were? Ruth's question stuck under her tongue.

"Go on," Jack said softly. "Tell her."

May raised a fluttery smile. "We joined the service together, our patriotic duty. He was a Navy chaplain. He was at Pearl Harbor. On the *Arizona*."

"Oh no." Ruth's voice tumbled out. "I'm so sorry."

"It's all right. He's with Jesus, and I've had a year and a half to heal. I'm fine."

"You *are* fine." Jack rolled onto his stomach, propped up on his elbows. "Which is why you should let me introduce you to Charlie de Groot. He's a strong Christian and he'd like to meet you."

Tiny May could pack a lot of power in those colorless eyes. "I told you. I don't want to meet anyone."

"Come on. I'll bring him on our next picnic two weeks from now." He turned to Ruth. "Isn't that fair? We made you suffer today. Next time shouldn't it be May's turn?"

"Sounds fair to me." Oh no, he'd tricked her into another picnic.

Surprise registered in his eyes and his smile. "Next time then."

She scowled at him. "When's it your turn to suffer?"

Jack rested his chin on his forearms. "Let's see. I got shot up, spent over six weeks in the hospital, and I'm fraternizing with two lovely officers who've seen my bare bum, as they say around here. I think I've suffered plenty."

May laughed, but Ruth saw opportunity in the white specks in his black mustache. "You have crumbs in your mustache, Major."

"Jack." He laughed and wiped his lip. "Call me Jack. And I'm not your patient."

"Once a patient, always a patient." She gave her most comforting nurse smile.

"Just as I suspected." He pushed himself up to sit cross-legged, leaned forward over his knees, and looked Ruth in the eye. "Validates my pastoral theory on why Lt. Ruth Doherty doesn't date."

Her breath mired in dread. "What's that?"

"You like your men helpless—horizontal, bandaged, and sedated."

Ruth managed to join May's laughter, but the truth of his insight put a painful dent in the iron shell around her heart.

8

Bury St. Edmunds Airfield

Monday, July 26, 1943

Jack drummed his fingers on the railing of the control tower balcony.

"Can't stand it, can you?" Charlie rocked his cigarette up and down in his mouth.

"What? The biggest air operation of the war? Blitz Week—a whole week of good weather forecast over Germany, a whole week of maximum effort missions, and I'm missing it? Of course, I can't stand it." He scanned the haze to the east for the bombers.

Dispatching a mission in overcast still seemed strange. Before this week, it had been impossible, but with the new "Splasher" radio beacons to guide group assembly over England, the local weather mattered less, and the Eighth Air Force could fly more missions.

Charlie's glowing embers bobbed to Jack's right. "Fifteen bomb groups now; 303 Forts dispatched today."

"Should be 304." Jack picked up the rhythm with his fingers. Five minutes until the estimated time of arrival.

Charlie whacked Jack's hand. "Stop it."

"You stop it." Jack laughed and flicked the wagging cigarette to the ground.

Charlie reached into his shirt pocket for his pack of Lucky Strikes. Despite the overcast it was shirtsleeve warm. "Might have to stop it permanently. Did you see how May wrinkled her nose when I lit up?"

"One thing about you, de Groot, you know how to make a first impression."

"Other than that, we got along great."

"Yeah." Jack crossed his arms on the railing. He'd spent most of the picnic focused on Ruth—how could he not?—but Charlie and May seemed to hit it off, in lively laughter one moment, in deep conversation another.

"She's a swell girl. Might be the one I've been waiting for. She seems fragile on the outside, but on the inside—wow, she's a powerhouse."

"Yep." On the other hand, Ruth had a tough exterior, but the more time he spent with her, the more vulnerability he glimpsed. In those moments when she let him see her weakness, he knew his plan was on target.

A new cigarette bobbed. "As for May's grief, well, at least I know what I'm up against. You, however, have no idea what you're up against."

"I'll figure it out." And he'd have fun doing so. Jack gazed across the runway to the field beyond, where a tractor cut a swath in tall golden wheat. Below him, in front of the control tower, the ground personnel tossed baseballs, shot craps, anything to take their minds off the incoming planes. Sweating out a mission could fray more nerves than flying one.

"It's got to be big," Charlie said.

"Huh?"

"With Ruth. Something about her makes me think she's been hurt and badly."

"Nothing I can't handle."

"Watch that pride."

"It's not pride. Really." Jack rolled his shoulders. "I have a strong feeling God led me to her. He wants me to teach her to love, to trust, something. And if he wants it, it'll happen."

Charlie's head turned to the east. Jack heard it too—the deep throaty pulse of Wright-Cyclone engines. "Remember that, Jack. God will make it happen. He doesn't need your mission plans."

Jack straightened up and squinted at the clouds. "Nothing wrong with plans. God doesn't want us to bumble around. Besides, when have my plans ever failed?"

Charlie chuckled. "Never. That's why I put up with you even when you do arrogant things like flying a B-17 under the Golden Gate Bridge."

Jack grinned. "That was swell."

"There they are," someone on the balcony cried. "One, two, three."

Jack lifted his binoculars. "Four, five, six." The flight passed on the downwind leg of the approach, parallel to the runway. They'd taken damage. One Fort had a hole blasted through the vertical stabilizer.

"Hey, they shot up our 'square A,'" Charlie said. Earlier that month, letters were painted on the tail fins as group identification, and the 94th sported a blue *A* on a white square. It boosted unit pride and helped distract the men from the loss of twenty-four planes, half the original crews, and several replacement crews.

"Seven, eight, nine."

The first flight completed the base leg and the final approach, and landed at spaced intervals.

"Ten, eleven, twelve, thirteen."

Jack frowned at the holes in the formation. Twenty Flying Fortresses had left Bury St. Edmunds at dawn to bomb a synthetic rubber factory in Hannover. How many had they lost?

"Fourteen, fifteen, sixteen."

Jack could hardly hear the count over the throb of engines, the screech of brakes, and the roar of propwash.

"Seventeen." Two red flares sprang from the plane to signal wounded on board.

"Oh boy." Jack knew what that was like.

The scene before him would look like chaos to the uninitiated eye—planes taxiing to their hardstands, pilots completing postflight checks with ground crews, trucks ferrying flight crews to the briefing room, ambulances racing. But all moved with precision and purpose, a symphony, but bigger, better, and with high stakes. To be part of the production was exciting, to know how it ran heightened the thrill, but to be the conductor—the thought made the adrenaline tingle warm in Jack's veins.

"We'd better get to the briefing room, find out how it went," he said.

Charlie peered through his binoculars. "Still three out."

"We'll get the word." Jack nudged him in the arm. "Come on. Coffee's waiting."

They trotted down the outside stairs, grabbed their bikes, and pedaled down the road that stuck the tower like a lollipop into the middle of the action. Jack pushed hard. Stretching the scar tissue, working the weak muscles, and pumping his heart felt good, even with prickles of pain as if slivers of shrapnel had defied the surgeon and the X-rays.

On the perimeter track, a crowd surrounded a B-17, and two olive drab ambulances parked by the rear fuselage door. Jack and Charlie stopped and planted their feet. A forest of hands lifted to help out a man with a bandaged thigh. Jack hoped it was just a flesh wound. He hated to see another man suffer amputation as Walt had. Mom's last letter said his younger brother was ill-humored, and he had to be a real grouch for her to say that.

Jack squinted at the shot-up Fort. Dad actually took pride in Jack for supporting Walt when he got the bad news, but Dad hadn't heard Jack fumble and waste all that mind-numbing seminary training.

A medic jumped out of the B-17, turned, and grasped a bloodied officer under the shoulders. The pilot, according to the crowd's murmurs. Another medic followed, supporting the man's feet.

Silence fell. Caps came off. Some of the men crossed themselves or muttered prayers. Jack's chest tightened, and he and Charlie exchanged a look and took off their hats. The medics laid the man on a gurney and pulled up a blanket. All the way.

The nose of the plane read *Dorothy Ann* and showed a pretty brunette in a yellow bathing suit. Somewhere in the States, a Dorothy Ann would receive a telegram in the next few days. Jack sighed as a warm breeze played with his hair, oblivious to the tragedy.

On the side of the fuselage, just forward of the Army Air Force's white star on a blue disk, gray letters read TS, the code for Jack's squadron. Jack hadn't even met the crew, who were probably on their first mission. This would be hard on the men. Somehow a body on a returning plane had a deeper effect than a crew of ten shot down in flames.

Both ambulances pulled away, one to Sick Quarters, where the wounded man would be stabilized and sent to the hospital, and the other to the morgue.

"We should go." Charlie's voice was thick.

"Yeah." They pedaled past Hangar Number One, the

workshops, and the supply stores. Jack had been unconscious when *Sunrise Serenade* put up red flares, but Charlie landed that plane and saw Jack hauled away to the hospital and poor Bill Chambers to the morgue.

He was a good man, de Groot.

When they reached the briefing room, they leaned their bikes on the stack by the door, returned the MP's salute, and entered the building.

Coffee. The smell wafted into Jack's nose, and he drew it in. Air crews stood in silent, fatigued groups and refueled on coffee and donuts while they waited their turn at inter-rogation.

Jack caught Charlie's eye and nodded to the long line at the Red Cross counter. "Coffee?"

Charlie gave a mock salute. "Right on it, Skipper."

"Thanks, pal." Jack clapped him on the back and headed into the briefing room. The noise energized him as much as the promised coffee. For the morning briefing, two hundred chairs had faced the map up front. Now the chairs surrounded a dozen tables, each with a crew and an intelligence officer recording every detail from the mission.

Jack walked the length of the room and extracted snip-pets of information. "Me 109s as thick as flies." "Flak? Sure, plenty." "Some of our bombs fell in the water." "I got him—a hundred yards. Right through the cockpit. Flipped head over tail all the way down." "Nine-tenths clouds over Hannover. Had to find a T/O."

Jack turned. The last statement came from Lt. Col. Louis Thorup, the executive officer, who had led the group on the mission. Which target of opportunity had they selected?

Exactly what the intelligence officer asked. "Wilhelms-haven" was the reply.

Jack spotted Joe Winchell's crew from his squadron. He

set his hand on Winchell's shoulder and leaned over. "Hiya, Winch. Hi, boys. How'd it go?"

"Great." A tired smile crossed Winchell's square face. "Hit those U-boat yards right on the button. Finnegan got himself an Fw 190 and an Me 109."

"Say, good job, Finn. Keep it up."

Captain Taylor, the intelligence officer, wore a snippy expression, so Jack gave him a nod. "I'll let you get back to work, Captain."

The snippy look dissolved. "Thanks, Major."

Jack went his way. All a matter of knowing each man, how to play up his strengths and play down his weaknesses. Let the clown joke, then make him get to business. Let the facts and figures man do his work, but get him to look up and smile once in a while.

At the front of the room, Colonel Castle stood talking to Maj. Jefferson Babcock Jr., temporary commander of Jack's squadron. What a work, Babcock. Cussingest man in the outfit until clean-mouthed Castle came along.

Jack approached Castle. "Sir, what's the word on the mission?" He knew better than to waste time on small talk with the hardworking, no-nonsense colonel.

"We have to wait for the final analysis, but the preliminary results look good." The CO stood shorter than Jack, with every feature, every gesture strong, neat, and sharp.

"We had two losses before the target." Babcock's soft tone echoed Castle's. "And one ditched 125 miles off Cromer."

A cold shudder ripped through Jack's bones. The day before, a crew from the 94th had ditched at sea, but both life rafts were spotted in the morning, and all ten men were rescued. "Another ditching?" Jack asked, his face composed. He couldn't let Castle know a ditching bothered him more than two lost aircraft and a man killed in action.

"They radioed coordinates," Castle said. "RAF Air-Sea Rescue is on the way."

"Thank goodness."

"You have a physical on Friday," Castle said. "Do you think you'll be cleared for active duty?"

"Yes, sir." Jack focused on his CO and tried not to smile at how Babcock adopted Castle's posture, hands clasped behind his back. To be different, Jack sank his hands in his trouser pockets. "I've been doubling up on calisthenics and passing up jeep rides. I'm more than ready."

"Good. As you know, we need another squadron commander, and I'd like to put Babcock in the spot as soon as possible."

"Congratulations." Jack shook Babcock's hand. The man smiled too much for someone who had advanced because a good man was either dead or imprisoned.

The colonel stepped to the side. "Well, Novak, I look forward to seeing you back in action."

"So do I, sir."

The CO left Jack with Babcock, whose smile dug deep grooves in his cheeks.

Jack put his hands back in his pockets. "Looking forward to your own squadron?"

"You bet." Babcock's voice rose to its usual level, and he ran his hand over his thick black hair, still ruffled from the flight helmet. "The job's a great stepping-stone."

"Stepping-stone?" The man hadn't even started as squadron commander, and he was already looking to the next promotion?

Babcock leaned forward, his dark eyes serious, as if explaining something to a child. "As a pastor, an advancement wouldn't do you much good, right?"

His laugh curdled Jack's stomach.

"But in a political career, promotions impress voters, and the more brass I work with, the more influence I'll have on Capitol Hill. My dad made a name for himself in the First World War, and you can see what it did for him." Babcock nodded, his lesson complete.

Jack tilted his head and narrowed his eyes. "I may be a simple country preacher, but seems to me we should focus on this job, not the next. As for promotions, we'll leave that to Castle."

Babcock's mouth remained in a smiling position, but the grooves in his cheeks flattened. The politician saw he had a rival, and Jack held his gaze firm until Babcock saw the rivalry was serious.

"Hiya, Skipper. Here's your coffee."

Jack broke his gaze only to take the coffee cup. "Thanks, buddy."

"You're welcome. Hi, Jeff. How was the mission?"

"My squadron did great." Babcock patted Jack's shoulder. "See you, Novak."

"See you." His squadron? What a jerk.

"Talking to your twin?"

Jack whipped around to face Charlie. "My twin?"

"Black hair, too handsome for your own good." Charlie held out a donut.

Jack took it, bit into it. "At least the similarities end with the looks."

"No, they don't." Charlie smiled as if he were amusing instead of annoying. "You're both 'juniors' following in your fathers' footsteps. You're both natural leaders, outgoing, ambitious."

Jack chewed the donut so hard he almost bit his tongue. "Ambitious? You can't compare my ambition and his."

"You both want the executive officer position, don't you?"

"Yeah, but I just want it. He—he's angling for it." He gestured in Babcock's direction and sent a spray of donut crumbs to the concrete floor. "Look at him mimicking Castle, glad-handing, and kissing babies. Next thing you know, he'll put up campaign posters."

"Want me to make posters too?" Charlie's face lit up, and he spread his hands wide toward the wall. "I've got it. How about 'No flak with Novak'? Say, that's not bad."

"Clever. Real clever." Jack let out a low grumble. "But I'm a commander, not a politician. Let him play his games. I'll just do my job."

"May the best man win?"

Jack glanced over at Babcock, who clapped Winchell on the back and ruffled Finnegan's hair. Castle would see through the baloney. Yeah, Jack would win.

9

12th Evacuation Hospital

Saturday, July 31, 1943

"I love this smell, don't you?" May said.

"Bichloride of mercury?" Ruth laughed and shook water from a pair of gloves. "Only a nurse would like this smell."

May rolled syringes in a pan of the blue green disinfectant. "In the orphanage I had no control over my life, but with soapy water and a stiff brush, I could scrub away the smells and pretend I lived in a castle."

Ruth draped the brown latex gloves over a clothesline to dry before being sterilized. "Cleanliness may not be next to godliness, but it beats back the demons of poverty."

"That it does."

Ruth inspected another glove for holes in need of patching. "Thank you for coming in early. It's so busy."

"Isn't it? If they keep flying such big missions, we won't have any beds left."

And the Eighth Air Force wouldn't have any men left. Ruth scrubbed at a stain on a glove. Jack wasn't in combat yet, was he? She didn't need that worry, nor did she like the fact that she would indeed worry.

"Tomorrow's Sunday," May said. "I don't suppose Jack and Charlie will come. They've sent up missions every day."

"I suppose not." Ruth kept her voice light although her heart felt heavy. Why was she still disappointed Jack hadn't come the previous Sunday to visit his men and worship in the chapel?

"I suppose I shouldn't pray for bad weather. The more they fly, the sooner this war will be over."

"I suppose so." Yet that morning, Ruth looked up and hoped for clouds. With Jack, she could almost be a normal woman. His looks and personality she could ignore, but not his character, his chivalry, his safety—a potent and lethal combination.

"We're doing a lot of supposing, aren't we?"

Ruth caught a rosy tint in May's cheeks. "Should I be supposing something?"

May snapped up her gaze. "Goodness, no. I don't want romance, and I just met Charlie. One picnic isn't enough to base any supposition on."

"But . . ."

May laughed. "But nothing. Sure, I trust Jack's judgment, but that doesn't mean Charlie's right for me, and that doesn't mean I'm ready, and that certainly doesn't make his job less dangerous."

"You won't get an argument from me. You know where I stand." So did Jack, yet the picnics smelled like a ruse, like a prelude to dating. All the more reason to get out of England and soon.

"Oh, Ruth, you'd better take your lunch. Are you going today?" May asked, eyes bright.

"Yes." Ruth rinsed her hands. She had an hour to ease her growling stomach and keep her appointment.

"I'll pray for you."

Ruth blinked at the strange sight of someone to talk to, someone who understood. "Thank you," she said to her roommate and—dare she say—her friend?

★

"Another one?" Lt. Agnes MacKinnon lifted her glasses, rubbed her eyes, and looked back down to Ruth's paperwork on her desk. "I can't afford to lose another nurse."

How many had applied to the flight nursing program? Nausea swept through Ruth's system as it had minutes before when she'd fled the mess hall. Sausage? She'd never be hungry enough to eat sausage.

The chief nurse's sigh made her thin chest collapse under her dark blue uniform jacket. "You're one of my best nurses. I don't want to lose you."

Ruth shifted her weight from one foot to the other. "Thank you, but I need this position. I support four brothers and sisters, and I can't do so on my current salary."

Lieutenant MacKinnon frowned at her.

Uh-oh. She'd think Ruth wanted the position only for the money. "It's not just for the extra pay. Flight nursing appeals to me for many reasons: the responsibility, the independence, the chance to participate in a new age for nursing."

The chief nurse tapped reedy fingers on the application. "Glamour, romance, adventure—that's all girls think about nowadays. What about the danger?"

"No more dangerous than if the 12th Evac were transferred to a combat zone."

"But hospitals are covered by the Geneva Conventions. Air evacuation isn't. It's performed in cargo planes. Cargo goes into the combat zone and casualties go out. Because the planes carry cargo, they can't be marked with the Red Cross, and they're legitimate targets for the enemy."

Ruth gripped her hands behind her back and forced a slow breath so she wouldn't hyperventilate. Her application had taken almost two months to arrive, and who knew how long it would take to be processed. Aunt Pauline's last letter complained of her sacrifices and the things she did without. Ruth couldn't afford delays from an apprehensive chief nurse.

"Ma'am, I joined the Army Nurse Corps aware of the risk. We're at war. Our men face the enemy without question. The least I can do is get the wounded out of danger, care for them, and take them home. I believe I would be an excellent flight nurse. I have the nursing skills, the ability to work independently, the desire to fly, and I am not afraid to be close to combat."

Lieutenant MacKinnon's lips pursed together.

Ruth clasped her hands in front of her stomach in a position just short of begging. "Please. Other than becoming a nurse, I've never wanted anything more than this. I need a recommendation from a highly respected nurse, which is why I came to you. I know your recommendation would carry weight."

The lips relaxed, but the eyes remained narrow.

Ruth offered a smile and a shrug. "Besides, my chance of acceptance is slim, isn't it?"

"Well, there is that."

"So, please—"

"All right." Lieutenant MacKinnon heaved a sigh and picked up the application. "I can't fight patriotism. What do you need?"

Ruth let out a puff of relief. "A letter. A letter, please. They need to know about my work habits and skills. Oh, and they also—they need a statement about my—my morality." Her throat pressed shut. A nurse was held to the highest standards and could be dismissed for morals violations. Somehow Ruth had always fooled everyone.

"Lieutenant Doherty?" The chief nurse gazed at Ruth over the top of her glasses. "Did your mother ever tell you to guard your reputation as a treasure?"

"Yes, ma'am," she choked out.

"Be glad you listened. Everyone talks of your high morals. This letter will be easy to write." She rubbed the bridge of her nose. "And very difficult. I'd hate to lose you."

"Thank you, ma'am." Ruth saluted and escaped, her heart straining against its iron shell.

High morals? She set a brisk pace down the pathway. Ten-Penny Doherty? High morals?

Ruth wanted to scream, and for a moment she thought she had, until she raised her head and saw a squadron of squat-nosed fighter planes—P-47 Thunderbolts, Jack called them.

She stretched one hand high as if she could grab hold and climb away from what she had done, from who she was.

10

Bury St. Edmunds

Monday, August 2, 1943

Jack glanced up Northgate Street to the red brick train station with its white Victorian scrollwork. Despite the fog, he had a complete view of the roundabout and he'd spot Ruth no matter which street she took downtown. Time for the next phase of the mission.

His plan had four stages. First came takeoff when he'd established a friendship with Ruth in the hospital.

The second stage, assembly—the group picnics—had gone well. In fact, yesterday's picnic exceeded expectations. They had all walked around the lake near the hospital, the one shaped like the squiggle over the *N* in Spanish—Ray would know what it was called. Charlie and May lagged, but Ruth stayed by his side, listened with compassion to his tales of the ravages of Blitz Week, and accepted his nudges with his jokes. Her bright laughter and smile goaded him into the third phase of his plan.

Time to cross the Channel and spend time alone with her, which wouldn't be easy. Ruth's defenses resembled the flak batteries on the European coast. Jack had to be subtle or he'd never reach the target, that gold ring around her heart.

Charlie thought Jack should slow down until he figured out Ruth's problem, but what did Charlie know? He'd only had two dates in three years.

Jack made out Ruth's shapely figure coming down Northgate Street. She couldn't afford the new olive drab uniforms some of the nurses wore, but she sure looked smart in the dark blue jacket and medium blue skirt.

Jack stepped back around the corner. He unzipped his lightweight leather flight jacket, made sure his shirt collar was open, and stuffed his hands into the pockets of his olive drab trousers. Had to look casual.

He let Ruth pass, then fell in behind her. "'One misty moisty morning.'"

Ruth looked over her shoulder and smiled.

"'When cloudy was the weather, I chanced to meet an old man clothed all in leather. He began to compliment and I began to grin. How do you do? And how do you do? And how do you do again?'"

Amusement crinkled her eyes. "It's afternoon."

"Yeah, but it's misty and moisty. Life in England has taught me what that means."

"No misty moisty mornings in California?"

"In January, not August." Jack proceeded down the flagstone sidewalk. "And look, you chanced to meet an old man clothed all in leather."

Ruth held her purse in front of her stomach. "I'm supposed to say, 'How do you do?'"

"With a grin, please."

She didn't. Her chin inched up, and she studied the two-storied houses crammed side by side. "First tell me why you're in town this misty moisty afternoon."

The first flak burst. Jack ducked his head to the side. "No mission today. Bad weather and too much damage from Blitz Week. We have to wait for replacement crews and let the mechanics do their work. Thought I'd explore town."

"Hmm." Ruth looked at a whitewashed brick house, her suspicion heavy as the fog.

What did he expect? He happened to explore town the same day he knew she'd run errands? No unbuttoned collar could mask that. "Would you mind if I walked with you?"

"As long as we're not together."

"All right." He strode into the street and spread his arms as wide as his grin. "There. We're not together."

"Jack!" she cried.

A honk. A delivery van lumbered all of five miles per hour down the street. Jack stepped out of the way and saluted the driver. In return he got a "Bloody Yank!"

"Get back up here." Ruth motioned frantically. "Don't make me fix you up again."

He hopped back onto the sidewalk. "Just as well, now that I'm cleared for active duty. Besides, I'd like your full-time company again, but I'd rather have this."

Too much. Ruth's eyes volleyed more flak at him.

He released a sigh. "Oh, come on. You've known me almost three months. I've never made a move on you, and I'm not about to start now." Nope, he had to wait a while.

Her eyes fluttered shut. "I'm sorry. I—it's a habit. I do—I do feel safe with you." She opened her eyes and revealed how fragile her trust was.

"Thanks." Time to change the subject. He tilted his head downhill, and they continued on their way. "What do you think of Charlie de Groot?"

"Charlie? Oh, he's wonderful."

"He's taken with May."

"I'm not surprised. She's a remarkable woman." A smile curved Ruth's pretty lips.

Jack was pleased that the two nurses were becoming friends. From what he could tell, Ruth hadn't had a friend in years. "Is May taken with Charlie?"

"Are you on a spy mission?"

"No." He laughed and plucked a handful of cherries from a branch overhead.

"He asked her out yesterday."

"Yep, and she turned him down, even though he gave up cigarettes for her."

"Do you blame her?"

"What?" Jack frowned. "First you say what a wonderful guy he is and then—"

"Yes, he's wonderful, and if we weren't at war, she'd be a fool to turn him down, but now?"

"Yeah." He popped a cherry in his mouth and almost spat it out. Sour. Was it even a cherry? "Not many men finish a twenty-five-mission tour. Charlie's up to eight, but still . . ."

"How many do you have?"

"One." He chucked the rest of the fruit into a shrub. He couldn't wait for the weather to clear. Jefferson Babcock Jr. had racked up lots of missions while Jack was grounded.

"One? What about all the missions you flew in the Pacific?"

"New tour. Start from zero." He grinned at her expression. "What? Worried about me? Better watch out. That looks like the concern of a friend, not just the concern of a nurse."

A GMC truck rumbled beside them, and Joe Winchell leaned out the window. "Hiya, Novak."

"Hi there, Winch. Hi, boys." The truck was crammed with a dozen men from his squadron. "Touring town?"

"Yep," Winchell said. "Want a ride downhill?"

"No, thanks. I'm enjoying the walk." He gazed down at the reason for his enjoyment.

She gave him a saucy tilt of her head. "I'd rather have a ride."

Several men cheered and scrambled to help Ruth, while Jack watched, dumbstruck. Once in the back of the truck, Ruth smiled down at him, a challenge in her eyes. She expected him to join her. She didn't want to be together, but she wanted him to follow like a lovesick schoolboy. Well, he wouldn't play along.

He saluted. "Enjoy the ride, Lieutenant Doherty. See you around."

The truck pulled away, and Jack laughed to himself at her stunned expression. Ten minutes later, he reached the Abbey Gate, a big square Norman tower. Although he'd sacrificed a walk into town with Ruth, he'd gained something better. Besides, the town wasn't that big, so he'd find her soon. Jack turned right onto Abbey Gate Street, where window boxes teemed with flowers in defiance of the war. Whatever made Hitler think he could defeat the British?

Jack poked his head into several shops until he found Ruth at the cash register of a bookstore. He leaned back against the counter next to her and crossed his arms. "'And how do you do again?'"

Ruth held out a trembling hand for her change. "Goodbye, *Major*."

He searched her stony face. "What's the matter?"

She gripped her book and stormed out the door.

He shook his head. This wasn't a burst of flak but a full-blown barrage. He jogged to catch up with her. "What's going on? Did I say something? What?"

"What?" She marched up the sidewalk. "You abandon me, and you have to ask what you did?"

"Abandoned you? What do you mean?" He stepped in front of her.

She edged past him. "Just that."

"Wait a minute. How could I abandon you if we weren't together in the first place?" He grabbed her arm.

"Don't touch me." Ruth flailed, and Jack dropped her arm in surprise. "How could you? How could you leave me?"

"I didn't. I didn't leave you. You left me, remember? You're the one who got in the truck. Not me. Be fair."

Ruth's head wagged from side to side. "How could you? How could you?"

Jack's gut twisted in anger. "Don't pin this on me. You're just mad 'cause I didn't play your game, 'cause I didn't heel like your pet dog, and now you're mad."

"No, I'm mad because you left me with those men." Her voice broke.

"Those men?" His anger detached, sent out feelers, and attached to something new. If anything happened, those men would be in the guardhouse—no, strapped to a bomb—an incendiary bomb. "Did they touch you? Tell me."

"No, but they could—" She pressed her hand over her eyes. "They could—there were so many . . ."

His lungs expanded with heat. "Then why on earth did you get in the truck?"

Ruth's face crumpled. "I thought—I thought you'd come."

She thought he'd come and protect her. The thought sliced into his lungs, and all the heat and pressure hissed out.

"I thought—I thought . . ." Her voice was tiny and cramped. "Why am I so stupid?"

Jack leaned back against the brick storefront, took off his cap, and ran his fingers through his hair. He'd never seen her scared before. In the hospital she was in control, the men helpless, but in the truck the situation was reversed. She wanted protection, and he hadn't provided it. He'd crushed the seed of trust he'd watered for three months. "Boy, did I blow it."

Her eyes—he couldn't stand it—anger, hurt, and fear jostled around in that gorgeous blue, all because of him.

"Listen, Ruth. I'm sorry. What was I thinking? A beautiful woman alone in a truck with a dozen men? Oh boy. Just because I know them and trust them doesn't mean you—oh boy."

Her jaw softened, and the anger washed from her eyes.

Jack leaned forward. "It won't happen again. You have my word. I will never leave you alone again."

Ruth looked up at him, eyes red and questioning.

"Never." He wanted to take her in his arms and show her what he meant, but the timing couldn't have been worse. Instead, he set his cap on his head and rubbed his chin. "If I'm going to keep an eye on you, I'd better get hospitalized again. Wait, what about your days off?"

Confusion overwhelmed the hurt and fear on her face. Good. Now to make her smile.

"Say, you think they'd take me in the Army Nurse Corps so we can work together? Wonder if those white dresses come in my size. Hmm. Guess I'll have to shave my legs." He hiked up one trouser leg and whistled. "That'll take a few days."

Ruth's mouth contorted, not quite a smile.

"Could you loan me a lipstick?"

"With—with your mustache? I can't—imagine." Ruth let out a flimsy bubble of a laugh. "You're crazy, Jack Novak."

He grinned. Out of the flak zone. Now to get back en route to the target. He gestured to the book in her hand. "What did you buy?"

Ruth uncrossed her arms and glanced at the book. "It's for my sister Anne. Her birthday's in September."

"You never miss a birthday, do you? They'd better return the favor."

"They'd better not," she said with a shaky smile. "It's my money."

Jack settled back against the wall and crossed his ankles. "When was the last time you got a gift?"

"Me?" Her eyes widened. "I don't know. High school graduation, I guess. My parents gave me a Bible."

Jack stared at her. How long had that been? Five years? Six? But she didn't have anyone to treat her, and she sure didn't treat herself. No nail polish or jewelry, not even a wristwatch. "When's your birthday?"

"Jack . . ." She glared at him, but he glared even harder until she broke away and sighed. "It's—it's August 3."

"Tomorrow?" He laughed good and hard, especially when he spotted the jeweler's sign overhead. "That settles it. I'll get you a watch as combination birthday present and guilt offering."

"A watch?" Ruth's jaw flopped open. "Jack, no. That's too expensive."

"You know how much I make? I don't have a family to support, not even a bad habit to support, and you need a watch."

"No, I don't." She clamped her hand over her wrist, the left one.

"Yeah, you do. How are you going to check pulses on a cargo plane? No clocks on those walls. Ever thought of that, Miss Flight Nurse?"

She blinked and frowned.

Jack held open the door to the shop. "You can stay out here, but if you want any say in the matter, you'd better come along."

Ruth groaned and headed into the store. "I wish I'd never met you."

Somehow he didn't believe her.

At the counter the jeweler displayed the limited selection of ladies' watches. Jack ruled out the cheapest, Ruth ruled out the fanciest, and they decided on a simple gold watch with a reddish brown strap, which Jack liked because it matched Ruth's hair.

After Jack paid, the jeweler held out the watch to Ruth, but Jack intercepted it. He buckled the strap around Ruth's slender wrist and let his fingers brush her skin. "There. Do you like it?"

"Yes. Thank you." She looked at her arm on the counter. "Thank you."

"You're welcome." A jagged scar curved around the watch face. He ran his finger over the scar. "How'd this happen?"

Ruth drew back her arm and tugged down the sleeve of her uniform jacket. "A long time ago."

She hadn't answered his question and she wouldn't. Oh yeah, Ruth Doherty was an intriguing little challenge.

When they stepped back outside, Jack nudged Ruth with his elbow. "What's your next errand?"

"Oh, no more errands. I was . . ." Her face went blank, and her eyes skittered about.

Fishing for an excuse. "Okay, what were you going to do before a thoughtless, bumbling pilot crashed into your day?"

One corner of her mouth crept up. "At least you're an honest, bumbling pilot."

"I'm a lousy liar. Always made my little brother lie for me. So what are your plans? And you're no good at lying either, so don't try."

"Well, I was—I had a quarter left over last month, so I thought I'd see a movie. Maybe."

"Sounds good to me."

"Jack . . ." There was that fire he loved.

He spread his arms wide. "What do you want me to do? If I go along, you'll think I'm finagling a date, but if I don't, I'll break my promise and abandon you. I have to wait around for you anyway, because I'm not about to let you go home by yourself. Might as well watch the movie."

The fire dimmed, but embers still flared.

"I'll sit on the far side of the theater," he said. "You won't even—"

"Oh brother. You can come, as long as I pay my way. Bad enough I let you buy me jewelry."

"Not jewelry—medical equipment." Nevertheless, Jack was pleased she saw the watch as the personal gift he intended.

The theater was almost empty, and they found seats center back. The men from the 94th preferred the first-run Hollywood movies shown on base, and in town they favored the pubs.

Ruth's laughter during the cartoons encouraged Jack, as did the newsreel showing the Allies' rapid advance across Sicily. Now that Italy's king had imprisoned Mussolini, GIs would soon storm over the Alps into Germany. With the Soviet drive west after the Battle of Kursk, and the American and Australian gains in New Guinea and the Solomons, the prospect of victory surged in Jack's veins.

However, the film, some song-and-dance B movie, grated on his nerves. When the hero sang about the moon, Jack whispered in Ruth's ear, "Betcha he'll rhyme it with June."

Ruth laughed softly. "You know what they say: moon, June, spoon."

"No imagination. What about tune, soon?"

Ruth's smile was visible even in the darkened theater. "Harpoon."

"Now that's more like it." For a moment he played with

lyrics, and then he leaned as close to Ruth as he dared and sang, "We stood beneath a moon in June. You skewered me with a harpoon. Then I got drunk in the saloon."

Ruth covered her mouth and her laugh. "I can't stand people who talk in movies."

"I can't stand you, either."

When she finished laughing, she uncovered her smile. "You goon."

"Loon." Jack savored the sound of their combined laughter. Eventually Ruth sighed and leaned back in her seat.

Jack rested his ankle on his knee. Maybe some of the day's damage had been repaired. He thought of another rhyme and turned to her, but at the same time she leaned closer, and before he could pull back, his lips brushed her ear.

Swell, now he really blew it. "I'm sorry," he said. "Sorry. Just wanted to say something."

"No. No, I'm sorry. I—I wanted to say something too. You go first."

Jack tried to read her expression in the gray light. The warmth on his lips was so sweet and fleeting, he wanted to kiss her for real.

"Jack?" she whispered. "What was it?"

He swallowed hard to clear his throat and his mind. "Raccoon."

"Raccoon?" Relief colored her laugh. "Don't start that nonsense again."

Good. She realized it was an accident. "What did you want to say?"

Ruth rested back in her seat. "Nothing, really. I—well, why do people in love lose their heads?" She nodded at the screen, where two lovers waltzed in bliss.

What an interesting question. "That's part of the fun. You can't take your eyes off each other, you have your own private language." Jack frowned at the screen. Why was she asking? Hadn't she ever . . . ?

He turned to her. "You've never been in love, have you?"

She shook her head, gaze fixed forward. "I bet you have, plenty of times." Her voice was too light, too high.

Very interesting. "A few times, but no one I should have married. And the girl I should have married—I couldn't manage to fall in love with her."

Finally Ruth faced him. "What do you mean?"

Jack slid nearer, under the pretense of keeping his voice low. "Alice was the daughter of one of my seminary professors. She was sweet on me. I dated her partly so I could pass Apologetics."

"You're awful."

"I know. And she was the ideal pastor's wife. Pretty, sweet, played the organ. But she had no fire in her. None. The Air Corps was my escape. Alice wanted me to take a church, said I was disobedient for joining up. She broke up with me and saved me the bother."

"Hmm."

He studied the curves of her forehead, nose, lips, chin, and how the contours changed as she thought. Did she realize Jack needed a woman with both character and fire? And she needed him too. He knew it.

Ruth shifted in her seat. "So it's against God's will for you to fly?"

"Well, no. There's a war on. But when the war's over . . ."

"You don't want to be a pastor, do you?"

Jack stared at the woman who had voiced what he never dared to think. With a groan he sank back in his seat. How had the subject changed from love? "It doesn't matter what I want, only what God wants."

"God wants you to be a pastor?" Ruth's eyes glowed in the light from the film. "You were called?"

Called? Dad talked about it, Ray talked about it, but what about him? Was he called? He shoved off the niggling thought. "Of course God wants me to be a pastor. I'm like my dad in every way. His namesake, the pastor—heard it all my life. Besides, I do want to serve the Lord." He held his forefinger to his lips. "Now hush. People who talk in movies—boy, I tell you."

Ruth smiled and faced forward.

Jack leaned on the armrest away from her. What was going on? He was supposed to shake up her world, not the other way around.

11

Bury St. Edmunds

Monday, August 16, 1943

"I'm so glad you came with me, May."

On the bus seat next to Ruth, May Jensen laughed. "I never thought I'd hear you say those words."

"Neither did I, but I am glad. I wanted to go into town today, but I promised Jack I wouldn't go alone, and then he didn't show by noon—he must be on a mission and—"

"I know." May glanced at Ruth's hands and smiled.

Ruth was stroking the leather of her watch strap again. May had noticed the watch immediately and figured out where it came from, to Ruth's dismay. She drew a deep breath to say what she needed to. "It'll also be fun to spend the afternoon with you." And necessary. She needed to write over the memories she'd replayed too often the past two weeks.

May's thin eyebrows elevated. "Orphans' day out?"

Ruth laughed. "Shall we go begging? Spare a tuppence, sir?"

The ladies stepped off the bus and headed down the hill, past two-storied houses standing shoulder to shoulder, neat and clean under black slate roofs. Ruth tipped her face to the warm blue sky laced with white tendrils. "A perfect day to fly."

"We spend too much time with Charlie and Jack."

"Perhaps." But the last few months were the best Ruth could remember. However, the war pressed on, and Jack was up in combat, possibly under fire while she walked in the sunshine. *Lord, please keep him safe.*

"I wonder how the mission's going." May's face mirrored Ruth's concern.

"Far too much time with them."

May groaned. "I can't believe this. I promised myself I wouldn't fall for one of the men, but Charlie—I can't help it. And you—you were more adamant about not dating than I was, and look at you."

Ruth's chest tightened. "I'm not dating Jack."

"And I'm not dating Charlie. We might as well, given how we feel."

At the moment, Ruth's mouth was the driest spot in England. She had to distract May. "Will you accept if Charlie asks you out again?"

"No." Wrinkles creased May's white forehead. "Oh, Ruth, his job is so dangerous, much more than Thomas's. I can't go through that again."

"I know." Ruth slipped her arm through May's. Their heels clicked in unison on the flagstone sidewalk.

May raised a wobbly smile. "What are the plans, oh great leader?"

How wonderful to have a friend—someone to lift her spirits, someone whose spirits also needed a lift. "Well, we're two happy-go-lucky women out on the town." Ruth flung out her arm and kicked her leg as high as her uniform skirt allowed. "Let's see a movie and weep during the funny parts and giggle during the sad parts."

May grabbed Ruth's hand and swung it back and forth. "Then we can dance through the streets and toss Hershey bars to the children."

"Smashing. Then we'll go to the center of town and play London Bridge until the MPs cart us home." Ruth ducked under their raised arms and twirled behind them to face—

"Jack!" she gasped. "Charlie!"

"Ladies." Jack's eyes crinkled at the corners.

A pencil dangled from Charlie's mouth. "So this is what women do when men aren't around."

May dropped a curtsey. "We dance *because* men aren't around."

Ruth laughed and readjusted her cap. "What are you doing here? I heard planes this morning and assumed you had a mission."

"We did," Jack said. "We're done. Early mission, short mission, easy mission."

"Dropped half our bombs on one airfield, half on another." The pencil jumped as Charlie talked. "Never done that before. Two targets on one trip. Boy, was that fun."

Jack stuffed his hands in the pockets of his flight jacket. "Now we're here. I can keep my promise."

Ruth never knew her heart fit in her esophagus, but apparently it did.

"And you." Charlie pulled the pencil from his mouth and pointed it at May. "You made me give up my smokes, and now I snap pencils by the bushel. Come on. We're shopping for pencils."

May's jaw fell open, and she looked at Ruth.

"Pencils?" Jack said. "I don't want to shop for pencils. Do you, Ruth?"

"Well, I—"

"Course not. Go on, you two." Jack tossed Charlie a coin. "Get me some ink while you're at it."

"Over and out." Charlie took May's arm and hauled her down the hill, while May shot Ruth a confused glance over her shoulder.

Ruth reeled from the change in plans and from Jack's warmth hovering behind her. "Pencils?"

"Stupid, huh? But he pulled it off."

So did Jack. She turned to face him. "You two are the sneakiest—"

"May didn't protest." Jack nodded toward the town center. "As for you, my friend, I believe the day's plans involve movies, dancing, and London Bridge."

"Oh no. Not with you." Ruth strolled down the sidewalk. "Now I have a yearning for one of those fussy porcelain figurines. Could take hours to find the right one."

Jack shook his head so hard Ruth thought his hat would fly off. "No shopping. I have two things to celebrate. Number one: I'm flying again, two days in a row."

"How was it?"

His eyes lit up. "Can't tell you how good it felt to get off the ground. And both missions were milk runs. What a difference those Thunderbolts make. Chased off the Luftwaffe. Just wish they had the range to escort us to Germany."

"How did you do sitting so long?"

"Fine, fine. Always the nurse." His glower faded with a sigh. "All right, I was mighty sore at the end."

She laughed. "Pun intended?"

"Pun?" His black brows drew together as if conferring on her statement. Then he grumbled. "The end. Swell. Glad my injuries amuse you."

"Not as much as your embarrassment." And what an opportunity to dispel any romance.

"You want to keep teasing me, or you want to hear the second reason to celebrate?" He pulled an envelope from inside his jacket and handed Ruth a piece of airmail stationery covered with jagged handwriting. "From my brother Walt. He's not used to writing with his left hand, but you can make it out."

> Well, Jack, for the first time in my life, I'm going to beat you at something.
>
> The other day at the hospital, I had a visit from Allie—the engaged woman I'd been writing to. After a few mishaps, I told her how I felt. Was I surprised to learn she'd broken her engagement and she's in love with—get this, Jack—your ugly kid brother! We're getting married next spring. Who would have thought I'd be the first Novak brother to tie the knot?
>
> Please tell Lieutenant Doherty if you see her. It's amazing we had the same nurse. But I don't believe in coincidences, only in God, and now more than ever I'm convinced God is good and merciful and generous beyond measure.

"This is wonderful," Ruth said.

"Yeah. I can't believe my baby brother's getting married. Of all the things to beat me at. I mean, the kid never dated, clammed up whenever he saw a girl."

Ruth couldn't decipher the gleam in Jack's eye. Was it joy? Or competition? He'd better not think he had to beat his brother, and if he did, he'd better not look at her.

Jack looked at her. "Today we celebrate. A movie, dinner,

my treat. Not a date. Boy, you're skittish. Can't a man and a woman eat together without it being a date?"

"I suppose so." She frowned. If dinner and a movie weren't a date, what was?

However, the movie was no more romantic than if she'd gone with May. No whispered rhymes, no accidental brush of lips, no nudges from a solid shoulder, and she couldn't deny her disappointment.

Out of the corner of her eye, she studied Jack's strong profile.

Why not? This voice had grown louder the last two weeks.

Why couldn't she? This unreasonable voice.

She could still provide for her family. This rebellious voice.

Wouldn't it be wonderful?

Jack glanced at her and smiled, as if he'd sensed her thoughts, as if he'd seen her stroking the watch strap and imagining his touch. *Why ever not?*

She pressed back in her seat. She knew perfectly well why not.

After the movie concluded, they walked outside and blinked at the sunshine.

"Okay, Lieutenant Skittish," Jack said. "To prove this isn't a date, we'll pick up some fish and chips and go eat at the abbey. Too nice to be cooped up indoors anyway."

"It is." A warm breeze wafted over her face. "And I've heard the fish and chips are wonderful."

"You don't eat out, do you?" His eyes widened. "Do you send every penny home?"

"Almost." Yet it still wasn't enough for Aunt Pauline. Ruth shrugged off the fear. "The Army feeds me and shelters me. What more do I need?"

"Everyone needs occasional pampering."

Ruth watched her uniform shoes tread the flagstones. "Not if you've never had it."

"About time someone pampered you." Jack's voice was so thick, Ruth glanced up. The determination in his jaw told her he planned to provide the pampering, and the tenderness in his eyes made her want to receive it.

"I'll start right here. This is a good place." He swung open a thick wooden door.

She forced herself to concentrate, to tamp down her emotions, and to adjust to the darkness of the pub. The scent of beer brought on a wash of nausea, but she made herself breathe evenly and followed Jack to the bar. A young woman with frizzy dark hair approached.

"We'd like some fish and chips to go," Jack said.

She flipped her hand. "You Yanks are always in a hurry."

Jack leaned on the bar and smiled. "We're in a hurry to help you win this war."

Red spots appeared on the girl's cheeks, and she patted down the frizz. "We have the freshest fish and chips in town, but may I recommend the bangers? They're lovely."

"Sounds good to me," Jack said. "Ruth?"

Her stomach balled up. "Bangers? That's sausage, right?"

"Yeah. Real good." He squinted at her in the murky light. "Are you okay?"

"Oh, I just—I can't stand sausage. The smell nauseates me."

Jack studied her, then turned to the barmaid. "Two orders of fish and chips, please."

With their dinner wrapped in newspaper, they strolled down the street and through the imposing Norman Gate Tower. Jack pointed out arrow slits in the thick stone walls.

Then they passed through a circular garden, where an old man sat playing a violin to a group of children.

"A GI!" The children jumped to their feet and ran over. "Any gum, chum? Any gum?"

Jack laughed and pulled a pack of Wrigley's from his pocket. He passed a stick to each child and sent them on their way.

Ruth had never seen him chew gum. "You buy that just for the children, don't you?"

"Sure. Why don't we sit on that wall over there?"

They padded through the grass to an ancient low wall, part of the ruined abbey. Jack laid his jacket down so Ruth wouldn't snag her stockings on the black, white, and gray stones protruding from the mortar.

Jack unwrapped his dinner. "The oldest buildings in Antioch aren't even a hundred years old, and here we are sitting on something over nine hundred years old."

"And Henry the Eighth tore it down in the Reformation." Ruth gazed around at the clumps of ruins in the grass, some rising ten, twenty feet to hint at a window or doorway. "The stupid things people do."

Jack chewed for a moment. "Speaking of stupid, did I ever tell you about the business I set up when I was a kid?"

"I don't think so."

"I sold rides in Grandpa Novak's old biplane. I must have taken up half the kids in Antioch, made a lot of money. Only problem was I didn't ask Grandpa's permission. When he found out, he gave me a memorable whipping, made me return every cent, and worst of all, he wouldn't let me fly for a whole year."

Ruth smiled at his forlorn expression. "Poor baby."

"Nah, I deserved it." He pointed a chip at her. "Okay, your turn."

She took a bite of fish and tried to think of a story. The crispy batter hit her tongue, and then the fish dissolved in her mouth, moist and flavorful, much better than what she used to fry up on the little coal stove.

The little stove. She swallowed and smiled. "There was the time I wanted to play at the beach. Pa couldn't afford El tickets for all of us, so Ellen and I made our own beach. We shoveled the ash out of the stove and onto the floor. You should have seen Ma's face. From then on, cleaning the stove was my job."

Jack's eyes shone so much, Ruth remembered another story, and they shared laughter over childhood misadventures while they ate. After they finished, they folded up the newspaper, unsure whether the grease disqualified it as scrap paper.

Jack put one foot up on the wall and draped his arm over his knee. "Your childhood was a lot like mine."

"Alike?"

"Sure. Kids having fun and getting in trouble. Parents who loved the Lord, loved each other, and loved us. What a blessing."

"I suppose so." The ruins glowed golden in the evening sun. Jack and May saw blessings everywhere. All Ruth could see was what God took away from her, not what he gave her. However, the blessings were there—her job, her daily bread, her brothers and sisters fed and clothed and cared for. *Lord, help me see the blessings.*

"Does the watch bother you?"

"Excuse me?" Ruth swung her gaze to Jack.

"You keep fiddling with it. Does it bother you?"

She glanced at the watch, a reminder of Jack's protective, giving friendship. Was it—yes, it was a blessing, and for once she didn't want to give him a sassy answer. "No, I like it. I like how it feels. I can't tell you how much it means to me."

She forced herself to look him in the eye, to let him know he had restored a piece of what she had lost.

"Does it keep good time?" He took her hand, stretched out her arm, and checked her watch against his.

Heat streamed up her arm, straight to her heart. She sucked in her breath, and her mouth and eyes flew open. She had to pull back, but his grip was both firm and strangely welcome.

"Does it?" He cocked an eyebrow at her.

Ruth clamped her mouth shut and nodded.

"Good." As if his touch weren't enough, he had to grin. "Your watch says it's time to dance."

"Dance?" she gasped.

"Can't celebrate without dancing. We even have that violin playing over there." He got to his feet and engulfed her hand in his. "Besides, this rock wall is killing me. Have pity."

"I—I don't know how to dance."

"Yeah, it's been a long time since cotillion, but—"

Ruth shook her head and wished she had the resolve to pull her hand free. "I didn't go. I had—odd jobs. After school—had to earn money—odd jobs."

"Then it's time you learned." With tender eyes and a tug on her hand, he led her to a level spot in the grass.

She struggled to breathe. "I—I—I don't—"

"Nothing to it. Put your hand here." At arm's length, Jack placed Ruth's left hand on his shoulder and set his hand on her waist. "Basic position. How's that?"

"I'm okay." White sparkles appeared before her eyes. She took a slow breath and concentrated on a button on Jack's khaki shirt.

"Just follow me. Nothing fancy. But I'll need to hold you closer."

The sheltering wall of his chest rose before her, the protective curve of his arm encircled her, and the button bobbed and blurred as through a glass of water. Pa used to hold her like this, so large and powerful and gentle. The button faded in the blur, Ruth's throat tightened, and a tear burned down her cheek.

She was crying? Oh no. She couldn't let Jack see, and she couldn't wipe her eyes without detection. Without thinking, she pressed her face to his shoulder. Oh, why did she do that?

Jack drew her closer with a deep murmur.

She fought for composure, but her tears ran unseparated onto his shirt. When was the last time she'd been held? Pa had been confined to bed. Ma and the children hugged her, but they didn't hold her like this, like a refuge.

Jack's muscles twitched under her face. "Say, you're not crying, are you?"

She shook her head, burrowed in his thick shoulder.

"Look at me and tell me that." He pulled back slightly and ducked his head to look her in the eye. "I knew it. I stepped on your toes."

"No." She released a strange sound, halfway between laugh and sob. With his face so close and accepting and encouraging, she had to tell the truth. She took a ragged breath. "My father—he was paralyzed when I was twelve. It's been twelve years since anyone held me, really held me."

Jack sighed, ran his hand up her back, and pressed her head to his chest. "Shirt's cotton. Washes easily."

He was giving her permission to cry? How long had it been? She was the strength in the hard times to ease her parents' burden. She was the support for the children when Pa and Ma died. Never once did she allow herself to cry.

Now the tears flowed in an unrelenting stream. Folded in Jack's arms, she could be weak, she could grieve, she could be nurtured.

Eventually the stream reduced to a trickle and dried. A sniff, a shaky breath, and peace. Still Jack hummed to the violin music and stroked her back. Ruth turned her face to the side and saw his jaw covered with the faint, dark stubble of evening. She had an urge to press her lips to that masculine roughness, to thank him for what he'd given her, but she couldn't.

"Thank you," she whispered.

"Any time, baboon."

She lifted her head and blinked, her eyelashes sticky from tears. "Baboon?"

"Moon, June, baboon." Mischief glinted in his eyes.

Ruth's laugh came out rough and wet.

"See. It was time to make you laugh again."

"I'll say." She touched the large damp spot on his shirt. "Oh dear."

"I don't mind." He planted a kiss on her forehead. "Now, do you want to dance?"

Ruth's mind tumbled and spun. "Dance?"

Jack's lips curved in a casual smile as if they hadn't just kissed her. "The violin, the celebration, remember?"

Unwilling to break the embrace, Ruth nodded. Dancing, however, didn't come easily. The beat eluded her and her feet betrayed her, but with Jack's patient good humor, the awkwardness slipped away, she relaxed in his arms, and her laughter mingled with his. Her chest felt lighter than it had in years, as if the salty tears had corroded the iron shell around her heart. She tried to summon her reservations, but every time he swung her around, another chunk fell off, until her heart lay exposed before him.

"Had enough?" he asked.

"Already?"

"I've got to get you home and return to base before eight

in case we fly tomorrow." He released her, returned to the wall, and slipped on his flight jacket.

The sudden emptiness made Ruth catch her breath. "What about London Bridge?"

"Huh?" Jack adjusted his jacket collar.

A surge of warmth made her want to surprise him, to please him, to give to him. She held out both hands. "A movie, dancing, London Bridge. You promised."

His eyes rounded, his smile rose, and he came and took her hands.

Ruth swung their clasped hands overhead. She knew her smile was coy, but she didn't care. "'London Bridge is falling down, falling down, falling down. London Bridge is falling down.'"

"'My fair lady.'" With a great laugh, Jack scooped her into his arms.

Ruth joined his laughter, overcome by his nearness, his breath on her face, *him*. And more than anything she wanted his kiss, his love, *him*.

"I don't date," she blurted out.

Jack looked as shocked by her words as she was. "Yeah," he said slowly. "That's why I never asked you out, my little macaroon." He waggled an eyebrow like Groucho Marx.

"Macaroon?" Her arms relaxed around his neck.

His face grew serious. "Ever had a macaroon?"

"Uh-uh."

"Funny things. They melt in your mouth, but if you're not careful, they crumble in your hand."

Ruth tried to analyze his analogy, but all she could concentrate on was how his lips moved. Eight years had passed since her last kiss, but she knew Jack would be a good kisser, like Eddie Reynolds. He wouldn't pucker or slobber or peck.

"I don't want to push too hard, Ruth. I don't. I care about

you. And I know, if I make the wrong move, you'll crumble. But if I'm careful . . ."

She'd melt in his mouth. That's what she wanted. No more pretending she didn't care for him. No more denying her blessings. She let her face rise toward him.

"Ruth." He gathered her close until their foreheads touched. "My darling Ruth."

"Oh, Jack." Her mind flooded with a liquid haze, as dark and warm and delicious as cocoa, until everything in her yearned for his kiss.

Then his lips molded against hers.

Trapped in the alley, three burly men, the crunch of her wristwatch on the brick wall, the sickening trickle of blood down her arm. "You're nothing but a whore."

Ruth gasped and flinched.

"Huh?" Jack stared at her. "What's the matter?"

"No. No. No." She squirmed out of his embrace. "Oh no."

He reached for her hand. "Oh, darling. That was your first kiss, wasn't it?"

Hysterical laughter burst out. She yanked away her hand and clapped it over her mouth. "No. Oh, you have no idea."

"Then what's the matter?"

His breath stank of beer and sausage. He ground the broken watch glass into her wrist, ground the truth into her head: "You'll never get rid of me. You'll always see my face."

Ruth backed away and turned around. Which way—which way should she go? She spotted the Gate Tower and headed for it.

"Ruth! What's going on?"

"Oh no. I can't believe I let this happen. I knew better. I knew this was a mistake."

Jack's footsteps thumped up beside her. "Mistake? I don't—"

"Yes, a mistake." She didn't look at him, only at the Gate, her escape. "I can't believe I let myself—oh, you're good, Jack. Really good. I can't believe—"

"What are you talking about?" He grabbed at her arm.

She shook him off. "No! I told you I don't date, but you didn't listen. Why didn't you listen?" Tears stung her eyes and her raw, exposed heart.

Jack swung in front of her and gripped her arms. "I'm trying to listen, but you're not making sense."

"Don't you understand?" Ruth's voice quivered. Her plans for life didn't include love or marriage, and now she knew why, with a crushing finality. She could never kiss a man again, not without remembering that day and her sin that caused it. "I hate kissing."

Jack's face scrunched up. "What?"

"Can't stand it." She broke away and strode for the Gate. "Hate it, hate it, hate it. Now do you see? Now do you understand why I don't date?"

"I've never known anyone . . ." Jack's voice diminished. He wouldn't follow her.

"Yeah, well, now you do. Now you can leave me alone. Do you understand? Leave me alone."

"Yeah. I'll do that."

Where—where was that iron shell now that she needed it most?

12

Jack threaded through the crowd in the Officers' Club, eyes averted.

"Last call for drinks, men. Mission tomorrow. Bar closes at eight."

Times like this, Jack almost wished he drank. With scotch in hand, the men seemed to forget the deaths of so many friends, the strong possibility they'd die the next day, and women. Nevertheless, alcohol didn't erase pain. It only postponed it.

Good thing no one was at the piano. Music was a better remedy than booze. Jack sat at the flimsy upright and thumbed through the sheet music: "Jersey Bounce," "I've Heard That Song Before," "Pistol Packin' Mama." Too cheerful, too likely to attract a crowd.

"Serenade in Blue." Yeah, appropriate. He played softly and let the tune lick his wounds. Just when he'd figured out Ruth's problem—grief for her parents and the strain of responsibility—everything blew up in his face. What on earth? Women always said he was a good kisser. What on earth was wrong with Ruth?

"You look like a man who needs a drink." Charlie plunked two Coke bottles on top of the piano.

Jack mustered a smile. "Thanks, pal."

Charlie popped the lids off the bottles. "'Serenade in Blue'? You usually pound out crowd pleasers. The doc will ground you for combat fatigue if you play 'As Time Goes By.'"

Jack released a wry chuckle. With Ruth Doherty a kiss was not just a kiss.

"What's up, Skipper?"

"See this?" He held up an open palm. "Macaroon crumbs."

"Huh?"

"Macaroon crumbs, and I don't even know why." Jack wiped his hand on his trousers and turned back to the sheet music. "You know, in all my life I've never failed to meet a goal. Not once."

"Wow. Proud of that, aren't you?"

"Yeah. But what if you set the wrong goal?"

★

Ruth's hands shook in the wash basin, rippling the water's surface. Ma always told her to wash her face after she cried, but tonight it didn't do any good. She hadn't shed a tear since she was fifteen. After that horrid day in the alley, she had cried, thrown up, cried some more, washed and washed and washed, and she'd never—ever—spoken of it, not even when her sister Ellen found her in the washtub behind the sheet hung in the corner of the apartment. Ellen figured out what happened. Ellen said she deserved it. Ellen was right.

Ruth buried her face in her towel and took deep breaths until the shakiness subsided. Then she wrapped her soap and toothbrush and toothpaste in her towel and strapped on her watch.

Should she even wear it anymore? A film passed over her

eyes. Jack's friendship had come to mean so much, and now she'd lost it.

"That sure is a nice watch." Pretty blonde Marian Willis smoothed cold cream into her cheeks. "Flo, did you see Ruth's watch?"

Ruth picked up her towel bundle. Oh no. She couldn't deal with Flo Oswald tonight.

Flo popped a toothbrush from her mouth and took Ruth's wrist. "Oh, nice. It's new?"

"Yes," Marian said. "She's never worn a watch. I always wondered why, because if I had a scar like that, I'd want to cover it. Oh, it doesn't cover the scar, does it?"

"Thanks for noticing." Ruth pulled her hand free and stepped toward the door, but Marian and Flo blocked her path.

"Who's it from?" Flo asked with bright, beady eyes.

Ruth looked at her watch, but she could only see Jack's tender smile as he buckled the strap. "It's a birthday present."

Marian chuckled. "Yeah, but from whom? Please tell me it's from a man."

"Oh, but she doesn't date," Flo said, eyes wide. "What do you think this is? The USO?"

Ruth shouldered past them. She couldn't possibly come up with a sharp-witted retort.

"Maybe it's from a former patient." Flo's voice followed her down the hallway. "Louise saw Ruth in town with a certain Major Novak."

Ruth whipped to face them. "I'm not dating him."

Marian smiled and crossed her arms over her nightgown. "You know what they say about protesting too much. Come on, tell us. Is it from that gorgeous major?"

Ruth made for her room. Her cheek twitched and her arms shook.

Marian squealed. "Oh, it is. How romantic."

No, no, no. Ruth dropped her towel on her cot and squeezed her burning eyes shut. Not tonight. She couldn't handle this tonight.

Two sets of footsteps drew up to her cot. "We're going about this the wrong way, Marian. You and I go out with any man who asks, and we never get gifts like that. Ruth plays hard to get, and lovesick fools shower her with gifts."

"Leave me alone," Ruth said, her voice quiet and trembling.

"Ooh, Ruth," Marian said. "If you actually dated, you'd get all sorts of presents."

Shakes spread through Ruth's whole body. This had to stop, had to stop.

"And for a kiss," Flo said. "I bet you could get cold, hard cash."

"No!" Ruth spun around, fists shaking at her sides. "Leave me alone!"

Marian stepped back.

Flo covered her mouth. "Goodness. We're just having a little fun."

"Leave me alone." Before Ruth's eyes, the nurses' faces darkened and stars flickered. She edged toward the door. So what if she wore her nightgown? She had to get out.

"What's the matter?" A touch to her arm. When had May come in?

May looked back and forth between the ladies. "What's going on?"

Flo blinked. "We just asked about her watch."

"I think you'd better go," May said with quiet power, and Marian and Flo left the room.

Ruth's breath came quick and shallow, and the white stars formed a swirling galaxy. She had to get out. The door— where was the door?

"Ruth?" May's face was almost black. "You're hyperventilating. You have to sit down."

"Gotta leave." She took a step and banged her shin on the cot.

"Sit." May grasped Ruth's shoulders and pressed her down to the thin mattress. "You know what to do. Put your head between your knees."

Ruth let her head drop. The floor swung up, and the boards spun and danced between her feet. She moaned.

May stroked her hair. "Deep breaths, honey. Deep breaths."

Ruth forced down her respiratory rate. In a few minutes, the white sparks fizzled out, and the floor righted itself.

"Kate, would you please get that glass of water on the table?"

Ruth ventured a glance. Four knees faced her. Oh no, she'd created a scene.

"How are you doing?" May asked, her hand gentle on Ruth's hair.

"Better. Thank you."

"Oh, thanks, Kate. Ruth, would you like some water?"

She had to face the world sometime. She straightened up, pushed the hair off her face, and took the glass. Kate Fletcher and Rosa Lomeli, two of her roommates, sat on May's cot across from her. Ruth offered a weak smile. "Thank you."

"It's the least I can do," Kate said. "I can't believe those two."

Rosa flapped her hand toward the door. "There's a word for gals like that, but I'm too much of a lady to say it."

"Ignore them," Kate said. "Marian feasts on gossip, and Flo's jealous you snagged such a handsome officer."

Ruth groaned and rubbed her eyes. Yeah, she snagged him and tore him to pieces.

May patted Ruth's shoulder. "Would you like some privacy?"

"Yes, please."

"We understand," Rosa said. "If you need anything— water, hankies, a posse to string up those wretched excuses for nurses—you let us know."

Ruth stared at Kate and Rosa as they left. Since she joined the 12th Evac, she'd had rare, businesslike conversations with the two women, yet they were being so kind.

"Would you like me to leave too?" May asked.

The word *yes* perched on her tongue, but May's expression was so sympathetic, Ruth didn't want to weld those chunks of iron back around her heart yet. "Please stay."

"All right." May locked her gaze on Ruth—eyes of the palest shade of blue, shot through with silver. "Now, remember, Flo and Marian don't really know you, and they don't know Jack. He gave you the watch because he cares about you, not because he expects anything from you."

Ruth's vision swam. Not again.

"So, did you have a nice day in town?" May said in a cheery voice, as if the change in topic would raise Ruth's spirits.

It didn't. Her face crumpled.

"Oh, honey, what's the matter?"

Ruth covered her eyes with her hand. Could she tell May about crying on Jack's shoulder? About flirting with him? About flinching from his kiss? About her hysterical flight? No, she'd already lost one friendship today.

She drew a breath, dropped her hand to her lap, and lifted her chin high. "Let's just say Jack knows I don't date, and he'll no longer try to change my mind."

13

Tuesday, August 17, 1943

"Say good-bye to the Thunderbolts," Harv Owens said from the top turret behind the pilots.

Jack had hoped they'd have escort for more than half an hour over enemy territory, but due to delays on takeoff and assembly, the P-47s had to turn back with low fuel. The Forts were on their own, an hour and a half from the target at Regensburg, deep within Germany.

"Left waist to pilot." Manny Souza's voice crackled on the interphone. "Enemy aircraft forming up at eight o'clock low. Looks like Me 109s."

"Figures," Jack said. Did they know the Fourth Bomb Wing was headed for the Messerschmitt plant to keep more Me 109s from the skies?

Even if they knew, they were in for a surprise. While seven groups in the Fourth Wing targeted Regensburg, nine groups in the First Wing aimed for the ball bearing factory at Schweinfurt. Then the brilliant part—First Wing would return to England, but Fourth Wing would swing south for North Africa. Boy, would the Germans be confused.

In addition to 500-pound bombs, the Fort carried mess kits and shaving kits, changes of clothing and blankets. Jack welcomed this first shuttle mission. He needed a few days away to chase off the memory of yesterday's fiasco and to purge his mind of Lt. Ruth Doherty.

"Those Me 109s are heading west for the tail-end combat box," Manny said.

"Again?" Several B-17s flying "Tail-End Charlie" had fallen since they crossed the Dutch border.

Each combat box carefully stacked and staggered bombers from two or three groups to maximize firepower and minimize danger. Colonel Castle led the 94th in the lead of the second of three combat boxes, a good spot but not immune. No one was immune.

"Fw 190s coming our way from two o'clock high." Gene Levitski, the new copilot, squinted at the clear sky from under gigantic brown eyebrows. "Remember, boys, don't forget to lead. Short bursts. Don't waste ammo. We've got a long mission."

Jack shifted in his seat. Yep, longest mission ever. At least eleven hours, and already his rear end ached. His mind flashed to Ruth's sweet laughter at his continuing discomfort. Just yesterday. He shoved the image away. He had more important things to consider, like the long haul with low fuel over the Mediterranean. Warmer water than the Channel, but no less deadly. And did the North African Theater have decent Air-Sea Rescue? Jack didn't want to find out.

"Here they come, boys," Levitski said. "Four of 'em."

Jack hoped his copilot stayed alive. He calmly called out bogies and let Jack concentrate on the plane and the formation. Still, Jack eyed the fighters coming straight for the nose. Years of experience kept him from following the instinct to wheel away, which would plow him into another ship in the tight formation.

At three hundred yards, tracers blinked toward him. "Get

'em," Jack said. *Sunrise Serenade* trembled as her .50 caliber machine guns opened up—Charlie's in the nose, and Harv's twin guns overhead.

The fighters pressed in, their propellers in round blurs. Bullets crossed paths in the sky. Three clunks rattled the right wing. Each Fw 190 did a split-S and disappeared under the Fort. Paul Klaus's guns joined the racket from the ball turret hanging from *Sunrise*'s belly.

Klaus whooped on the interphone. "I got one. Tore his wing right off. Don't you dare call me a Kraut again, Owens."

"Taking away all my fun." Harv kicked shell casings off his turret platform. "Come on, Jerry. Send up some more. Gotta beat Klaus."

Jack didn't share Harv's eagerness. Every bullet carried risk to men, to electrical and control cables, and to fuel and hydraulic lines. He checked the fuel and oil in engines three and four. Looked okay. He couldn't afford the loss of even one engine, not with all that water ahead.

Klaus let out an expletive. "There goes one of our Forts. *Dear Mom*, it says."

"Chutes?" Jack asked.

"One, two." Silence. "Cockpit on fire. She's in a spin."

"Come on, you guys," Jack said. "Get out."

"Three, four." This from Everett, the tail gunner. Then he cursed. "She exploded."

"Oh Lord." Jack didn't even know how to pray. Despite the black heaviness in his chest, he adjusted his throttles to maintain airspeed at 180 miles per hour.

"Whole cloud of twin-engined fighters," Manny said from the waist. "They're passing us up."

They were aiming for the final combat box, which was too far back to benefit from the firepower of the forward boxes. From Jack's estimation, the 146 B-17s spread over an unacceptable fifteen miles. When they reached Africa, Col. Curtis LeMay—the commander of Fourth Wing, the developer of the combat box, and never a man to mince words—would have plenty to say.

Jack took careful note of how LeMay and Castle led. Neither commander had to fly such a rugged mission, but both did. The men respected things like that.

Over the next hour the tail gunner called out the demise of half a dozen Forts from the final groups, as well as the explosions of many enemy fighters. The 94th missed out on most of the action, which provoked colorful language from the top turret. Nevertheless, half of the remaining twenty planes in Jack's group bore wounds—a feathered engine here, a chunk out of a wing there, punctured fuselages everywhere.

Sunrise had three holes close to the Tokyo tanks. Only the B-17s in the Fourth Wing bore the extra fuel tanks in their wingtips, which extended their range all the way to North Africa.

"We're at the Initial Point," Norman Findlay said from down in the nose.

Jack smiled as he made the dogleg turn to start the bomb run. The navigator's dislike of nicknames included abbreviations. Everyone else called it the IP.

Jack leaned down to the low panel on the center console and activated the AFCE so Charlie could fly the plane, the Automatic Flight Control Equipment, as Norman would call it. What a lot of syllables the boy wasted.

"Okay, Charlie, she's all yours."

"Thanks, Skipper." Charlie's voice sparkled. As lead bombardier for the squadron, he'd line up the target in his Norden bombsight. Every adjustment he made in the bombsight altered the plane's course until positioned over the target. The rest of the bombardiers in the squadron would keep their eyes on *Sunrise* and release their bombs when Charlie did.

SARAH SUNDIN

The Luftwaffe abandoned them, which meant flak ahead. Jack squinted into the distance at the leading groups. No black puffs of flak, only dark specks plummeting eighteen thousand feet to earth.

"That's one beautiful target," Charlie said.

Jack didn't have Charlie's view through the clear Plexiglas nose, but in a few minutes he saw what his friend meant. The Danube River made an unmistakable bend, as in the slides at briefing, and an aircraft factory snuggled in the bend, complete with workshops, hangars, and an airfield. Best of all, a column of smoke rose thick and dark from the center. Only a few smudges of flak spoiled the picture.

"Just aim for that smoke, huh, Charlie?"

"That's . . . what . . . I'm . . . bombs away."

Jack had that heavy rising-in-an-elevator feeling as the load fell from the bomb bay. "Okay, Charlie, I'm taking back my girl." He turned off the AFCE. "Let's continue our European tour, men."

He followed Castle east to the Rally Point. The combat boxes formed up again, and Jack's low squadron flew neater and tighter than Babcock's high squadron. Good. Castle would notice.

Now for the southern leg, the fun part. All those Fw 190s and Me 109s would be refueled and ready to hit them over western Germany, not over the Alps and across Italy. Let them search and burn up that fuel.

Fuel. The holes in his wing made him nervous. "Levitski, check the fuel in the Tokyos."

The copilot flipped the fuel indicator switch on the far right of the panel. His thick eyebrows bunched together over his oxygen mask. He flipped the switch some more. "The right tank's down to 390 gallons. Left tank's still at 540."

"Oh boy." Jack looked out the right window toward the

wingtip. "Must have a slow leak." It wouldn't show up in the engine fuel pressure, because they couldn't transfer from the auxiliary tanks until each engine fell below one hundred gallons.

"I see it," Levitski said.

A golden dotted line bled away in the slipstream, and nothing could stanch the flow. Jack had lost 150 gallons in about an hour and a half. He couldn't afford to lose all 540 gallons, 20 percent of total fuel capacity. Jack's lungs strained against the pressure, the waters threatening to swamp him.

"Novak?" Levitski said. "What do you want to do?"

Jack coughed away the sensation. "Can't do anything. Can't even transfer what's left until the main engines fall below one hundred gallons. Where are we at now?"

"About 155 in each."

Over two hundred gallons total to burn before he could transfer. One whole hour. He would lose another hundred gallons by then, which could mean the difference between landing in Africa and ditching in Mediterranean waters.

Jack forced his mind to focus. He couldn't lose that much fuel. If only he could—yes! Jack rapped his thigh with his palm. "I've got it. Okay, Harv, fuel transfer. Pump off sixty gallons from engine four into engine two. Then another sixty from three to one."

The flight engineer extracted his big frame from his turret and gave Jack a curious look, but at Jack's nod, he crouched over the fuel transfer switches on the threshold of the door to the bomb bay.

After the fuel transfer, Jack retrimmed the ailerons to maintain level flight with the wings unbalanced. Then he sent Harv with a portable oxygen bottle into the bomb bay to drain the leaking Tokyo tanks into the emptied tanks of engines three and four.

"Good thinking, Novak," Levitski said. "We might make it now."

Jack shrugged, but he took pride in his clever, lifesaving idea, one of many in his career. Top leaders needed ingenuity, and Jack knew he had it even under pressure.

"Say, fellows, look below," Charlie said from the nose.

Jagged hills built up to majestic, frosted peaks, and Jack let out a low whistle. "Okay, boys—the Alps, sunny Italy, a Mediterranean beach vacation—don't say I never take you anywhere nice."

"I feel a song coming on," Charlie said. "'I've flown around the world in a plane.'"

Jack smiled at the appropriate lyrics. Today he'd add another continent to his list—North America, Australia, Europe, and now Africa.

"'I've settled revolutions in Spain. And the North Pole I have charted. Still I can't get started with you.'"

Jack squirmed on his sore backside. He couldn't get started with Ruth, no matter what he did or said or planned. Just as well, because something was wrong with the girl. She told him to leave her alone? Fine. That's what he planned to do.

14

Redgrave Park

Thursday, August 19, 1943

"Chicken again?" May said with a wrinkled nose and whiny voice, a perfect imitation of the other nurses.

Ruth smiled and scooped the last bite of chicken à la king onto her fork, bland but filling. "I wonder where those girls were during the Depression."

"Their memories must be shorter than ours." May scraped her plate clean of her second helping, yet she was just a slip of a thing. "I wonder if we'll hear anything tonight."

"I didn't hear planes today. With this weather . . ."

May stood and picked up her tray. "Africa. I can't believe they're in Africa."

If they made it. Ruth followed her friend, returned her tray, and stepped out into the misty evening. "'*One misty moisty morning.*'" She could still see Jack's confident grin as he sauntered toward her. That was before he knew, and he knew only the smallest part.

"I hope it's clear tomorrow." May threw her cape around her shoulders. "This waiting—oh, it's unnerving."

Ruth smiled at the role reversal. "Don't you always tell me to trust in the Lord?"

May let out a small laugh. "I know, but I wish I knew Charlie was all right, and Jack too. My goodness, 60 planes lost out of 376. That's 600 men. We've never lost even half that many before. The odds—"

"Hush." Ruth put her arm around May's shoulder. "Don't get worked up. I know you're worried. I am too, but we have to be strong for our patients."

"I know, and hundreds of Bible verses tell us not to fear, and I do trust God. I do. No matter what, his will is best."

Was it? Ruth tensed as they turned onto the pathway into the woods behind Redgrave Hall for their evening walk. Was it best for Pa and Ma to die? For those men—

"If Charlie and Jack are in heaven now, we should rejoice for them, and if they're alive, we should rejoice to have more time with them."

Ruth's heart drifted down. She had no more time with Jack, but she forced a smile and jiggled May's shoulder. "So when Charlie comes home, will you go out with him?"

"Yes." May's smile twitched about. "I've been praying. I thought I was sparing my heart, but look at me. Am I less worried than I would be if he were my boyfriend? No. I'm only depriving each of us of happiness, however short it may be."

At least Charlie and May would have that happiness. Her heart rose back into position.

"Will you patch up things with Jack?"

Ruth let her arm fall and hugged her cape about her. "There's nothing to patch up."

"Nonsense. He's crazy about you, and you're crazy about him, even if you won't admit it."

Ruth sighed. How had she convinced herself both she and Jack only wanted friendship? How had she let it progress so far?

"One thing about Jack Novak." May trailed her hand on a tree trunk. "He doesn't give up."

"He did."

"I can't see him giving up so easily."

Black leaves mottled the leaden sky, as thick and wet as the sadness that had been her companion for several days. "You didn't hear his voice."

"Why? What did he say?" May asked, not with Flo's malignancy or Marian's lust for gossip, but with confidential compassion.

Ruth picked up her pace. "Come on. I have my physical for the flight nursing program tomorrow and I want to be in shape." Now more than ever she needed to get off the island.

"Ruth, I'm not giving up."

She groaned. "Jack didn't say anything, do anything."

May came alongside. In the last few weeks she kept any pace Ruth set. "What happened? You'll feel better if you talk about it."

"Is that right, Freud?"

May chuckled. "Freud has nothing to do with it. It's what friends do."

The branches tangled in a web overhead. Exactly why Ruth avoided friendship.

"Let's start from the beginning. Charlie and Jack caught us dancing in the street, and then Charlie hauled me away under the pretense of buying pencils. Pencils?"

Ruth had to smile. "Transparent, wasn't he?"

"Oh, it was a team effort. See, any man who'd conspire in such a scheme won't give up. So, what did you and Jack do after we left on our pencil hunt?"

Ruth grumbled. "We saw a movie and ate fish and chips in the abbey ruins. Nothing happened, okay?"

"Until . . . ?"

Something flared in Ruth's chest. If she couldn't freeze out May Jensen, then she'd scare her off with craziness. "Fine. Jack talked me into dancing, and I cried on his shoulder because no one had held me for twelve years, and I bawled like a baby. There. Satisfied?"

May still walked in step. "Oh dear. Men can't handle women's tears."

"No, that's not it." The annoyance washed away at the remembrance. "He was sweet. He let me—he encouraged me to cry. He held me. He was kind, tender."

"Oh?" A note of surprise elevated her voice. "So . . . ?"

Might as well get this over with. Ruth faced her friend on the path. "He kissed me."

May's eyebrows jumped and then settled into a compassionate curve. "You weren't ready."

"I'll never be ready." Now for the crazy part. "I hate kissing. I can't stand it."

May pursed her lips and rearranged her cape. "Maybe you need to be patient with him. Some men—well, I loved Thomas dearly, but he was so tense when—"

Ruth huffed. "That's not it. He had excellent technique. It's me. I don't like anything about it. Nothing. Makes my skin crawl, okay? Do you understand? Do you see why I don't date? Between my family and kissing and—" What was she saying? And why on earth had she analyzed Jack's technique?

Instead of running away as she was supposed to, May set her tiny hand on Ruth's arm. "If Jack is half the man I think he is, he'll come to understand."

Yeah. He'd understand enough to leave her alone, which was best for her and her family, yet the sadness soaked thicker and wetter than ever.

15

Tunisia

Friday, August 20, 1943

A donkey with an oxygen mask?

Jack walked closer. Sure enough, Dan Finnegan, Manny Souza, and Paul Klaus restrained a black Arab donkey, while Joe Winchell strapped an oxygen mask on the animal.

Winchell yelped, drew back his hand, and cussed. "She bit me."

"Don't blame her," Jack said.

"Hiya, Novak." Winchell flipped sandy hair off his forehead. "I could sure use your help."

Jack's unbuttoned shirt rippled in the hot, dry wind. He shoved the shirttails back and sank his hands in his pockets. "Don't tell me you want to take that donkey home."

"Course I do. Paid good money for my Sahara Sue." He lengthened a strap on the harness for the mask. "I think that Arab won out in the bartering, but so what?"

"Come on, Winch. A desert donkey in rainy England? Worse, on the mission home in a B-17? What if she bucks under fighter attack?"

Winchell cocked an eyebrow at Jack. "Since when have you become Major Regulation?"

"I'm not." Jack studied the harness. He saw where Winchell had gone wrong, but he wasn't about to show him. "But you didn't think this through."

"Ah, you can't think when you're in love." Winchell threw his arms around the donkey's neck. "Look at that face. Just look."

The donkey brayed, tossed back her head, and flung Winchell into the sand. The other men broke down in laughter, and the donkey trotted, hee-hawing, to the end of her tether.

Winchell got up and dusted the seat of his pants. "I love a girl with spunk and fire."

Jack's stomach swirled with acid. "One problem with fire, Winch—you get burned." He turned and walked away.

"What's up with Novak?" Finnegan's hushed voice carried downwind. "Normally he'd be laughing, helping us out."

Yeah, he would, wouldn't he? Jack's shoes kicked up sand. The grains hit his calves below his rolled-up pants.

"Ah, who knows?" Winchell said. "He's been grumpy the last few days."

Ever since Monday night. Jack passed a gunner washing his mess kit in a two-gallon bucket. "Don't forget to scrub with sand. Don't want to be stuck with dysentery at twenty thousand feet. It's a long way home." If they ever got to go home. The weather had been lousy over Europe, and the forecasts didn't look any better.

The gunner glanced up. "Thanks. That's what Major Babcock said."

Babcock—more than one donkey on the field.

There he was, not a hundred feet away, braying to the reporters again. Babcock stood with his hand on the nose of a

B-17, buttoned up in khakis. Half a dozen newsmen scribbled his boasts on their notepads.

To hear Babcock tell it, he alone was responsible for the destruction of the Messerschmitt complex, for the loss in production of about two thousand Me 109s, for the loss of only one plane in the 94th Bomb Group. Never stated outright, but implied. Did he honestly think if he'd been in the trailing group, the 100th wouldn't have lost a whopping nine planes?

Jack grimaced and glanced away to where a dozen airmen stood in line for camel rides. A young American rider hollered like a buckaroo, while the camel plodded along and ground its jaw in a circular motion as if chewing its cud. Did camels have cuds?

The old man leading the camel wore a long tan robe. Looked awfully hot. Other than Babcock, the airmen were as close to naked as possible, with nothing but pants rolled up to the knee. Some threw shirts over sunburned shoulders. Jack wore his only as a token of authority.

He headed for *Sunrise*, lined up with the other Forts gathering sand in the desert sun. The morning of the Regensburg mission, he'd grabbed the first khaki shirt he found, the shirt he'd worn the night before, the shirt Ruth cried on.

Her tears lay heavy on his shoulder, brittle and edged with a salty, white rim. What had he been thinking? Kissing her right after she broke down and poured out her heart? Oh yeah, such a great shoulder to cry on.

Jack shrugged off the shirt and ducked under *Sunrise*'s wing. At least the kiss revealed her bizarre phobia before he invested another couple of months and fell even harder for her.

He stuffed his shirt into his bedroll and pulled out his stationery box and pen. What was her phobia about anyway? Some nurse obsession with hygiene? That cute blonde nurse he'd dated in Australia certainly didn't share Ruth's aversion.

Jack set his things on the wing and hiked himself up. What he'd sacrifice in comfort, he'd gain in privacy. He sat cross-legged and composed his thoughts. Somehow he needed to write Walt and congratulate him on his success in love.

Dear Walt,

Heartiest congratulations on your engagement. How did you get her to say yes? Flowers? Bribery? Blackmail?

I can't wait to meet this Allie of yours. Any woman willing to put up with a lifetime of Novak stubbornness must be amazing. Give her a kiss for me. On the cheek, you numbskull! What kind of a fellow do you think I am?

By the way, I ran into Lieutenant Doherty, and she sends her congratulations.

Jack looked up to the blazing sky. He ran into her? More like he ran over her.

"Ahoy there, Skipper."

So much for privacy. Jack sighed as Charlie hoisted himself onto the wing.

Charlie sat down and leaned back against the fuselage. "What are you doing?"

"Letters."

"How can you stand it up here? I've spent my day under wings, not on top of them." A rivulet of sweat ran down Charlie's pink face.

Jack shrugged. The sun felt good on his bare back.

"How long are you going to pout?"

"Excuse me?"

Charlie stuck a shiny new pencil between his teeth. "Yeah, pout. How long? The great Jack Novak struck out with a girl for the first time ever, and now he pouts."

Jack glared at him. "I didn't strike out. I decided not to go to bat."

"Yeah, that sounds better."

Jack rolled his eyes. "What's your point?"

"My point is dozens of men look to you for leadership, and you're in a sulk. It's bad for morale. They think you're down about the mission."

"Shouldn't I be?" He capped his pen so it wouldn't dry out. "First Wing lost thirty-six planes, Fourth Wing lost twenty-four. Sixteen percent losses on both legs. We would've lost even more if we hadn't surprised them with the shuttle. We can't continue deep penetrations of Germany without fighter escort. We can't sustain losses like this."

"Of course not. But since when have you let mission losses keep you down? You always focus on success. You'd be clapping the men on the back and congratulating them on putting Messerschmitt out of business if it weren't for Ruth."

Jack closed his eyes. "I don't want to talk about her."

"Yeah, but I'm sick of the pouting. What happened?"

"She told me to leave her alone."

Charlie laughed. "She probably told you that the day you met. Never stopped you before. Why now?"

Jack rolled the pen between his palms. "I don't know. The girl—she's got problems."

"Don't we all?"

"Not like hers. Don't know what's wrong with her."

"I thought your pastoral task was to figure it out."

"You don't understand. She's completely . . ." What? Completely opposed to romance? The woman who laughed in his embrace? The woman who enticed him back into her arms?

The woman who raised her lips to him? Yeah, she initiated that kiss. Why would a girl who hated kisses ask for one?

Jack shook his head. "I don't know, Charlie. One minute we're moving to kiss, and she's shooting green flares, but as soon as our lips touch, she acts as if I'd slapped her."

Charlie's face puckered. "I could give you some pointers."

"It wasn't me. She said I was good—really good, in fact. But she doesn't like kissing. Hates it, she said."

"Wow." The laughter drained from Charlie's face. "Is that why she doesn't date?"

"Yeah." His insides coiled. He'd betrayed Ruth's confidence, hadn't he?

"I see why you gave up on her."

"Yep."

Charlie tipped the pencil up in his mouth. "What good's a woman who doesn't like to kiss?"

Jack narrowed his eyes. "That's not what I said."

"Sure it is. The only reason you gave up is she won't kiss you."

"Oh, come on." Jack squirmed under grilling hotter than the Sahara sun. "What do you expect? Ever had a girlfriend you couldn't kiss?"

"No, but once you said God led you to her. You wanted to teach her to trust and to love, if I recall. When you told me that, kissing never came up."

Jack's chest simmered. What did Charlie know? He hadn't heard her rant.

"Pride's your weakness, Skipper. Don't let it keep you from doing God's work—"

"That's enough, Captain." For once, Jack pulled rank. He gathered his papers and slid off the wing to the ground. "Excuse me, but I have some men to cheer up."

16

Redgrave Park

Tuesday, August 24, 1943

May frowned at the twilight sky above the Nissen hut that served as the PX. "A good day for flying."

"Yes, it was." Ruth fingered the box of airmail stationery she'd bought while May stocked up on candy bars.

"On my break I saw planes coming in." May chomped down on a Mars Bar.

Ruth had heard May's report three times already. Each time May became more nervous, which fed Ruth's worry. "Maybe Charlie will come on Sunday. In fact, I'm sure he will."

May's smile held a smudge of chocolate. "I can't wait to see them."

Them? No, not Jack. Ruth would never see him again. Even though it was for the best, she couldn't shake the hollowness, the dampness.

Ruth looped her arm through May's, but her smile faltered. "Where do you want to go for our walk? The lake? The orangery?"

"The lake." A male voice hit from her left. "Moon, June, lagoon."

Ruth's heart ricocheted about in her chest. Jack and Char-lie leaned against the last Nissen hut before the road, about twenty feet away. Praise the Lord, they were alive! Then Ruth dropped her gaze. Why had Jack come?

May screamed and flung herself into Charlie's arms. "Yes, yes, yes. Everything you asked me—yes."

Charlie laughed and swung her around. "Ouch! Watch the sunburn."

"Oh dear." May stepped back, reached for his crimson cheeks, and stopped herself. "I'm sorry. Look at you."

"Right now it doesn't bother me." He pulled her close. "Are you sure? You're sure you're ready?"

"Very much so."

Despite her turmoil, Ruth's heart stirred for her friends, and if she watched them, she didn't have to look at Jack.

"See you later, you two." Charlie steered May down the road to the right toward Redgrave Hall, and May wiggled her fingers over her shoulder at Ruth.

She gaped at their retreating backs. How could they leave her alone with Jack?

"Well?" His voice rumbled into her ear. "Do I get a hug?"

"What?" She snapped her gaze to him.

"A hug?" He smiled and gestured down the road. "Charlie got one. How about me?"

A lead weight sank in her stomach. He thought he could change her mind. He thought if he was patient and charming and romantic, she'd come to love his kisses.

He walked toward her, his arms and smile spread wide.

Ruth stepped back. "Are you out of your mind? Didn't you hear what I said?"

Jack sobered and lowered his arms. "Yeah, I heard, but now I'm listening. For the last week, the sun beat on me,

Charlie beat on me, and God beat on me. Takes a while to get through this thick skull sometimes."

An ambulance turned onto the road. Ruth had to step closer to Jack, but she gazed toward the refuge of the Hall. "It's almost dark. I need to go home."

"Not yet. We're going for a walk." He took her arm and led her across the road toward the lake. While not restrictive, his grip couldn't be resisted. How could he always do that? How could he make her do what she didn't want to?

"I don't want to go for a walk. I want to go home."

"Not yet. We'll walk by the lagoon, and you can skewer me with that harpoon."

"Harpoon? Jack—I don't—"

"Because I'm a buffoon, that's why. A jerk." He stopped under a broad-spreading tree and faced Ruth with eyes filled with regret. "I came here to apologize."

"Apologize?"

He tilted his head toward the lake and released her arm. "Let's walk."

Ruth followed, but her mind spun. Why was he apologizing? She was the one who should apologize.

Jack sighed and put his hands in the pockets of his flight jacket. "Listen, Ruth. From the day we met, you made it clear you wanted nothing to do with romance."

She stared at his lowered face in the fading light. Nothing? Had he forgotten how she acted in the abbey?

"The friendship was going great, and—well, you're a beautiful woman, and I thought maybe—well, I got carried away."

He got carried away? He wasn't the only one. Why did he take all the blame?

"I will never try to kiss you again. I promise."

Again? He sounded as if they'd continue to see each other.

Ruth couldn't speak; she could only watch the strange scene unfold.

"Can you forgive me? If I promise to be the gentleman you thought I was?"

Her breath caught. Chivalry—that's why he took the blame. To avoid an awkward talk about her behavior, he was pretending the whole thing was only an unwelcome kiss.

"Ruth?" He glanced over at her.

"Of course, I forgive you, but can you—"

"Good, because this week was miserable. I messed up a great friendship and I missed you."

Leaves rustled overhead, their shoes swished in the grass, and warmth filled the hollowness in Ruth's chest. "Jack?" she said. "I missed you too."

"Can't imagine why you'd miss a goon like me."

A laugh bubbled off the last of the dampness. "I didn't miss those rhymes."

One black eyebrow arched.

She laughed again. "Okay, maybe I did."

"Good, because I had a dilemma. If I left you alone as you asked, how could I keep my promise never to leave you alone?"

"Mm, that is a dilemma." Pinpoints of light pricked the indigo sky.

"And now Charlie and May are a couple. He's my best friend, she's yours, and if you couldn't stand the sight of me . . . well, it'd be a lot easier if we could be friends."

Ruth's chest tightened again. "Can we?"

"Yes." He faced her, a respectful three feet away. "I won't lie to you. I find you extremely attractive, but I can control myself." A note of humor rang in his voice.

Ruth studied his extremely attractive silhouette. Jack's control was only half of the problem.

A whining scream, and Ruth jumped. "The air raid siren? Again?"

Jack turned back toward the hospital complex. "Where's a shelter?"

"I haven't gone in a shelter in ages," she shouted over the blare.

"You're going tonight."

"Nonsense. They're all false alarms." Nonetheless, Ruth followed.

"Not always. Sometimes they break through and do some strafing. Just last night the RAF shot down four Me 110s around here." He beckoned. "Come on, slowpoke. I talked you into being friends again. I'm not about to let you get perforated."

"Perforated?" She laughed and led him through the complex, to an earthen lump of a shelter, and down the steps. One nurse, the new girl, sat wide-eyed on a cot while half a dozen of her ambulatory patients played poker.

Ruth leveled a glare at Jack. "See? Almost deserted."

"Fine by me." He sat on a cot, leaned back against the tin wall, and patted the canvas beside him.

Ruth sat with a humph.

Jack pulled his legs up and set his heels on the frame of the cot. "Feels good. I'm beat."

The single lightbulb illuminated the fatigue and weathering of his face. "Hard day?"

"Mm-hmm." He opened his eyes, even bluer against a deep tan. "Reveille at 0400. We stayed up late removing sand from engine parts and pumping 2,400 gallons of gas by hand from 55-gallon drums."

"Oh my. And how was today?"

Jack draped his arms over his knees. "Good. Dropped a load of presents on an airfield in Bordeaux on the way home. Not much opposition, but a long flight."

"Then you came up here."

"Showered first. Be glad. A week without laundry or showers—boy, I tell you."

"I am glad." She smiled and relaxed against the wall. "And—and I'm glad you came here, especially after a long mission. Goodness."

He turned his eyes to her, a bit too close and much too warm, but he'd keep his promise. "How was your week?"

Ruth crossed her arms over the stationery box on her stomach. Should she be as honest as he'd been? She raised half a smile. "Miserable."

Sympathy and amusement flowed between them. The friendship was restored. What a blessing. Yes, a blessing.

Ruth opened her eyes wide. "Oh, I passed my physical."

"The Form 64? Wow. Lots of men can't pass that. So, now you wait to hear?"

"Well, no, I still have to do . . . um, a test flight." How awkward.

"Yeah?" Jack laced his fingers behind his head. "Do they take you up in a C-47? C-54?"

"Any plane will do." She rubbed her thumb over the stationery box. "But I have to—I have to arrange it myself. I have to find a—a pilot."

He laughed. "I may be a buffoon, but I'm a mighty good pilot. If you'd like—"

"Oh, would you? Could you?"

"Sure. I'll clear it with Castle, take you on a local practice mission. Say, you think May would like to go?"

"Would she?" Ruth almost crushed the box. "If she were five pounds heavier, she'd apply too."

"Okay, I'll get back to you with the details." He nodded at her box. "Now, you seem eager to write letters, and I'm beat. I'm going to nap until they sound the all clear."

"Good idea." How thoughtful he was to want to save the friendship, and how clever to figure out a way.

Jack pulled his cap over his face and crossed his arms.

"That doesn't look comfortable."

One corner of his mustache edged up. "After a week sleeping in a blanket on the ground under the wing of my ship, this is heaven, believe me."

"I'll wake you if the siren doesn't." She pulled out a gossamer sheet. Stationery and ink consumed a great deal of her spending money, although she wrote in tiny script. Today she wanted to fill many sheets. She'd write Bert first. Her youngest brother would be thrilled with the news of her test flight.

Ruth pulled her pen from her purse and started to write "Dear Bert," but she was out of ink. "Oh dear."

"Wassa matter?" One blue eye peeked from under the service cap.

"I forgot I was going to refill my ink cartridge tonight."

"Here. Use mine." Jack reached inside his shirt pocket and handed her a silver pen.

"Thank you." When she removed the cap, it made a gritty, scraping sound. She took out a new pen wipe she'd bought at the PX. What a strange war this was. A Chicago slum girl sat underneath English manor grounds, wiping Sahara sand from the pen of a war hero pilot from California.

Once she'd wiped the pen cleaner than it had probably been in years, she wrote her letter. She would ride in an airplane. Not just any airplane, but the famous B-17 Flying Fortress. Not just any pilot, but a man who'd flown over Pearl Harbor, New Guinea, and now Regensburg and Tunisia. Not just a good pilot, but a good friend.

Ruth gazed at Jack. Soft snores rumbled from his drooping

mouth. She smiled at the sound, familiar from his hospital days.

She had two friends now, two good friends who liked her just as she was.

Ruth's heart seized up. No. No, they didn't. They didn't know who she really was.

17

Bury St. Edmunds Airfield

Monday, August 30, 1943

Thousand-pound general purpose bombs lay stacked under camouflage netting in the grass under a gnarled oak, but Jack paid them little attention.

"How are things going out here?" he asked.

Lieutenant Mulroney wore a testy expression. As a new ordnance officer, he wasn't accustomed to Jack's visits to dispersal sites. The bomb dump was isolated at the far northeastern corner of the base to minimize damage in case of an explosion. They didn't get visitors.

Jack set one foot on a crate and rested his arms on his knee. "Have enough personnel?"

Mulroney glanced around and switched his weight from one leg to the other. "Yeah, sure."

"How about supplies?"

"Fine." Then he frowned. "Except—well . . ."

"Go ahead."

"Pencils. Seems we never have enough. We have so many forms to fill out and—"

"I'll let Quartermasters know. Of course they'll make you

fill out more forms to get them." Jack pulled a pad and pencil from his pocket and scribbled a note. Then he grinned and handed Mulroney his pencil. "Here. Not much, but a start."

The lieutenant's eyes lit up as if Jack had given him a whole case. "Don't you need it?"

"Nah, I've got a pen." He patted his chest pocket. A very clean pen.

It didn't take much to win over Mulroney. Jack stayed at the bomb dump for half an hour to talk to the men about work and life. He'd never learn the names of all three thousand men at Bury St. Edmunds, but he'd try. Flight crews came and went and took all the glory, but ground personnel stayed for the duration without accolades. Any discontent on base affected morale, but to be content, most men just needed notice, appreciation, and response.

Jack mounted his bike and headed south on the road to the living sites. As a squadron commander, he could use a jeep, but he preferred the exercise. Besides, Major Babcock whizzed around in a jeep with his adjutant at the wheel, like a president on parade. Ridiculous. Jack refused to abuse the privileges of command—or his adjutant.

He stood on the pedals to build speed down the quiet road. He planned to hit five sites in the interval between his daily squadron meeting and the lunch meeting with Castle and the other squadron commanders. Then this afternoon . . .

He smiled and coasted down an incline. This afternoon, Ruth would meet him on the base for her test flight while he checked out his newest pilot.

His plan was back on target, now that he'd figured out her problem. Her dad had been paralyzed when she was twelve, which took Ruth from carefree girl to responsible young woman. About that time she'd last had a boyfriend—eighth grade, she'd said—probably a fumbling kid of thirteen. No wonder she hated kissing.

Jack could change that.

Once they were crazy in love, he'd arrange another intimate moment like in the abbey. Then he'd remind her of his promise not to kiss her, and she'd beg him to break it, or maybe she'd break it for him.

Jack grinned and hit the brakes at the crossroads to let a GMC truck pass. For now, he'd pull back, keep his hands to himself, and let the friendship grow to trust, then love.

Charlie said Jack's plan was driven by wounded pride because he couldn't stand a strikeout on his batting record. Baloney. Now that Charlie finally had a girlfriend, he acted as if he were an expert on women. Nothing but baloney.

When Jack reached the enlisted men's mess, he leaned the bike against the wall and went inside. The smell of oatmeal lingered in the air, and men on KP duty wiped down the tables. Jack walked up to a hulking man with thin blond hair. "Corporal Boyd, back again?"

Boyd's thick face broke into a smile. "Hiya, Major. Listen, you gotta talk to my sergeant. It's my wristwatch, sir, I swear. It blinks out on me. Only reason I'm late."

Jack leaned his hip on a table. "You know I can't do that. Get it fixed, get a new one, or at least throw the old one away. We rely on you being on time."

Boyd slapped a rag on the table. "Oh yeah, the great Quartermaster war hero."

"That's right. You are—when you do your job."

An eye roll.

Jack laced his fingers together in front of him. "Don't you see? We're all linked together. It takes ten men on the ground to put one in the air. I can't bomb Germany unless ordnance loads bombs, and guess what? Ordnance is low on pencils. They can't do their jobs unless you do yours."

A slow smile cracked Boyd's face. "Then you'd better get me off KP so I can go to work."

Jack laughed and clapped him on the back. He spotted Pvt. Ed Reynolds, another regular on KP. Reynolds swished a rag in languid circles on a table. When he saw Jack, he raised a grin that made him look about ten years old.

Jack opened his mouth to ask what he was in for but then caught a whiff of the private's breath. The kid had shown up for duty either drunk or hung over. Again. Jack gave him a nod. "How are things at the laundry?"

Reynolds swiped brown hair off his forehead, but it flopped back over one eye. "Same as here, sir. Warsh, warsh, warsh, all day long."

Jack smiled at how he said *wash* with an *R*, as Ruth said it.

"Never have time to relax, have some fun." The private dunked the rag in the bucket, gave it a token wring, and flung the dripping mess onto the table. "Least I'm not up to my neck in jungle muck, getting shot at."

"Remember that." If he kept up the boozing, he'd find himself in that very position.

Jack headed into the kitchen, greeted the staff, and sampled the mashed potatoes. Sticky, but passable. Nothing brought down morale faster than bad grub. No matter what, he always included one of the messes on his rounds.

Next he proceeded to the parachute packing plant, where dozens of white silk parachutes hung from the fifty-foot ceiling for inspection. He never took for granted his parachute or the men who packed it.

After a while he retrieved his bike and pressed through the mud on the path to Hangar One, where he would check out progress on repairs and spend time with the maintenance men.

A horn tooted behind him. Maj. Jefferson Babcock Jr. rolled up in his motorcade. The jeep stopped beside Jack. "Good morning, Novak."

"Morning." Jack planted his feet.

Babcock draped his arm along the top of the windshield. "Out pressing the flesh?"

"Making my rounds."

"You should use a jeep, get out of this mud." Babcock threw in several profane adjectives before *mud*.

Jack snapped to attention and saluted an imaginary point behind Babcock. "Good morning, Colonel."

Babcock whipped around, then turned back with a faint smile. "You're a funny man, Novak."

"If you want Castle to buy this wholesome act of yours, you have to be consistent."

"Good point." The man actually saw it as advice, not a jab. "This is a lot like my dad's campaigns. You have to present the right image, feign interest." He dropped a conspiratorial wink.

Conversation with Babcock always killed Jack's appetite. He dug in his heels and crossed his arms. "I see it more like how my dad cares for his congregation. You minister to needs and encourage everyone to work together—with genuine interest."

Babcock's mouth twitched. "Fine. You be a preacher; I'll be a leader." He motioned his adjutant to drive away.

Jack grumbled as he pedaled down the road. He wanted to be executive officer for the group's sake, because he'd be good at it, but Babcock wanted it for his own sake. At least Castle saw through the baloney. Didn't he?

18

May turned around in the front seat of the jeep to face Ruth. "Please tell me I don't look as ridiculous as you do."

"Sorry. It's a tie."

"I think you look cute." In the driver's seat, Charlie fingered a strand of May's hair.

Her cheeks turned pink. "We'd be cuter if you had flight suits in our size."

"No kidding." Ruth tightened the belt holding up the voluminous olive drab jumpsuit. When the ladies arrived at the airfield in dress blues, Charlie had laughed good and hard, then taken them to get flight suits and leather jackets. Skirts were not practical in a bomber.

Jack had sent Charlie with a jeep while he walked his new pilot through the preflight inspection, and Ruth appreciated the ride past all the buildings and away from all the men. Two women on the air base had attracted attention, whistles, and at least one bicycle accident.

"A donkey?" May pointed at a man leading a black donkey with a blue blanket over its back.

"Sahara Sue, Joe Winchell's souvenir from Tunisia." Charlie hummed the tune of "Sierra Sue."

Ruth stared. She'd heard of groups adopting dogs, but a donkey? From Africa?

"Straight ahead—that's the control tower." Charlie turned right onto a wide paved road. "Each plane has its own hardstand—its own personal parking pad—dispersed around this perimeter track to minimize loss in case of air raid."

Ruth leaned forward in her seat. She understood why Jack loved his job. The airfield buzzed with activity and throbbed with purpose. The heady scent of metal and fuel and adventure, that's what she smelled on Jack.

Charlie turned left and parked the jeep. "Here's our ship, *Sunrise Serenade*."

Jack's plane, and it was beautiful. He'd described it so often, she felt as if she were meeting one of his friends. Ruth climbed out of the jeep and scanned the length of the olive drab plane. Behind the clear nose, yellow letters spelled out *Sunrise Serenade* in an arch over a rising sun with musical notes for rays. No naked ladies on the pastor's plane.

Up in the cockpit, Jack sat in the copilot's seat, head bent.

"Jack's running through the cockpit check with Silverberg." Charlie leaned into the jeep. "Can't forget the Thermos. Heaven forbid the great Jack Novak has to fetch his own coffee."

Ruth raised her eyebrows. Sarcasm from Charlie?

He headed under the wing. "Want to see something?"

She followed, awed by the enormous engines right overhead. Heat had discolored the metal in a mottled rainbow like an oil slick.

Charlie patted a section on the underside of the plane where the gray paint didn't quite match. "This is how we all met. The hole from the flak burst that put Jack in the hospital."

Ruth fingered the cool aluminum patch and tried not to think of shells piercing this skin, then Jack's, but she'd seen the damage.

"Okay, gals, let's go." Charlie picked up a wooden crate, set it by a door near the tail, and made a gallant sweep of his arm. "All aboard."

Ruth followed May inside. She had room to stand, but not much more.

Charlie joined them. "This is the waist compartment. Two gunners, one at each window, and down there is the tail gunner's station."

Ruth peered down a narrow tunnel to a small seat in front of the rear window. "Isolated, isn't it?"

"That's why we have the interphone system." Charlie patted a dome in the floor. "Here's the ball turret. The gunner doesn't get in until we're over the Channel. Pretty snug in there."

May held onto the metal post connecting the ball turret to the ceiling. "Spinney snug?"

Charlie gave her a sheepish smile. Must have been a personal joke. As Jack said, people falling in love had their own language. A sigh grew in Ruth's chest, but she absorbed it back into her lungs. If she were normal, she and Jack might be exchanging glances and private sayings.

She passed through a metal doorway. *Lord, could you possibly—could you ever forgive me and make me normal?*

"The radio room," Charlie said. "Technical Sergeant Rosetti, the radioman. Rosetti, meet Lieutenant Jensen, Lieutenant Doherty, our passengers today."

Sergeant Rosetti wore a garrison cap and a headset over thick black curls. "Welcome, ladies. We should do this more often, de Groot." His gaze bounced around, but not quickly enough to conceal a scan of Ruth's figure. Thank goodness for the shapeless flight suit.

Charlie led them through another doorway and along a narrow aluminum walkway. "The bomb bay. We load these racks with goodies for the Nazis. By the way, if you come back here when we're in flight, watch your step. The bomb bay doors won't hold your weight."

Ruth didn't want to test that theory.

Yet another doorway. "The cockpit. Make your way around the top turret, and squeeze on in." Right inside the door stood a round platform with two poles leading up to a Plexiglas dome in the ceiling.

Jack turned around in the copilot's seat and eyed the ladies' outfits. His mustache flicked up on one side. "Still think flight nursing is a glamorous profession?"

Ruth eased behind his seat. "Who cares about fashion when you have a chance to fly?"

Charlie introduced Lieutenant Silverberg in the pilot's seat. The lanky pilot patted the instrument panel. "This is how we get this baby in the air and keep her there."

Ruth had never seen so many dials and gauges and buttons and switches—at least a hundred on the panel, and more cascading onto a center console, still more on the walls by the pilots' seats and overhead.

"How do you . . . ?" She stopped. Her question sounded daft and eyelash-batting.

Jack smiled. "Same way you know all those medications and procedures and patients. Training and practice."

"See why I hold our skipper in such high esteem?" Charlie said. "This is the toughest, most important job on the base."

"Baloney. Charlie's got the most important job. I'm nothing but his glorified chauffeur."

"Don't even try, Jack. You don't wear modesty well."

Jack's eye twitched, but then he laughed.

"Well, well, well." Behind Ruth, a large man gripped the top rim of the doorway, like a gorilla hanging from a branch. "When did we switch from ferrying bombs to ferrying bombshells?"

Ruth crossed her arms over her chest and held her chin high.

"Can it, Owens, they outrank you," Jack said, a growl in his voice. "Ladies, this is Technical Sergeant Owens, a fine flight engineer and top turret gunner, if not a gentleman. Now, Charlie, why don't you show our passengers to the nose so we can finish the cockpit check?"

"On our way." Charlie stepped down into a hole between the seats.

"Okay, Silverberg," Jack said. "Control check. Full right aileron."

Lieutenant Silverberg shoved the wheel forward and to the right.

Jack twisted around to look out his window. "Right aileron up. Right elevator down."

"Left aileron down. Left elevator down," Lieutenant Silverberg said.

Ruth dropped into the passageway behind May. Why was she disappointed? What did she expect from Jack? A half hour's devoted conversation? He had a job to do.

She got to her knees and crawled after Charlie and May, glad she wasn't wearing a skirt.

"Best room in the house—the nose compartment."

Ruth straightened up. A man with sandy hair hunched over a plywood desk to her left. Lieutenant Findlay, the navigator, gave the briefest salute and returned to his maps and charts and rulers.

Charlie buckled a throat microphone around May's neck, while Ruth struggled with her own. Would Jack have helped as he did with her watch strap, gaze intent, touch lingering? No, of course not. True to his word, he hadn't laid a finger on her since he'd hauled her across the hospital road to apologize to her. He was less attentive, but wasn't that what she wanted? And if not what she wanted, wasn't it what she needed?

Charlie glanced out the clear nose. "Why don't you take a seat? They're about to start the engines."

Ruth and May sat on the floor and leaned back against the rounded wall.

A sudden cough and sputter. The compartment filled with the engine's roar, and Ruth's heart quickened.

May gripped Ruth's arm. "I hope I don't get sick."

Another engine added to the din. The purpose of the test flight was to see if Ruth could handle flying. *Please, Lord, help me through this. You saw Aunt Pauline's letter, and you know she can't manage much longer. I need this.*

The third engine started, then the fourth, and vibrations tickled Ruth's back.

Charlie sat across from them, beside the navigator's desk, a pencil sticking up from his mouth like Roosevelt's cigarette holder. "So far, so good?"

Ruth gave a quick succession of nods. "This is so exciting."

"Isn't it?" May shouted over the noise. "And we aren't even moving."

Lieutenant Findlay glared at them over his shoulder.

Ruth lifted May's earphone and spoke in her ear. "I don't think he likes hens in his roost."

"Clear for taxiing." Lieutenant Silverberg's voice crackled in Ruth's headset.

A release, and the plane rolled forward. May's grip on Ruth's arm tightened.

Taxiing seemed to take forever. Planes, sheds, and trees

passed by, and then the B-17 swung in a quarter circle and faced a stretch of pavement bounded by green grass.

"Pilot to crew. Clear for takeoff."

The engines built to a whine, as if protesting the extra work, and Ruth's fingers tingled in May's grasp. She wiggled her fingers to loosen the grip and patted her friend's hand.

"Oh, Ruth, what are we doing?"

"We're having an adventure."

The Flying Fortress inched forward. Shouldn't it be moving faster? But then it did, faster and faster than Ruth had ever been, bouncing and jostling, faster than a car or a train, and how could it possibly stay on the ground? A cottage stood in the way, straight ahead. Ruth pressed back, as if a few inches would help in a collision.

With a swooping feeling, the bouncing stopped, and the nose pointed up, over the cottage. Smooth. Free.

"Flight," Ruth whispered.

"Wheels up," Lieutenant Silverberg said.

"Check," Jack said, his voice warm in Ruth's ear. "Up right."

"Up left."

"Tail wheel up."

Charlie cocked his head toward the nose. "Come enjoy the view. The bombsight and gun aren't installed, so nothing's in your way."

Ruth crawled up onto a platform and around the bombardier's chair.

"Don't worry. You can't fall out." He climbed right into the conical glass.

"Charlie!" May gasped.

"Oh brother. I know my plane." He slid out. "You've got to see."

Ruth craned her neck forward. In an instant she knew she

had to fly again and again. Blue sky soared above her as always, but the earth rolled beneath her, a crazy quilt of green and gold, stitched with black roads and deep green hedgerows, appliquéd with miniature houses and people and farm animals. "Oh my. I've never seen anything so beautiful."

"Never," May said. "It's wonderful."

"Bombardier to the skipper," Charlie said. "Two cases of love at first sight down here."

"Oh yes," May and Ruth said simultaneously, which made them laugh.

"Make that three cases." Charlie gave May a slow wink.

Ruth glanced down and out the window, where a river lay crumpled like a silver ribbon dropped by a careless girl. If she hadn't flinched from Jack's kiss, they'd be acting like Charlie and May by now.

She stroked the cool Plexiglas, a barrier between her and open sky, between her and certain death. Her aversion to kissing served as a similar barrier between her and loving intimacy, between her and devastating revelation.

Was the aversion a curse or a blessing?

19

London

Sunday, September 26, 1943

"'Mind the gap'?" Jack studied the sign on the Underground train. "I say, old chap, do they take us for a bunch of blithering idiots?"

"Brilliant deduction, Novak." Charlie peered down his nose and held a pencil like a pipe. "I do believe they consider us incapable of differentiating platform from open space and—"

"Just get off the train." May gave Charlie a playful shove.

Jack pointed a warning finger at Ruth. "Don't even think about it. The gap—mind the gap."

She stepped off the train. "The doors, Sherlock—mind the doors."

Jack hopped through, but the door banged his shoulder.

She shook her head at him. "Buffoon."

He rubbed his shoulder and smiled. Yeah, things were going great.

"Enough, you two," Charlie said. "Jack, you've got the map. Where to?"

Jack pulled the map from the inside pocket of his service jacket and scanned the Underground station's walls and corridors and tracks and swarms of people. "First we've got to figure out how to get out of this place."

"You're such a greenhorn." Ruth pointed to a sign suspended from the ceiling that read "Way Out."

"'Way Out'?" he said. "Way out where? Way out in the middle of nowhere?"

"Come on, country boy, follow the sign." She wrapped her hand around Jack's elbow and pulled him toward the Way Out.

He'd follow that sign. Warmth coursed through his arm. He'd been so good the last month. He hadn't touched her, not once, but now she was touching him.

The city girl led the way through the crowd, and Jack let her. At the base of the stairs, she dropped his arm to trot ahead, but maybe she'd guide him again if he played Little Boy Lost. He stepped outside into a canyon of gray stone buildings. He wouldn't have to pretend he was lost.

"Let me get my bearings." Jack unfolded the map and searched for the Tower of London along the bend of the Thames.

"Didn't you come here with Walt?" Charlie asked, his arm around May's waist.

"Yeah, but we must have come a different way."

Ruth stepped closer and peered at the map. "Good thing you're a pilot, not a navigator."

He lost all interest in the map. Ruth's auburn hair floated inches from his cheek, and her clean scent tangled his thoughts. She raised her head, her gaze bounced about, and her red lips moved. If only . . .

She met his eyes. "Well?"

Well—well, what? What did she say?

"I vote with Ruth." Charlie led May down a road to the right, sent Jack a sly wink over his shoulder, and sang "The Nearness of You."

Jack shot him a murderous glare.

Charlie swung his gaze to the petite blonde under his arm and continued singing.

May rested her head on his shoulder. Good. If she thought the song was meant for her, Ruth would too.

"He has a nice voice," Ruth said by Jack's side.

"Yeah, but he uses it too much." He flipped the tails of his jacket out of the way and put his hands in his pockets so he wouldn't be tempted to take her hand.

"May doesn't mind. She adores it."

The couple snuggled as they walked down the street, and Jack tamped down a surge of jealousy and impatience. He had to wait and let Ruth fall for him. This trip would help. Even Ruth couldn't resist the romance of a forty-eight-hour pass in London. Despite Charlie's concerns about Jack's pride and Ruth's problems, Jack knew time and subtlety would get him to his goal.

"Do you think your group's flying today?" Ruth asked.

"I'm sure of it." Only scattered cumulus and silver barrage balloons dotted the sky. Right now Babcock would be up in that blue, earning points with Castle.

"Things have been going well lately?"

"Yeah. Since Regensburg we've had only one rugged mission, and the 94th hasn't lost a plane all month. The P-47s get us all the way to the German border now."

"Good. I hate to think of you getting shot up again."

"Yeah?" He studied her expression and found a new element of tenderness. If she wasn't in love, she was awfully close.

Her chin jutted out. "One more reason to hate the Nazis. How could anyone shoot at *Sunrise*? She's beautiful."

Jack laughed. "You're in love with my plane."

"You introduced us."

He stuck his tongue hard between his molars. Now was no time to joke about how she didn't date. "Be glad I didn't introduce you two days ago."

"Why, what happened?"

Jack frowned. He couldn't tell her they had tested British H2S radar, which would enable them to bomb through cloud cover. "The Fourth Wing—I mean, the Third Bombardment Division—can't get the new name straight. Well, we were on a practice mission over the North Sea, got jumped by Me 109s. Good thing we had some guns installed."

"Oh my goodness."

"Lost a Fort in another group, but we escaped with a few holes."

"In *Sunrise*?" Alarm, anger—boy, was it cute.

"Vertical stabilizer."

"Why, those—"

Jack stepped in front of her and set his hands on her shoulders. "Hold it there, buckaroo. Leave the gunslingin' to the sheriff."

"And you're the—"

"Howdy, ma'am." He touched the bill of his service cap with his fingertips.

"Oh brother." She headed downhill.

Jack caught up to her, stuffed his hands in his pockets, and gripped the pocket lining. Had to make sure he didn't swing her into his arms for a little do-si-do.

"There's the Tower," Charlie said. The four turrets of the White Tower protruded above the treetops. The group passed a clump of trees and came to a fence overlooking the outer wall studded with round towers. They leaned on the railing.

"Can you imagine?" Ruth said. "William the Conqueror, Sir Walter Raleigh, Henry the Eighth, and poor Anne Boleyn."

May clutched Charlie's arm on one side, Ruth's on the other. "Too bad it's closed to visitors. Wouldn't it be wonderful to see the ravens? The crown jewels?"

"But they carted the jewels away," Charlie said. "Hid them somewhere."

Jack pointed to the northern wall. "Good thing. Look at the bomb damage."

Everyone murmured what a shame it was, and then Ruth glanced down into the moat and laughed. "Is that what I think it is? A Victory Garden?"

Jack peered at the vegetables in their proper English rows. Then he made a ghoulish face at Ruth. "Must be well fertilized—with poor Anne Boleyn's blood."

"Quit it, Jack." Ruth bumped his shoulder. "You can't disgust us. We're nurses."

"Ah, what good's a girl if you can't make her squeal?"

May squealed. "Look! London Bridge. Remember, Ruth? Remember that day in town?"

Oh no, of all the lousy things.

And lousier still—May clasped Ruth's hands and raised them overhead. Jack could still see Ruth in the abbey, in the same position, flirting with him. Now Ruth's eyes widened and her face grew pale.

He had to stop this. He grasped May's shoulders and turned her to face the bridge. "That's the Tower Bridge. Not London Bridge, the Tower Bridge. Let's get a closer look." He marched her down the sidewalk.

May laughed. "Charlie, he's abducting me."

"Your knight to the rescue, my fair damsel." Charlie strode in front of them and struck a gallant pose, hands on hips. "Unhand her, you ruffian."

Jack stepped back and swept a low bow. Only then did he venture a look at Ruth. She followed, her brow furrowed, her purse clutched tight.

Jack's stomach balled up. May's innocent mistake could set him back weeks if he didn't lighten things up. "Say, Ruth, did you hear that? He called me a ruffian." There, he'd given her a chance to tease him.

Her gaze flicked up. "He's wrong. You're a gentleman."

Wow. He hadn't expected a compliment.

When they reached the Thames, Jack hung back and directed his gaze up to the giant stone towers, the blue swoop of cables, and the catwalks several stories up, all sky blue and white and gold.

"That looks like fun." Charlie pointed to a boat loaded with GIs, which turned under the bridge and headed for a pier close by.

No, thanks. Jack would leave the boat rides to Walt and Allie. After Walt's medical discharge from the Army Air Forces, he'd taken an engineering job at Boeing in Seattle while his fiancée worked in the business office. For fun they rode the ferries. Fine. They could have them.

May headed for the pier. "If we hurry, we can catch it."

Jack's chest clenched, but he laughed it off. "Come on, boats are slow. If we take the Underground, we'll have time to see the Westminster area before dinner."

"We have all day tomorrow," May said.

"And just imagine floating on the Thames," Ruth said with a dreamy look Jack wanted directed at him someday. The look faded. "Oh, I wonder how much it costs."

A chance to pamper her? A chance for romance? Jack dug in his pocket and handed Charlie a handful of British coins. "Here. Go get four tickets." The stupid things he did for love.

When it was time to board, he kept his eyes on the boat and away from the river bucking beneath him. His friends went to the railing, but Jack found a bench up against the cabin.

Charlie sent him a curious look. "The view's great."

"I can see fine from here. Want to rest my legs." Jack laced his hands behind his head and leaned back. If he watched the sky, maybe he could pretend he was flying. As the boat pulled away from the pier, Jack concentrated on the engine sounds, but he preferred the pulse of Wright Cyclones, and the sound of air against aluminum to water against wood.

Ruth's laughter drew his gaze and held it. Since the crowd at the railing obscured the sight of water, he tuned in to the conversation. Charlie related his experiences crabbing on Chesapeake Bay, and he spoke with animation of storms and fishermen and learning Dutch from his dad and granddad to pass time.

Ruth leaned close, one hand on her garrison cap, wisps of russet hair whipping around, her body a blue-uniformed figure eight, one heel raised and swinging back and forth like a metronome. Beauty, intelligence, character, and fire—no wonder he was in love.

He'd never been in love like this. Love always followed dates and kisses, but now none of those things swayed him, and he loved Ruth for herself.

She glanced over her shoulder and gave him a smile. "Aren't you going to join us?"

"No, thanks."

"Why not?" She leaned back with her elbows on the railing, her heel still waving back and forth, beckoning him to come over, throw his arms around that slender waist, and kiss her so well, she'd forget she hated it.

"Hmm? Why not?"

Jack readjusted his hands behind his head. "I don't like boats. I like planes."

One side of her mouth crept up. "What's the matter? Sea-sick?"

"I don't get seasick."

"Can't swim?"

Too close. "Of course I can swim. I grew up on the river."

"Oh yes. I remember the stories." Ruth walked over and sat beside him on the bench. "You and your brothers in the San Joaquin River without any suits."

Of all the things for her to remember. He smiled. "Mm-hmm."

"So why does a boy who grew up in the water dislike it now?" Her eyes glinted with friendly teasing and something more—she knew she was on to something.

"No reason." Jack shrugged off his annoyance. "I prefer sky to sea, okay?"

Her eyes narrowed. "Okay."

Words formed, but he blocked them. Reminding her she also disliked certain things would sound childish and pet-ulant. Instead he leaned closer and pointed up. "Can you blame me? Look at that sky. Remember what those clouds are called?"

"Cumulus." She smiled and patted his arm. "I'm going back."

Jack rapped his knuckles on his thighs. Stupid river, keeping him from the woman he loved.

20

London

Monday, September 27, 1943

Westminster chimes in Westminster. Ruth imprinted the sound into her memory.

"That's one big clock."

She glanced up to Jack's mischievous face. "That's Big Ben, you goon."

"Is it now?" He looked at the map, then pointed left. "This way."

"Only if you want to fall into the Thames," Charlie said with a laugh. "Ruth?"

She shook her head at Jack and studied the map, which wasn't easy with his breath on her ear. "We go straight ahead on this road to the right."

Charlie and May led the way down the sidewalk. Jack touched the small of Ruth's back to ease her in front of him so a group could pass, and electric shimmers ran through her. But why? He was just as likely to clap Charlie on the back or pat May's shoulder.

She had to control these emotions that had propelled her so disastrously into his arms before.

Jack looked over his shoulder to Big Ben. "My mom has always wanted a grandfather clock. Whenever she pined about it, Ray played the Westminster chimes on the piano for her."

Ruth smiled up at him. "I think I'd like your brother."

"Who doesn't? Even the cadets he washes out of pilot training like him. I'm surprised he eliminates anyone. He's too nice. Gets him in trouble." Jack shook his head and huffed. "That Dolores, what a number. Good thing he had a broken engagement, not a broken marriage. She sure fooled him, made him think she was a virtuous woman."

Ruth frowned. She understood why someone would conceal a lack of virtue.

Charlie came to a stop. "Here we are. Houses of Parliament. Wow. Look at the bomb damage." The rubble had been cleared long ago, but boards still covered holes in the walls.

"Parliament. Babcock would be right at home here," Jack said. "Suppose we could get the Brits to elect him, take him off our hands?"

"I don't understand why you can't get along with Jeff," Charlie said. "You get along with everyone else."

"Let's see. Naked ambition, manipulation, glad-handing, phoniness, and pride bigger than his home state." Jack ticked off points on his fingers.

"I see the problem. Other than the phoniness, it hits too close to home, doesn't it?" Charlie laughed and led May down the street.

Jack's eyes burned in a face set like stone. Ruth had never seen that expression and never wanted it pointed at her. What was going on with the men? Charlie always played the role of loyal sidekick, but lately she detected acid in his tone.

"If it's any consolation," Ruth said, making Jack's gaze turn to her and soften, "I think your pride's smaller than your home state."

He broke into a smile. "Thanks a lot. California's bigger than Illinois."

"Mm. Only in land, not in population or importance."

"Fine. Charlie insults me, you insult my home state."

She nudged him in the arm. "For the record, no Doherty ever voted for 'Baby-Face' Babcock."

"Yeah? Would you vote for me?"

"Oh, you're too noble to enter the base profession of politics."

Jack laughed. "At least I have one friend," he said loudly for Charlie's benefit.

He'd called her his friend again, a compliment rich in meaning. Yet as Charlie and May studied a building with their hands entwined, friendship seemed second-rate. It could have been more.

If she were virtuous.

"Wow," Jack said. "Must be impressive with windows."

Ruth focused on the side of an ancient building of pale gray stone with a regal façade rising to her right. Westminster Abbey, of course. Every window was boarded up. "I heard they removed the stained glass to storage during the Blitz."

"Smart," Jack said. "The Nazis target historic sites. At least the U.S. aims for military targets. Sure, there's civilian damage, but not on purpose."

"The RAF, on the other hand," Charlie said. "Carpet bombing at night, not that I blame them."

Jack looked around at the razed lots and boarded windows, his jaw set forward. "Yep. Hitler started it."

In her mind, Ruth replaced Westminster Abbey's boards with stained glass. "I'm glad we don't deliberately cause damage like this, don't try to kill innocent people."

"Compassion makes you a great nurse," Jack said. "But you'd make a lousy bombardier."

"We already have a bombardier on this crew," Charlie said. "She's our navigator. Speaking of which . . ."

Jack pulled out the map and unfolded it for Ruth.

"Come on, Novak, give her the map."

"It's mine."

Ruth studied the map. Two months ago, she would have suspected he kept the map for these moments of closeness, but now he kept it only from masculine pride. "This road to the right takes us to a street that runs along St. James's Park to Buckingham Palace." She drew back, and her arm cooled away from Jack's touch. Ridiculous.

She strode ahead at full pace, passing Charlie and May.

Jack's footsteps thumped up beside her. "Hold yer horses there, ma'am."

"Since when have you turned into a cowpoke?"

"Can't rightly say, little filly. Somethin' 'bout this here town brings out the rebellious Yank in me." He pursed up his mouth. "Got me an urge to spit. Maybe get a little gun-fight goin'."

"Don't you dare. You'll get us kicked out of town, and I'll never see the palace."

"You're an enthusiastic little tourist, aren't you?"

Ruth gave him a glare for the patronizing *little*. "Can you blame me? We're in London. London! All these places I've read about all my life, but I never dreamed I'd see. These two days have been the best of my life."

"Mine too."

Ruth's mouth went dry. He'd been to London before, so he had to mean the company. At the corner, sharp stone buildings gave way to a broad avenue with greenery on the far side. They waited for shining black taxis to pass, then crossed the road and turned onto a path that edged the park.

"Jack?" She cleared her throat and willed her stomach to

stop hopping around. "You and May and Charlie—well, you're part of the reason this trip is special. I never imagined I'd have friends like this." She looked back to where Charlie and May lagged behind, then to Jack's face, full of affection.

Ruth tripped on a flagstone, and Jack caught her elbow. "Watch it, there."

She managed to laugh, but her ankles wobbled until he let go.

They walked under the partial canopy of trees, the sun warm on her back, and they discussed the American breakout at Salerno. If Italy was a boot, the Allies controlled the shoe portion. Jack thought an invasion of France was necessary but would be easier with the bombing campaign weakening German defenses, the Soviets reclaiming Russia in the east, and the Allies marching up Italy.

What really made Jack light up was the progress in the Pacific. The Americans and Australians had almost secured the Solomons and were pushing across New Guinea, land he'd flown over and watched friends die over.

Ruth studied this man who thrived on adventure. "Sometimes I have a hard time picturing you in the pulpit."

His face twitched. "Any news from your family?"

Once again he avoided the topic by addressing her favorite subject, except today it made her stomach knot up. "I had a letter from Aunt Pauline."

"She has your youngest sister, Maggie, right?"

"Right." She glanced through the trees to a lake—could those be swans on the lake? They'd have to walk down there on the way back. "My aunt can't make ends meet. My contribution isn't enough."

"Forty-two bucks a month isn't enough?" Jack's eyes flashed. "Come on. A man can support a family on twenty-five a week."

Ruth didn't dare indulge in the same line of thought. "Uncle Clancy doesn't make much, and Maggie's growing. She needs food, clothing, schoolbooks."

"Still—"

"Still they need more, and they can't make it until Chuck graduates in June."

Jack groaned. "And your aunt has legal control over your sister."

"Yes." Her voice cracked, and she hated that.

"Don't worry. You'll get into the flight nursing program." He gave her a look so full of compassion her throat ached.

If only she shared his confidence. Every day the dread grew. What if she didn't get in and couldn't care for her family? What if she did get in and had to leave her friends?

At the end of the park lay a roundabout with a monument in the center. To the left stood Buckingham Palace, far larger than any home had a right to be. They headed for a wrought-iron fence, tipped with gold, which separated the common from the royal. Ruth grasped the bars and peeked through. Hundreds of windows, and unimaginable grandeur inside.

"Makes Redgrave Hall look tiny, doesn't it?" May said.

Ruth nodded, her throat tight. Behind those walls people still got sick and died and hurt each other. But behind those walls people never went to bed hungry, never watched their loved ones work themselves to death, never turned to immoral means in order to eat. Behind those walls people never worried about little girls being sent to orphanages, never had to leave their friends to pay the bills, never had to spurn a wonderful man because they were filthy. She'd sold her affections, sold them away, and now she had none left to give.

Jack nudged her shoulder, smiled down at her, his lips in motion. Conversation volleyed light and frothy over her head.

She uncurled her hands from her prison bars and followed the group across the roundabout to the monument.

So many GIs in London. So many. How many from Chicago? From her neighborhood? Could they recognize her? She wore an officer's uniform and a different hairstyle, but she was still that tramp selling her kisses.

Many of the soldiers eyed her, violated her in their minds. They knew. They knew what she was.

She dragged her feet up the steps of the monument and circled the marble rising in carved splendor to golden winged figures on top. Ruth gazed up at Queen Victoria bright in the midday sun in all her marble purity. The queen looked down her pure white nose with disdain in her pure white eyes. She knew. She saw Ten-Penny Doherty in her filthy shame, sullying her beautiful land.

Ruth broke the gaze and whipped around, breathing hard.

A group of enlisted men sauntered by, their shoulders sporting patches of the Eighth Air Force, a yellow winged 8 encircling a red-and-white star on a blue field. The men didn't look at her, thank goodness, but at a group of English girls to her left.

One of the men—there was something about his lazy walk, the fall of brown hair over his forehead, the set of his boyish smile in profile.

Eddie Reynolds.

Dear Lord in heaven, no!

Ten years before, she and Eddie had sneaked to the alley to share some kisses after school, after she'd spent another fruitless afternoon begging for work, any work. Ma couldn't support them all cleaning that big old office building at night. The level in the money jar fell lower every day. But no one would hire an unskilled thirteen-year-old girl.

"You're the best kisser in the whole eighth grade," Eddie had said with that great wide grin.

Too bad kissing didn't pay. Or could it? "Eddie, would you pay to kiss me?"

His grin fell. "Pay? Money?"

"Not you. You're my boyfriend. But if you weren't, would you pay?"

His face constricted. He let go of her and leaned back against the brick wall. "Yeah, I guess so."

"How much would you pay? For a kiss like the last one." A ten-minute kiss.

"Oh, that's worth a dime."

A dime. In an hour, she could earn sixty cents. That was a whole lot of money. "Kissing lessons. Most boys kiss too puckery or too slobbery or too pecky. I could teach them."

He crossed his arms. "Penny, you're talking crazy."

Not crazy, smart. She'd tell her parents she'd found odd jobs. Since God didn't provide for her family or her future, she'd do it herself. She had raised a wobbly smile. "Ten cents for ten minutes. Has a nice ring, don't you think?"

Under the British sun, Eddie's gaze swept the length of the palace, closer and closer.

No! No, she couldn't lose all this. If her secret were revealed—a morals violation—she could lose her job, her commission, her license, and her ability to provide for her family.

Ruth grabbed Jack's arm. "The park. I have to see the park." She dashed across the roundabout with Jack's body as a shield from Eddie's knowing eyes. *Oh God, please no*.

She thought she heard Jack say, "Whoa, there, little filly," thought she heard May's laughter follow behind, thought the road threw up white sparks, taunting her with unattainable purity.

An opening. Stairs. Ruth ran down, out of Eddie's view, into the park. Now to get away, farther away. She pushed through the grass, the dark grass, past dark trees, in dark, heavy air.

Her knees buckled. She stumbled.

"Ruth?" Jack caught her under the arm, his voice in a fog.

Oh no, she was hyperventilating. She staggered to a black tree. Jack's voice echoed in the fog, incomprehensible. She heaved herself back against the tree, let her head fall over her trembling knees, squeezed her eyes shut, blew out her breath, and sucked it in past swollen throat tissue.

"Ruth? Ruth?" Jack's voice came from down in front of her, his hands strong and supportive on her shoulders. "Darling, what's the matter?"

"Ruth? Jack? What happened?" May laid a calming hand on Ruth's back. "Oh dear. Is she hyperventilating again?"

"I—I don't—"

Ruth nodded and concentrated on her breathing.

"What happened to upset her?"

"I—I don't know," Jack said, his voice thick. "We were having fun at the palace, the memorial. Suddenly she broke out running, and now this. Darling, what's the matter?"

Darling. He'd called her that twice in a row. Not a chummy *honey*, or a paternal *sweetie*, but a lover's *darling*, what he'd called her in the abbey. What had she gotten him into? He thought she was virtuous. He didn't know who she was or what she'd done to pay for nursing school. He deserved better. She opened her eyes, and the grass stood green and still around her black Oxfords.

"That's it," May said. "Slow and steady. Feel better?"

She nodded, ashamed of her behavior and still fighting the terror that her secret could have been revealed to destroy all she'd worked for, sacrificed for, and sinned for.

Jack's fingers eased up her chin. His face swam into focus, tender, concerned—loving. "Can you tell me what happened?"

No. Never. She pulled in a breath to speak. "Too much excitement, I guess. I've seen so much, done so much, and then—I must have run too fast."

He brushed hair out of her face. "Be careful, okay? You scared me."

She locked onto his gaze to show how much she meant her words. "I'm so sorry, Jack."

21

Bury St. Edmunds Airfield
Saturday, October 9, 1943

The briefing room resounded with groans and nervous laughter, but Jack grinned. He knew the details from helping Colonel Castle and the senior officers plan the mission late into the night.

On the map, red ribbons stretched from England to Nazi targets. The lowest ribbon, representing two First Division B-17 wings, reached to the Arado aircraft component works in Anklam on the German coast. Ribbons for the B-24s of Second Division and two more B-17 wings passed over Denmark, then down to the ports of Gdynia and Danzig. Two wings from Third Division would proceed farther, to the Focke-Wulf factory in Marienburg in East Prussia.

"Marienburg," Charlie said. "Great target."

"Yep." Jack slung his elbow over the back of Charlie's chair.

Lt. Col. Louis Thorup, the executive officer, stated how the target factory produced 50 percent of Fw 190s. A slide flashed on the screen, a map of the target area with landmark towns, roads, waterways, and railroads.

Charlie and Norman studied the map, their eyes in rapid motion. Norman fidgeted in his seat. "Fifteen hundred miles round-trip."

The longest mission to date, but that was part of the brilliance. Since the Eighth wouldn't be expected, they could bomb from eleven thousand feet. More groans circled the room, but Charlie's eyes widened. The lower the altitude, the higher the accuracy.

Thorup stood as straight as the pointer he tapped between his feet. He told the group each plane would carry three 1,000-pound general purpose bombs plus five 100-pound M-47A incendiary bombs, all fused one-tenth nose and one-hundredth tail. He didn't use notes.

Jack admired that. He could see himself giving a briefing. He'd relay information in a calm and precise manner, add gravity to impress the importance of the job, mix in humor to ease the tension, and end with a bang of confidence-building enthusiasm.

"I'll be up there before you know it," he murmured, but Charlie didn't respond.

Jack leaned back in his chair as the flak officer took the floor. No flak batteries at Marienburg. None. The Germans thought they were safe, but they were wrong.

"This is our day to shine." Again no response, but Jack brushed it off. He couldn't have designed a better opportunity—a major mission with everything pointing to success, and Jack would lead the group. He'd had the chance only a handful of times, since the squadron commanders rotated the lead and the CO or executive officer flew the big missions.

Not today. To sweeten the deal, Babcock wasn't flying. Everything stacked in Jack's favor. Castle seemed to prefer him, he'd logged a solid fourteen missions, and now the

Marienburg mission would glow on his record. Maybe Jack would get that promotion before he finished his tour.

The weather officer showed charts of predicted cloud cover—patches of fog over England, three-tenths to five-tenths medium and high clouds over the North Sea, clearing over the target. Ideal for bombing.

"Do your best for me, buddy," Jack said. "I've got you for only three more missions."

Charlie's cheek twitched. The bombardier had his future lined up. When he finished his tour, he'd be promoted to major, forsake the one-month furlough offered to entice men to volunteer for a second combat tour, and take a ground job training lead bombardiers.

Colonel Castle stood, gave words of encouragement, and dismissed the men to their specialized briefings. Conversation picked up as the men filed out of the briefing room, tones quiet in expectation of a long haul, but eyes bright in anticipation of success.

Jack looked over his shoulder to Charlie as they edged down the aisle. "Boy, will this be good. What a shame Babcock has to miss it."

Charlie connected the zipper on his sheepskin-lined flight jacket. "Are you gunning for Hitler? Or Babcock?"

Jack rolled his eyes. "Come on, buddy. I know the difference between an enemy and a rival."

Charlie's grumbling reply was lost in the chatter. Just as well. Today was Jack's shining day, and he wouldn't let Charlie's morning grouchiness mar its luster.

☆

"What'll it be, Winch?" Jack stretched tired fingers over the piano keyboard in the Officers' Club. "One more song, then I'm taking a break."

"'Take the A Plane—Train.'" Joe Winchell sputtered a laugh and sloshed scotch on the piano top. "Ha! That's us, the A planes. Square A? A Plane? Get it?"

"Got it." He smiled and searched through the sheet music for the Duke Ellington hit. Tonight he'd cut Winchell some slack. Jack was in too good a mood after the mission, and Winchell deserved a celebration, even if Jack thought little of drunkenness as celebration.

Not many men survived twenty-five missions. In fact, very few. But today Winchell and the men in his crew had 25 painted in blue on their foreheads.

"I tell you, Novak." Winchell leaned on the piano top, his gray eyes bleary. "What a way to finish. I tell you, I saw that map this morning, thought Sahara Sue would be a poor little orphaned donkey. 'Bout breaks my heart. How many fellows get it on their last mission? How many, I ask you?"

"All too many."

"All too many. That's right, my friend, all too many. You're a good man, Novak. A good man. It's been a prib—prib— privilege flying with you." His head bobbled his sincerity.

"Same here, Winch. You'll do a great job in Intelligence." Then he grinned. "Once you're sober."

Winchell exploded in laughter, and his drunken crewmates jostled him. More whiskey dribbled on the piano top. Mom's piano at home never had such a baptism.

Jack launched into the song and jiggled his knee to the beat despite creeping fatigue. Up at 0300, takeoff at 0700, a ten-hour mission, then debriefing and dinner. It was only 2000, but after this song and some time with Charlie, he'd hit the sack to rest for tomorrow's mission.

The song and the day's success pumped energy back into him. Although Castle was never one for flattery or exaggeration, he called it the bombing of the year. Strike photos showed 58 percent of the bombs fell within one thousand feet of the aiming point, the best percentage ever.

As predicted, the southern Anklam leg drew the Luftwaffe's attention and took most of the losses. On the Marienburg leg, only two planes fell, none from the 94th.

Jack finished the song, shook floppy hands in congratulation, and scanned the club for Charlie, who wasn't in his usual spot by the piano. There he was, across the room with Norman Findlay and Gene Levitski. A tentacle of smoke rose over Charlie's head.

Jack spun a chair around and straddled it backwards. "Fell off the wagon, huh? Guess it's good you won't see May tomorrow after all."

Gene and Norman got to their feet. "Good night," Gene said. "Hate to go, but tomorrow's early, you know."

An abrupt departure, but Jack couldn't fault them. "Night, boys. See you at briefing."

"Yeah." Gene and Norman exchanged a look and turned to leave.

Jack watched Charlie tap a cigarette into an ashtray. "Run out of pencils?"

Charlie stuck the cigarette in his mouth and inhaled deeply.

Jack studied his friend's face. He couldn't be down about the mission, so he had to be down about missing tomorrow's Sunday picnic. "You know, buddy, it's not so bad missing a date with the ladies. Every time we do, they worry a bit, get a little sentimental and a lot more appreciative."

Charlie stared at the ashtray and blew smoke out his nose.

"Besides, May's already crazy about you. Of the two of us, I'm the one who should be blue. Ruth's not in love with me yet—close, but not quite."

Charlie let out a smoky huff. "Still won't let up with that plan of yours, will you?"

"Why would I? It's working."

"Working? The woman—" He closed his eyes and shook his head. "She runs off in London, she hyperventilates, she—she—something's wrong, but you keep pushing. You treat her like a project, not a person."

Jack leaned back, "Oh, come on. I treat her like a person. More than that. I love her."

"No, you think you love her. You love the challenge, the plotting, the manipulation."

"Manipu—" His mouth drew up. "Oh, come on."

"What's the goal you're after? A kiss. Since when is that the most important part of love?"

Jack stared at Charlie de Groot, a man he'd known for three years, a man who knew him well, or so he thought. "You've got my motives mixed up. I'm in love with her, and if I want her to fall in love with me, what's wrong with that?"

Charlie pounded his cigarette into a little accordion in the ashtray.

Jack blew off the steam in his chest. Charlie had never been in a worse mood—he was tired, disappointed not to see his girl, and anxious about his two remaining missions. He needed rest, and so did Jack. Now was no time for an argument. He shifted his feet to push himself to standing.

"Hiya, fellas." Nate Silverberg grasped Charlie's shoulders from behind. "Great mission today, wasn't it?"

"The best." Jack grinned. Silverberg had proved an excellent pilot, and Jack had moved him to deputy lead. He'd command the squadron well someday—in the near future, Jack hoped.

"Well, de Groot, I'm looking forward to flying with you tomorrow." Silverberg thumped Charlie on the back. "Thanks for sharing the wealth, Novak." He tipped a salute and was gone.

Jack shook his head to clear his ears. "What's he talking about?"

"I was about to tell you."

"Tell me what?"

Charlie lit another cigarette. "I'm flying my last two missions with Silverberg. Crew lists are posted for tomorrow. It's set."

"What?" Jack gripped the chair back in front of his chest. "Who switched the crews around? That's my responsibility. I make the crew lists."

"Jack . . ."

He scanned the room. "Babcock. I should've known. He won't get away with this."

"Stop it. This is why I switched."

"What?"

"I went to Castle and requested a crew change. It was my doing. Mine alone."

"Huh?" A sick feeling oozed into his stomach.

"I know. I only have two missions left, but I had to get off your crew, and now."

The sickness crept, green and vile, up to his chest. "Off my crew, but—I don't—why?"

"Your pride." Charlie raised his eyes, resolved and self-righteous. "I've never minded before, because you're a good pilot and a good friend. But lately, that pride's grown. You're so consumed with beating Babcock, you're more focused on the promotion than the job, just what you accuse Jeff of doing."

Jack gaped at the lies spewing from Charlie's mouth.

"At some point your pride will make you do something dangerous. I don't want to be around."

Anger ignited in the green mess in his stomach, but he

laughed it off. "Come on, we're a team. You and I. Since primary flying school."

"I know, but I can't fly with you again. You're too good, Jack. That's your problem. Because you're good, you've never let yourself down, and you trust in yourself. You can't do that. You have to trust in God alone."

"I do." He drummed his knuckles on the chair back. "Of course I do."

Charlie sighed, ground out his cigarette, and got to his feet. "I've got to go."

"Come on. We've been friends too long." Jack dug in his pocket, pulled out a dime, and pressed it into Charlie's hand. "Go get us some coffee, and we'll talk about this."

Charlie stared at the dime in his hand. "You know, for once I'd like to see you get your own drink."

Jack blinked. "What do you mean? I'm paying."

Charlie laid the coin on the table. "You don't understand, do you?"

Understand? He glared at Charlie's retreating back. It was a bunch of baloney. How could you understand baloney?

22

12th Evacuation Hospital

Tuesday, October 12, 1943

"Thank you, Sergeant." Ruth took the basin of Dakin's solution from the medic and set it on the table next to Lieutenant Baker's bed. The smell of bleach wafted up from the basin. Ruth tried to smile away the nervous look in her patient's eyes. "Let's clean that wound."

When she removed the dressing, Lieutenant Baker howled. "Look at that big hole in my thigh. That doc didn't even stitch me up."

"Dr. Hoffman used the latest technique, developed at Pearl Harbor." Ruth irrigated the wound left by a Luftwaffe cannon shell, which brought more howls. One of her whiniest patients ever. "Open wounds rarely develop gas gangrene, because the bacteria can't grow when exposed to oxygen. If Dr. Hoffman had closed your wound, as they did in the First World War, you might have lost your leg or your life."

"But the hole." He arched his neck on the pillow when she patted the wound dry with gauze. Most men barely flinched.

"God designed your body to heal itself. Before you know it, all you'll have left is a scar."

He whimpered. "A scar?"

She smiled to disguise a sigh. "Think how it'll impress the folks back home. And your children. And grandchildren."

"Hmm." Lieutenant Baker's eyes narrowed. The thought of milking sympathy fifty years into the future seemed to distract him, because he didn't protest when Ruth applied a clean dressing. He yelped, however, when she injected a quarter grain of morphine into his deltoid.

Ruth gathered the soiled dressings and dumped them in the workroom. She tried to ignore the envelope stiff in the pocket of her white dress. She should have opened it at lunch. Now she didn't dare open it until after her shift.

A narcotics count would keep her occupied. She unlocked the narcotics cabinet and counted vials of morphine, phenobarbital, and the new wonder drug, Pentothal. Now anesthesia could be induced by injection, not just by inhalation. Dr. Hoffman had used Pentothal for an emergency procedure in the ward, and the patient had been knocked unconscious in ten seconds flat.

On her last round she took vital signs, charted her notes, and turned down Captain Heller's marriage proposal. If it weren't for the fluttery feeling in her stomach, she might have convinced herself the envelope was forgotten.

Seven o'clock arrived, and so did Flo Oswald for the shift change. After Ruth gave report, she stepped into the cool autumn evening. The envelope crinkled like the leaves underfoot.

She fastened her cape around her neck and explored the letter in her pocket. It was thick. Rejection would require only one thin piece of stationery.

Her heart and stomach tumbled so she couldn't tell which

organ was in which position. She should be thrilled. This was her dream—to fly, to be independent, to wear the golden wings. She could provide for her family and keep Maggie out of the orphanage. This was a blessing from God. A blessing.

Yet as she walked between the rows of Nissen huts, a sense of loss hollowed out her soul.

She finally had a girlfriend, someone to talk to and laugh with, someone she could trust. Even if she made a new friend at Bowman Field, she would never find someone like May, who shared Ruth's history of pain and loss yet kept her faith and serenity.

She'd also lose her group of friends. On Monday, while Jack stayed home with paperwork, Charlie had taken May and Ruth to Cambridge to see ancient university buildings, majestic cathedrals, and charming boats on the river, all more meaningful when shared.

Ruth turned onto the path toward Redgrave Hall, in too much turmoil to eat.

Jack. She'd put off thinking about him until last. Why was the thought of losing him the most painful? After the trip to London, she knew he cared too deeply for her, and now he could find the nice, normal girlfriend he deserved. But she also felt too deeply for him. She loved being with him, loved everything about him.

"Ruth!" May called behind her. "There you are. I saw you pass my ward. Aren't you going to dinner?"

"I'm not hungry." Her eyelashes were wet, her vision blurry.

May gave her the probing look. "Are you all right?"

Ruth drew the letter from her pocket and blinked away the moisture in her eyes. "I heard from the School of Air Evacuation."

"Oh." May's face drooped. "Oh, I thought you'd get in."

"I think—I think I did." She examined the return address. Kentucky—she'd never been to Kentucky.

"You haven't opened it yet? Goodness, what are you waiting for?"

Then she knew. She'd been waiting for May, for support and assurance. She slid a shaky finger under the lip of the envelope, tore it open, and pulled out three sheets of paper. The first was an order to report to duty at Bowman Field for an eight-week program starting November 28, the second was a list of items to bring, and the third contained instructions to obtain travel vouchers.

Joy illuminated May's face, and she threw her arms around Ruth. "You got in! You got in! Congratulations."

"Thank you." Ruth hugged her friend, but her face crumpled.

"I'll miss you so much. I'm sorry. I know it's selfish. I know how much you want to go, but I will miss you."

"I'll miss you too." Selfish—yes, that also described Ruth's thoughts. She had a duty to her family. They needed Ruth far more than Ruth needed friends.

23

Thursday, October 14, 1943

Jack made a ninety-degree turn at the Initial Point over Würzburg and guided his high squadron northeast toward the target.

Schweinfurt.

No matter what he'd said, Jack hadn't been able to bolster morale that morning. On August 17, half of the Eighth Air Force had been pummeled over Regensburg, and the other half over Schweinfurt. The veterans remembered; the rookies had heard.

Now both First and Third Divisions, with 320 Flying Fortresses, were out to bomb the ball bearing plants. Fighters made sporadic attacks when they crossed Luxembourg, and Third Division had lost a couple of Forts from the 96th in the lead.

Jack activated the AFCE. "She's all yours, Char—" The sickness returned and twined around his gut. "Vickers, all yours."

"Bombardier to pilot. Roger."

Don Vickers was good, but he wasn't Charlie de Groot. Three years flying together, and Charlie broke it up over a stupid difference in perspective. Charlie called it pride; Jack called it confidence. Charlie said Jack didn't trust God; Jack knew he trusted in his God-given abilities. And what was the problem with the coffee? Jack hated standing in line; Charlie never minded. They always did it that way. Always. Now he had a problem with it?

Jack flexed his gloved fingers to keep them limber although it was minus forty degrees outside. Gray smoke rose from the bombs of First Division, six minutes ahead of them. Would the smoke obscure the target? Charlie knew how to aim in the smoke, but today on his last mission, he shirked his responsibility and flew deputy lead in Silverberg's plane.

Charlie had broken up the foursome as well, which cut Jack's time with Ruth in half, but he wouldn't give up tomorrow night's dance at the air base. With Ruth leaving for Kentucky in a few weeks, he wouldn't waste the opportunity to hold her again. He'd been magnanimous and encouraged her goal although it ran contrary to his goal. Now he didn't have much time. He wanted a long-distance romance, not a long-distance friendship.

A barrage of flak opened about a half mile ahead, like burnt popcorn scattered over the sky. In the lead, the 96th wobbled under the impact.

"Coming up on the target." Vickers's voice seemed high and foreign to Jack's ear. "Bomb bay doors opening." A metallic cranking sounded to the rear.

"Check. Bomb bay doors open," Paul Klaus said from down in the ball turret.

More flak and closer. Behind Jack in the top turret, Harv Owens let out his own profane barrage. "Stay away, Jerry. I'm on mission twenty-five and I'm not going down."

"Shut up, Owens. It's bad luck," Klaus said.

Jack pushed the interphone button on the control wheel.

"That's enough, boys. No luck, no superstition, and no chatter. Watch for fighters."

He wished this superstition didn't hold truth, but it did. A man stood the highest risk on the first five missions, and the last one. Other than Levitski and Vickers, all his crewmen were on number twenty-five, and of all targets, they got stuck with Schweinfurt, over four hours in enemy territory, most of it without P-47 Thunderbolt escort.

The steel bombs of the 96th dropped through black puffs of flak. Twenty-five thousand feet below, smoke roiled over the VKF ball bearing works. If the Eighth Air Force did their job today, Hitler would lose 50 percent of his ball bearing production for months, which would slow manufacture of all sorts of equipment, including fighter planes.

Jack leaned forward to get a better view. On the ground, explosions flashed bright like firecrackers, and then lumps of earth and smoke added to the mess.

The lead squadron of the 94th let their bombs loose. "Bombs away," Vickers said.

Jack disengaged the AFCE and took back control of his plane from Vickers. "Okay, boys, let's go home." He tried to sound cheerful, but they wouldn't rendezvous with the Thunderbolts for over an hour.

At the Rally Point, Jack turned west and eased his squadron back into the high position, to the left and slightly behind the lead squadron. Babcock flew the dreaded low slot. Jack didn't envy his rival, but he didn't gloat either, despite what Charlie thought.

"Okay, men," Levitski said, his voice muffled by the oxygen mask. "Enemy aircraft at two o'clock high, also ten o'clock level."

Had to be over a hundred fighters. Jack squeezed the bag on his oxygen mask to make sure ice hadn't built up. "Levitski, better do an oxygen check before things get hot."

He nodded and called through the stations on the inter-phone. Everyone was conscious.

Jack kneaded the throttles in his hand to keep his airspeed steady. Me 109s and Fw 190s peeled off from the black mass of fighters to rip through the combat boxes. To the south, twin-engined Me 110s paralleled the Fortresses, out of range of the Americans' .50 caliber machine guns.

One of the Me 110s jiggled. A rocket shot from its wing and smashed into the side of a Fort in the 96th. A horrible explosion shook the formation. Chunks of metal fell. Not one parachute. Eighth Air Force Intelligence said the Luftwaffe had trouble aiming the rockets, but what did they know?

"Here they come, boys." The bag on Levitski's mask pulsed quickly, his only sign of anxiety.

Jack glanced down. His bag kept time with Levitski's.

"Four bogies. Ten o'clock level," Vickers said. "What I wouldn't give for my chin turret."

Silverberg flew a new B-17G model with two .50s in a chin turret below the bombardier's position. A B-17F, *Sunrise Serenade* had a single .50 straight out the nose. Today Charlie operated Vickers's chin turret.

One, two, three, four, the Me 109s rolled in, spitting bullets. *Sunrise*'s guns rattled into action, but the fighters concentrated on the low elements in the squadron.

"Nine o'clock high. Two of 'em."

"Three o'clock level. Four Fw 190s."

Dividing their fire. The Fort shivered with so many guns firing at once. The acrid smell of cordite filled the cockpit.

"Fogerty's hit," Manny Souza called from back in the waist section.

"Mission twenty-five." Harv hurled curses at the Germans.

"Enough, Harv. Souza, how's Fogerty?"

"You won't believe this. Flak vest saved his life. He got knocked flat on his rump, but that bullet's sticking out from the vest."

"Fogerty, how do you feel?"

A cough. "Okay. Got me a fine souvenir. Let go of me, Souza. Gotta get 'em back."

Jack exchanged a relieved look with Levitski and patted the cloth-covered steel plates of his flak vest, its weight reassuring on his torso. Too bad he hadn't had one back in May. Of course, it wouldn't have covered his backside, and if it had, he wouldn't have met Ruth.

Bullets raced toward *Sunrise* and away from *Sunrise* through air electrified with tracers. A sharp crack kicked up the right wing—a twenty-millimeter cannon shell. The propeller hub for engine three was gone, and black oil spewed out. Jack groaned. "Shut down three."

Levitski pulled the mixture control lever on the center console. "Engine three off. Booster off."

Jack turned the ignition switch on the console. "Engine three off."

"Cowl flaps closed."

"Throttle closed. Harv, when you've got a moment, transfer fuel from three to two."

"When I've got a moment? Tell that to Jerry." Harv swung his guns overhead after a yellow-nosed Fw 190.

Jack looked outside. Chaos. Fighters in every direction, hundreds of them. Forts lagging and tumbling, fighters in flames, white American parachutes and brown German ones.

"Nine o'clock low. Keep an eye on him, Klaus."

"Fort going down. Six, seven chutes. Eight."

"I got him. Wow! Look at him fall."

Jack trimmed the ailerons, wiped sweat from his forehead,

A MEMORY BETWEEN US

and glanced at the clock—1528, only thirty minutes off the target and ages until they met the P-47s.

"We are passing south of Giessen as briefed," Norman Findlay said from the navigator's desk. "Our estimated time of arrival is in three hours and twenty-seven minutes."

"ETA." A battle raged, and the man tied up the interphone with full terminology.

"Here comes another wave," Vickers said. "I see them in the distance."

Swell. They were using a relay system. Would they keep this up all the way to the coast?

"One o'clock high. Ten o'clock high." The clock numbers spun in Jack's ears; fighters spun before his eyes.

Harv whooped. "Two 109s collided. They're both going— oh no! Watch out!" He ducked out of his turret.

Jack looked up. A hunk of wing tumbled toward him. He yanked the wheel and barrel-rolled to the right. As the top plane in the squadron, he had a bit of room to maneuver.

He didn't have time.

The debris slapped the left wing down. Jack fought the wheel. Felt as if *Sunrise* hit a wall.

He snapped his gaze to the wing. A jagged triangle of metal stuck up—one corner pierced the nacelle of engine one, one corner jammed between the props, and one shimmied in the slipstream.

Levitski spat out an expletive.

Jack wished he could join him. He and Levitski ran through the procedure to shut down number one, but they couldn't feather the props with that chunk of metal wedged in, and those unfeathered blades pressed flat against the wind and acted as brakes.

Airspeed down to 137. *Sunrise* drifted back in formation. Jack flipped the overhead radio switch and told Silverberg to take the lead, but Silverberg lagged too, his left elevators shot away and engine one windmilling, unable to be feathered. Charlie thought he'd avoid trouble by switching crews, but he hadn't, and Jack's problems today had nothing to do with pride.

On the ground, smoke and flames from crashed bombers and fighters marked a straight line from Schweinfurt toward Holland.

Holland. Jack's feet went cold. The course took them over the Rhine Delta with dozens of watery inlets and marshy islands. He couldn't think of a worse place to crash or bail.

The 94th Bomb Group passed by. Five planes lagged in the gap between combat wings, easy prey for the Luftwaffe. The last wing of three groups pulled even before the next wave of fighters hit. One of the stragglers fell and several added to their number.

By the time they threaded the narrow corridor between the flak batteries at Bonn and Cologne, the Third Division left Jack and Silverberg behind with ten other planes too scattered to benefit from mutual firepower. If the P-47s didn't arrive, the enemy would finish them off.

Unless . . .

"That's it. We'll form our own combat box." Bomber Command frowned on ships helping stragglers, but why couldn't the wounded band together? Jack called the other B-17s on the radio, and before long a raggedy combat box limped over Germany.

A short-lived victory. They'd passed the rendezvous point for the P-47 escort. How long could they survive? They'd be discovered, hunted, forced into the water to drown.

Jack stuck one finger under the strap of his throat mike to ease the choking sensation.

"Levitski, take the wheel." He unplugged his headset and

oxygen, hooked a portable oxygen bottle to his mask, and dropped into the passageway between the pilots' seats. He scrambled on hands and knees into the nose compartment. "Findlay, we need a new course."

"A new course?" he shouted over the engine roar.

Jack leaned over the map on the navigator's desk with Findlay's lines penciled in. "Next wave of fighters, we're dead, all of us. We need to get away."

Norman stammered about his carefully plotted course, but Jack ignored him and studied the map. If they flew north of the Delta and south of the Zuider Zee, they'd avoid all that inland water.

Jack lined up his course with a ruler. "Here. When we get to the Dutch border, these woods here, we'll jog northeast about thirty miles, get away from the main bomber stream. Then swing back northwest. Plot it."

Norman put a gloved finger over the nice solid Dutch land. "But—but there's Rotterdam, Utrecht, Amsterdam—antiair-craft batteries everywhere."

"Plot around it." He put a firm hand on Norman's shoulder. "You're the best navigator around. I know you can do it." Jack returned to the cockpit, where he informed the other pilots that his navigator would radio them a new set of co-ordinates.

With the skies clear for the moment, Jack trimmed *Sunrise* and had Harv transfer every available drop of fuel from the dead engines.

"Navigator to pilot. I have the coordinates. I transmitted them in coded form to the other aircraft."

"Thanks, Findlay."

"Radio to pilot," Rosetti said. "Silverberg wants to talk to you."

Jack flipped the radio switch. "Cedar lead to Cedar two."

"Cedar two. We—well, we have a question about the course. It appears to add some—some distance, not to mention higher flak concentrations."

"Flak over the coast no matter what. This way we avoid interception."

"Maybe, but we'll—we'll miss our escort."

"We already have." How many dissenters were there? Couldn't they see the beauty of his plan? "We're on our own, and this is the best course. Trust me."

"But we're not sure . . ."

Jack rolled his eyes. "Listen, have I ever let you down? Trust me."

"Roger. Wait—I'm sorry. Excuse me." Silence. "I have a message from de Groot. He says to—to trust in God, not in yourself. That was from de Groot."

Jack's lips pulled in tight under his mask. Good thing Charlie had broken up the friendship and saved Jack the bother. "Roger. You have your coordinates, your orders. See you at home."

He flipped the switch back to interphone and guided his flock northeast. The tail fins bore letters from half a dozen bomb groups, but they were his now. He'd get them home.

Twenty miles after the turn, a plane from the 390th fell back. They'd have to bail soon, but they'd do so over solid ground. Eleven planes made the second turn into Dutch territory.

They had company.

Six Me 109s appeared to the southwest, then altered course to intercept. "Okay, men, here we go. Eleven o'clock low. Let's hope they're low on gas."

"Better hope so," Harv said. "'Cause I'm low on ammo."

Please help us, Lord. Jack's breath snagged on the thought.

He hadn't prayed much today, hadn't prayed before he charged in a new direction. Could Charlie be right?

The fighters climbed above the bombers. Three of them careened through the formation, spraying bullets every which way.

Pop! Pop! Pop! Down the right side of the fuselage.

"Left waist to pilot. Fogerty's hit again. For real. In the knee." Screams in the background confirmed the words.

Levitski's thick eyebrows drew together. "First aid has to wait. Man your gun, Souza. Here come the next three."

"Tail to pilot. The first flight is heading home, not coming around for another pass."

Jack eyed the second flight. *Lord, let this bunch do the same.*

The first two spun for the low element, but the last plane headed straight at Jack. Head-on. "Get him, Vickers."

Vickers did. The Me 109's cockpit exploded. The plane's carcass rolled to the side, still coming head-on. Collision course.

Jack cried out and shoved the wheel forward. The fighter wheeled toward him, flaming, breaking apart.

Sunrise's left wing jerked down and back. A shudder ripped through the plane and threw Jack's hands off the wheel. He grabbed hold, wrestled the wheel up and to the right, Levitski with him. Couldn't let her go into a spin. Could not.

"Come on, girl." He stared at the flight indicator on the panel. With all his will and all his muscle, he forced it back to the horizontal position.

Levitski heaved a sigh. Jack pressed his hand to his forehead, but it slipped right off. His hands shook something fierce. He glanced out the window to an intact left wing. How on earth, with a collision like that? The wing should have been shorn clean off.

"Ha!" Harv leaned over Jack's left shoulder. "Would you look at that? Lost our passenger."

Passenger? What was he talking about? Then it registered. The triangular chunk of debris had been knocked out of engine one. Gone! He laughed, a strange sound, shuddering as the B-17 had only moments before. "Would you look at that?"

The loss of debris eased up some of the drag and allowed him to gain enough airspeed to climb back into formation.

"Everett?" Jack called to the tail gunner. "How's the formation?"

"Fighters are gone. We lost another Fort. 96th Bomb Group. Two chutes."

Jack let out a sigh. Still ten left. "Manny, how's Fogerty?"

"He's with me," Rosetti said from the radio room. "Gave him some morphine, so he ain't whining as much now. Ordered him to stop bleeding over my clean floor. It took me this long to get your blood scrubbed out."

Jack laughed. "I'll put your name in for the Army Nurse Corps."

His laughter stopped. Black puffs ahead. Despite the undercast, they'd been spotted. "Findlay, what's our position?"

"I tried, sir. I tried."

"I know, but where are we? How far from the coast?" Jack looked through a hole in the low clouds to buildings and roads. Oh no, a city.

"I think—I think it's Rotterdam."

Dear Lord, help us. They had ten to twenty miles to the coast, and Rotterdam was famous for its flak batteries.

Five bursts to his rear. Jack massaged the rudder pedals under his feet to control the yawing.

"Silverberg's hit," Manny said. "Get out. Get out, you guys."

Oh no. Charlie. Jack rocked back and forth to see around Levitski. "What's going on? Manny, what's going on?"

"They—they lost most of the tail. Hole in the nose. Oh no."

Jack slammed his fist into his leg, made his foot jump. "Come on, Silverberg."

"Oh no, they're in a flat spin. Get out, you guys."

"Lord, no." A flat spin? Almost impossible to pull out of. Worse, centrifugal force built up and pressed the men to the sides. "Charlie, get out of there. Get out!"

Whatever he'd felt in his stomach the last few days was nothing. This—this was true sickness—vile, green sickness.

"Manny?" Jack forced the word out.

"She's still in a spin, heading north."

Jack pressed his fist against his steel-plated stomach. He had to ask, but he couldn't, couldn't say it.

Levitski asked for him. "Any chutes?"

Jack knew the answer. None. Charlie, his best friend, was hurtling five miles down to his death. Terrified. Trapped.

24

Redgrave Hall

Friday, October 15, 1943

"You've got to wear my dress, Ruth." Rosa Lomeli held up a slinky black number and sashayed around.

Ruth sat on her cot in dress blues and smiled at her roommate. "Dress uniform is appropriate for formal occasions."

"But this is a pawty."

Ruth laughed at Rosa's Bostonian accent. "Would you like me to loan you an *R*?"

"What? So I can sound like you and warsh up for the party?" Rosa's mouth twisted over the extra consonants. "Now, the dress. Think how you'd make the major's eyes bug out."

Part of Ruth wanted to wear the dress, and watch Jack's eyes bug out, and dance in his arms all night, but it wasn't fair to Jack. She cared for him too much to toy with his affections. Besides, she'd never worn a party dress or bared her shoulders.

May adjusted the straps of her gown, in a soft shade of pink that brought color to her cheeks without overwhelming her.

"You look lovely, May."

Rosa stepped in front of Ruth. "Don't change the subject. The dress."

One of the nurses poked her head into the room. "May, Ruth, you have company."

"Sorry, Rosa. Too late."

When they left, Ruth's military uniform didn't swish and sway like May's gown, but Ruth needed to dispel all romance from the evening. She'd only accepted because Jack said she didn't have to dance. Still, the thought of the party, the music, and the time with Jack made her heart flip around.

Then she reached the top of the stairs, and all flipping ceased. Jack was alone. He stood with his hands at his sides, and his fingers worked the hem of his service jacket. She'd never seen him in that posture. Each step brought his face into clearer focus—pale, haggard.

Oh no. Ruth's breath caught, and she stopped on the stairs. She'd heard the talk all day—sixty planes lost on the Schweinfurt mission. Six hundred men hadn't come home.

May trotted down the stairs. "Hi there. Where's Charlie?"

Jack looked up at Ruth, his eyes so hollow she saw through to something wretched in his soul. Charlie was one of the six hundred. "Oh no," she whispered.

"He—he didn't make it."

Ruth clutched the banister, but she had to be strong for May as she had for her brothers and sisters. She forced her feet down the steps.

May glanced toward the front door. "Is he meeting us there?"

"He didn't make it. Yesterday. The mission. His plane was—was shot down."

May gave a thin little laugh. "Don't be silly. You're here."

Fresh pain ripped through Jack's face. "He wasn't—he didn't fly with me. He flew with Silverberg. We hit flak over Holland. They went down."

May covered her mouth. "Oh no. Poor Charlie, a prisoner. Unless—unless he's evading. He could do that. Holland? He speaks Dutch, you know."

Jack shot Ruth a devastated glance, and her chest caved in. Charlie was dead.

"No." Jack's eyes flicked back and forth, one moment engaging May, the next avoiding her. "He couldn't have—he couldn't have made it. He didn't survive."

Another laugh, thinner and tighter. "He can't be dead. It's impossible."

A silent plea from Jack, and Ruth set a hand on her friend's shoulder. "May . . ."

"No." She stepped away and glared at Ruth, then Jack. "You don't understand. I'd know. When Thomas died, I knew, I felt it." She thumped her fist over her heart.

Jack took her by the shoulders and struggled to control his face. "May, he couldn't—"

"Yes, he could. He bailed out. I know it."

"He couldn't. There was a hole in the nose. He probably didn't—but even if—they were in a flat spin. A flat spin. You can't get out. Centrifugal force presses you to the sides. You can't get out. There were no chutes. None. We watched until they dropped through the clouds."

May wrenched out of his grasp. "So you didn't see. He still had time."

"No time. Low clouds, and he couldn't. There's no way."

"There's always a way." Her voice rang fierce and strong.

Ruth and Jack exchanged a look, full of mutual grief and worry for May. Ruth recognized this reaction. Her brother

Bert had denied Ma's death for days. She gave Jack a slight shake of her head to tell him no logic would convince May tonight. She needed time.

Jack turned to May again, his face etched with pain. "I'm so sorry."

Her eyes shot silver darts at Jack. "Don't feel sorry for me. I'll miss him, but I'll be fine. Feel sorry for Charlie. He's in a German prison camp or hiding in Holland, all alone, and even more so because you've given up on him. Well, I won't. He needs me. Now, I'm going off to pray for him." She pulled her wrap tight and headed for the door.

Jack went after her. "May—"

"No." She spun around and pointed a finger at him. "No more of your lies."

Ruth set a hand on his shoulder, which twitched with tension. "I'll go with her."

May turned a softer gaze to Ruth. "No, stay and talk some sense into him. Besides, he needs you more than I do."

Ruth glanced between her friends, one almost mad in denial, the other shattered in grief. They both needed her, Jack more so tonight. Oh, how could she leave England? In three short weeks she'd be gone, but they would still be mourning.

"All right," Ruth said. "Go pray. I'll see you later tonight."

After May left, Ruth studied Jack's face—the tics in his cheeks and around his eyes. What did he need in his grief? To talk, to rage, to contemplate, to cry, to be distracted? She'd seen six children through two deaths. She'd find Jack's needs and guide him through.

Clusters of women stood in the entryway, wide-eyed with concern. Ruth needed to take Jack somewhere private. She put her arm around his waist and led him out the front door. To her left in the twilight, a figure in pink turned behind Redgrave Hall. Most likely, May was headed to Charlie's

favorite spinney of trees near the orangery. Ruth led Jack
south to the park around the lake and tried to rub out the
spasms in his back.

When they reached a wooded area far from prying eyes,
she asked in her gentlest voice, "Do you want to tell me
about it?"

He grimaced. "It's my fault, all my fault."

"Oh, Jack, don't say that. The Germans—they're the ones
who shot him down."

"He shouldn't have been there, not with Silverberg, not
over Rotterdam. My fault."

Could she help him unravel the guilt from the grief? "Tell
me what happened. Why was he with Silverberg?"

Jack groaned, pulled away from Ruth, and slammed back
against a massive oak. "It's me, my pride. He said he couldn't
fly with me again, not even for two measly missions. He
couldn't stand it, said my pride would make me do something dangerous some day. He was right." He let out a cry
and pressed his palms to his forehead, his fingers coiled as if
to dig out the memory.

Ruth couldn't bear to see him like that. She wrapped her
hands around his and eased them down from his face.

"Shouldn't have. I shouldn't have." He directed tortured eyes to the branches above. "It was longer, more flak.
Should've stayed with the group, but no, thought I was so
smart, so clever. Wouldn't listen to anyone, wouldn't even
pray. For heaven's sake, I'm a pastor, and I didn't pray. Charlie
was right—nothing but filthy, stinking pride."

She gripped his hands, unsure what had happened. "Please
don't do this. I'm sure you had good reasons."

He lowered his gaze to her—a flash of what looked like fear,
then more pain. "My reasons don't matter. I didn't pray. Pride,
nothing but pride. I lost four planes over Rotterdam."

She rolled his hands in hers, trying to loosen all those muscles. "They might have been lost if you'd—if you'd stayed with the group. Isn't that possible?"

Jack squeezed his eyes shut. "Maybe. I don't know. All I know is Charlie's dead."

"There really is no way?"

"None." He stared hard into her eyes. "You have to understand. A flat spin, it's a pilot's nightmare. You can't pull out, and you can't escape. The centrifugal force—you can't get to the hatches. You're trapped. Charlie was trapped."

Ruth released one of his hands and stroked his hair. "Maybe he didn't know. Maybe he was—maybe it was instant. You said there was a hole." Her voice choked. Was death in an explosion better than death from a fall?

His face scrunched up. "Two minutes, Ruth. It takes over two minutes from that altitude. You know how long that is? Knowing he was trapped, knowing he was going to die, knowing it was my fault."

"Oh, darling, please don't. You know Charlie wouldn't blame you. You know that. He was probably worried about you, that you'd blame yourself. You mustn't. For Charlie's sake, you mustn't blame yourself."

Jack's face contorted. He buried his face in her shoulder and clutched her tight around the waist. Although he almost lifted her off her feet, she had to adjust her footing to bear his weight.

Ruth murmured comfort in his ear. A broken little boy.

His breath puffed on her neck. "You're right. Charlie was a good man, too good to blame me."

"That's right." She ran her fingers through the soft waves of his hair. "He wouldn't."

"He was so good, so good. He kept me in line, never let me get too full of myself. Except . . . except . . ."

"Ssh. Ssh." He'd lost his best friend. The men had been through so much together and followed each other all over the world. Jack had maneuvered Charlie and May together. Now Charlie was dead, and May, when she accepted it, would be in mourning again. With good reason—Charlie was a fine man. Ruth's eyes felt wet and sticky. "Poor, dear Charlie."

Jack nodded against her neck. "At least—at least we know he's with Jesus."

Ruth's eyes stretched wide. She'd heard those words when Pa died, when Ma died, and the sentiment had angered her. What good did it do? She was stuck on earth alone. However, the thought seemed to comfort Jack. His grip lightened, and her heels settled to the ground.

"But what about us?" she said.

"We'll see him again someday." Jack's voice lost its rough edge.

"What about now? What about May and you and me? Stuck here alone."

"We're not alone. We have God. We have each other." His words tingled on her skin.

"I—I suppose so," she whispered.

Jack pulled taller in her arms. Ruth sensed, almost heard, the swoosh of power shifting. The broken little boy returned to full-grown man.

"Thank God I have you." His lips nuzzled the spot between her collar and her ear. "What would I do without you?"

Even though Ruth knew better, she leaned into his kiss and played with his hair. "You—you'd manage."

"I don't want to," he said right into her ear. "I love you, Ruth."

She should have been stunned, but she already knew.

His mouth inched across her cheek, and panic swelled in

her chest. "Please don't," she tried to say, but he smothered her words with his kiss.

She pushed herself back, and the air tumbled out of her lungs. "Oh, Jack, no."

"Please, darling, please." His hands gripped her waist. His eyes, his mouth grasped for a shred of love and joy in all this death and despair.

"I can't." She shoved out the words, hating what she was doing to him. "Don't you understand?"

"No, I don't. Help me understand, so I can fix it."

"You can't. No one can." She'd prayed for God to forgive her, to fix her, but he wouldn't remove the punishment she'd earned. She'd kissed too many boys for the wrong reason, and now she couldn't kiss the man she cared for most.

"But I love you. Let me help."

The desperation in his eyes made her heart ache. She lifted a shaky hand to his cheek. "Oh, darling, I'm so sorry."

His gaze steadied, penetrated, comprehended. "You love me too, don't you?"

Ruth felt her heart would rip in two, torn between the truth Jack had seen and the truth she needed to tell him. "I can't. Not as you deserve, not as you want me to."

"But . . . but . . ." His arguments dissolved into pain and regret. He pulled her close and sighed over her shoulder. "Oh, darling, I broke my promise. Oh no. I'm sorry."

"Please don't. I'm the one who's sorry." Why should this wonderful man have to apologize for kissing the woman he loved? Why was he punished for her sins?

25

Bury St. Edmunds Airfield

Monday, October 25, 1943

Jack took a seat in Colonel Castle's office and crossed his ankle over his knee. After a week's R & R he was supposed to be rested and relaxed, and he'd do his best to look it, although he'd barely slept the past eleven nights.

The CO stood with his arms crossed and studied Jack. "How was your week?"

He plastered on a grin. "Great. Got the hang of croquet, but now I'm ready to get back to work." Hard work would take his mind off Charlie's death, the loss of four planes and forty men, and his love for a woman who couldn't love him back.

Castle shuffled papers down on his desk. "Bomber Command has made some changes. We're increasing each squadron from nine to twelve aircraft, and to handle the increase, we need two group executive officers, a ground executive and an air executive."

A position was open? Now?

Castle tented his fingers on the desk. "This has been a difficult decision. You're qualified and you'd be an outstanding executive officer."

Jack gripped his shin so hard it hurt. He'd lost it. First he'd killed Charlie, now he'd lost everything he'd worked for, all due to his stupid pride.

"I can't give it to you." Castle fixed a sad gaze on Jack. "Not after Schweinfurt. I can't reward a rogue decision that cost us four planes. Your men have lost confidence in you."

Jack's lips felt glued together, but he managed to speak. "I understand, sir."

"Thorup will be air exec, and Jeff Babcock will be ground exec. He hasn't been informed yet. I wanted you to hear the news from me."

"Thank you, sir." Babcock—insult to injury.

Castle sat down and folded his arms on the desk. "Your tour is almost up."

"Yes, sir." Eight meager missions to undo the damage. Impossible.

"You have two options. You could take a noncombat position here, at the division level, or stateside. With your credentials, a single reprimand won't affect your career."

A bureaucratic job away from planes and command? A part of his life drained away, same as it did when he contemplated a life in the ministry.

"The other option would be to take a month furlough, spend Christmas at home perhaps, then return as squadron commander. You'd have another chance for promotion in the future."

Another tour? His chance of survival would be next to nothing. He swallowed hard. "I want to command, sir, and I need to fly."

The first smile Jack had seen that morning. "I thought so. I hoped so."

Jack left the office and forced his shoulders straight. Babcock passed him on his way to get the news Jack should have gotten. Jack gave him a nod, glad he didn't have to congratulate him yet.

Then he escaped, out of HQ, out into the cool fog. He drank it deep. How many hits could he take before he went down? He was skimming the deck. He had to fight his way up and gain some altitude.

First, with Ruth. He was meeting her today, and it was time for an honest talk. She said she couldn't love him—not that she didn't, but that she couldn't. Why? Because of her family? But he'd be honored to care for them.

She couldn't love him as he deserved? Did she think she wasn't good enough for him? Baloney. And she couldn't love him as he wanted her to? That was his fault, pushing for a kiss. It didn't matter. He could be patient and wait until she was ready.

Jack turned onto the road to the communal sites. His other order of business was to earn back the men's respect. If he had to remain a squadron commander, he'd be the best ever and he'd start right now at the mess hall.

He entered the back door into the kitchen, which smelled of chicken and dumplings and peas. Pots clattered and spraying water hissed. Since the men weren't combat personnel, they still respected Jack, and their smiles did him more good than a dozen games of croquet.

Private Reynolds was back. The kid couldn't keep himself off KP. His sergeant was fed up with him, but Jack knew he was the sort motivated by encouragement, not punishment.

"Hi there, Reynolds." Jack leaned back against the counter next to the sink where the private washed dishes. "How are things going?"

"Sick of KP, sir. Bad enough Sarge has it out for me. Now the MPs are on my case."

Jack hadn't intended to discuss his infraction, but now he had no choice. "What happened?"

"Ah, they call it 'drunk and disorderly.' I call it 'a little fun in town.'"

Jack sighed. He hated to play disciplinarian when Sergeant Masterson did such a stern job of it. "Look at things from the British point of view. Their quiet country town has been overrun by three thousand brash young Americans, all wanting a little fun."

Reynolds shrugged. "Still, it ain't fair, getting KP 'most every day. A man gets sick of all this warshing and scrubbing."

Warsh. Jack smiled at the chance to change the subject. "So, where's home? The Midwest?"

"Chicago. Filthy slum near the stockyards." He gave a tray a partial wipe with a rag.

"Yeah? I have a friend from that area, Ruth Doherty."

Reynolds squinted at the ceiling. "Knew some Dohertys, but I don't remember a Ruth. Dated one of them in eighth grade. Wow, what a dame."

"Yeah?" Jack settled back against the counter a safe distance from the splashing.

"Gorgeous redhead. Too smart for a girl, you know, but boy, did she love to kiss."

Jack smiled grimly. There the similarity ended.

Reynolds plunged a pot into the sudsy water and slopped the rag inside. "In fact, she was so good at it, she turned it into a business."

"A business? Kissing?"

"Yep. Needed the money. Family had more kids than cash. Something wrong with her dad, couldn't work. Kissing lessons, she called them. Gave the boys pointers."

"Kissing lessons?" Jack shook his head. The stupid things people did for money.

Reynolds set the pot upside-down on the counter, and suds ran down the side. "Yeah. The boys would line up in the alley after school for lessons. Charged ten cents for ten minutes. Ten-Penny Doherty, we called her, 'cause her name was Penny. Wow. I haven't thought of her for years."

Penny. Penny Doherty. Jack's stomach filled with something heavy and cold and slimy, as if he had swallowed mud. He spoke over the thick slab of his tongue. "What happened to her?"

"Ah, who knows? Probably running her own brothel. I heard one of the fellas at the plant call her Dollar Doherty. Did it all for a buck. Best buck he ever spent, he said."

It couldn't be. It could not be. Mud oozed up his throat, choked him, blinded him, polluted his mind. He had to get out, had to clear his mind.

He pushed for the door, his feet mired in the mud, past the kitchen staff and out the door, took gulps of moist air to cleanse his mind of the filth, the invasion of filth.

Jack made his way down the crowded road and barged into a spinney of trees. He had to pull himself together, get to the hospital, and straighten it out with Ruth, his Ruth, his virtuous Ruth who hated kissing, hated it.

He gripped a tree and pressed his forehead hard against the bark, as if the roughness could scrape away the mud, let him see it was all a misunderstanding.

Couldn't be the same girl. Could not. Chicago was a big city. Real big. There had to be two Penny Dohertys, maybe even more. It couldn't be her. Not Ruth, not his Ruth.

Smart. Gorgeous. Redhead.

Jack's fingers dug into the tree bark. Coincidence, just coincidence.

Boyfriend in eighth grade. Big family. Dad couldn't work.

His grip tightened and pried off chunks of bark into his fists. Too many coincidences. Too many.

She hated the name Penny. She'd gone by Ruth ever since she left home.

A sound arose, deep and animal and raging, and expelled all the mud until he saw clearly, thought clearly for the first time in months.

26

Redgrave Park

Trees emerged from the fog on either side of the road as Ruth walked to the park gate. "I'm surprised Jack isn't here. They can't be flying."

"Maybe he has too much paperwork after his R & R," May said.

"Maybe." Ruth's sigh blended with the mist. This was her last day off before she left. If Jack didn't come today, she would only see him Sunday at church, maybe an evening if he could spare one, or she might not see him at all. She needed to see how he was doing. *Please, Lord, help him in his grief. Help him stop blaming himself.*

If only she could have comforted him instead of adding to his pain.

He loved her. This wasn't the infatuation of one of her patients based on her looks. She'd never known this kind of love from someone who knew her well.

Ruth made out a silhouette on the road with Jack's build and gait. "There he is."

"Good. I could use an afternoon to catch up on my letters. I'll see you later." May retreated toward Redgrave Hall. Poor thing. Unable to accept Charlie's death, she wrote daily letters to mail when she found out where he was imprisoned, or to hand him when he returned to England. She still couldn't forgive Jack for what she considered betrayal at best, a lie at worst.

Gravel crunched under Jack's shoes, and Ruth wanted to rush into his arms. But then his face became clearer—the hard set of his jaw, the cut of his mouth, the steel of his eyes.

Contempt.

Her heart stopped. Her feet stopped. He couldn't know.

Jack marched off the road and between the trees into the grass beyond. "Over here."

His voice sliced through her. He knew? How could he know?

Once she'd seen a movie where a woman was led to the guillotine. Ruth had wondered why the woman didn't run, fight, go limp—anything. Yet Ruth now walked in the same resigned manner.

Jack faced her, a good ten feet away in the dewy grass. Coldness remained in his eyes, but his expression rotated between confusion, hurt, and anger.

Ruth pinched her cape together as if to keep her secret shrouded. *Please, Lord, no. Please.*

"Does . . ." He paused and made a face. "Does the name Ed Reynolds ring a bell?"

Not a bell, but a gong crashing in her head. Her hands flew from the folds of her cape to her clanging temples. Eddie Reynolds! She'd seen him in London, seen the Eighth Air Force patch on his sleeve, but there were two dozen groups in England, thousands of men at each base. Why? Why did he and Jack have to meet?

A desperate plea pierced through Jack's fury. "Please tell me he's a liar."

"Oh-h-h." Her moan merged into the fog, heavy and gray.

Jack registered her response with a grimace and a sharp turn of his head.

"No, no, no," she said, over and over, in time to the gong in her head.

His face worked as if to twist his emotions into words. "All this time, all this time I thought you were virtuous, too virtuous to date, too virtuous to kiss. I thought you didn't like kissing. Boy, was I a fool. You just don't like kissing me."

Her head wagged. The mist transformed into white darts aimed at her eyes, her soul.

"Oh, that's right. They paid you. Why didn't you tell me? You want money? I've got money. Here." He thrust his fist into his pocket, his face dark and getting darker.

"No." Not money, anything but money.

"Here, I owe you. Two kisses. I stole two kisses. Yeah, with you it really is stealing. Why didn't you tell me, huh?" He jabbed at the change in his palm. "A dime. A dime. Here, two dimes."

Jack hurled black coins into the black grass in front of her.

A black knife sliced into her heart. She cried out and stumbled back.

"What kind of a girl does such a thing? What kind of a girl even thinks of such a thing? How old were you anyway?"

"Thir—teen." The word cost too much. Blackness settled thick about her and shot pain through her head.

"Thirteen? Thirteen? You should have been playing—I don't know—hopscotch or something, not—not—how could you?"

Ruth moaned. Her legs buckled. She slumped down to her knees and dropped her head. Her breath raced.

"Virtuous?" He spat it out. "A virtuous woman doesn't sell kisses."

Each word plunged a knife into her body and spirit.

"A virtuous woman keeps herself for the man she loves."

Crushed her with the burden of who she was.

"A virtuous woman doesn't sell her body for a dollar."

"What?" Ruth raised her head. Blackness throbbed at the edge of her vision. "I—I never."

Jack stood dark in all the darkness. "You deny it?"

"The—the lessons—I did that. But not—not—"

"He called you Dollar Doherty." He sounded as if he had something vile in his mouth.

Not as vile as the memory. Six lessons a day had been her rule—no more, no less—and for safety, every boy stayed the whole hour, even when his lesson was over. But that day Bud Lewis from her tenement and two of his friends from the meat-packing plant had chased off the boys.

Bud waved a dollar bill in her face. "So, Ten-Penny, what's a dollar get me?"

A great nauseating tremble ran through her body, but she managed to speak. "One ten-minute lesson and ninety cents change."

But that didn't stop them. Nothing and no one could stop them. Afterward, three horrid dollar bills had rained down on her ruined body.

Ruth's fingers dug into the grass. "Oh no, Jack. No, it's not what you think."

"Tell me. What should I think?"

She collapsed over her knees. She'd never spoken the word, never even formed it in her thoughts. "I was—I was—raped." The word tore a bilious path through her throat and out her mouth.

Jack stood silent and still before her for a while. "Yeah?" His voice lost its hard edge but not its chill.

She pressed fists to her eyes. "I was fifteen. The alley. There were three of them." She grabbed the knife implanted in her soul, took it in her own hand, and if she cut deep enough, everything would spill out, and maybe she'd die and get it over with. "They were big, strong. I couldn't get away, couldn't stop them, and they raped me, over and over and over, all three of them, and they wouldn't stop, and I couldn't—I couldn't get away, and over and over and over." Her chest heaved out long, low sobs.

No sound or motion from the man before her, the man who once thought he loved her, but he hadn't known what she was.

Ruth's sobs deepened. Her hands slid over her slippery eyes. "Oh, Jack, I'm so sorry. So sorry."

"Yeah, me too." He disappeared into the fog.

27

Ruth clenched grass in her fists, watered it with her tears, and tore it out by the roots.

Footsteps sounded behind her, and she clamped off her sobs. She couldn't let anyone else see her like this.

"Ruth? Ruth!" May dropped to her knees and put her hand on Ruth's back. "Oh my goodness. What happened?"

"Go away. Leave me alone."

"Oh dear. I knew I didn't like Jack's tone. That's why I stayed around. He sounded so angry, and then I heard you— oh my goodness. What happened?"

"Leave me alone." She grabbed fresh handfuls of grass. She liked the ripping sound.

"Oh no. Did he—did he hit you?"

She shook her head, and the grass in her fists brushed her forehead.

"What did he do?"

"He said the truth, that's all. Now, go away."

"The truth?" May sounded so naïve, Ruth wanted to blast her with the truth and drive her away forever.

She pressed her face into her fists and spewed out the truth, all of it, in a voice that sounded foreign, childlike, and dis-embodied. She cut even deeper now, a strange pleasure, like lancing a boil, releasing the pressure, spraying it all over May, poisoning her, infecting her, shocking her.

Then the pain of the surgery hit.

A moan worked its way out. What had she done? She'd lost Jack and now she'd lose May. Would May tell the others, the chief? This was a serious morals violation. What could be worse than selling one's affections repeatedly? She'd lose her position at Bowman, her commission in the Army Nurse Corps, and her nursing license. Wouldn't it be ironic if what she had done to feed her family stripped away her ability to provide for them?

Oh Lord, no. Please. But why did she bother praying? Every time she prayed, God did the opposite to spite her, to punish her. She'd never finish paying for her sins, never.

"There, there. That's better now, isn't it?" May spoke in cooing tones and stroked Ruth's back.

Ruth opened her eyes and looked into the grass and dirt. Then she unfolded herself to sitting and tried to focus her blurry eyes on May.

"Oh, Ruth. Now I understand." Trails shimmered down May's cheeks.

Ruth ran the back of her fist across her eyes and stared harder. "Understand?"

"I knew it had to be more than the loss of your parents. You carry so much shame. Now I understand."

Where was the disgust and indignation? "How could you understand?"

May wiped her cheeks. "I often wondered what I'd do if—well, if the orphanage closed, or if I did something awful and they threw me out, if I had to take care of myself. You never know what you'd do."

"You wouldn't do what I did."

"Of course not. I'm not pretty." She gave a faint smile. "But I understand."

"How could you?" Ruth stared at her in all her pale purity. "What I did was wrong, don't you see? It was immoral. I played with the boys' emotions, took advantage of them."

"Yes, but that doesn't justify what those men did to you."

This was nonsense, went against everything she knew about her sin and her punishment. "I asked for it. I led them to believe I was easy, and—"

"No." May's eyes flashed. "They're the criminals. Yes, you put yourself in a dangerous situation, but they committed the crime, not you."

Ruth glanced around the grass-floored dome in the fog, a soft-walled prison. "Not a crime, a sin. A morals violation. My job. Oh, my job."

"Honey, don't worry. I'd never say anything. It's in the past. You live an upstanding life now."

A glint in the grass drew Ruth's gaze. Jack's dimes. Her chest collapsed. "Jack."

"Never mind him." May's voice chilled. "Not after how he treated you."

He treated her as she deserved, but would he turn her in? He was a man of integrity, an officer, a pastor. Was it his duty to report her violation? Would he consider her family and how she supported them?

"I wish we didn't have to wait two weeks before leaving for Kentucky."

Ruth blinked away the haze in her eyes. "We?"

May gave a twitching little smile. "I received my letter this morning. I was accepted."

"Accepted? I didn't know you applied."

"I never said anything, because I didn't think they'd take me. For one thing, I had to stuff myself to meet the weight requirement."

"But—but why?"

May shrugged. "Same reasons as you. I applied when you did, before the boys went to Tunisia. Things were going too well with Charlie, and I wanted to get away."

Ruth understood that sentiment. "But after Tunisia?"

"Charlie and I decided we wouldn't be any different than most couples nowadays, separated by thousands of miles. Geography can't divide us—it still can't. Besides, you need me more than Charlie does."

"Me?" A flame sparked in her chest. "Need you? I don't need a friend. Look what friendship's gotten me." She lifted her fists, grass still clenched inside, and flung it away.

"You do need friends."

"No. No, I never did." She pushed herself to standing, her legs numb. "I don't need anyone. No one."

"Ruth—"

"You hear me? No one." She tottered away and cringed from the electric jolts in her legs. "I don't need anyone, and I certainly don't need you, May Jensen."

"Maybe—maybe I need you."

The tremor in May's voice shocked Ruth more than her prickling legs. She turned around. "What?"

May's face turned a deep pink and contracted. "Did you ever consider for one moment that maybe I need a friend?"

"You?" Ruth swept her arm in the direction of Redgrave Hall. "You have friends, lots of friends. You had plenty of friends before me."

"But I want you for a friend. I don't know why. Goodness knows you've been cold to me, prickly, often downright rude." May crossed her arms, and her face buckled.

Ruth's face buckled too. "Why me?"

"I don't know." May swiped at her eyes. "I thought you'd understand, not just cold and hunger, but loneliness and—

and ostracism and having too much care on your shoulders. Understand fear and—and grief." Her voice cracked. She pressed her hand over her eyes.

More tears trickled down Ruth's cheeks. "I—I do. Oh, May, I'm sorry."

She lowered her hand to reveal eyes as red as Ruth's had to be. Unlike Ruth's hard, brittle shell, May's was soft and resilient, but underneath lay someone as vulnerable as Ruth, someone who needed a friend.

Just as Ruth did.

She stared at the wet, grassy mess on her hands. "Someone better warn the School of Air Evacuation to make way for two poor little orphan girls."

28

Bury St. Edmunds Airfield

Saturday, November 20, 1943

Jack studied the men who stood at attention before his desk at Squadron Headquarters. Fresh from the Combat Crew Replacement Center, the four lieutenants and six sergeants hailed from cities and farms and small towns all over the U.S. The youngest were eighteen, the oldest was twenty-two. Some looked eager, some tough, one looked terrified.

Jack leaned his forearms on his desk and lifted a smile he hoped would instill enthusiasm. This got harder every day. He'd lost his touch this month, and he didn't know how to fix it.

"Well, boys, you've come at an exciting time for the Eighth Air Force. We're able to dispatch over five hundred bombers on each mission. A year ago we could barely send up a hundred." Of course, losses ran high as ever.

He stood and pressed his fingertips to the desk. "Now we have Pathfinder Force aircraft in each combat wing with radar so we can bomb through the clouds." When the fool equipment worked.

"With P-38 Lightnings now in the theater, we have escort for a hundred miles farther." At least the brass learned the lesson of Schweinfurt and no longer sent them on deep pen-etrations without escort. This limited target selection, but then the weather had been too lousy to fly anyway.

Jack hefted up another smile. "This squadron's always been a family. Even though we've grown from nine crews to twelve, we're still a family." He hated the words while still in his mouth. He'd never told his men that before because they'd figured it out for themselves. If he had to convince them, it wasn't true anymore.

He dismissed the men, returned to his desk, and dropped his head into his hands. *Lord, three more missions. Let me finish this tour so I can take a furlough. Christmas at home, Mom's cooking, Grandpa's farm, and I'll be back to normal.*

"Hiya, Novak." Joe Winchell entered his office, took a seat, and propped his feet on the desk.

Jack shuffled some papers to look busy. "Hi, Winch."

The new intelligence officer watched in silence for a moment. "A little scotch would do you a lot of good."

Jack rolled his eyes. The thought had occurred to him many times in the past month. Oblivion sounded good, but it wouldn't bring back Charlie or the other men, wouldn't give him that promotion, and wouldn't erase Ruth's dirty little secret.

"How 'bout a dame? I know a lot of girls in town. Muster up one of your old smiles and you're in."

"Last thing I need is a girl." He needed to stay away from women until fire no longer lured him.

He stuffed papers in the stapler and pounded it harder than necessary. Twice. Yeah, he'd found that ring around Ruth's heart, but it wasn't gold, it was iron pyrite—fool's gold—and he was the fool.

"I know what you need."

"Winch." Jack speared him with his gaze. "All I need is a furlough. Meanwhile . . ."

Winchell held up his hands. "Roger and out."

"Thanks, pal."

"Hmm. Furlough in sunny California. Just the kind of weather—"

"I told you I'd take her." Sahara Sue wasn't doing well in England, and Jack—he still couldn't believe he'd agreed—would take the tranquilized donkey on a cargo plane, then a train, to Grandpa's farm.

Winchell put his feet down, leaned over the desk, and turned a paper so he could read it. "'Memorandum 36: Mud Control'?"

Jack groaned. "Goes out tomorrow. According to Lt. Col. Jefferson Babcock Jr., the greatest threat to the 94th Bombardment Group is neither flak nor fighters, but mud."

"Mud?" Winchell laughed and scanned the memo. "He wants to outlaw mud? In England? In November? He's got to be kidding."

"I wish he were. Look at the new regulations to reduce mud on the base. Ridiculous. He actually expects us to sweep the highways."

"The men will hate this. It's—"

"I know." Jack cut him off before the profanity. "The kind of baloney that makes men hate military life and disrespect authority."

"What are you going to do?"

"Me? I have no choice but to follow the blasted memo." He stood, pulled his overcoat off the coatrack, and slipped it over his olive drabs.

"Just ignore it."

"Can't do that." Jack belted his coat against the rain tapping on the windows of the Nissen hut. "I know it's unenforceable and futile, but I've got to go through the stinking motions."

The men left the office, hunkered against the rain, and

headed down the rock-edged pathway past the sign for Squadron HQ. Mounted on bomb casings, the sign displayed the squadron emblem, a winged bomb against a blue background with lightning bolts in a *V* for Victory.

Victory? No victory over mud in weather like this. He wanted to hurl a glob of mud at the ground exec's jeep. "Power's gone to Babcock's head. Thinks he can control the weather."

Winchell shook his finger at the dripping sky. "Hear that, Lord? Babcock's going to put you on KP."

Jack laughed for the first time in weeks, but the good feeling didn't last. He could still hear Charlie's reprimands for his rivalry with Babcock. Did Jack dislike the memo because it was stupid, or out of jealousy? Maybe both. He sighed over the aching lump in his chest. He strained to hear Charlie's voice in his head—the pitch and cadence, but mostly the words. Winchell was fun, but no moral compass.

Charlie kept him in line. Jack hated to admit it, but the night after Marienburg, Charlie had spoken the truth about a lot of things. Not everything, but a lot.

At the Officers' Mess for dinner, Jack picked over the shepherd's pie and made a halfhearted attempt at conversation. Then he walked to the Officers' Club. The piano bench beckoned. He pulled change from his pocket and looked around for Charlie's yellow hair and round pink face.

Jack sank to the bench, his chest crushed. Not only had he killed his best friend, but he'd mistreated him when he was alive. Jack the hero, Charlie the sidekick. Jack the major, Charlie the captain. Jack the charismatic leader, Charlie the cheerful follower.

He plunged through the circle of men gathering for a song and joined the crowd at the bar. His impatience with lines was no excuse for always sending Charlie. What was he thinking? Too important a man to get his own drink?

At least fifteen minutes passed before he returned to the piano with a hot cup of coffee. The young lieutenant at the keyboard jumped to his feet. Because Jack was a better player, or because Jack outranked him? Didn't matter. Jack wanted to play, needed to play.

The men called out requests, and Jack took the young lieutenant's—"Tonight We Love." He had learned the piece in junior high at Mom's side before Tchaikovsky's "Piano Concerto in B-Flat" became a big band hit.

The powerful chords drummed out his grief and anger.

Anger at Ruth. No matter how hungry she'd been, how could she sell herself?

Now he understood why she hated kissing. It had lost all meaning for her, just a business transaction. And if she felt bad about what she'd done, as she should, Jack's kisses would have dredged up shame.

They probably also dredged up memories of what those men did to her.

Jack tripped over his fingers, and he stopped to find his place. He wanted to hammer the images out of his mind. Two images intermingled—Ruth screaming, pinned down by three men—and Ruth sobbing, pinned down by Jack's wrath.

Guilt strangled his heart. No one deserved rape, and no one deserved to be abandoned weeping on the ground. He could still see her with her cape spread over her crumpled, violated body. "Clothed in shame"—he'd seen that phrase in the Bible, and it certainly applied to Ruth.

Jack pounded the final chord but found his anger unresolved.

A cloak of shame? She'd earned it.

29

Bowman Field, Louisville, Kentucky

Sunday, November 28, 1943

Ruth pointed to the orientation material as she and May walked from the barracks to the classroom building. "Talk about expecting the worst. Crash procedures, ditching procedures, field survival, the use of side arms."

"Because the Japanese don't follow the Geneva Conventions. At least those subjects are practical. What about military customs and courtesy?"

"We're in the Army Air Force now." Ruth still smarted from the morning bunk inspection. The hospital corner on her cot was one-quarter inch off, and she had to start all over. The Army Nurse Corps hadn't put her through these boot camp hoops when she joined. This was like the first months of nursing school before she got capped, but with calisthenics.

"And look at these academic subjects: aeromedical physiology, neuropsychiatry . . ."

"I don't know what will hurt more—our brains or our bodies."

About twenty feet behind Ruth, a nurse belted out "Oh,

What a Beautiful Mornin'." The roar of a twin-engined C-47 cargo plane overhead couldn't drown out the girl's big voice.

Yes, it was a beautiful day, crisp and cool, without England's smothering dampness and grief, without Chicago's biting cold and shame. What a blessing.

A new trace of pink colored May's pale cheeks. Would the taxing eight-week program help her come to terms with Charlie's death? With Charlie listed as Missing in Action, she might deny his fate indefinitely.

"Charlie loves to sing," May said with a sigh. "I sure miss his voice."

Ruth looped her arm through May's and gritted her teeth. Time for another push. "What if—what if he doesn't come home?"

For once May didn't reprove her, which was progress. "Then I won't hear his voice until I get to heaven, but oh, how lovely it'll be then."

"But how will you manage?"

"Same as now, by leaning hard on God's arms."

Every one of Ruth's facial muscles tightened. "How can you trust him? He took your parents. He took Thomas. He took Charlie."

May stopped on the concrete walkway and turned those penetrating eyes to Ruth. "He let you be raped? He let Jack find out your secret?"

Ruth clamped her lips together and gave a sharp nod. "I know why I was punished, but you—"

"Punished? You think the rape was punishment?"

"I know it was, and Jack, and everything."

May closed her eyes and pressed her hand over Ruth's for so long that the alto passed them singing about Oklahoma corn.

"Oh, honey," May whispered. "A child playing with fire gets burned, but that's not punishment."

Ruth's stomach simmered. "The Lord could have stopped it. I prayed."

"Yes, and he could have kept Charlie's plane aloft, but he didn't. I don't know why, but he has a reason—to teach us to rely on him alone, to get us to change direction."

Ruth curled her free arm around her roiling stomach. "Well, he certainly got me to change direction, but why did Jack have to find out? I've changed."

"Mm-hmm. Have you asked God to forgive you?"

"So many times I've lost count." Her mouth puckered. No, she would not cry her first day at the School of Air Evacuation.

"Then he's already forgiven you. Now you can heal."

Ruth's head shook from side to side. As a nurse, she knew of no procedure or medication or surgery to remove shame.

"God can heal you. Trust him." May patted Ruth's hand. "The first step was taken for you. Your secret's out in the open."

She rolled her eyes and tried to laugh. "Oh yeah, that helped."

"Didn't it?"

Ruth held her breath. Hadn't she told whiny Lieutenant Baker how a closed wound festered? Her wound had been closed for eight gangrenous years, but now it had been lanced, now it was exposed to oxygen, and now perhaps it could heal.

Footsteps and laughter sounded behind them, and a group of five nurses approached across the green lawn. "Hi, ladies, are you going in?"

Ruth's watch read five to nine. If they were late, they could end up with push-ups or KP or who knew what. "Yes, we're coming."

Still they lingered and let the group pass. "Ruthie? I'm praying for you," May said.

She squeezed May's arm, her heart full. "I'm praying for you too."

They entered the classroom building. Ruth stole one more glance at her watch and stroked the soft russet leather. A quick, sharp pain dulled to the familiar, unrelenting ache. She slid the watch up her wrist. It didn't cover her scar. It never would.

Her mind reeled at the thought. Just as Jack's watch didn't cover her scar, his love hadn't healed her wounds. Wasn't that what she had wanted, even if she'd never admitted it? For Jack to be her Boaz, to heal her?

That wasn't Jack's role, nor was it Boaz's role. Although Boaz spread his cloak over Ruth and accepted her, she came to trust under the wings of the Lord, not Boaz.

Ruth wrapped her hand over the watch and closed her eyes. *Oh Lord, I don't know if I can. I want to. I want to trust you. Help me.*

"What size, Lieutenant?"

She opened her eyes. A clerk sat at a desk, bored and impatient. Ruth had followed the line unaware. She stammered her size to the clerk, and he handed her a stack of clothing, including jackets, trousers, skirts, and a garrison cap, all in gray blue wool, and white undershirts with black trim that read "U.S. Air Forces" over a caduceus, representing the medical services.

Behind the clerk stood a nurse with a matronly figure and a smile to match. Silver bars glinted on her shoulders—a first lieutenant. "I hope you're more attentive on the job, Lieutenant . . . ?"

Swell, the chief nurse. Ruth snapped herself up straight. "Lt. Ruth Doherty, ma'am, and I'm very attentive on the job."

"Good." The chief swiveled her gaze to the next in line.

Ruth groaned, clutched her pile of clothing, and stepped aside to join May. How long would it take to overcome that first impression?

"That's the color I wanted." Someone touched Ruth's hair—the alto, her brown eyes as big as her voice. "I wanted auburn." The nurse's garrison cap and snood couldn't hide the green streaks in her brown hair.

"Oh dear," Ruth said. "That's too bad."

"I dyed it before my last audition." She heaved a sigh. "No roles on Broadway for mousy brunettes, only for flashy redheads and sunny blondes and raven-haired beauties. Of course, they don't want green-feathered songbirds either. So I came here instead."

For Ruth flight nursing was a dream, but for this girl it was a consolation prize.

"Isn't this exciting?" The actress looked around the room filled with the twenty-four nurses and twenty-four surgical technicians of the new 815th Medical Air Evacuation Transport Squadron. "My hospital job was so dull. Paid the bills between auditions, but so dull. I need drama. This—this has drama."

May exchanged a glance with Ruth. "We've had enough drama, haven't we?"

"Why are you gals here? Adventure? Glamour?" She winked. "Handsome pilots?"

Ruth laughed, surprising herself. "We've also had enough of flyboys, thank you."

"Glad to hear it," a male voice said behind her. "How about a handsome technician?"

She turned. The speaker was indeed handsome, with a square jaw and blond curls that fell over his forehead in a studied way. He draped his arms over the shoulders of two other men, but he looked at Ruth, only at Ruth.

"Don't forget the nonfraternization rules—Sergeant," she said with a sweet smile. At least the prohibition on dating between officers and enlisted men kept half her suitors away.

"Ah, you'll change your mind once you get to know me." He still looked only at Ruth, although May and the actress stood next to her. "Staff Sgt. William D. Burns at your service, but you can call me Burnsey. Everyone does."

"You can call me Lieutenant Doherty." To break his bold gaze, she turned to the other women. "This is Lieutenant Jensen and Lieutenant—"

"Dorothy La Rue." She darted forward and stuck out her hand. "Call me Dottie."

Sergeant Burns untangled his arms from his friends' necks to shake Dottie's hand. "Pleasure to meet you. And this is— what's your name, pal?"

"Sergeant Morrison."

"Sergeant Dugan."

They seemed uncomfortable with their new buddy's flirtation, so Ruth gave them genuine smiles. To her relief, the classroom doors opened. The nurses filed into one room and the techs into another.

Dottie sat at a desk next to Ruth and rested her chin on her stack of clothing. "That Burnsey's a real looker, isn't he? I wouldn't mind him for a partner."

"I would," Ruth said.

Dottie's eyes grew even rounder. "But why?"

"Ruth and I like to keep our professional distance," May said. "Remember, the nonfraternization rules are for our protection."

"Yeah, I know," Dottie said. "Think how awkward it'd be to date someone you bossed around. Still, he'd be awful nice to look at on those long flights."

Ruth frowned. The evacuation leg of a flight would be crowded with patients, but not the cargo leg. She'd better get a tech who could act like a gentleman.

30

Antioch, California

Thursday, December 9, 1943

Jack closed his eyes and let Mr. Noia do his job with shaving cream and razor.

On his last furlough home in February, he'd picked the busiest time to get a haircut so he'd have a big audience for his stories. Today he went midmorning when most men were at work. Still, word spread that young Jack Novak was home, and Antioch's old-timers packed the Central Barber Shop.

Jack didn't need a haircut as much as he needed an escape. His train had arrived yesterday, and he chafed at how Mom clucked over him and made his favorite meals as if he'd lost a ball game. Why did it bother him? Hadn't he longed for Mom's pampering back in England?

"So, boy, were you at Schweinfurt?"

Jack murmured his reply.

Expressions of awe bounced around the barbershop and drowned Jack's groans. He didn't deserve this. He was no hero. Mr. Noia slapped aftershave on Jack's cheeks, and Jack wished he'd slap harder.

"Tell us about it, son."

What could he say? He was supposed to assure those on the home front that their hard work would lead to a victory parade any day now, but he couldn't lie. For every Nazi they shot down, two more met them the next day.

"You sure are lucky to be alive, young man."

"Lucky?" Even if he believed in luck, which he didn't, was it lucky to cause your best friend to plummet to his death?

Mr. Noia whisked away the towels.

"Sorry, gentlemen. Some other time." Jack pressed a quarter into Mr. Noia's hand and left the shop.

A stiff wind blew down Second Street, and Jack clapped his hand over his service cap as he passed El Campanil Theater. Too early for a show. Wouldn't it be great to sink into a plush seat in the ornate theater alone in the darkness with Bob Hope and Bing Crosby and Dorothy Lamour on the road to anywhere?

He looked both ways before crossing, still not used to downtown with so few cars. A horse even stood tied in front of Palace Drugs. He wandered up G Street. Why did so many people roam downtown? Each needed a tip of the hat and a cheery "good morning." Couldn't let the town whisper about Pastor Novak's middle son, who had always been such a nice boy.

Some wanted to talk, but Jack explained he was in a hurry. Yeah, a hurry to get away.

The door to Della's Dress Shop banged open. A young woman burst out and ran smack into Jack. He caught her by the elbows. "Whoa, there."

"I'm sorry. Oh, Jack, hi. I heard you were home."

He smiled. Helen Carlisle, Dr. Jamison's daughter, belonged to Walt's gang of friends and had a knack for accidents. "Where are you off to in such a hurry?"

"Oh, I need to pick up Jay-Jay at my sister's, and run to

the bank and post office before lunch." The wind whipped dark blonde strands of hair around her face, and she tucked them under her hat.

"Jay-Jay—how's that baby of yours?"

"Not much of a baby anymore. He's twenty-one months old and cute as can be."

"I'm sure he is. And how have you been?" Helen's husband, Jim, had been killed off Guadalcanal about a year before.

"I keep busy." She gave a shaky laugh. "I have two meetings this afternoon. I wasn't supposed to help at the dress shop today, but no. Oh, I could strangle Jeannie Llewellyn."

"Yeah?" Jack didn't mind her stories as long as he didn't have to tell his.

"We worked late nights all week on a gown for her, used up the last of our silk. She insisted she needed the dress by Friday—insisted. Well, today was her final fitting—and it fit perfectly, by the way—but she decided the blue did nothing for her coloring and she'd wear the red dress she bought in San Francisco—black market, no doubt. All our hard work for nothing. Mrs. Carlisle won't even charge her, doesn't want to get on the Llewellyns' bad side. I hope someone buys it." Helen motioned to the store window. "Well, I have to run. I'll see you around."

Jack mumbled something, but he couldn't tear his gaze from the evening dress in the window, from the striking shade of blue, the same color as Ruth Doherty's eyes.

He could imagine her in that dress, but he didn't want to. He'd never seen her in an evening gown or any civilian clothes. Had she ever dressed up? In her life?

A nasty feeling squeezed his belly. Any girl who sold kisses to buy food wouldn't have money for fancy clothes.

Jack leaned his forehead against the cool glass. What did he know about poverty? Sure, the Novaks had struggled in the Depression, but they never missed a meal. Ruth, however, knew hunger and did what she thought necessary for her family. Yes, it was stupid and wrong, but she was only thirteen.

He peeled away from the glass and strode down the street. Thirteen? That's how old he was when he sold rides in Grandpa's biplane. Stupid and wrong, and not even for a noble cause.

Would he have kept it up for two years? Sure, but he'd been caught.

Ruth hadn't been until those three rats caught her in the alley.

Jack whipped around the corner onto his parents' street. He could still see Ruth pounded into the grass by his anger, his pride, his self-righteousness. She didn't need confrontation—she was no longer sinning. And she didn't need punishment. She punished herself and denied herself any small luxury. She didn't need Jack's help.

Up the driveway, behind the house, and he flung open the garage door to find his old Schwinn with tires pumped full. Dad must have been using it. A clergyman's E rationing card for unlimited gasoline didn't do any good when the stations had no gas at all.

He coasted down the driveway.

Mom stood on the front porch, drying her hands on her apron. "I thought I heard you. Where are you going?"

"The farm." He didn't know it until he said it. Grandpa Novak never made a fuss.

"Oh good. Your grandparents will be glad to see you. Have fun."

Jack sent a wave over his shoulder. Fun? What a lousy goal. Charlie had him pegged. Jack loved the game with Ruth, the challenge—yes, the manipulation.

When he reached A Street, he turned right. Ruth told him straight out she didn't date, hated kissing, couldn't love him, but no, he was convinced he'd change her mind. Why? 'Cause he was such a swell guy? Yeah, how could she resist?

He slammed his fist on the handlebar and made the bike wobble. Pride! All about what Jack wanted, not about what Ruth wanted, what she needed. Fine thing he called love.

Fighting the wind, Jack pedaled hard down A Street, down Lone Tree Way, past farms and ranches and rounded hills and green grass passing last year's dried-out growth. Despite the cool air, he worked up a sweat under his flight jacket. If only he could sweat out his pride.

He let his bike fall in a clatter next to the barn and marched inside, where Grandpa groomed Winchell's blasted donkey. "Put me to work."

Even though he hadn't even gotten a hello, Grandpa just tossed Jack a pitchfork. "Stalls need mucking out."

Jack threw his jacket over a railing, rolled up his sleeves, and dug in with vigor. In blessed silence he cleaned stall after stall. The smell of ammonia made his eyes water, but his pride stank worse. He wiped sweat from his mustache, took off his shirt, and dug in harder.

"Sure am glad you brought home this little miss," Grandpa said. "Coyotes have been getting the chickens. Nothing like a donkey to chase off coyotes."

Jack groaned. No amount of chicken dinners could make up for carting that beast.

"Things not going well over there?" Grandpa asked.

"No, they're not."

Grandpa grunted.

"We need fighter escort all the way to the target. Too many good men dying. A waste—a stinking, bloody waste." The pitchfork clanged into wood. Jack heaved out the forkful and moved on to the last stall. For the first time in his life, he wished for more manure.

"Home to stay?"

"No. I've gotta fly, gotta be with my men. I made a mistake—a stupid, prideful mistake, and I paid for it. But it's what I'm good at, where I do some good in this stinking, lousy world."

"So, you figured it out."

Jack drove the pitchfork into the pile and leaned his elbow on top, panting. "Figured out what?"

"You're meant to be a military man, not a pastor."

Jack's pride had to be located in his chest, because that's where he felt the punch. "I'll—I'll be ready for the ministry after the war."

Grandpa fed Sahara Sue a carrot. "Why? You've found what you're good at, where you do some good. Some people live their whole lives, never find that."

Jack's mouth flapped open and shut. "But . . . but . . ."

"But that son of mine's got you filled with the notion you can only serve God in the pulpit. Balderdash." Grandpa stomped up to him, and his hazel eyes flashed. "Can't all of us be pastors. Even the Good Book says that. Someone's gotta farm the earth and build the houses and care for the sick. Now, your brother Walt—that boy was made to be an engineer, no doubt about it. He uses the gifts the good Lord gave him for a good purpose. So do you. Don't you think we need godly men on the farms, at Boeing Aircraft, on your air base?"

Jack's mind whirled as he stared at his grandfather in his overalls and barn jacket with a crumpled hat over his gray hair. "Yeah, but—"

"Jack Novak, you share your dad's name, but you do not have to share his profession. God has a purpose for you, boy, and you've found it. Now, be a man and trust God to work in his way, not your dad's."

Jack had never heard his grandfather give a long speech. Ever. Could Jack do that? Could he abandon the ministry and stay in the military?

Would it be a failure? Or a victory?

31

Bowman Field

Monday, December 13, 1943

Ruth scrambled up the wall and hoisted herself over the edge.
For the first time, she landed on her feet. She sprinted forward, dropped to her belly, and slithered under camouflage
netting. When they went on bivouac in a few weeks, they'd
dodge live ammo, so Ruth tucked in her chin.

"Keep that backside down, Doherty. You'll get it shot
off."

She grimaced and splayed her knees to do as she was told.
Free of the netting, she sprang to her feet and raced for the
finish.

The sergeant hit the stopwatch. "Better. You shaved three
seconds off yesterday's time."

Ruth set her hands on her knees and let her chest heave.
"Didn't fall today."

"About time." He glanced at his clipboard. "La Rue, you're
next."

Dottie took off at a fast clip. All that singing must have
strengthened her lungs.

"Good job, Ruthie."

She smiled up at May over her shoulder. "Not as good as you."

"I'm just little and wiry."

"You're getting strong too."

May grinned and flexed her bicep. "I look like Rosie the Riveter, don't I? Won't Charlie be surprised when he gets back?"

Ruth pretended to be too winded to answer. Charlie's name hadn't appeared on the POW lists, but since evadees took many months to work their way back to England, May's hope was artificially prolonged. *Lord, let her see the truth, and let me help her when she sees it.*

"Your best time yet, La Rue." The sergeant sent the nurses back to the barracks.

Showers had never felt better than they did at Bowman Field, where mud and sweat rolled off Ruth's body and down the drain. She wrapped her towel around herself and shook her hair out of her shower cap.

On the bench, Dottie fluffed her curls, cut short to get rid of most of the green. "You really should let me give you a permanent, Ruth. It'd be so much easier. Doesn't May look cute?"

Ruth couldn't afford a perm, but May did look darling with her face framed by platinum curls.

After they dressed in their U.S. Air Forces T-shirts and olive drab trousers, they went to the mess for breakfast, then to the airfield, where a dozen nurses were scheduled to train inside a C-47.

Ruth climbed through the cargo door in the rear of the plane and sniffed in the oily, metallic smell. When she graduated, she would work in either a C-47 or a C-54, a larger plane designed for transoceanic flights. She passed aluminum ribs in the tubular fuselage. To the front a door led to the radio room and the cockpit.

The instructor, Staff Sergeant Rawlinson, greeted them in an authoritative voice that contrasted with his soft eyes. Ruth settled into a canvas seat next to May, and her knee jiggled in anticipation.

A C-47 accommodated twenty-four patients on their litters straight from the battlefield, and a well-trained team could load the plane in under ten minutes. Sergeant Rawlinson reached up to a canvas storage bag on the ceiling, emptied its load of web strapping, and anchored the webbing to a bar on the floor. Then he demonstrated how to insert the poles of a litter into the strap.

The nurses divided into pairs, and Ruth and May received four litters to arrange like a bunk bed.

May strained to slip a pole through the top loop. "I see why they don't take nurses shorter than I."

"And why they make us do all these calisthenics." Ruth looped the strap through the buckle. "Imagine a 250-pound man on this litter."

May groaned. "Does the Army take them that big?"

"Only as officers." Sergeant Rawlinson inspected their work. "Tighter."

Ruth grunted and tugged the strap, even as she smiled at the sergeant's joke.

The instructor paced the aisle. "As Lieutenant Jensen noticed, the top litter is hard to reach. Reserve those positions for patients who require minimal care. Arrange your patients so anything that needs attention during the flight faces the aisle—wounds, drains, casts. Put men with heavy casts on the bottom. Yes, you'll have a technician with you, as well as ground personnel to help load and unload, but ultimately, this is the flight nurse's responsibility."

Ruth and May guided the next litter into its slot at chest level.

"Speed is vital." Sergeant Rawlinson unbuckled Norma Carpenter's strap and made the willowy blonde start over. "You may load your plane near a combat zone and come under fire. You may need to unload after a crash or ditching. Your speed, your calmness, your efficiency will be the difference between life and death for your patients."

Norma's eyebrows shot up, but Ruth felt a thrill. This was what she'd signed up for.

May stopped to catch her breath. "After all this, the flight will seem dull."

"Oh no," Ruth said. "We're allowed to use Pentothal. That could be fun."

"Fun? Putting patients under?"

"Yeah." Ruth used all her weight to tighten a strap. "Any man makes a pass at me, I'll threaten him with Pentothal."

"We're done, Sarge." Dottie stood on the lowest litter and swung into the aisle with a sweep of her arm. "'Off we go into the wild blue yonder.'"

"Take it down, and put it up again. Faster. Tighter."

"But when do we get to fly?"

He jiggled the litter. "When you realize this is the Army Air Force, not the Navy. No hammocks."

Dottie pouted and hopped down. "But I wanted my flight pay to buy Christmas presents."

Flight pay. Ruth sighed. She had to fly forty hours a month to earn it, so Aunt Pauline wouldn't get a higher check until January. One end of the litter slipped down with a clatter.

Sergeant Rawlinson fixed a stern look on her.

"Sorry, Sergeant," Ruth said. "The patient was in shock. I had to put his head down in Trendelenburg position."

He chuckled and turned away. "Women in the Army—whose bright idea?"

Ruth smiled, but May sighed.

"I hope we can fly soon. Remember, Ruth? Wasn't it wonderful?"

The question knocked out her breath. Her memory of flying was tied to her memories of Jack, but every thought of Jack cast her to the ground in the fog. "I wish we could fly again and get above the gray days."

"Do you remember that talk we had about gray days?" May asked in a quiet voice. "The Fourth of July, I think."

Ruth nodded and fumbled with the strap. She could still see Jack stretched out on the blanket, goading her to take the ham and cheese, say his name, and accept his friendship. Her whole chest ached, missing him, knowing he didn't miss her one bit.

May's forehead creased. Denial protected her from grief, but not from worry.

Ruth knelt to insert the lowest litter. "We can't get away from those gray days, can we?"

"No, we can't."

"What? You're not going to rhapsodize about how prayer drives away the gray clouds?"

May frowned, her hands wrapped around the canvas-covered pole. "Well, no. Prayer takes you above the gray. It doesn't always take it away."

Ruth's head spun. All her prayers, all her life, had been for God to take away her problems, to snatch her from the valley of the shadow of death. She said the verse in her head, then heard it as if for the first time: *"Yea, though I walk through the valley of the shadow of death, I will fear no evil: for thou art with me; thy rod and thy staff they comfort me."*

God never promised to take her out of the valley, but to be with her, guide her, and comfort her—*in* the valley.

Oh Lord. Ruth's prayer stumbled. She didn't trust God

because she thought he had abandoned her. But he hadn't. She had rejected him. *Oh Lord, forgive me.*

May nudged her. "Ruth? You strapped in your belt."

Ruth was indeed well secured. She let out a shaky laugh and scratched at a tickle on her cheek. Her finger came back wet. She whipped out a handkerchief and dabbed her eyes. All those years without a single tear, and now she'd turned into a fountain.

"All right. Class is over," Sergeant Rawlinson said.

On her way off the plane, Ruth kept her head down to conceal any redness in her eyes, but a commotion on the ground made her look up. The chief nurse, Lt. Erma Shepard, stood with a list in hand. The 815th MAETS consisted of four flights, each with one flight surgeon and six pairs of nurses and surgical technicians. Today they'd find out who their partners were.

"Lt. Norma Carpenter, you'll be with Sgt. Michael Dugan. Lt. Ruth Doherty, you'll work with Sgt. William Burns."

Ruth couldn't even hear the rest of the list. Burnsey? She'd been teamed with Burnsey?

After the chief nurse finished, a private passed out mail, but Lieutenant Shepard headed toward the classroom building. Ruth trotted to catch up, and she offered the chief a salute. "Lieutenant Shepard? I put in a request not to work with Sergeant Burns."

Lieutenant Shepard gave her a motherly smile. She had kindly brown eyes and a sharp nose with slits for nostrils. "That's why I put you together."

Ruth's mouth dropped open.

The chief nurse laughed. "Everyone else wanted to work with him, for good reason. He's distinguished himself as an excellent tech, our best. But he's also handsome and popular, so to maintain professionalism, I paired him with the one person in the squadron who isn't swayed by his charms—you, my dear."

Ruth couldn't close her mouth. She couldn't say why she didn't want to work with him, because she couldn't put it in words. He'd never said anything inappropriate, never touched her, never asked her out. He just made her nervous. "There must be someone—"

"No. Haven't you seen how the girls flirt with him? With you, I can be sure there won't be any hanky-panky." Her mouth drew up as tight as her nostrils.

"But—"

"My decision is final. Now, we shall all get along splendidly, shall we not?"

Ruth recognized an order when she heard one. "Yes, ma'am."

Lieutenant Shepard walked away, and Ruth turned toward the group by the C-47.

May met her halfway. She'd lost all the color she'd earned from three weeks of calisthenics. "I got a letter from Jack."

"Jack?" His name tasted strange in Ruth's mouth.

"I gave him my address and asked him to contact me if he heard anything. Read it."

Ruth hesitated, but she had no choice. She felt woozy at the sight of Jack's firm hand with its confident, oversized capitals. She steeled herself to hear his voice in her head.

November 30, 1943

Dear May,

I have postponed this letter as long as possible, since I know how much you hope for Charlie's return.

Today we received a prisoner of war list

containing more names of men lost on the
Schweinfurt mission. Charlie's name was not
among them. May, I'm afraid not one man
from his crew is on any of the lists. While the
men must officially be classified as missing
in action, the Eighth Air Force has contacted the
men's families. Given the circumstances, we are
certain the entire crew was killed in action.

   Please accept my condolences on your loss.
I knew Charlie for three years and I never saw
him as happy as he was with you. I hope you
know how much he loved you and how much
you enriched his life. Please take comfort in
knowing he is home with the Lord he loved and
served.

Ruth's heart weighed heavy, so heavy she was surprised it
still beat. Would May accept Jack's statement?

May's face was carved from marble, her chin high, her
eyes dry. "Well, that's that. I was wrong. Come along, Ruth.
We'll be late for class."

32

Antioch

Sunday, December 19, 1943

In the faint dawn light, Jack sat cross-legged on the sand and stared at the greenish gray water in the cove. The San Joaquin River streamed west from the Sierras, through Stockton and past Antioch, joined the Sacramento River at Pittsburg, and then flowed into San Francisco Bay.

Jack knew the smell, the currents, and the tides, but he hadn't swum in the river or anywhere else since he'd been pulled half-conscious from its grasp by some Portuguese fishermen. After that, at beach parties he stoked the campfires, entertained the beachcombers, and wooed the girls. His fear of water had little impact on his life. Until Schweinfurt.

He reached forward and let the cold liquid rush between his fingers. Such innocuous stuff, water, yet it was the stuff of life, the stuff of death.

A shiver ran through him. He'd never thought of himself as a coward, but only a coward would risk the lives of over a hundred men so he wouldn't have to face his fear.

Jack slipped both hands under the water and onto the firm sand, then curled his fingers in. Dirt clouded the water as pride had clouded his judgment over Schweinfurt. Fear had sparked his fatal decision, but pride fueled it. He thought he could pull it off. He always had before.

"You're too good, Jack. That's your problem." Charlie was right. Even in seminary, when Jack should have failed, he'd squeaked by on charm and dogged hard work.

It wasn't that he didn't trust God, but that he'd never had to.

Jack ran damp hands over his face and into his hair. "Lord, forgive me. I trusted myself more than you. Please don't let Charlie's death be in vain. Help me put aside my pride and learn to trust you."

Before long, God's forgiveness warmed him more than the pale sun could, but Jack had a long way to go. The sin of pride had hundreds of tentacles tunneled deep in his soul.

He wandered home through streets deserted except for boys tossing the *Ledger* onto porches, and Mr. Fortner in his horse-drawn milk wagon, pressed back into service. At home, Jack washed up, changed into dress uniform for church, and joined his family in the kitchen. His brothers and future sister-in-law had arrived the day before.

Mom smiled over her shoulder as she scrambled eggs. "Good morning, dear. Pull up a chair wherever you can."

"Morning, everyone." Jack squeezed a chair in place. Dad, Ray, Walt, and Allie sat around a table heaped with biscuits, jam, and eggs from Grandpa's farm. For the first time in weeks, Jack felt hungry.

Walt grinned across the table at him. "We saved half a sausage link for you."

"Nope," Ray said. "Just ate it."

Mom clucked her tongue at them. "Nonsense. I have plenty. Granted, I used a wad of ration stamps, but I wanted your first breakfast together to be special."

Jack had joined the Air Corps in 1940, and Ray and Walt followed soon after. Training took them all over the country, and then Jack and Walt went overseas. The whole family hadn't sat under one roof for three years.

Jack studied his older brother beside him. Ray still wore the single bars of a lieutenant since he didn't have combat experience. Back in 1940, the Air Corps had been desperate for instructors and had tapped members of each graduating class to teach the next. Ray had gladly obliged. His job in pilot training would never lead to advancement, but Ray didn't care about such things.

"So, Ray," Dad said. "Have you met any nice girls down in Texas?"

Jack winced and stuffed a bite of sausage in his mouth.

"Haven't been looking." Ray had a rough recovery from his second broken engagement.

"Just wait. God will send the right woman." Walt had never looked so good. He'd even lost the nervous habit of shoving back the black curl over his forehead. Jack tried not to stare as Walt used the silver hook on his right arm to brace a sausage with a fork while he sliced. At first, Walt wanted nothing to do with prosthetics, but his recent letters described the tasks the artificial arm helped him with. Ever the engineer, he saw it as a fun toy.

Jack nudged Ray in the side. "If our ugly kid brother can find someone, so can you." He shot Walt a grin, which was returned with interest.

"Oh my. I see where you learned to tease, Walt." Those were the first words that morning from Allie Miller. She struck Jack as a long-faced librarian, a girl most fellows wouldn't give a second look, but she did have the pretty green eyes Walt raved about.

"Say, Allie," Walt said. "Tell the story about your arrival in Seattle."

She gave him a withering glance.

Jack smiled and chewed his biscuit. She had some fire in that prim head after all.

"Come on, sweetheart. Jack hasn't heard it. I couldn't tell him in a letter. Loses its punch unless he sees how proper and ladylike you are."

Allie turned to Jack with light in her eyes. "Did he tell you he abandoned me at the train station?"

Jack's smile grew. Walt had met his match. Jack leaned forward on the table and gave Allie his most sympathetic look. "I can't believe it. What a jerk."

Walt laughed. "Hey, I had to work. I sent a taxi."

Jack frowned and shook his head. "Horrible, just horrible. Please continue."

Allie smiled back and forth between the brothers. "Horrible. I agree. Well, Bill Perkins was one of Walt's crewmates, and his family offered to rent me a room. When I arrived at the house, a couple greeted me at the door, and I thanked them profusely for their hospitality. They brought me in and served me tea, but they seemed uncomfortable, which made me nervous."

Walt dipped a spoon in the strawberry jam. "And when she's nervous, she talks a blue streak."

"Yes, I do. I chatted about how lovely Seattle was, and how happy I was to be there and to work at Boeing and to see my fiancé again. Then I glimpsed Walt coming down the sidewalk, except he went to the house across the street. So I looked at the address Walt gave me—number forty-two, or was it forty-three?"

"You know how bad my handwriting is now," Walt said.

Jack nodded. Poor girl. Just the kind who would die of mortification.

Sure enough, Allie's cheeks turned pink, but she smiled.

"You see, I introduced myself but never asked their names. This sweet couple entertained a complete stranger."

Jack joined his family in laughter. Allie laughed too, and any girl who could laugh at herself was okay in his book.

Walt gathered her hand in his. "May 6—we've set the date."

"Congratulations." Then Jack pointed at Allie. "I meant that for him, not you. I know what you're getting stuck with."

"So do I, and I couldn't be happier."

Now Jack smiled at Walt. "You've done well for yourself, kid."

Half an hour later, Jack sat in the pew between his brothers, sharing a hymnal with Ray while Mom played Christmas carols on the organ.

Then Dad started his sermon with the mannerisms and intonations Jack had practiced in front of the bathroom mirror as a boy. His professors at seminary praised his delivery but not his messages.

Jack shifted in the pew. Good speaking skills didn't make him a good pastor.

His sermons lacked depth and originality and insight, he knew that even as he wrote them. But sermons weren't his only failing in the ministry. Pastors needed to be calm and strong in a crisis and offer solace from Scripture. Jack had faced four crises the past year and failed at all four.

First, he'd been in Texas with Ray when Dolores broke their engagement. Jack had fumbled, his words tangled in his own dislike of Dolores. Then he'd been in the hospital with Walt when he saw his stump for the first time. Once again, he fumbled.

He hadn't done any better breaking the news of Charlie's death to May. She didn't even believe him. Good thing Ruth had been there for May—and for him.

Jack slammed his eyes shut, remembering his worst failure of all, but he couldn't block the image of Ruth bowed under his condemnation. Condemnation? A good pastor would have offered compassion and forgiveness.

He squeezed the Bible in his lap. He could hear Dad telling him he just needed to try harder. *Is that it, Lord? Am I disobedient to your call? Do I need to accept your will and apply myself?*

Then Grandpa's words rang louder, telling him he was meant for the military, not the ministry. *Or is that it, Lord? Is pride making me stick with a goal that was never your will for me in the first place?*

Jack glanced between his father in the pulpit and his grandfather in the pew in front of him, both godly men who loved him. Which man was right?

Only God knew the answer. *Lord, help me follow your will—not Dad's, not Grandpa's, not mine—only yours.*

33

Bowman Field

Wednesday, December 22, 1943

Ruth readjusted her pack over her aching back. "Remind me why we applied in the summer so we could go on a five-day bivouac in December," she whispered to May.

"It was the glamour."

Ruth clamped off her laugh. She wore fatigues, her hair hung in two short braids under her helmet, she was filthy, and she stank. She had never been less glamorous.

"How much longer, do you think?" May's curls clung to her forehead.

"If I look at my watch, Sergeant Sadistic will send me on a fifty-mile run." Out of the corner of her eye, she saw Sergeant Sanderson driving alongside. His heckling was bad enough, but to do it from a jeep? He'd earned his nickname. "At least we're almost halfway through."

"Only half?" May's voice rose. "I thought we'd come at least six miles."

"No, the bivouac," she whispered. "It's Wednesday. At noon we're half done."

"Doherty! Jensen!"

Oh no. Ruth and May exchanged a glance.

Sergeant Sanderson leaned over the steering wheel of the jeep. "Shut your traps. Haven't you learned your lesson? This ain't a tea party. You think this is a tea party?"

"No, sir."

"Get over here and give me twenty." He pointed to a mud hole next to the jeep.

The rest of the nurses kept marching. They knew the routine. Ruth and May fell out of line and shrugged off their packs.

"Packs on," he barked. "This ain't the Girl Scouts. You think this is the Girl Scouts?"

"No, sir." Ruth pulled on her pack. Without being obvious, she searched for a dry spot to put her hands. She failed. The sergeant yelled off the count. Each push-up drove Ruth's fingers deeper into the clammy mud. By ten her arms burned, by fifteen they shook, by eighteen they felt like gelatin.

Sergeant Sanderson revved the jeep's motor. The wheels kicked mud into Ruth's face. She squeezed her eyes shut against the sting and spat out mud. No matter what, she wouldn't let this man get in the way of her goal.

"Twenty."

Ruth groaned, pushed herself back onto her knees, and wiped her hands and face.

"Now, quit your yakking. You wanna yak, you quit the Army Air Force and go back to the kitchen where you belong. This ain't a quilting bee. You think this is a quilting bee?"

"No, sir." Ruth chewed her muddy lip so she wouldn't laugh. The penalty for giggling was even higher than for yakking.

"You dames wanna be in a man's world, you do things a man's way." He threw in profanities to make his point. "Look how far behind you are. On the double."

"Yes, sir." The ladies jogged to catch up. The jeep passed and splattered mud on their fatigues.

Ruth waited until he was out of earshot. "This ain't glamorous. You think this is glamorous?"

May stifled a giggle. "Quit your yakking."

By the time they returned to position, the nurses had reached the day's campsite. One hundred women from the four squadrons at Bowman were on their own in the Kentucky wilderness. Before they could sit down to K rations for lunch, they had to dig "sanitary installations" and slit trenches. The night before, fireworks had simulated an enemy attack, sent the nurses into the trenches, and then forced a retreat.

Dottie screwed a shovel head onto a handle. "I don't care what Sergeant Sadistic says. Good thing I was a Girl Scout. I'm used to hard work in the out-of-doors."

Ruth set her foot on the top of her shovel head and pushed it into the earth. "Good thing I grew up in a slum. I'm used to filth and stench."

"Good thing I'm an orphan. I'm used to being unloved and unappreciated." May gave a big, fake sniff, which made Ruth laugh.

Dottie sank her shovel into the dirt. "I don't see why we can't bivouac with the technicians. I sure wouldn't mind some strong male muscles right now."

May smiled. "So you've seen Rosenberg's merits?"

"Rosie?" Dottie rolled her eyes. "I'd never cast him in my play."

"Oh, but he's sweet," Ruth said. "And you're the fastest team in the squadron."

"I'd rather be with Burnsey. Who can blame you for going so slowly? I'd make the most of every minute with him."

"Believe me, that's not the problem." Ruth set her teeth. They were the slowest team in the flight, because the tech interfered with Ruth's duties and neglected his own. It was easier to work with a man who hated taking orders from a woman than one who used chivalry to mask condescension. When she complained to Lieutenant Shepard, the chief nurse wrinkled her sharp nose and said, "If you performed your duties in a timely manner, he wouldn't have to help." In all her years as a nurse, Ruth had never had difficulty performing her duties in a timely manner.

"I can't see why you don't like him. He's awful cute."

"Dottie, we've been over this," May said.

"Yeah, yeah, I know. Professional distance." She adjusted her helmet and added a handprint to the smudges. "We've got to get you two on some dates."

"Absolutely no dates." Ruth tossed a shovelful of dirt behind her.

"Why not? Did you leave boyfriends back in England?"

Ruth sent her an anxious look and a shake of her head to tell her to drop the subject.

It didn't work. "How about you, May? Do you have a fellow?"

May kept digging, her forehead wrinkled under the dirt. "My boyfriend was a bombardier. He was killed when his B-17 was shot down over Schweinfurt."

Ruth felt as if someone whacked her in the chest with her own shovel. Since Jack's letter arrived, May hadn't mentioned Charlie. Not one word, not one teardrop, not even a change in mood.

"Oh no." Dottie's face turned as white as May's. "I'm sorry. That's the day they call 'Black Thursday,' isn't it?"

Ruth nodded. Black indeed.

"You too?" Dottie asked Ruth in a small voice.

"No." She frowned and chucked a rock from the trench. Did Jack still live, or had he been killed the day after he wrote that letter? Had he finished his tour and gotten his promotion? Was he still wracked by grief and guilt for Charlie's death?

"So . . . ?" Dottie asked.

Ruth wanted to give the stock answer she'd given several physicians and C-47 crewmen in the past month, that she didn't date, but it felt incomplete, almost dishonest. She hadn't dated Jack, but they'd had something precious. "We had an argument, a horrible one."

"Mm." Dottie heaved out more dirt. "Whose fault?"

"Mine," Ruth said as May said, "His."

"What?" Ruth stared at her friend. "I'm the one who did wrong."

"No." May snapped up her gaze. "God forgave you. Why can't Jack? Does he think he's better than God?"

Ruth's jaw dropped open.

"I think he does. He's proud, that Jack Novak. He always held himself above Charlie, thought he was better, but who could be better than Charlie—sweet, kind, thoughtful Charlie?" Her voice broke.

The shovel fell from Ruth's hand. Never had she seen May in such a state.

Her eyes were silver daggers. "Then Jack thought he'd found a girl worthy of him but—oh no!—you didn't meet his lofty standards, so he yelled at you and insulted you and abandoned you."

Ruth's head shook from side to side. No, his anger was justified.

"He didn't even ask about you. Did you notice? In his letter? Not one word about you. He doesn't even care how you are, after he left you broken. Did you notice?"

Ruth nodded, and her eyes watered.

"And you defend him?" Tears cut pink trails over May's dirty cheeks.

"I—I understand why—"

May let out an exasperated cry. "Of course you understand why he can't forgive you, because you can't forgive yourself. You don't even believe God forgave you."

"Yes, I—"

"No, you don't." May hurled down her shovel. "If you did, you'd shove off that shame. Jesus forgave you. Why can't you? Why can't Jack?"

Ruth's thoughts whipped into a tornado. She kept asking God to forgive her over and over, as if once weren't enough. Why? Did she think her sins were too big for God? A single drop of Christ's blood was enough to wipe out the sins of all mankind, she knew that. Yet she believed it wasn't enough for her.

She pressed her filthy hands over her face. *I'm sorry, Lord. I do—I do believe you've forgiven me. I believe you've taken away my sin. Please take away my shame. Please help me trust you.*

"May! Ruth!" Dottie whispered fiercely. "Sergeant Sadistic."

Ruth groped for her shovel, thrust it into the trench, and pitched out mounds of earth. After the jeep rumbled past, she ventured a glance up.

May's face stretched long. "I—I'm sorry, Ruthie. I don't know what came over me."

She considered the great shaking and settling in her soul. "I think—I think it might have been the Holy Spirit."

May's eyebrows disappeared under the rim of her helmet, and Ruth had to laugh. May joined her in strange, elated laughter.

"Quit your giggling," Sergeant Sanderson yelled. "This ain't a beauty parlor. You think this is a beauty parlor?"

"No, sir!"

Ruth clamped her lips between her teeth, but May looked so funny with her red face streaked with mud and tears, that Ruth gave in to great, joyous, forgiven rolls of laughter, worth any number of push-ups.

"You're right." Dottie shoveled hard, her eyes gigantic. "Absolutely no dates for you."

34

Antioch

Saturday, December 25, 1943

"*Christian Behaviour* by C. S. Lewis." Ray flipped through the slim book. "You can't get this in America yet. Thanks, Jack."

"You're welcome." He smiled at the delight on his brother's and his father's faces.

"Two years in a row," Dad said. "Walt sent us *Broadcast Talks* last year."

"Yep." Jack still hadn't read it. He glanced around the parlor. Walt pored over the pictorial book of England and tried to get Allie's attention to show her sights he had seen, but Allie and Mom were busy unwrapping English china from old *Stars and Stripes* newspapers.

"Have you heard his BBC broadcasts?" Ray asked.

Whose broadcasts? Oh, C. S. Lewis's. Jack adjusted his service jacket. "Can't say I have. The Germans keep me awful busy."

"Of course." Ray's smile flickered. "Still, what I wouldn't give to hear him."

Jack looked away, as if fascinated with how Mom folded

the wrapping paper to use next year. Ray would never take his place, not even to hear the noted theologian. All his life, Ray had talked his way out of fights. He was the last man Jack could imagine facing the Luftwaffe.

Jack tried to ignore the sting of Ray's statement, unintentional, but it still stung. Any pastor worth his salt would catch those broadcasts and read those books, not because he had to, but because he wanted to.

"Here you go, Jack. From your mother and me. Merry Christmas." Dad handed him two gifts in red paper creased from many years' use. Books. Thick theological tomes to gather dust on his bookshelf upstairs.

Jack unwrapped them. Luther in German and Augustine in Latin. "Thanks," he said, although memories throbbed in his head of trying to comprehend Augustine, falling asleep over Luther, and sneaking peeks at English translations in the library so he wouldn't have to struggle with foreign languages and deep thoughts simultaneously.

"I searched through the books in your room to get ideas. I'm surprised how few you have. I know you had these in seminary."

"Oh yeah."

Ray leaned to the floor to straighten his pile of gifts. "Dad, I told you he sold his books to save money."

"Yep." Sold them and murdered them, yet here they were back from the dead.

Dad chuckled. "The shortsighted actions of youth. You'll need these as a pastor."

"Unless I'm not going to be a pastor." Jack sucked in his breath. He hadn't meant to say that out loud. Silence hummed. Mom's forehead furrowed as she flattened paper. A grin climbed Walt's face, and Ray gave him a slight nod. Jack would consider that later.

Dad eyed him, and Jack returned his look steadily, respect-fully, and carefully. He shared so much with his father, not only his name, but his personality and talents.

Dad let out a laugh. "Not be a pastor? What else would you do?"

Jack shrugged. "I'm a good pilot, a good commander. I could stay in the military."

"The military?" Dad smiled around the room, but everyone ducked his gaze. "Always the family joker. You'd waste three years of seminary education?"

A jab in the chest. Dad and Mom skimped and saved to put three boys through the University of California, then two of them through seminary, all during the Depression when the tithe often came in as a bushel of tomatoes or asparagus.

"I didn't say I'd do it. I'm just thinking about it."

"Thinking about it?" Dad leaned forward on his knees and fixed Jack with the strong stare he used with such effect in the pulpit. "You'd better do more than think about it, son. You'd better pray about it."

"I do."

"Good. The Lord will show you the error of your thinking. Isn't that right, Edie?"

Mom looked up from the wrapping paper. "Oh, John, please. It's Christmas."

Dad huffed, sat back in his chair, and waved toward the piano. "Fine. It's Christmas. So let's have Christmas music. How about it, Allie? Walt says you're a fine player."

The girl's eyes grew as big as the china plate in her hands.

"Come on, sweetheart," Walt said. "Let's do that number we practiced."

"Do—do you think now is a good time?"

"Now is the perfect time." Walt grabbed his fiancée's hand

and led her to the piano. "This is a new song called 'I'll Be Home for Christmas.'"

Yeah, perfect. Jack smiled at the back of his brother's head. The song would remind Dad to be thankful his boys were alive, no matter their career choices.

Rather than a traditional duet, the couple played with Walt's left hand and Allie's right, two people as one. With her free hand, Allie cradled what remained of Walt's right arm.

Jack's eyes felt funny, and his nose stuffed up. He remembered Walt in the hospital, his voice husky as he proclaimed no woman would ever love him.

"You can sing, you know," Walt said with a grin. "This isn't a concert."

The family sang. Everyone knew the song, because it played almost continuously on the radio, but their voices sounded thick and throaty.

Jack was home for Christmas, next to the piano crowned with doilies and the brothers' service portraits. How long until they all sang around this piano again? Would they ever? Ray and Walt were safe. Next year Walt and Allie would be married, and Ray would find a wife before long. Little Novaks would soon add to the music.

Would Jack be there to see it? Or would he be frozen in time as a black-and-white portrait?

Why not? Charlie was already frozen in time, and Bill Chambers and Nate Silverberg and countless others. In Maryland the de Groots were spending their first Christmas without their youngest son, and May Jensen was deprived of the man she loved and a home to long for.

What about Ruth? Jack stared at his stack of gifts, meager due to shortages, but Ruth would have none. What kind of holiday would she have in Kentucky? Was she still friends with May, or had Jack made her close her heart again?

Jack studied Walt and Allie at the piano. Their love was unconditional, but Jack's love—one mistake and he snatched it away.

Who was he to hold Ruth's mistakes against her? He'd failed her countless times, but she kept forgiving him. She forgave him when he left her on the truck with his men in Bury St. Edmunds, and what could be more terrifying for a woman with her history? She forgave him for kissing her, when a kiss meant trauma to her, not love.

Jack realized the music had stopped. He brought his eyes into focus. Walt whispered in Allie's ear. She nodded, shaking her brown curls. Then she turned to Walt with a trembling smile and tears on her cheeks.

Walt brushed them away. "We're your family now."

Jack blew out a sigh. This was Allie's first Christmas away from her home and the family who had disowned her for refusing to marry the man they had chosen.

"Then I'd better go help in the kitchen." Allie stood and bent over to kiss Walt on the forehead. He tipped back his head and kissed her on the lips. She blushed, laughed, and walked away with green velvet swishing around her ankles.

Mom was gone to the kitchen, judging by the intensified smell of roasting turkey. Dad was gone too, probably to polish tomorrow's sermon. When had they left? And Ray—he studied Jack.

Jack tensed. No longer could he dodge pastoral counsel.

"You leave on Monday, huh, Jack?" Walt spoke first, thank goodness. Small talk.

"Yeah. Figured I'd get an early start with this railroad strike. Can you believe it? Men are fighting and dying, and our railroad men refuse to work, all for a couple bucks."

"It's not right," Ray said.

"No kidding. So I'll catch military planes. I'll have to hop, skip, jump all over the country before I can get overseas."

Ray leaned forward on his knees. "Are you ready to go back?"

"Sure am. Can't wait."

Ray didn't look convinced, and Walt looked downright skeptical.

Jack sighed. "The war's tough, I'll give you that, but there's no place I'd rather be."

Ray's eyebrows bunched together. "Are you sure? You seem—well, you're not yourself."

"Yeah," Walt said. "You've barely insulted us all week. We wondered—"

"Am I flak-happy? No, not that. It's other stuff, okay?"

"The military versus the ministry?" Ray asked.

Jack groaned. "That's just a part of it, a small part."

"Would you—"

"Fine. You want to know what my problem is? It's my pride. You know Charlie got shot down. What I didn't tell you is he died because of my stupid decision. Not just Charlie, but twenty-seven men killed and thirteen POWs because of my pride."

"Oh, wow." Walt looked as if he'd been slugged in the chest. He'd also lost his best friend over Europe, but it wasn't Walt's fault.

"I got reprimanded and lost out on a promotion I'd worked for all year."

"Oh, wow."

"Yeah, and that's not all." Jack felt manic glee in dumping this on his brothers. "My pride cost me the woman I love."

Walt frowned. "Who? Lieutenant Doherty? I didn't know you were dating."

"We weren't. Didn't stop me from falling in love."

"What happened?" Ray wore that firm but gentle look a pastor should have.

Jack hesitated. Walt had met Ruth, so he needed to be discreet. "I lashed out at her. I found out she—she had a past."

"Mm." Ray nodded slowly. "Does she have a present?"

A dagger right in his gut. "No. Absolutely not."

Ray shifted his gaze up, right over Jack's head. "Terrible thing, a past. No matter what you do in the present, your past never changes. You confess, you repent, you turn your life around, but your past remains. Always."

A heavy band encircled Jack's chest. Even if he uprooted every weed of pride, he'd always be responsible for those deaths and for condemning Ruth.

Now he understood what Ruth lived with. Now he had a past.

35

Bowman Field

Friday, December 31, 1943

Ruth buckled the leather flight helmet under her chin and tugged at her scalp to loosen hairs pulled by the headset and helmet.

Across from her, wedged on a metal bench in the altitude chamber, May and Dottie giggled. In green oxygen masks, the six nurses and six techs of their flight looked like long-nosed grasshoppers.

Ruth pressed her mask over her mouth and nose. The smell of rubber made her cough. She fumbled to strap the mask onto a ring on the helmet over her cheek.

"Here, let me help you." Sergeant Burns reached for the strap.

Ruth twisted her shoulder to block him. "If you want to help, let me learn to do it myself."

Burnsey's sabotage was so subtle, no one saw it but her. During C-47 drills, he stood in her way, bumped against her, reached in front of her, and handed her things backwards or upside-down. Each act wasted precious seconds. Whenever she confronted him, he gave the same response: "We'd get along better if we spent more time together." Ruth knew what he really meant, and the way his gaze drifted over her body when they were alone confirmed it.

"These A-14 oxygen masks are an improvement over the A-8." The instructor, Lieutenant Brown, stood in the door of the chamber. "The A-8 is a continuous flow model with a rebreather bag, but the A-14 has a demand flow regulator with a diaphragm that closes on exhalation."

Ruth nudged her mask higher to relieve pressure on the bridge of her nose.

"An aneroid in the regulator expands as altitude increases, shutting the port for air and opening the oxygen port. Thus, the percentage of oxygen automatically rises to meet higher requirements at altitude."

May quirked an eyebrow at Ruth, and Ruth smiled. Yes, she also wished Lieutenant Brown would stop droning and start the simulated flight to 25,000 feet.

"The A-14 also has a built-in microphone, so throat microphones are no longer necessary."

Ruth's stomach twisted at the reminder of her test flight, and May's eyelashes fluttered. That night on the bivouac, huddled in their pup tent, May had finally cried for Charlie. As Ruth had never allowed herself to grieve so she could be strong for her family, May had trained herself never to demonstrate anger or sadness or discontent for fear of losing favor in the orphanage. But that night May cried—jerky, unpracticed sobs—and Ruth held her and listened to her and laughed with her because they had nothing clean to use as a handkerchief.

Muffled laughter sounded in her headphones. Burnsey wrapped his hands around the corrugated hose connected to the chin of his mask and pretended to play it like a clarinet.

She sighed. Burnsey was the darling of the squadron with

his quick wit and his access to items in short supply. His family ran a wholesale business, and whatever the PX lacked, Burnsey seemed to receive. He sold the items at cost, which endeared him more.

Lieutenant Brown sealed the hatch of the cramped metal compartment. Over the next hour, the air would be pumped out to produce the rarefied atmosphere experienced at high altitude.

"One thousand feet," Lieutenant Brown said on the intercom from his station outside the chamber.

Air hissed through the hose and into Ruth's lungs, heavy with the taste of rubber. On evacuation flights she would rarely, if ever, fly high enough to need oxygen, but on bombing missions the men stayed on oxygen for long hours. Right then, Jack could be wearing a similar mask, if he was still alive.

"Two thousand feet."

Ruth swallowed to pop her ears, and made a note on her clipboard. Why did she allow herself to care for Jack? May was right. He didn't care for her, not one bit. He was proud and unforgiving. God wanted to remove her shame, but Jack added to it. Her stomach soured, and she wrote so hard her pencil tip snapped.

Burnsey nudged her and held out a pencil. "Here, I always bring a spare."

So sour, but she had to take it to complete her work.

"Three thousand feet."

In her mind, Ruth repeated a passage from Psalm 34: *"I sought the Lord, and he heard me, and delivered me from all my fears. They looked unto him, and were lightened: and their faces were not ashamed."*

God wanted her to be lightened, to glow with his love, free from shame. How could she not love God and trust him, when he treated her, in her vile sin, with such mercy?

✭

May hooked arms with Dottie and Ruth as they walked to the mess for lunch. "My New Year's resolution for 1944 is to find makeup to cover the rims those oxygen masks leave." The rims shone red on May's fair skin, but Dottie's had faded. Ruth didn't care if she had rims or not.

"I resolve to take up smoking," Dottie said. "All the great actresses smoke. They look daring and glamorous."

"Sickly," May said. "Stinky, raspy voiced."

Dottie's hand flew to her throat. "My voice. Oh no. I'll need a new resolution."

Ruth had a ludicrous thought. "You could give tap dancing lessons to us orphans."

Dottie's face lit up. "Wouldn't that be fun? Look. This is a shuffle. This is a ball change." Her black Oxfords kicked up dust on the pathway.

May clutched Ruth's arm. "Oh, what have you done?"

Ruth shook her off and tried to copy Dottie's footwork. "Come on, expand your horizons."

"I'll fall on my face and break my nose." But May tried a shuffle.

"More snap on the shuffle," Dottie said. "That's it. Keep moving. Lunch awaits."

Ruth laughed at her own awkwardness as she shuffled and ball changed down the path.

"Try this—the time step." Dottie's feet flew into a frenzy. "It looks hard, but the components are easy. I'll break it down."

Ruth could hardly speak through her laughter. "Break it way down."

"Stomp, hop, step, shuffle, ball, stomp—you just keep going. Come on, try. Stomp, hop . . ."

Too many steps. Ruth stomped and hopped any old way.

May broke down in giggles, and Dottie spluttered correc-
tions. They rounded the corner of the mess hall, and Ruth
paused mid-stomp.

A man leaned back against the wall of the mess, his head
slumped. He wore a flight jacket, olive drab trousers, and a
pilot's crush cap over black hair. If she didn't know Jack was
an ocean away . . .

"Don't stop now," Dottie said. "You've almost got it,
Ruth."

The man's head snapped up. Jack.

"Oh my goodness," May said.

"Stomp, hop, step . . ." Dottie's voice trailed off.

Ruth struggled to catch her breath, from the dancing and
from the sight of a man she never imagined she'd see again,
a man who treated her like filth. Something flamed in her
chest. "What are you doing here?"

He jerked his thumb over his shoulder. "Furlough. I was
home—for Christmas—home. The railroad strike. I flew—
skip, hop, brought me here. I wanted that. I've got a—yeah,
an hour. C-47—La Guardia."

Ruth had never seen him with stammering speech and
halting gestures.

May marched up to him. "The nerve of you. Haven't you
said enough to her?"

Jack flinched, and then his face twisted. "No, I haven't.
I didn't say one thing I should have, and everything I did
say . . ."

Ruth remembered. He'd beaten in her shame, while Christ
had been beaten for her shame. She pulled her chin high and
set her jaw.

May pointed toward the airfield. "Go catch that plane."

He dragged his gaze to Ruth. "I came to apologize. You
deserve an apology."

"Go catch—"

"No, let him." Ruth's voice came out strong, although her throat was tight, her stomach in a knot, and her hands balled at her sides. She strode past him to the privacy beside the mess. "Over here." How satisfying to hurl his words back at him.

At the back corner of the building, she faced him and steeled herself against his forlorn expression. She would not pity him. Why? He'd shown her no pity.

"I—I came to apologize."

She nodded, determined not to speak.

Jack looked down at a red paper bundle in his hands and pursed his lips. "Everything I said that day came from pride. Pride alone. Because you kissed them, but you wouldn't kiss me. But now I understand why you don't date, why you don't kiss. It makes sense now."

His understanding threatened her defenses, and she clenched her fists to stop the softening in her heart.

"I had a goal with you, and my pride wouldn't let me give up. I tried so hard not to fail with you, but I did a far worse thing—I failed you. When I think of what I said to you, how I left you . . ." His face contorted.

Ruth crossed her arms across her blue wool flight jacket. No. No pity. He'd experienced only a fraction of the pain he'd inflicted.

"I condemned you when I should have shown compassion, compassion for being in a position where you felt you had to do such a thing. You were so young. And then what those rats—and then me. You've been through enough, and then I condemned you."

No, Ruth would not be moved by his words or his emotion.

"What I said was wrong, every word. What's past is past. You truly are a virtuous woman."

Oh yes, he was good and he was smooth, but she knew better.

Jack lifted devastated eyes. "I know nothing can erase what I said that day. I'm not looking for forgiveness. For once I'm doing something for you, not for me. I came only to apologize, to let you know I was wrong and I'm sorry."

How could she reply? Should she tell him in a fierce voice that he didn't deserve forgiveness? Should she throw herself in his arms, have a good cry, and forgive him as God forgave her? Should she scream at him and beat him down as he beat her down?

She opened her mouth, unsure of what would come out. "Go catch your plane."

He blinked, nodded, and turned away.

No, that wasn't what she wanted to say, but she couldn't move or breathe or speak.

Jack set the red parcel on the stoop for the side door. "Your Christmas present. It's not—I can't use it. It's strange, I know. Please read the note." He straightened up and met her eye. "Good-bye, Ruth."

Her mouth was glued shut, and he was gone, and May and Dottie rushed around the corner.

May's eyes stretched wide and frantic. "Ruth! Ruthie, are you okay?"

She nodded, her gaze fixed on Jack's diminishing form. She should run after him, and scream or cry or hit him, but not let him walk away. Anything but that.

"What happened?" May wouldn't be ignored.

"He apologized. He was—he was sincere." And humble. She'd never seen him so humble.

"What's this? A present?" Dottie asked. "Oh, a guilt of-fering. What fun."

Ruth couldn't see Jack anymore. Never again.

"Might as well open it. You can't leave it here." Dottie pressed the package into Ruth's hands.

She couldn't follow Jack. What could she say or do? She sighed and examined the package wrapped in red paper ridged from previous use. She tried to work off the string, but her hands shook, and May had to help her. They unfolded the paper to reveal peacock blue fabric.

Dottie lifted it. With a swoosh, the fabric cascaded almost to the ground. "Oh, isn't it lovely?"

Ruth's mouth hung open, and she reached out and fingered the silk. An evening gown? What on earth was she supposed to do with an evening gown?

"Here's a note." May dusted off a piece of paper.

> Dearest Ruth,
> I can't explain why I'm giving this to you, but once I saw it, I couldn't rest until I bought it. You may burn it, tear it to shreds, give it away, whatever you wish. I'm not even sure about the size. I just had to get it for you.
> With eternal regret and highest regard, Jack

Ruth stared at the gown, the note, the gown again. Why on earth did Jack feel compelled to buy it? She'd gone twenty-four years without a fancy dress, and she hardly needed one now.

The silk caressed her hand, as cool and slippery as water. Jack knew she'd never owned anything this nice. He was trying to fill a hole in her life, Boaz lifting the corner of his robe to cover her.

36

"Can you verify that recall message?"

Recall? Jack glanced to his right. Lt. Col. Louis Thorup, the air executive of the 94th, sat in the copilot's seat, leading not just the group, but the Fourth Combat Bombardment Wing and the whole Third Division. Jack appreciated Castle's vote of confidence, the bold move to let Jack fly the command ship.

Thorup had the faraway look men had on the radio. "I need to verify that recall."

Jack shook his head. A recall message when they were only twenty-five miles from the target? Likely a bogus signal sent by the Germans.

The Nazis would love to call off the 663 bombers bearing down on them. First Division headed for the Fw 190 plant at Oschersleben and the Junkers plant at Halberstadt. The Third Division, with the B-24s of Second Division right behind, aimed for three aircraft plants at Brunswick.

"Weather is worsening," Thorup said to Jack. "They think we can't make a visual attack."

Jack frowned at the clear sky. "Even if it clouds over, we have the PFF planes." The Pathfinder Force bombers of the

482nd Group carried either British H2S radar, or H2X, the improved American version. Two of these planes flew with Fourth Wing.

Thorup sighed. "I know, but Second Division is turning back, and so are the other wings in our division."

"Oh boy."

"If Fourth Wing goes, we go alone and without escort. That's the other reason for the recall. The weather grounded the P-38s. They won't meet us over Brunswick."

If the seats were reversed, what would Jack do? Only moderate flak dirtied the sky, but scores of enemy fighters lined up, ready to strike after the bomb run. If they turned back, they might not locate a target of opportunity in worsening weather, and the day's efforts would be in vain. But if they ignored the recall, they could take heavy losses.

Jack studied the instrument panel. *Lord, help Thorup make the right decision.*

"Fifty-four unescorted B-17s." Thorup's tone said he was considering it.

A sense of lightness rose in Jack's chest despite layers of flight gear. Walt had never had escort over the target, and Jack had only enjoyed it a handful of times. "No escort? When has that ever stopped the Eighth Air Force?"

"A year ago fifty-four planes would have been considered maximum effort." Thorup fiddled with the radio knobs overhead.

"Bombardier to pilot." Lt. Ogden Drake's nasal voice came through the interphone. "We're over Wolfenbüttel. Target coming up."

"Roger. How's the formation, Bob?"

In the command ship, the copilot rode in the tail gunner's position to monitor the formation. "High element of the low squadron is too far out, and the other wings are heading home."

Jack snorted. "Bunch of yellow-bellied, lily-livered—"

Thorup cocked an eyebrow.

Jack chuckled. "They're following a recall order, but we can't verify. Besides, the 94th has never turned back in the face of the enemy, and we're not about to start now."

A whoop rang in his ear. "That's the way to tell 'em," Bob Ecklund said.

When Jack returned to Bury St. Edmunds, he had received a new crew, men with no memories of Schweinfurt. Sure, it would take time to regain respect in his squadron, but his men would get a better version of him now that he was determined to let God run his life.

"Bombardier to pilot. I'm having difficulty locating the target."

Jack frowned and glanced down through the whirring propellers. "Why? No undercast."

"I must have missed a landmark."

Jack winced. The briefing slides showed subtle landmarks leading to the factory where twin-engined Messerschmitt 110s were produced. Charlie would have found it.

"I know where I went wrong. If I had another shot . . ."

Jack and Thorup exchanged a glance. Another shot? A 360-degree turn and a second bomb run under fire?

Jack's stomach contracted. Pride demanded another chance at success, but how many lives would be lost? No. Too much like Schweinfurt.

Or did he have it backward? Was pride telling him to play it safe and protect his reputation at the expense of the mission objective? *Oh Lord, give us wisdom. But I'm glad this isn't my decision to make.*

"Roger." Thorup turned to Jack. "The 447th thinks they've got it."

Jack turned off the AFCE and took control of the ship. He

needed to peel off, either to lead the wing home or to circle for another run after the 447th and the 385th Groups bombed.

"Sir, I'd like another chance," Drake said from down in the nose. "Before I joined up I was a mailman, and I've never failed to make a delivery."

Jack smiled. "Neither rain nor snow nor flak nor Me 109s?"

"Yes, sir. Those bombs are addressed to Herr Goering at Brunswick and must be delivered."

They'd already come through heavy rain on takeoff and assembly, flak over Amsterdam and Hannover, and the fighters would attack whether they bombed or not. "Why are we here anyway?" he whispered.

"To deliver those bombs," Thorup said. "Take us around, Novak."

Jack snapped his gaze to the right. He hadn't meant for that comment to be heard, but Thorup's look told him the decision had already been made. After the command went through to the other planes, Jack put the Fort into a neat turn.

He had a new plane, since *Sunrise Serenade* had been shot down with another crew while he was on furlough. "You know, Drake, I haven't named this bird. How about we call her *Special Delivery*?"

"I'd be honored, sir. The mail must go through."

The 94th Bomb Group did the intricate dance of turning in formation, and Jack adjusted the throttles to compensate for a strong headwind. In the distance, Me 110s approached from nine o'clock, but Jack felt warm inside. Even if he gained a reputation as a dangerous man to fly with, he knew they'd made the right decision.

Strange thing about swallowing pride—it tasted nasty and went down hard, but once digested, a sweet, nourishing strength resulted.

Jack noticed it when he visited the de Groots in Maryland on his way back to England. Boy, was it hard to knock on that door, see those faces, and admit his role in Charlie's death. But they had long since accepted their son's fate and they assured Jack of their forgiveness. They even shared laughter over family pictures and pineapple upside-down cake.

His visit to Bowman Field made him feel even better. No forgiveness, no laughter, no upside-down cake, but that wasn't why he'd gone. His only purpose was to apologize and offer a hand to lift Ruth from the grass. To his relief, she already stood strong.

Rockets exploded outside, fighters dived, and the Fort shook from her own guns, but Jack didn't care. If he died today, he'd die at peace.

★

Jack walked around the B-17. No doubt about it, *Frenesi* was Category E, damaged beyond repair—one wingtip shot off, number two engine out, horizontal stabilizer ripped to shreds, and so many holes she resembled a cheese grater. The destruction of the interphone and oxygen systems had led five crewmen and a photographer to bail out over the continent, while the pilot and copilot wrestled the Fort home with three wounded gunners aboard. Pilot William Cely was sure to earn a Silver Star.

Jack mounted his bicycle and pedaled to HQ in a light rain.

The 94th had lost eight of twenty-five planes, and all but one were damaged, yet the mission's success elevated morale. Ogden Drake had been true to his word, and on the second run he delivered his packages straight into Goering's mailbox.

Jack waved to his men, and sent out words of praise and

appreciation. He passed a small group. One fellow spread a hand wide to mimic a swooping fighter, while the other hand vibrated a bomber's .50 caliber response. "Outnumbered three to one . . . ninety-mph headwind . . . shot that Jerry right out of the sky."

Two gunners walked past Jack. "Me 110s, Fw 190s, Me 109s, Ju 88s. Even took a shot at an Me 210. They hurled everything at us, but you can't stop the Big Square A."

Jack smiled and leaned his bike against the wall at HQ. The building buzzed with men talking, teletypes printing, and phones ringing. Jack breathed in the postmission adrenaline and went to the room where Colonel Castle and the senior officers pored over the strike photos.

"Outstanding," Castle muttered, his eyes pressed to a magnifier over a photo on a table.

"Best I've ever seen." Jeff Babcock wore a smug smile as if his mud memo were responsible.

Jack shoved aside the peevish thought. "Do we have a percentage?"

Thorup glanced up. "We dropped 73 percent within a thousand feet of the MPI and 100 percent within two thousand feet."

Jack whistled. All of the bombs so close to the Main Point of Impact? Unparalleled accuracy.

Castle shifted the magnifier. "Looks as if we hit every single building in the installation. Many appear destroyed."

"Thank goodness," Jack said. "I'd rather not go back."

The men chuckled their agreement.

Castle straightened up. "This is what daylight bombing is supposed to achieve—precise destruction of strategic targets. Go get your dinner, men. You've earned it. We don't have a mission tomorrow, so we'll meet at 0900. Major Novak, I'd like a word with you."

The officers headed out. Babcock gave Jack a sympathetic look, and Jack tamped down his irritation. Why was Babcock convinced Castle wanted a negative word with him?

In fact, Castle smiled. "Thorup told me what a good job you did."

Jack shrugged. "I've been flying all my life."

Castle nodded and glanced down at the photos of craters and smoke. "I can't have reckless officers. We have too many lives in our hands, not to mention two-hundred-thousand-dollar planes paid for by the American people."

Jack felt a twinge in his stomach. Did Castle think he was reckless? "I understand, sir."

Castle lifted his square jaw and looked at Jack. "But a good officer knows when to take risks. Our purpose is not to protect our own lives but to smash Nazi Germany. After Schweinfurt, I was afraid you might become overly cautious, indecisive even, but today you showed the traits of a first-rate officer."

Jack released a deep breath. "Thank you, sir."

The CO nodded to the door. "Now, go get some dinner. It's good to have you back."

"It's good to be back, sir."

37

Chicago

Monday, January 24, 1944

Ruth stepped off the El and pulled her cape against the bitter wind. She coughed at the smell. She'd lived in hospital sterility so long she'd forgotten the smoke from the meatpacking plants, the stink from the stockyards, and the stench of poverty.

She tramped across the platform and down the stairs, vigilant for ice. Then she followed the familiar path through gray slush. Her brothers and sisters lived in different neighborhoods now, away from this slum and its rumors. Ruth didn't have to come here.

On Friday her squadron had graduated from the School of Air Evacuation. Eleanor Roosevelt attended, and Ruth shook her hand—the first lady herself. Then her squadron shipped to Camp Kilmer, New Jersey, for overseas processing. Everyone would get a forty-eight-hour pass to explore New York City, but Ruth took her pass en route and diverted to Chicago for the day.

Ruth attracted stares in her uniform. She passed a group of teenagers on the corner. A black-haired girl laughed, gave one of the boys a playful push, and brushed her body against his. Ruth cast her gaze to the side. That's what she used to be.

An older woman plodded along, her hair dull under a ratty cap, and she raised hard eyes—she was no older than thirty. Ruth inhaled sharply. That's what she would have become.

She picked up the pace past shops, some familiar and some changed. *Thank you, Lord, for getting me out of here.*

Now she knew it was the Lord's doing, not hers. Ma always said God would provide, and he did. How much more would he have provided if she'd trusted him? She'd been too impatient to wait for him, like Sarah giving Abraham her handmaid, like Jacob stealing his father's blessing. God still provided in spite of their sin, in spite of hers, but with long-reaching consequences and broken relationships.

Ruth turned onto her old street. She'd never see Jack again, and their friendship could never be restored, but his apology had worked its clumsy way into her soul and removed another stone of shame.

Her old tenement. Her gaze climbed the soot-stained red bricks three stories up, then two grubby windows to the right. In a way, she wanted to see the two-room apartment, but she didn't want to be appalled by the squalor. She wanted to keep her memory filled with the light of Ma's faith, Pa's humor, and seven laughing, well-loved children.

Would Pa and Ma be proud of her, of how she cared for the children, of the gold flight nurse's wings she wore on her new olive drab dress uniform? She imagined they would, but what would please them most was how she was coming under the Lord's wings.

That window held her. If only she could stay with the happy memories, but that wasn't why she'd come. She ripped her gaze down and away, and set her feet in the dreaded direction.

In the entrance to the alley, she halted, overcome by the reek of garbage. That never figured into her nightmares. She must have been accustomed to it.

One step. Two steps. Brick walls towered over her. Decrepit staircases crowded about her. Nothing had changed. The line there, the lessons there, the rape there. Shouldn't the place be crimson with blood and black with shame?

She took a slow breath to prevent hyperventilation.

Bud Lewis loomed over her, his face red with lust and rage, his breath rancid with beer and sausage. *"Time for the kissing whore to become a full-fledged whore."*

White spots prickled her eyes, but she blew them away. "Lord Jesus, I'm in the valley of the shadow of death, but you are with me. I know you are."

Ruth turned in circles, needing to take it all in. This was her past. Nothing could ever change that, but she would not let it consume her.

Isaiah 54:4 ran through her head. She said it out loud and declared it to her past. "'Fear not; for thou shalt not be ashamed: neither be thou confounded; for thou shalt not be put to shame: for thou shalt forget the shame of thy youth.'"

The shame of her youth screamed at her from every brick, but Jesus silenced it. "Christ died for me. That's all I need to know. Thank you, Lord. Thank you."

She had dreaded this moment for weeks, but God was so powerful. In the very place of her worst sin and deepest pain, his peace billowed through her soul.

★

Ruth stood in front of the house—a real house on a clean Chicago street lined with snow-draped trees. She checked the address again. Yes, this was where Uncle George and Aunt

Gloria lived now. How wonderful for her brother Bert to be raised in such a place. Trees—imagine that.

She drew a deep breath and rang the doorbell. How much had her brothers and sisters changed? She hadn't seen them since her departure for England in December '42.

Bert opened the door. "Hi, Penny," he said in a deep voice. Last year he had been taller than she, but still a boy. Now he was fifteen, and Ruth saw the man he was becoming, tall and handsome with his childhood red hair deepened to auburn.

"Bert, oh my goodness." She ignored his outstretched hand and reached up to hug him.

A blush overpowered his freckles. "Come on in. Chuck, Anne, and Maggie just got out of school, but they'll be here soon." He hung up Ruth's cape and led her into the living room.

"How's school?" she asked. "Are you still enjoying your sophomore year?"

"Oh yeah." He sank into the sofa. "I love biology. Wow, it's so interesting. Uncle George thinks I should be a doctor."

Ruth lowered herself into an upholstered chair. A doctor? Chuck and Anne didn't have an academic bent, but Maggie did. Could she put two of them through college, then medical school for Bert? One look at his bright and gentle face, and she knew she had to. "I can't imagine anyone who'd make a finer physician."

"That's Chuck." Bert sprang for the front door. Only his red ears betrayed his embarrassment.

Ruth stood as the young men approached. Almost eighteen, with brilliant red hair and green eyes, Chuck looked so much like Pa that Ruth's chest hurt.

"Hiya, Penny." Chuck pumped her hand up and down. "Say, look at those wings. Those are something, aren't they? You and Harold have all the fun. What I wouldn't give to be in San Diego with Harold. The stories he tells—boy, oh boy."

Ruth frowned. The stories she heard involved oppressive work and frustration that the Navy kept him stateside. Apparently, he painted a partial picture.

"The Navy recruiter said they'd take me now, but Uncle Nolan says if I don't finish high school, I have to pay you back every cent, so I don't have a choice, but boy, I can't wait to have money of my own." He grinned, oblivious how his statement affected Ruth.

Heaviness settled in her chest. Chuck would spend his entire salary on himself as Harold did, but at least she'd have his portion to divide between Bert, Anne, and Maggie.

"Albert Doherty, what are you thinking, leaving the door cracked in January?" Aunt Pauline entered and shrugged off a dumpy brown coat over a dumpy brown dress.

Bert's ears flamed red. "I—I'm sorry. I thought it was shut."

She lifted her gray-streaked head and sniffed the air. "I'm glad George Doherty has money to burn, unlike the rest of us."

Chuck made a face over his aunt's head, and Ruth gave her a peck on the cheek. "So good to see you, Aunt Pauline."

"Penny."

Ruth peeked around her aunt's matronly form. "Hi, Maggie."

"Hi." Maggie gave her a shy wave.

Ruth gathered her in her arms. The baby girl who once snuggled under her chin now reached that chin. The eleven-year-old wore a beige sweater with shiny elbows over a gray skirt several inches above her knees. Still, she had a glow in her cheeks, burnished brown braids, and new saddle shoes. Money was tight for Uncle Clancy and Aunt Pauline, but Maggie was far from starving.

Aunt Pauline sat in the center of the sofa. "I'm surprised you're here, Penny. I didn't realize you had money to squander on train tickets."

Heat rushed up Ruth's chest. Those tickets cost her a whole month's spending money. Meanwhile, her fellow nurses enjoyed fine dinners and Broadway plays. "It's not squandering money to visit my family for the first time in a year, especially since I don't know when I'll return stateside."

Maggie guided Ruth into a chair and knelt beside her. "Tell me, Penny—"

"Ellen can't come," Aunt Pauline said. "Too busy with the babies. You understand."

"Of course." Ruth hated the strain in her voice. Her oldest sister had barely spoken to her since she found out about the kissing lessons, but at least her aunt didn't know the cause of the estrangement.

"Penny, Penny, tell us. Do you know where you're going?" Maggie lifted anxious eyes. Even as an infant, she'd disliked arguments.

Ruth smiled at her. "We won't find out until we get on the ship. We'll go east—Africa or Italy, maybe England." But she hoped not.

"How exciting." Maggie's eyes shone with Ma's soft light. "I want to be a nurse too. I want to be just like you."

No, she didn't. Ruth glanced away. Bert sat in a wing chair, with Chuck perched on the arm, leaving Aunt Pauline alone on the couch. "How's Uncle Clancy?"

Aunt Pauline clucked her tongue. "He wears himself out in the office, day in, day out, with no appreciation whatsoever. All that hard work for peanuts."

"I like peanuts," Maggie said.

Ruth swallowed a laugh and gave a sympathetic murmur.

Maggie tugged on her uniform sleeve. "Don't you like peanuts? I like them so much better than bacon."

"Bacon?" Ruth smiled at the childish non sequitur.

"Uncle Clancy says he's bringing home big wads of bacon with the war on."

"Maggie!" Aunt Pauline snapped.

"Well, he says that all the time. Though I don't understand, 'cause I can't find any bacon in the icebox, and bacon's rationed."

"You misunderstood," Aunt Pauline said. "Now, don't interrupt."

A chill stole Ruth's breath. Could Aunt Pauline be exaggerating their financial difficulties? She wouldn't lie. She was Ma's sister, and Ma never spoke a false word in her life.

"Who started the party without me?" Anne stood in the doorway with hands on hips—yes, hips. Then she burst into a grin.

Ruth rose to give her a hug, and a big red bow in Anne's dark hair poked Ruth in the nose. "Look how you've grown."

"Thank you." Anne straightened her cardigan, her blue eyes twinkling. She had a figure, and a nice one. Ruth returned to her chair, her throat clamped shut. Thirteen. Anne was thirteen. But she was so young, so innocent.

Across the room, Chuck pulled Bert's hair into "Dagwood" points on each side. Bert elbowed him and sent him sprawling to the floor. Aunt Pauline scolded, but Ruth smiled. The affection between her brothers and sisters had survived despite her painful, necessary decision to split them up.

Anne flounced to the floor and fingered her little sister's skirt. "Oh, Maggie, why are you wearing these old things? What happened to all the darling outfits you got for Christmas?"

Maggie groaned. "Aunt Pauline made me wear this to school. I nearly died of embarrassment."

Ruth stared at the woman on the couch. What was going on?

Aunt Pauline glared at Maggie. "That's enough, young lady. Money is tight. You'll wear what you have and be thankful."

Maggie opened her mouth, then closed it. "Yes, ma'am."

Ruth's stomach twisted and sickened. Maggie had plenty of nice clothes purchased with Ruth's money, but her aunt made her wear outgrown, worn-out things? Why? To deceive Ruth?

"All caught up? I don't want to intrude." Aunt Gloria peeked out of the kitchen.

Ruth set aside her concerns and walked over to give her favorite aunt a hug. "It's your home. You can't intrude."

"Don't you look wonderful? So smart and polished. Your parents would be so proud."

Ruth swallowed hard. She hoped her aunt was correct.

"Come, see the cake before I cut it. Your aunts Peggy and Ruby pitched in some butter and sugar." Aunt Gloria led her into the shiny little kitchen. On the counter sat a cake iced in blue, decorated with yellow wings similar to the ones Ruth wore on her uniform.

A cake for Ruth? The yellow and blue wavered into green. "I'm glad Bert's with you."

"So am I. I wish we could do more." Aunt Gloria glanced to the kitchen door. "Don't worry. Maggie's not too unhappy. She has your spirit. She'll turn out just like you."

Ruth wiped her eyes. Successful at a price? Forgiven but damaged? She wished so much more for her baby sister.

38

Bury St. Edmunds Airfield

Wednesday, February 16, 1944

Jack let out a low whistle. She was naked and she was blindingly beautiful.

The brand-new B-17 stood on the hardstand, flaunting her silver skin.

Some muck-a-muck in Army Air Force HQ decided camouflage paint slowed down the planes, but Jack suspected the calculation involved dollars rather than miles per hour.

"Some rookie's gonna get stuck with her," the man next to him said.

"Poor fella," came a voice from behind. "That'll attract every gun in Nutsy-Land."

Colonel Castle walked over, his forehead furrowed. More of these silver birds were coming, most likely, and the grousing would build—Uncle Sam didn't know what it was like, didn't care, and wanted to kill them all.

Jack had to nip it in the bud. He laid a hand on the chin turret. "Let some rookie crash this beauty? Not if I can help it. I want her for myself."

"What? Are you flak-happy, Novak?"

"I'm the only sane man here." Jack strode down the length of the plane, ducked under the wing, and stroked the cool aluminum skin. "Look at this baby. Fresh off the assembly line, no dings, no patches, and look at these waist windows."

Reluctant murmurs of agreement rose from the crowd.

"Boeing listened to us." He patted the Plexiglas with its square hole for a gun. "They enclosed the windows. Less wind, less frostbite. And they staggered the windows, so the gunners won't bump backsides anymore."

"What'll you name her, Major—*Target Practice*?"

Jack studied the men's laughing faces. "Come on, boys. How many times have you been in a pinch and prayed for a few more mph? I'll already have it."

"You'll need it. Call her *Clay Pigeon*."

"Yeah?" Jack walked back and forth in front of the men. "Do you honestly think camouflage paint protects us? Does it stop bullets? Does it fool the Fw 190s? Come on, olive drab at twenty thousand feet? What are we trying to blend in with?"

"What about the gray paint underneath? The flak worries me, not the fighters."

Jack turned to the gangly lieutenant, who had an awfully good point. "Our contrails give us away most of the time anyway. I'm convinced the natural finish will not make a difference."

The CO stood by the tail of the plane with a trace of a smile. He cocked his head to one side, summoning Jack.

"See you later, boys," Jack said. "Don't get your grubby fingerprints all over my new girl."

He trotted after Castle. His friends insisted he needed a new girl, but Jack knew better. He still needed to drill the lesson of his failure into his thick head.

When Jack caught up, Castle chuckled. "Give them a day,

and they'll be grumbling about how Major Novak got dibs on that swell plane."

"I hope so. I gather she's the first of many."

Castle nodded. "Many changes coming."

Jack strolled by his CO's side. The new year brought lots of change when Gen. Dwight Eisenhower took command of the European Theater of Operations. To command the Eighth Air Force, Eisenhower appointed Gen. Jimmy Doolittle, one of Jack's heroes for his aviation racing records and his leadership of the daring bombing raid on Tokyo in April 1942. Doolittle inherited twenty-eight bomb groups and eleven fighter groups, some with sleek new P-51 Mustangs with the range to cover any target.

Castle cleared his throat. "Some of the changes might affect you."

Jack snapped his gaze to the colonel, then gave an indifferent mumble. Although he was finished with angling and manipulation, his heart picked up a notch. Thorup had served as executive officer for many months and deserved a higher position.

In front of the control tower, Castle stopped and faced Jack. "I have two things to discuss with you. The first concerns your career. I know you put in long years of training to be a pastor."

"Yes, sir." Three very long years.

"However, I'd like you to consider a military career. You're the sort of man we want in the Army Air Force after the war is over."

Jack's tongue dried out and stuck to his teeth.

"Have you considered staying in?"

He pulled his tongue free. "Sometimes I—I think about it."

"At some point soon, you'll have to decide. Certain positions would be better for a man who won't leave after the victory parade."

"That makes sense." His mind whirled. Colonel Castle thought he'd do well in the military, but he could feel Dad's strong stare. "*You'd better do more than think about it, son. You'd better pray about it.*"

Jack swallowed hard. "I'll think about it. I'll pray about it."

"Good. Now, for the second matter. I received a call from High Wycombe. Another evadee from Bury has returned to England."

Jack grinned. Nothing like returning evadees to boost morale.

"I need you to head down to identify the man—standard policy to make sure German spies don't creep in."

Jack's grin broadened. "From my squadron?"

"Your crew."

"My crew?" His smile drifted back down. "Impossible."

"The man claims to be Capt. Charles de Groot."

39

Prestwick Air Base, Scotland

Thursday, February 24, 1944

Ruth fastened a strap across her mock patient's chest to secure him for unloading. "There you go, Private. Thank you for pretending to fly with us."

The supply clerk grinned. "A nurse like you makes a fella want to get hurt."

She smiled, although she'd heard similar comments on countless occasions. "Don't do anything rash. Wouldn't Hitler love to see all our men in the hospital?" She placed her foot in a stirrup to climb up and check the man in the top tier.

Brisk, salty Scottish air billowed through the cargo door of the C-54. While nurses were dying, pinned down on the beach at Anzio in Italy, Ruth ran drills, drills, drills. After the 815th MAETS arrived in southern England, Ruth's flight was sent on Temporary Duty to Prestwick to help the 811th begin trans-Atlantic evacuation. However, they were grounded by bickering brass. Gen. David Grant, the Air Surgeon, pressed for air evacuation, but Gen. Paul Hawley, who ran the U.S. Army hospitals in Britain, wanted none of it. Meanwhile, the hospitals teemed with men who needed long convalescence or could never return to duty.

"Watch his head, boys." Sergeant Burns directed two men with a litter toward the door.

When Ruth moved her foot to a lower stirrup, someone fondled her bottom. She whipped around—Burnsey. "Hey!" She kicked at him, slipped, clipped her head on the top litter, and collapsed over the supply clerk.

He braced her shoulders. "What a nice surprise."

Ruth groped with her toe for the stirrup. "Sergeant Burns, how dare—"

"When a girl's this pretty, she doesn't have to be graceful." He set his hands on her waist.

"Ain't that the truth?" the clerk said. "You can trip over me any time, doll."

Ruth struggled to climb down without Burnsey's help. She knew where his hands would go. Just helping, he'd say. Feet on the floor, she shook him off. "Sergeant—"

"Make it fast." He strode down the aisle to the door. "We're being timed."

The jerk, always making it her fault. Ruth stamped her foot and loosened the clamp on the next litter. She had to work faster than ever, and by the time the last litter was out, she was breathing hard. On the tarmac, she circulated among the pretend patients, unfastened straps, and folded blankets.

Burnsey stood on the steps to the cargo door and stretched his hands wide over the men. "'Arise, and take up thy bed, and walk.'"

The men chuckled and got to their feet. Ruth carried a pile of blankets to a truck parked by the C-54. The nerve of him, quoting Jesus Christ.

Footsteps pounded behind her. "Well, gorgeous, impressed by the Bible verse?"

"I'd be impressed if you obeyed the Bible." She plopped the blankets in the back of the truck.

Burnsey draped his arm over the tailgate. "Anything to win you over."

She sent him an acidic glare. "Start by watching where you put your hands."

"My pleasure." His gray-green eyes glinted. "I'll watch where I put my hands—very closely."

Her chest contracted in a crush of terror, but frustration battled to the top. She'd tried direct orders, coldness, laughing him off, and reporting to the chief, but Burnsey grew bolder every day.

"How was their time?"

Ruth whipped around. Lieutenant Shepard addressed a sergeant with a stopwatch.

"Thirteen minutes and eight seconds." Even slower than usual.

Burnsey trotted up to the chief nurse and saluted. "In our defense, ma'am, we made a great comeback. Lieutenant Doherty had a little fall, but we pulled together after that."

Lieutenant Shepard directed motherly disappointment at her, and Ruth slammed her tongue against the roof of her mouth so she could sift her words. "Lieutenant Shepard, Sergeant—"

"No need to thank me." Burnsey patted her on the back. "We're a team."

"You should be grateful to have such a good partner, Lieutenant. Now, come with me." The chief nurse turned and walked away.

Ruth glanced around at the stretchers and blankets. Burnsey would have to clean up, and boy, would she hear about it. She followed Lieutenant Shepard to the next C-54.

"Lieutenant Jensen?" the chief called. "Please come with me, dear."

May exchanged words with her tech and joined Ruth about twenty feet behind the chief. "What's up?"

"I have no idea."

"How was your drill?"

A groan rumbled out. "Over thirteen minutes. Burns made me fall."

"He made you fall?"

"He grabbed—he grabbed my bottom."

"Oh, Ruth, maybe it was an accident."

"An accident? His hand, my bottom." She cupped her hand to demonstrate.

May tucked a curl behind her ear and frowned. "Did you tell Lieutenant Shepard?"

"Not yet."

"Good."

"Good?" Ruth stared at May. "What on earth do you mean?"

May's mouth squirmed. "I'm—well, I'm concerned. You need to be careful. People are talking."

"People are talking because Burnsey's a snake. Everything he says has a double meaning, and he twists things—"

"Ruth." Her brow creased. "I think your dislike for him is affecting your work."

How could she say such a thing? "My dislike? You think my—my reaction is the problem? No, it's his actions."

May shifted her feet, glanced over Ruth's shoulder, then returned her gaze. "I'm afraid—well, I know what horrible things you've been through. You know—you have to know it affects how you relate to men. Your judgment of Burnsey may be based on your past, not on reality."

"Is that right, Freud? I'm insane, am I?"

"No." May pressed her fingertips together and set them against her lips. "No, you're not insane. You're just—well, you're still healing."

Like a slap to the face, but was it the slap of betrayal or the slap of truth?

"Ladies? Come with me, please." Lieutenant Shepard inclined her head.

Ruth moved her feet in a mechanical way after the chief. May had the annoying ability to always be right, but was she right about this? Yes, her past affected how she dealt with men, but was that why she saw lechery in Burnsey when everyone else saw friendliness?

She glanced over the airfield, the major trans-Atlantic hub, where new bombers and fighters and crews arrived from the U.S., along with mail and cargo. Her stomach rose and fell like the dunes that separated the airfield from the Firth of Clyde. *Lord, is May right? You know what Burnsey really means. If I'm wrong, please show me, but if I'm right, please help me.*

Lieutenant Shepard led them into the Nissen hut that served as HQ for the evacuation squadrons. When she reached her office, she smiled at May. "I like many things about flight nursing—leaving the physicians on the ground, making the decisions in flight, and wearing trousers on the job. Today I found a new benefit. I've seen nurses sweat out missions men flew, but today I watched men sweat out a mission nurses flew, or pretended to fly."

Ruth and May exchanged a puzzled glance.

Lieutenant Shepard opened the door. In a chair by the window, silhouetted against the afternoon sunlight, sat a man. He stood slowly, a skinny man in an Army officer's uniform, walking with a limp, and as he approached, the light receded and his features came into focus.

"Hello, May," he said in a familiar bass.

Ruth gasped. As always, May had been right all along.

May gripped Ruth's arm. "No, it can't—it can't be. Charlie?"

The face was thinner and paler, but the kind eyes and smile hadn't changed. "It's me."

May's fingers dug into Ruth's flesh. "I thought—I thought—oh, Charlie, I'm so sorry."

His smile sagged, but he hiked it back into place. "It's okay. You thought I was dead."

Oh no, he thought she'd found someone else. Ruth pried May's fingers off her arm. "What are you waiting for, honey? Go to him."

May closed the gap with halting steps, and she pressed shaky hands to his cheeks. "I'm sorry. I'm so sorry I gave up on you. I never should have given up."

"It's okay. I understand."

"I'm glad God never gave up on you." She flung her arms around his neck and burrowed kisses into his cheek.

Over her shoulder, Charlie's eyes widened. "You still love me?"

"Of course. Of course."

He stumbled under her kisses, and a man dashed from the corner to support him. "Careful, May. He's still weak. He's had a rugged run of it."

Oh goodness, it was Jack. Ruth's heart seized, and she grasped the doorjamb.

Charlie laughed. "Back off, Skipper. For four months I dreamed of this moment."

Jack guided them toward the window. "At least take this moment to a chair."

Charlie eased himself down, May sat on his lap, and they kissed and murmured their love to each other.

Airy bubbles lifted Ruth's chest, but Jack's presence stirred them into a frenzy. She glanced down the corridor. Charlie and May needed privacy, and she needed to get away.

"Come here, Ruth." Charlie grinned at her, one arm stretched out.

Her escape would have to wait. Ruth smiled and crossed the room, conscious of Jack in the back corner of the room, and she hugged Charlie. "I can't believe it. I'm so glad you're alive."

"Isn't this wonderful?" May said.

Ruth straightened up and squeezed May's hand, overcome by the joy on the face of the person who deserved it most.

"Look at you two. Flight nurses." Charlie played with May's curls. "And look at your hair, Shirley Temple."

"I'm also learning to tap dance." She put one finger under his drooping chin. "But don't you dare talk about me. Last I heard you were in a flat spin. Jack said it was impossible to get out."

"I've never been so glad to be wrong in my life," Jack said.

"What happened?"

Charlie bobbed his head from side to side. "Ah, I'm no good at telling stories. Jack, you've heard it a hundred times. You tell it."

"Sorry, buddy. It's your story."

Ruth shot him a glance. It wasn't like Jack Novak to shun the limelight. He stood against the wall with a smile aimed at Charlie, but then his gaze flicked to Ruth. His smile sputtered, his shoulders slumped, and he looked down.

The regret in his eyes turned her insides to mush. She knew shame and so did he, but she knew forgiveness. He should too.

"Oh, all right," Charlie said. "Pull up a chair, Ruth."

She couldn't get away, but she did want to hear his story after all. She rotated the chair in front of Lieutenant Shepard's desk, a chair she knew too well, and faced Charlie.

"Flat spin," May said. "Impossible to get out."

"Pretty much. You can't pull away from the fuselage, but with great effort, you can slide along it." Charlie frowned. "The copilot was injured, and I headed back to the cockpit to help Silverberg. A shell hit the nose, almost blew away the Plexiglas, and I went back to investigate. The navigator was—he was killed. The next shell hit the tail, sent us into a spin. I didn't think I could make it out. The cloud level was six, seven thousand feet, and by the time I got to the hole in the nose, we were in pea soup. Then it sure took some wriggling to get out. Yanked that rip cord as soon as I got clear. We mustn't have been high, because I wasn't in my chute long. Never saw the ground in the fog. Landed hard and broke my leg."

"Oh, Charlie!" May sprang from his lap.

He pulled her back down. "Other leg."

Ruth leaned forward on her knees. "How on earth did you evade with a broken leg?"

Charlie chuckled. "Believe me, that wasn't my plan, but it was my patriotic duty to try. The Lord plopped me ten feet from a haystack, so I dragged myself and my chute inside. Never been so itchy in my life. At nightfall I worked my way to the farmhouse. Turns out the family had helped several Allied airmen evade. Of course, when they saw my condition, they wanted to turn me in."

May stroked his hair. "Thank goodness you talked them out of it."

Charlie laughed and squeezed her waist. "I didn't. I told them it was a wise idea. If they turned me in, the Nazis would think they were loyal, which would make it easier to help other evadees. Well, they just stared at me. Guess my dad taught me passable Dutch. By sunrise, we had it worked out. I became their simpleton cousin from town, who fell down a ladder and broke his leg."

"Simpleton?" May asked with a laugh.

"Explained my funny accent and limited vocabulary. Not a hard part for me to play, huh, Skipper?"

Jack, however, only let out a low chuckle.

Ruth resisted the urge to glance his way, which would increase their mutual discomfort.

"They got me clothes and papers, called in a doctor to set my leg, gave me some simpleton chores, and let me heal for two months. Those people risked their lives for me, gave up food for me, and they don't get enough as is. The Nazis haul away all the food from Holland's farms to the Fatherland. The Germans get fat, and the Dutch starve."

"Are they okay?" May asked. "Did they get caught?"

"Not that I know. They sent me off with the Resistance in December. Traveled mostly at night, but sometimes on the train with the Gestapo. The hardest part was hiking over the Pyrenees into Spain in the snow. I almost gave up, but you kept me going, May."

"Me?" She sat up straight in his lap. "Not me. The Lord."

"Yes, he strengthened me, but you motivated me. God would always be with me, but if I wanted to see you anytime soon, I had to plow forward."

"Oh, darling." May leaned her forehead against Charlie's, and her cheeks glistened.

Ruth sighed. They deserved this tender reunion, and now they deserved some privacy. One deep breath, and she stood to face Jack. "Why don't we give them some time alone?"

His eyebrows jumped, but then he motioned for her to

lead. She left the office, and as soon as they stepped out into the cool air and the door shut behind them, Jack's footsteps halted. He'd given her the opportunity to return to quarters—tempting, but not what she needed to do.

Ruth turned and gave Jack her best attempt at a smile. "I can't believe Charlie's back. How amazing."

Jack's eyebrows leaped again. He blinked. "Yeah."

"I'm so happy for him and for May."

"Me too." He huffed and looked away. "Listen, I'm sorry. I shouldn't be here. I know this is difficult for you, but Charlie's not up to full strength, and the doc insisted someone had to come with him, and Charlie insisted it had to be me."

Ruth regarded his stiff posture and pained expression. The poor man had punished himself for months. He shouldn't have to suffer eight years as she had. The last residue of her anger melted away. "I'm glad you came. I need to tell you I forgive you."

One more shock and Jack's eyebrows would fly from his head. "Huh?"

"I forgive you," she said. "Besides, I can understand why you were so angry with me. I can imagine how shocked, how hurt—"

"No." He locked eyes with her. "Don't justify what I did. It was wrong. Wrong and cruel. What you did—how was it any different than a kissing booth at the county fair? And you were young. You wanted to take care of—"

"Don't justify what I did either. It was also wrong." She lifted her chin in challenge. "I didn't trust God to provide for my family, and I took advantage of those boys. Wrong."

For a long time they stared each other down. She absorbed his remorse and mercy and reflected it back to him.

"Forgiveness doesn't require approval," she said. "God never approves of sin, but he still forgives us."

Jack nodded without breaking his gaze. "True."

Ruth glanced at the Nissen hut. Charlie and May would be a while. "Would you like to go for a walk?"

"A walk? I—I'd like that, but you—just because you forgave me doesn't mean you have to spend time with me."

She kept her gaze on the office window. "What if I want to? I missed you, you goon."

A laugh tumbled from his mouth. "Goon? You're the only one who insults me as well as my brothers do."

Ruth turned back, which was a mistake. She'd forgotten how disturbingly gorgeous his grin was.

"If you're willing to put up with me," he said, "why don't you show me the town?"

"All right." She indicated the way. The sky spread pale blue above them, striped with white contrails. Ruth folded her arms to combat the cold penetrating the gray blue wool of her jacket. Trousers were warmer than stockings, but she still felt uncomfortable wearing them into town.

After a few minutes of awkward silence, Jack asked about the flight nursing program. At first Ruth related the academic subjects, drills, and training. As she relaxed, she told him about Dottie and Sergeant Sadistic and Burnsey, but only how the technician slowed her down.

They reached the edge of town, and Jack talked of his trip home, his failures, and his faults. He had changed. They both had. Ruth couldn't decide if she had renewed an old acquaintance or made a new one.

She stopped at the intersection where Monkton Street became Main Street and showed Jack the Prestwick Town Hall with its Gothic stone spire, the ancient Mercat Cross, and the Boydfield Gardens across the street. Jack wanted to see the beach, so Ruth led him down Station Road.

At the Esplanade along the shore, they stood on the grass

and gazed across the sand to the Firth of Clyde and beyond to the Isle of Arran, the "Sleeping Giant." Three children in thick creamy wool sweaters played tag with the waves while their mother scolded them not to get wet. A group of teenagers jostled one another and tried to push a red-haired boy into the icy bay. He broke free and grabbed one of the girls as a laughing, screaming hostage.

"I never told you why I prefer sky to sea." Below Jack's mustache, his lips pressed into a thin line.

"Makes sense for a pilot."

He shook his head once, his gaze fixed on the ocean. "When I was fourteen, I tried to swim across the San Joaquin River to show off for the girls. I was certain I could do it. I couldn't. I almost drowned."

"Oh my."

"I haven't swum since."

The sea breeze blew hair in Ruth's face, and she pushed it back to see Jack as he was, imperfect and wounded. "That's why you didn't want to go on the boat in London."

He turned to her, his eyes a blend of the blue sky above and the gray sea beyond. "That's why I made the decision over Schweinfurt."

Her breath caught halfway in. "I don't understand."

"I plotted a longer route to avoid the Rhine Delta and the Zuider Zee, because I'd rather crash in flames than drown."

"Oh, Jack."

"Twenty-six men died, thirteen are POWs, and Charlie—you heard what he went through—because of my fear and pride."

"I'm sure—I know Charlie's forgiven you."

"I haven't told him yet."

"He'll understand." To break the intensity of his gaze, Ruth glanced down. Once again her hand was wrapped around her watch. "I never told you how I got the scar."

"On your wrist?"

She nodded and rubbed the leather. "For my twelfth birthday my parents gave me a watch, when Pa still had his job. I loved that watch. I also—I used it to time the lessons." Shame rushed like bile up her throat. She swallowed it and ventured a glance at Jack.

His face went limp, and his eyes grew hazy. "Oh boy. If I'd known, I never would have bought—"

"No, I'm glad you did. You—you filled a hole, something those men took from me."

"What? They stole your watch? After what they did to you?"

"No, they broke it. That's—that's how I got the scar."

"Ruth." His eyes slipped shut. His arms were folded, and he kneaded his upper arms with his fingers.

Four months ago he would have taken her in his arms, and to her alarm, that's where she wanted to be.

Jack's eyes flew open, his jaw set. "Please give me another chance."

Ruth edged back. Another chance? What was he thinking?

"I promised never to leave you alone, and then I left in the worst possible way. And I promised I wouldn't kiss you, and I never even meant it." He let out an angry laugh. "I was so full of myself. I thought you'd beg me for a kiss. What a crock." He whipped his gaze to the ocean.

Ruth could still feel his embrace and his breath on her neck. She wrapped her arms around her middle. "It's all right. You—you cared for me, and you didn't know."

"Now I know." He shook his hand at the sea. "It's like—a kiss for you is like a dunk in the ocean for me. I understand now. I do."

"I know you do," she whispered.

Jack stepped closer, his face earnest. "Do you see? I could never do that to you again. Never."

Ruth stared up at him, struck again by his power and his security. She knew what she had to say, but it took an extreme act of will to open her mouth. "I trust you."

His eyes brimmed. "You are the most amazing woman I've ever known, Penelope Ruth Doherty."

Her heart jumped and stalled. He'd never called her by her full name before. He accepted her, all of her, past and present.

40

Bury St. Edmunds Airfield
Monday, March 6, 1944

Flashbulbs popped, movie cameras whirred, and reporters jostled for position beside Jack's plane. "So, Major, how's Berlin?"

Jack shrugged. "I'm ashamed to say, but we left it in worse condition than we found it."

That got a laugh. More cameras snapped. "The first big strike on the German capital. How's that—"

"The first big *American* strike. The RAF has been hitting Berlin since the Blitz. However, they haven't bombed during the day in over a year." He held up his gloved hand. "But now Hitler will get no rest from Allied bombs, day or night."

The reporters scribbled, flipped pages, and nodded.

The last week in February, the Eighth pummeled German aircraft factories. "Big Week" was now followed by a visit to the "Big B." Air superiority had once seemed an elusive dream, but now Jack smelled it. Soon they'd grasp it and never let go.

With rapid speech and staccato laughter, Jack's crew shed harnesses and life vests. He, too, felt as if he'd downed six cups of coffee. What a historic mission. Too bad Charlie missed it, but he was done with combat and on assignment with the Pathfinder Squadron at Alconbury. Knowing Charlie, he would have sung from the Spike Jones hit, "Der Fuehrer's Face."

For Charlie's sake, Jack grinned at the reporters. "'Ven Herr Goering says, "Dey'll never bomb dis place," we "Heil! Heil!" right in Herr Goering's face.' Insert your own raspberries," he said about the verbal salute after each "Heil!"

He decided to leave them laughing. "If you'll excuse me, gentlemen, I have a pile of forms waiting for me."

From under the canvas canopy of a GMC truck, he peered at his plane. *Special Delivery* had been passed to a rookie, and Jack named his new ship *Silver Salvo*. Some prankster changed the lettering to read *Silver Salvage*, but Jack repainted it. As he liked to point out, *Silver* had no more holes than the camouflaged planes.

The light snow that had fluttered around the Forts on takeoff now squished under the truck tires on the way to interrogation. The men piled out, picked up coffee and donuts at the Red Cross counter, and entered the briefing room.

Joe Winchell waved Jack's crew over to his table. "Hiya, fellas. How was the mission?" He sent the bottle of scotch past Jack.

"Never been so disappointed." Fred Garrett, the right waist gunner, poured a shot of whiskey. "Came back with our gun barrels still taped. Not one bullet fired."

Winchell made a note on his form. "Did you see any enemy aircraft?"

"Only from a distance." Bob Ecklund, the copilot, warmed his square hands on his coffee cup. "The Little Friends kept them away. We saw some dogfights."

Jack chewed on his donut, and bits plunked into his empty stomach. Flight rations didn't substitute for a full lunch.

"What a difference an escort makes," Oggie Drake said in his nasal voice.

"Dead right," Jack said. On this mission 801 fighters accompanied 750 bombers. After escort duty, the fighters hit the deck and strafed airfields. The new procedure made the bomber boys worry the fighter jockeys would abandon them to seek ace status, but Jack agreed with General Doolittle's order—to destroy the Luftwaffe in the air, on the ground, and in the factory.

The crew related every detail of the mission—the heavy flak, the inability to bomb the primary target of the Bosch Electrical Equipment factory, the dropping of *Silver*'s salvo on the city center, and the loss of the command ship with Brig. Gen. Russ Wilson, CO of the Fourth Combat Bombardment Wing.

After Winchell gathered his data, Jack and his crew went to the equipment shed, turned in flight gear, and retrieved personal items. On the walk to the mess, Jack lagged behind to review letters he had received the day before.

Ruth's letter came first. She wrote him frequently and deeply. Jack savored her forgiveness and the unwarranted second chance, but where was this going? Physical intimacy was impossible, but did that rule out a future together? All he knew was a visceral urge to love her, protect her, and provide for her.

Yesterday's letter heightened that urge. Jack scanned her strong, tiny script. Ruth suspected her Aunt Pauline was taking advantage of her, and Jack didn't doubt it. Despite Ruth's sacrifices, this hag swung the ax of the orphanage and demanded more, more, more.

The next section of the letter made his blood boil. He

couldn't punch out Aunt Pauline, but his fist itched for Burns's chin. In the hospital Ruth had brushed off propositions unfazed, but this fellow fazed her. She described his harassment in cautious terms, but behind her self-doubt, Jack saw fear.

"Hi there, Major Novak."

Jack glanced behind him. Lieutenant Polansky, his newest pilot, approached with an officer he didn't know. "Hi, Polansky. Great job today. You kept her in tight formation."

"Thanks, Major." The kid's round face broke into a grin, and Jack had an urge to give him a lollipop.

The two men passed Jack up on their way to the mess. "Your squadron commander?"

"Yeah," Polansky said, his voice low but not low enough. "There's a born leader. The right man in the right job."

Was it prideful to glean satisfaction from those words? Surely it wasn't wrong to love your job and want to do it well.

Jack fanned out three more letters, one addressed by Dad's typewriter, one in Ray's script, and one in Walt's jagged capitals.

Walt encouraged him to stay in the military, not a surprise. When Walt had decided to become an engineer, he had to stand up to Dad. The rebel supported another rebellion, but was that what Jack needed to hear?

On the other hand, Ray's letter stunned him. Jack opened it again.

> I've been thinking about your career dilemma.
> I pray God will make his will clear, and I'll
> support whatever choice you make. Remember,
> the pulpit is only one place to serve the Lord.
> You can also serve him on your base, where you

interact with men who would never set foot in church.

Please pardon my bluntness, but were you called to be a pastor? I've never known you to struggle, not in high school or at Cal or in the Army Air Force. However, in seminary it seemed as if you forced yourself to fit and to succeed. I wonder, if you were not the namesake and image of a gifted and strong-willed pastor, whether you would have pursued the ministry.

Jack frowned and folded the letter. Dad thought Jack was meant to be a pastor, but Ray didn't, and both men loved the ministry.

Then the last letter. Dad encouraged his prayer and obedience and insisted Jack's desire for adventure would fade over time.

Jack stopped under a tree. Crews sauntered into the mess hall for a first-class combat meal, clapping each other on the back, joking, and reliving the mission. Jack relished the smell of steak, snow, aviation fuel, and something better and deeper—the smell of fear faced and overcome, of competence discovered, of camaraderie developed—the excitement Dad thought he'd outgrow.

Would he?

When the war ended, would he suddenly have a passion for the ministry? Would he be ready to leave the vigor of military life?

Jack tucked the letters in his flight jacket and headed for the mess. He was twenty-nine years old. He doubted he would change that much.

41

Friday, March 10, 1944

Ruth inserted a glass straw into Lieutenant Halperin's mouth. He murmured his thanks and drank chicken broth from the Thermos, not much of a lunch, but it had to do for the ten patients confined to litters. Up front, Sergeant Burns distributed sandwiches to twenty-two ambulatory patients in folding metal bucket seats.

"Nurse?" In the top litter, Lieutenant Grodzicki leaned over the edge, and a sheet of black hair flopped over his forehead. "I need a bedpan."

Ruth winced. "We'll land at Meeks in an hour. Can you wait?"

"I suppose so."

She sighed. The first evacuation flight was bound to have glitches, but this was a monster of a glitch—no bedpans or urinals in the seventy-five-pound medical chest. Did they expect the patients to hold it for fifteen hours from Prestwick to New York? At least they were stopping at Meeks Field in Iceland and at Harmon Field in Stephenville, Newfoundland.

Lieutenant Halperin nudged the straw out of his mouth. "Thank you, ma'am."

"Delicious?"

His wide-set brown eyes twitched. "I'm thankful for what the good Lord gave me."

"But . . . ?"

He squirmed. "Well, it tasted odd, ma'am, and it had stuff in it."

"Stuff?" Ruth angled the jug toward the window and peered inside. Flakes floated in the bouillon, but what were they? She twisted the Thermos. A crack ran up the inside.

"Oh boy." The altitude and temperature must have cracked the lining and leaked insulation into the soup. The second glitch. In the rear of the C-54, Ruth inspected the empty containers and found cracks in half of them.

"Nurse?" Lieutenant Grodzicki called down the aisle. "I can't wait."

"An hour. You can wait."

"You said an hour ten minutes ago. I can't wait."

The other men made suggestions, all of them crude. Ruth had to improvise, but how? Her gaze fell on the Thermos jugs, and she smiled. Why not?

She picked one up and returned to Lieutenant Grodzicki. "Use this."

His eyes flew open, and then he drew back, his lip curled.

Ruth laughed. "It's all right. We have to throw it away. The lining leaks."

"Never in all my livelong days." He shook his head and pulled the Thermos under his heavy pile of blankets.

Ruth retrieved the flight manifest, then put on her headset and plugged it into the wall jack at the rear of the plane. "Flight nurse to navigator, requesting altitude and temperature."

"Navigator to flight nurse. Altitude 7,100 feet, temperature minus twenty."

Ruth logged the information, thankful for her fleece-lined leather flight suit. The cabin heater only raised the temperature to a balmy zero degrees.

She ducked down and gazed out the rearmost window. Before her, the propellers of the two right engines left circular smudges on the clear sky. Below, the ocean curved, its surface nubbly like the skin of an orange. The sound of conversation and the drone of engines faded as she took in the expanse of blue.

Finally, flight. The brass had decided to send home men who needed at least 120 days of convalescence, a sign the big invasion was imminent. They were emptying hospital beds to make room for casualties.

With flight came flight pay, which would silence Aunt Pauline and delay a confrontation about how she had deceived Ruth. Shame had led Ruth to carry the whole burden for her family, and it had blinded her to her aunt's lies. But now she saw clearly. While stateside wages rose, prices were controlled—and Uncle Clancy and Aunt Pauline prospered. Regardless, as Maggie's legal guardians, they required cautious handling.

"What's up, gorgeous?" Hands snaked around her waist from behind.

Ruth jumped and whipped around. "Don't touch me."

Burnsey held up his hands in surrender. "Need help with vitals?"

"Of course. It's your job."

He stepped closer and backed her against the chill aluminum. "Why don't you start with me? Whenever you're near, my heart rate goes up."

Ruth swallowed a nasty taste in her mouth and shouldered past him. "Whenever you're near, my blood pressure goes up."

He laughed. "I love a girl with spunk."

Her pulse throbbed against the collar of her jacket. Everything she did encouraged him. He took silence as acceptance, comments as banter, and insults as spunk.

Burnsey loved spunk. Jack loved fire. Both men were handsome, charming, and persistent, yet with Jack she felt safe, while with Burnsey she felt threatened.

Ruth used a stirrup to reach the top litter. She smiled at her patient and checked his Emergency Medical Tag, which noted the loss of both legs below the knee when his P-47 crashed on takeoff. "Lt. John Grodzicki," she said to Burnsey to check on the flight manifest.

"What do I do with this?" The patient raised the edge of his blanket to reveal the Thermos.

"I'll take it." She handed it down to Burnsey. "Please put this in the back. Careful, it's almost full."

He peered inside. "You didn't want your broth? Say, anyone still hungry?"

"No!" Ruth flung up one hand, and Lieutenant Grodzicki howled with laughter.

Ruth laughed too. "That's not broth. It's—we don't have a bedpan. The Thermos—the lining cracked. Most of them did. They're ruined anyway. I figured . . ."

Burnsey did a double take and lifted a grin. "Aren't you a clever little girl?"

Wasn't he a condescending little boy? When Ruth's patient stopped laughing, she put a thermometer in his mouth and wrapped her fingers around his wrist to time his pulse.

Jack was right that she needed a watch in this job. He wrote every day, sometimes only a few scrawled lines after a mission, and sometimes pages. All his letters revealed a humbler man, no less able, but learning his own strength wasn't enough, nor was it meant to be. Every day she found more in him to enjoy, to admire . . . to love?

No, she couldn't let that happen. There was no happily ever after. She was forgiven but damaged. And Jack understood. Never again would he hold her or kiss her or love her, which filled her with sad relief. Yet she closed her eyes. *Lord, I wish you would make me normal.*

"Nursh?"

Ruth's eyes popped open. Lieutenant Grodzicki grimaced and twisted his wrist in her grip. She loosened her hold. "I'm sorry. Heart rate—um, 72." She plucked out the thermometer and rolled it until the ribbon of mercury appeared. "Temperature 98.5."

"Check," Burnsey said.

Ruth folded back the blankets to check the bandages around his stumps. "No signs of bleeding or infection. Any pain, Lieutenant?"

"Yeah, it's coming back something fierce."

"Sergeant Burns, when was his last shot of morphine?"

"Let's see, at 0500. Over five hours ago."

Ruth tucked the blankets around the lieutenant. "I'd say it's time for another dose. Sergeant Burns, would you draw up a quarter grain please?"

Ruth lowered herself to the floor so she could check on Lieutenant Halperin. She logged his vitals on the manifest and checked the casts on both arms.

Burnsey returned and wagged a syringe in front of his chest. "I have to load cargo from my uncle when we land at La Guardia, but then I'm free. How would you like a fancy dinner in New York?"

She held out her hand for the syringe. "I'd rather starve."

Something unsettling flickered in his eyes. "Too bad."

Glass shattered and tinkled on the metal floor. Ruth glanced down to shards of glass, a tiny puddle of liquid, a needle, and a plunger. She gaped at Burnsey.

One corner of his mouth lifted. "Too bad you dropped it."

"Me?"

"I'll draw up another syringe."

"Don't you dare." She marched to the rear of the plane. "Clean up your mess, Sergeant. I'll get the med."

However, when she reached the medical chest, her hands shook so hard she couldn't insert the needle through the rubber stopper. The man was dangerous. Why wouldn't anyone believe her?

★

Ruth stepped out of the bathroom at Meeks Field. She'd have to avoid fluids to make it to Newfoundland. She crossed the airfield with its fine layer of snow. Never had she dreamed of being in Iceland.

May jogged to catch up. "How was the first leg?"

Ruth smiled at the glow that hadn't left May's face since Charlie's return. "It would have been better if we had bedpans."

"I know. Can you believe it?"

"No, and did your Thermoses leak?"

"Leak?"

"You'd better check. One of my patients complained about a funny taste, and sure enough, the lining was cracked."

May's pale eyebrows bunched up. "The men griped, but I attributed it to Army food. I'll check."

"At least it solved the bedpan problem."

May looked puzzled. Then she clapped her hand over her mouth and laughed.

Ruth hooked her arm through May's. "Any problems on your flight?"

"None. And Lieutenant Shepard is rounding up bedpans. I'm glad she came along."

"Me too. I need to talk to her."

"What about?" May's voice sounded strained.

Ruth paused. After all May's hardships, she deserved to enjoy this idyllic time unblemished by worry for Ruth. May couldn't help but hear the nurses side with Burnsey and snipe about Ruth, but must she hear Ruth's complaints as well?

"I—I want to tell her about the Thermoses." With that lie, a wall slammed between them. Ruth almost gasped from the pain, but it was a selfish pain. May needed peace and protection more than Ruth needed a confidante.

"Are you okay, Ruthie?"

She turned away and scanned the airfield. By a tanker truck refueling a C-54, Lieutenant Shepard stood with Sergeant Burns. "I need to—I'll see you later." She headed across the tarmac, and with each step separation ripped at her.

The chief and the tech had their backs to Ruth. Burnsey held up a Thermos for inspection. "See? After I discovered they were cracked, I realized they were good for nothing— except as urinals."

Lieutenant Shepard laughed and patted his arm. "How resourceful of you. That's the kind of independent thinking we want on our evac teams."

Ruth stopped. Her jaw flopped open. Never had she expected accolades, but how despicable of Burnsey to steal credit. Of course, if Lieutenant Shepard knew it was Ruth's idea, she'd proclaim it unhygienic and a misuse of government resources.

The chief leaned closer. "Any problems with Lieutenant Doherty?"

Ruth stood stock still.

Burnsey shifted his weight from one foot to the other. "I hate to get her in trouble. She really is a good nurse. You should see her—"

"Sergeant, you know I rely on your assessment of her."

"Well, it's nothing much. She just dropped a syringe. I cleaned—"

"That's a lie," Ruth cried.

They spun to face her.

Ruth strode forward. "He's lying. He dropped that syringe and on purpose, because I refused to go out to dinner with him."

The chief raised her eyebrows and turned to Burnsey.

He spread his hands wide and shrugged. "I know better. I know the rules."

Ruth stamped her foot. "You know them but you flaunt—I mean, flout them."

"Lieutenant Doherty, come with me." The chief grabbed her arm and pulled her down to the nose of the plane. "I have had enough of these—these ridiculous accusations."

"They're not ridi—"

"Enough. Now you've called him a liar. That's slander."

Ruth sucked her lips between her teeth. Temper would not help her case. "You will remember," she said carefully, "I requested not to work with Sergeant Burns. Once again, I'd like to request to work with a different technician."

"I fail to see how you could work with any man. You can't work with the most amiable, the most competent, the most resourceful technician in the squadron."

Ruth reminded herself to breathe evenly. In the distance, May stood across a snowy gulf. May had followed her to Bowman because they needed each other, but now that Charlie was back, May didn't need her. And Ruth needed—Burnsey gave her a smile so smug it brought pains to her stomach—Ruth needed to get away from him no matter what.

Heaviness settled in her chest. "When we return to Prestwick, I'll request a transfer to another squadron."

The chief's thin nostrils closed. "They'll never approve it, not with the evaluations I've given you. Lieutenant Doherty, I'm afraid you're not suited for flight nursing. Perhaps a return to the wards would be best for you—and for us."

White flakes flurried about her. Back to the wards? She'd lose her flight pay and everything she'd worked for. She'd promised Ma she'd take care of the children. If Ruth failed, their futures would become as dark as the nose of the C-54, as Lieutenant Shepard's face.

"I'll—I'll make it work here." Her lips tingled. Her head whirled.

"See to it that you do." Lieutenant Shepard walked away. "No more complaints. Not one."

Ruth braced her hands on her knees and sucked in drafts of air as icy as the knowledge that she couldn't get away.

42

Bury St. Edmunds Airfield

Thursday, March 30, 1944

Jack swallowed hard. Ruth wore the evening gown that matched her eyes. Curves that were alluring in wool were downright eye-popping in silk. Every man at the party would want her. Jack would have to keep her close to his side.

Ruth chewed her lips and clutched one elbow, her bare arms forming the numeral four.

His brother Walt used to complain about clamming up around women, but now Walt was about to get married, and Jack was struck dumb. However, Ruth was nervous about the party and the dress, and Jack had to say something. Not a compliment. She'd received too many compliments from too many men with impure motives. Instead, he grinned at her. "You didn't burn the dress."

She laughed, and her posture relaxed. "How could I? It's beautiful."

Jack crossed the floor of the air base's Aeroclub, where May and Ruth were staying with the Red Cross girls. He took Ruth's hands in his. "I'm glad you came."

Her chin edged up. "I just came for May, you know."

"I know." He suppressed a smile. Sure, she came to escort May on the train, but Jack caught a whiff of perfume, borrowed, no doubt. She never wore perfume.

He turned to Charlie, who helped May put on her cape over a long pink dress. "Got your pistol, de Groot? No man comes within twenty feet of these ladies."

Ruth laughed. "Won't that be hard on the dance floor?"

He turned back. She'd only accepted the invitation because Ed Reynolds's drinking finally got him booted to infantry, and because Jack promised she wouldn't have to dance. "Remember—"

"This is your party. One hundred missions for the 94th is something to celebrate." She whisked her cape around her shoulders before he could help her.

"Poor Jack's flown almost half of them." Charlie held open the door for May.

"No kidding." Twenty-five on the first tour, twenty on the second, and ten to go. With missions escalating and losses falling, the Eighth Air Force had increased the length of a tour to thirty missions.

Jack offered his elbow to Ruth and led her out into the cool, damp evening. He'd hoped she'd dance with him ever since his visit to Prestwick a few weeks before, the day she returned from her first evacuation flight. When she saw him, she clapped her hand over her mouth, then walked to him, then ran to him. He held her and let her cry and offered to beat up that Burns jerk.

That's when he developed his new plan, designed for her, not him, and he had prayed over it—a lot.

Jack tucked Ruth's arm close to his side. "How are things at Prestwick?"

"Busy. We're evacuating two hundred patients a day."

Jack nodded. Clearing the hospitals. The invasion would

come as soon as weather permitted. "Any more problems?" He kept his voice low, although Charlie and May fell several paces behind.

Ruth sighed. "The same. Innuendoes, double entendres, but I don't dare complain, not with my job in jeopardy. I have to make do."

"I don't trust this guy. Did you check? Can you do anything about the return leg?"

She shook her head and released a hint of perfume. "Lieutenant Shepard is so fed up with me, she won't let me return on another plane, and the air crews say I'd get in the way up front. But he hasn't bothered me on the cargo leg. He clacks away on his typewriter, doing paperwork for his business, and then he sleeps."

"Good," Jack grumbled. "I still wish you'd let me beat him up."

Ruth's laughter mingled with the music from Hangar Number One. "A sweet thought. But you do more good just listening to me. You're the only one I can talk to."

She followed the "no complaining" order so strictly she wouldn't even confide in May, which bothered Jack at first. Now he agreed. Why dim May's light? Besides, being Ruth's only confidant had benefits, like the stars in her eyes right then, which did funny things to his stomach.

He led her through the gigantic hangar doors, open enough to let people in but keep the cold out.

Hundreds of men in dress uniform milled about, and almost as many women—American nurses and Red Cross personnel, and British girls trucked in from local villages. A makeshift bar stood along one wall, tables dotted the concrete floor, and the base band played on a stage decorated with red, white, and blue bunting. The Latin tune "Frenesi" bounced off the high ceiling, and the clarinet soloist did a fair imitation of Artie Shaw.

Jack checked in his overcoat and Ruth's cape, and then took her arm. "What do you think?"

"A lot of people." Her face seemed pale.

That great, protective urge swelled inside him. "And you're stuck with me, poor kid."

She didn't look up, but her cheeks rounded in a smile. He had to get her on the dance floor before she changed her mind. Why did the band have to be at the far end of the hangar?

Jack plotted a course through the crowd to avoid men from his squadron. Along the way, Ruth left a trail of dropped jaws, but Jack made sure the men knew she was with him.

At the back of the hangar, couples jitterbugged to "American Patrol." Jack pulled Ruth into his arms and relished how she drew in her breath. Good, he still had an effect on her.

"Remember, just follow me." He led her in a simple fox-trot as he had in the abbey months before, and she slowly relaxed, and soon he could swing her around and make her laugh. Now he needed a slow song, but "American Patrol" kept up its lively pace.

"Do you like the band?" he asked.

"Oh yes, and the stage. It's . . ." She grinned and tilted her head. "It's festooned."

He laughed at their rhyming game and swung her around. "Over by the bar—spittoons."

"You're kidding."

"Ah, you never know around here. One big muddy pig-sty. Even when we dress things up, this is still a greasy old hangar."

The music slowed, and Ruth scowled at him. "You planned this."

The band played "Sleepy Lagoon." Jack shook his head hard. "Honestly, I—"

Then she laughed, and Jack drew her close, and she didn't

even stiffen, and he rubbed his cheek against her soft hair and filled his lungs with her perfumed cleanness. "I do love you, Ruth Doherty."

Now she stiffened. She pulled back to look him in the eye. "What?"

He kept his arm around the silky curve of her waist. "Back in October I said I loved you, but I only loved a woman I had imagined. Now I know you, and I love you more each day."

"Jack . . ." Her gaze slipped over his shoulder, toward the exit.

He rocked her around until she faced the bandstand. "I have something to discuss with you. No protests until I'm done. Then after a reasonable time of protest, we'll continue to enjoy the evening. Agreed?"

"Jack, I—"

"Agreed?"

She sighed, and creases striped her forehead. "Agreed."

His heart accelerated, an engine raring to go, but he held back the throttle. *Lord, if this isn't your will, stop me now.*

"Jack, what is this about?"

"I want to marry you."

Her eyes widened, the same greenish blue as the dress.

"I've thought this out, and I've covered all your objections. First of all, we won't get married until the war's over. We both have jobs to do."

"Jack—"

"No protests yet." He brought their clasped hands in front of her face and lifted one finger. "Hear me out. Now, you're worried about kisses and—well, not to embarrass you—but the things that go on in marriage, but I promised you. I know now. I understand. I don't need any of that. I just need you. We'll have separate rooms, and if you want children, we can adopt. Goodness knows, this war is making too many orphans. We can take in your sister Maggie for starters."

Her entire face agitated. "This—"

"I'm not done yet." He swayed to the music, although it was like dancing with a concrete post. "Once you told me you could never marry because of your family, but I'd be honored to provide for them. Your family will be my own."

Ruth's face twitched a million protests, but she kept her mouth shut.

"I love you so much." Jack's voice deepened, and his throat felt thick. He pressed his lips to her fingers until his throat loosened. "I want to provide for you. I want to protect you. I want to love you for the rest of my life."

She stared at his chest as if she could see how hard his heart beat, and her eyelids fluttered. "I—I don't know what to say."

He drew her close and nuzzled in waves of auburn. "Say yes."

She burrowed her face in his shoulder. "No, I can't. This is crazy."

"No, it's—"

"Yes, it is. It's wrong, all the way through. I don't even know why. It's just wrong."

"Ruth . . ."

She shook her head and clutched his shoulder. "It's not fair to you."

"Of course, it is."

"No, it's not. You deserve a normal wife and children of your own if God provides."

Jack held the smooth body that would never be his, but he didn't care. "Darling, I don't want any of that. I just want to love you. Please let me love you."

"If God provides." She lifted her head and squinted. "That's why it's wrong."

"Huh?"

"If God provides." She looked him in the eye. "That's it. You want to provide for me, to protect me, to love me, but that's God's job. I'm finally turning to him for provision and protection and love, and to turn to you would be wrong. I have to trust the Lord, not you."

Jack's balloon pricked and the air rushed out, but he made himself smile. "What a coincidence. I have to learn to trust him too. We can learn together."

Those pretty, untouchable lips bent in compassion. "Not as man and wife."

"Someday." He swung her around until his confidence and her laughter returned. "Someday, my little macaroon. Someday I'll convince you to be my wife."

★

On the stage, colonels and generals read introductions and citations and congratulations, but all Ruth noticed was Jack's presence behind her and the warmth of his hands on her waist. If only she could sink back onto his chest and let him encircle her with his arms and his love. If only she could bolt for the door.

The two emotions hacked at each other, taking chunks of her heart.

"That's General Curtis LeMay," Jack murmured in her ear. "CO of Third Division. A hard man, but boy, is he good."

Ruth nodded. The man at the microphone had an uncompromising look in his face and an immovable set to his stocky frame. He read off the Distinguished Unit Citation, the highest award an outfit could receive, for a January mission to Brunswick.

The general read an account of the mission, which involved a recall order, a 360-degree turn, and heavy fighter attacks the group faced alone. "Through a display of extraordinary heroism and exemplary devotion to duty above and beyond that of all other units participating in the same engagement, and by striking a decisive blow at hostile industries, the 94th Bombardment Group rendered a truly outstanding service, which reflects the highest credit on itself and the Army Air Forces."

"Oh my goodness." Ruth glanced over her shoulder. "Were you on that mission?"

Jack nodded, his gaze on the stage. Then he applauded. Whoops and whistles broke out as a colonel came to the microphone. Although he wasn't tall, no one would ever call him short, not the way he held himself with quiet authority.

"That's Castle," Jack said and added his whistle to the din. "Best CO ever."

The colonel accepted the citation and addressed the crowd. When he finished, a man clapped Jack on the back. "Good job, Novak."

Another man lifted his drink. "Here's to you, Major."

"What's that about?" Ruth asked.

Jack shrugged. "They're in my squadron."

He hadn't told her why they congratulated him. No doubt about it, Jack Novak was a changed man.

The ceremony concluded, and the band struck up "Stars and Stripes Forever."

Jack took Ruth's arm. "I see Charlie and May. Let's take a rest." He waved at Charlie, and the men exchanged hand signals, finishing with a thumbs-up.

Ruth laughed. "What was that?"

"I told him to find a table while I get the drinks." He weaved through the crowd. "The cockpit's loud in combat. Sometimes the interphone goes out. You get by with hand signals."

"I can imagine. When the flak is bursting and the fighters

are diving, it's important to know who'll find the table and who'll get the drinks."

He looked down at her and laughed. "I have the best date in the room."

She groaned. The other men had dates who knew how to dance and were accustomed to long gowns and bare shoulders. Ruth kept getting tangled in her skirts, she couldn't get used to the air tingling her arms and chest, and several women had smirked at her clunky Army shoes.

At the bar, Jack ordered four Cokes. Two blond lieutenants leaned against the bar, identical in looks, and each man's gaze rolled over Ruth's body. She pressed closer to Jack. The twins glanced at him, and four blond eyebrows twanged as if struck by the glare off the major's oak leaves.

Ruth gazed at the major, who conversed with the bartender. What an impressive man. His looks and personality commanded attention, but his ability and character earned respect. With little or no effort, he could have any woman in the room. Ruth saw how the ladies watched him, how they trailed their fingers down their throats.

Jack pressed a chilly bottle into her hand. He stuffed two more bottles in his jacket pockets, took her elbow, and directed her across the hangar.

"Why me, Jack?"

"Hm?" He looked down at her, confused, and then he smiled and waggled his eyebrows at her. "Because I love you, my little macaroon."

Ruth countered the squishy feeling in her heart with an eye roll. "No. Why me? Look around. Any of these women would marry you in a heartbeat."

"Nah." He pointed to a brunette in a red dress. "See the jewelry on that gal? She'd never settle for the salary of a pastor or a career military man."

"Oh, but a poor little orphan girl . . ."

"Yep." His eyes crinkled. "Look at me, proposing marriage when I don't even know what I want to be when I grow up."

"Still can't make up your mind?"

"What do you think? Would you rather be a pastor's wife or a military wife?"

She laughed. "Neither. Besides, it's up to God, not me, right?"

Jack navigated around a loud circle of men. "Yeah, but he hasn't given me a clear answer."

"Maybe he has."

Jack stopped and faced her with a frown.

She frowned back. Who was she to tell him about God?

"Go ahead," he said.

Ruth sighed. "Well, you tried. You tried so hard to fit into your father's mold, but you don't fit. Here—this is where you fit. I see it in your eyes when you talk about your work. And everyone who knows you best thinks you should stay, except your father. But he's only a man, Jack."

His eyes flickered. For the longest time, he looked in her direction without looking at her. Ruth rearranged her fingers on the cola bottle. Would she want someone to tell her Ma was only a woman? Ma meant so much to her, and Jack's father meant so much to him, the man he identified with, admired, and emulated.

"I'm a lousy pastor." Jack focused on her, his expression sad but settled. "Because I'm not meant to be a pastor."

Ruth puckered one corner of her mouth with empathy.

Slowly his expression changed, and starry lines radiated through the blue of his eyes. "You asked, 'Why me?' I'll tell you—you're a godly woman with fire, and I'm madly in love with you." He leaned forward and placed a tender kiss on her forehead.

Her body and her heart swayed toward him. She forced herself straight. "You promised."

Jack narrowed his eyes. "Hold your horses, pardner. That promise applies to your lips. I've kissed your forehead before, and you didn't complain. Right?"

Ruth had to nod.

"I just have to keep my lips away from this area." He traced a circle from her nose to her chin.

Her mouth fell slack, but she tightened it again. "No, keep your lips over there." She pressed her fingers to those lips.

Bad idea. Jack kissed her fingertips and sent warmth rushing into every cell of her body. He loved her, all of her, and that was sweeter and more effervescent than the soda in her hand.

"You love me too, don't you?" He worked his arm around her waist and pulled her close until all she saw, all she felt, all she wanted was him.

Someone jostled Ruth and apologized in a Southern accent, and she became aware of the crowd, the hangar, and the singer crooning "I'm Getting Sentimental over You," and even more aware of the danger of losing her whole heart, her whole life to this man.

"Huh? Huh? You love me, don't you?" Jack's tone was light now, joking.

Ruth wiggled out of his embrace. "You're so full of yourself. You say you've changed, but it's the same old thing—pride, pride, pride." She headed for the table and sent him a teasing look over her shoulder.

His smiling reply said he knew the truth.

She loved him.

Now that he knew it, he'd never give up until she gave in. But a crushing pain in her chest told her she loved him too much to let him marry her.

43

Bury St. Edmunds Airfield

Friday, March 31, 1944

Jack leaned over his desk and jotted down names from his squadron: Polansky, Berardi, Davis, maybe Markowitz. For the other squadrons, he had to rely on the commanders' evaluations, and they weren't pleased Jack was skimming the cream of their crews.

It was an honor to have his squadron selected to become the Pathfinder Squadron for Fourth Wing. An honor.

It just wasn't the honor he wanted.

When Castle had called him in to the office that morning, Jack entered flush with the knowledge he was meant for the military and about to be named Lt. Col. John Novak Jr., air executive.

He wasn't. He was still a major, still a squadron commander, just a glorified squadron commander.

"An honor." He said it, wrote it in bold gray letters, then scratched it out. It looked stupid.

Jack tapped his pencil on the desk. Criteria, criteria. Over five missions to prove they could handle combat, but no more than fifteen. The Eighth couldn't train a crew in radar-guided bombing only to have them finish their tour in a month.

This was no temporary assignment for Jack while Castle waited to promote him.

More tapping. "An honor."

"Ahoy there, Skipper." Charlie strode through the office door. "You got the news?"

One look at that jovial face, and Jack knew Charlie played a part in the decision. He forced his mouth into a smile. "Sure did."

Charlie plopped into a chair. Every day he gained strength and weight, although he was still down ten to twenty pounds. "Won't it be swell? We'll have four weeks together at Alconbury, just like old times."

"Yeah, swell." He looked down at the list so Charlie wouldn't see his phony smile. "Need to pick my crews today. We start Monday."

"Wait and see what H2X can do when we put a squadron in every wing, eventually every group. Hitler will never get rest, rain or shine."

"That's the idea." Jack put pencil to paper: Kirby, Johnson, Carter.

"When I think about what the Dutch go through—starvation rations, getting hauled away for slave labor, living in constant fear of the Gestapo. And that's nothing compared to what the Jews endure—concentration camps and who knows what else."

Jack set down his pencil. Why on earth did he fuss about his stupid career when a whole continent needed liberation from tyranny?

He cracked a smile. "How's the coffee at Alconbury?"

"Awful. You'll feel right at home."

"Speaking of coffee." Jack peered at the sludge in his cup. "Ready for lunch?"

"That's why I'm here." Charlie stood and tossed Jack his overcoat from the coatrack. "Still drizzling out."

"At least it didn't drizzle last night on the girls in their fancy dresses." He buckled his coat around his waist. "You saw them off at the train station?"

"Yep." Charlie led him out of the office. "They understood why you couldn't come."

Jack gave a sharp nod. "Think I'll get a forty-eight-hour pass when I'm at Alconbury?"

Charlie laughed. "In training?"

Jack stepped outside and added his sigh to the mist. Could he convince Ruth to marry him through letters alone?

A jeep crunched to a stop on the muddy pavement beside them. Jeff Babcock waved from the passenger seat.

"Hiya, Jeff." Charlie shook the ground executive's hand. "Good to see another old-timer around here."

"Not many left. Everyone finished his tour or was promoted away. Right, Novak?"

He knew what Babcock meant. Of the combat crewmen who came over almost a year before, only Jack remained in his original position. He gave a grim smile. "Everyone who survived."

Babcock's grin flickered, then flew back into place. "Say, Novak, that was one hot cookie you were with last night. My, oh my. Not the sort of woman I'd picture with a pastor, but then you've got to sow those wild oats while you can, huh, pal?"

Jack's fists balled up in the pockets of his coat, and he marched right up to the jeep. "Lieutenant Doherty is neither a cookie nor an oat. She is a woman of exceptional virtue, more than good enough for any pastor, so loudmouth politicians better watch—"

"Come on, boys." Charlie wedged himself between the men.

Babcock leaned back so far his cap slipped off. "I didn't mean anything by that, pal."

Jack grasped Charlie's shoulders and shoved past him, fire in his chest. "I'm not your pal, never have been. And yes, you did mean something."

"Jack, stop it." Charlie grasped his upper arms.

His fists strained for Babcock, for Burns, for the men who raped Ruth and scarred her for life. "You meant she's a tramp, just 'cause she's beautiful. I've had it—"

The jeep almost ran over Jack's toes. Babcock waved over his shoulder. "I only wanted to congratulate you on ending the dry spell in your love life. Maybe your career dry spell will be next."

Jeep or no jeep, Jefferson Babcock Jr. needed a black eye to match his heart. Jack wrenched his arms free and took off running.

"Jack! What do you think you're doing? You're a senior officer, for crying out loud."

A senior officer. He stopped in his tracks, turned to Charlie, and became aware of his heavy breathing and the knot of rookies watching.

Charlie's face was red, and he massaged one of his hands. "What are you thinking? You're acting like a schoolboy."

Jack bit back the "he started it" on his lips, because Charlie was right. He couldn't get in a fight. He had to set an example. And like it or not, Babcock outranked him.

"I know you've never gotten along with him, but you've never let him get to you before. I thought you were working on your pride."

"My pride?" Jack shook a finger at Babcock's little motorcade. "This isn't about me, it's about Ruth. He can't talk that way about my future wife."

"Wife?"

"Yeah." His arm drifted down. "I asked her last night. She didn't say yes, but she will."

Everything about Charlie narrowed—his mouth, his eyes, even his cheeks pulled in. "Not this again."

"It's not what you think." Jack strode up to his friend. "It's not like before. I don't want to change her. I just want to love her."

Still that skeptical look.

Jack held his hands before him as if he held the answer in a box. "I finally got it. Love isn't getting her to meet my needs. No." He shook the box. "Love is meeting her needs."

Charlie's face relaxed. "She's fine with this?"

Jack groaned and looked away to a dribbling tree next to squadron HQ. "Not yet. I have to admit, the idea of a—a platonic marriage—it takes some getting used to. But she'll see. I have to do some romancing and a whole lot of praying, but she'll see."

Charlie puffed out his breath and walked around Jack. "I've got to hand it to you. You never give up, do you?"

"Dead right. I thought I was in love before, but no, this—this is love." He walked next to Charlie and lifted his chin to let the rain tickle his face. "I can't tell you how good it feels to do something for her, not for myself."

Charlie grunted. He'd worn the same expression the night he said he wouldn't fly with Jack again.

Annoyance surged up, but Jack wrestled it down. Charlie had been right that night, and today he deserved a hearing. "Say it, Charlie."

He shrugged. "How can it be for her if she doesn't want it?"

Jack stuffed his tongue in his cheek. Charlie hadn't seen the way Ruth melted in his arms the night before. He hadn't seen the love in her eyes.

It might take a while to convince her. It might take longer than the lousy war. But someday she'd see.

44

Prestwick

Saturday, April 15, 1944

"Nurse? Got an aspirin? Ethel Merman's giving me a head-ache." The corporal pointed across the airfield tent hospital to Dottie, who sang "Oh, What a Beautiful Mornin'" with gusto.

Ruth smiled down at the boy on the cot. With his red hair and green eyes, he resembled her brother Chuck, and he couldn't be much older. "Do you really need an aspirin?"

"Not really, but it ain't even morning yet. Can you make her stop?"

"No, but if you figure out a way . . ."

He grinned. "I'll be sure and let you know."

"I'd appreciate that." Ruth had already received the doctor's preflight report on Cpl. Arthur Thompson. While loading 500-pound bombs into the belly of a B-24 Liberator, the corporal had been pinned by a loose bomb, which crushed his pelvis and femur.

Ruth squatted beside his cot. "Have you ever flown before, Corporal?"

"No, ma'am. Been inside a bomber a million times, but

never in the air. To tell the truth, a man's meant to stay on the ground. I'm a farmer, ma'am. A man of the earth."

She smiled. His farming experience probably consisted of riding on Pa's knee on the tractor. "How long did it take you to get to England?"

"Almost two months, ma'am, zigzagging around them U-boats."

"Mm-hmm. Well, tonight you'll have dinner in New York. You may change your mind about flying. And wait till you see the view."

"Oh, I won't look down, ma'am." His skin became almost as green as his eyes.

Just the kind who might get airsick. She'd only had one case among her patients so far, but the smell led half the other men to throw up. Corporal Thompson would go toward the front of the plane where the motion was calmer.

Ruth laid a hand on his arm. "You have nothing to fear. The Air Transport Command pilots are gentler than the bomber boys you're used to. They go out of their way to avoid turbulence."

"Turbulence—that's rough air, right?"

"Mm-hmm. Sometimes it feels as if you're on a rocky road in an old jalopy, but you're not. Besides, there's nothing to hit up there." She gave him a big smile.

"Still . . ." He rolled the brown blanket between his fingers.

"We also have life rafts and jackets, full emergency equipment, and hours upon hours of training, which we've never once put into practice."

The corporal's face relaxed. And if he got worked up on the flight, that's what phenobarbital was for.

"I tell you, ma'am. Your boyfriend's a right lucky man."

"Thank you." Ruth stood, and a rush of dizziness made

her stumble. She'd responded to that line many times but never with a "thank you." What was that supposed to mean? Jack wasn't her boyfriend.

She lifted her stethoscope from around her neck to take the corporal's vitals. Wouldn't Jack have loved her response? He remained convinced she'd marry him, and he wrote such romantic letters they broke her heart, because someday his heart would be broken.

She loved him too much to let him deceive himself, but how could she persuade him? He'd disemboweled her two best arguments, her family and her aversion, and he'd stuck his knife in the third. His last letter reminded her how God used people to do his work, so why couldn't he use Jack to protect Ruth, provide for her, and love her?

It was too logical. It wouldn't do.

All that remained was the flimsy, indefensible gut knowledge that she could not marry him. She couldn't even explain it to herself. She just knew it.

Ruth wrote Corporal Thompson's vitals on the flight manifest and checked the cast that encased most of his lower body. He'd go in the forward lower left bunk.

Only distancing would work with Jack, but how could she bear to lose his friendship? Since she held May at arm's length, Jack was the only one she could confide in, who believed her and supported her.

Ruth groaned and tucked the blankets around her patient. "Is there anything you need before your trip home, Corporal?"

"I could use a smoke, ma'am. Might settle my nerves."

She groaned again. "I'm sorry. We're out of cigarettes. The last shipment was short." That was Army life. One week quartermasters had to drive all over the U.K. scrounging up scraps of gauze, and the next week they had so much gauze the nurses joked about making it into curtains for the barracks.

"You need some cigs?" Sergeant Dugan walked down the next aisle with a tray piled with bandages. "Burnsey's in the med room. He's got a crate."

"Oh, she wouldn't go to Burnsey," Dottie called out with a glare at Ruth. "She'd have to say something nice about him for a change."

Ruth glanced toward the med room. "Black market, I bet," she muttered.

"What was that?" Dottie said.

Corporal Thompson tugged her sleeve. "Black market, white market, I don't care. I just want a smoke."

Ruth held her breath. They'd heard her? Would that be considered a complaint? What if it got back to Lieutenant Shepard? Ruth plastered on a smile for the boy who looked like her brother. "If cigarettes will help you through your first flight, I'll be glad to get them."

She headed down the aisle and pushed through a flap into the medication room. Burnsey was alone, his blond head bent over rolls of gauze.

He looked up. "Well, hi there. What's up?"

It hurt to speak. "I heard you have cigarettes."

A smile stretched across his face. "Only a matter of time until you came to me to meet your needs."

Bile rose thick in her throat. "Not for me. For a patient. Do you have them or not?"

"I have everything you need." He reached into a crate by the supply cabinet. "What do you want? Camels, Lucky—"

"I don't care. Whatever the men like." She pulled her coin purse from her pocket and fumbled with the clasp. She refused to have a patient pay for something the Army was supposed to supply as rations.

Burnsey sauntered over with a pack. "I tell you what. I'll give it to you for free if you go out on the town with me tonight."

Ruth stepped back and bumped into the steel supply cabinet. Why hadn't she moved toward the door flap?

"You get yourself dolled up, no one will know you're an
officer. And I'll show you a swell time—New York's finest
dining, dancing, a Broadway show, whatever you want."

"I want—you to leave me—alone." Her breath puffed out
in short bursts, and she held out a quarter with a trembling
hand.

"How can I? I can't resist girls who play hard to get."

He stood so close, Ruth smelled his toothpaste. "Leave
me—alone."

"No one plays hard to get better than you do, gorgeous."

Ruth molded her back to the cabinet and stepped to the
side, but Burnsey took her arm and blocked her. The bile
congealed and plugged her throat.

"Keep your money. You'll pay me back someday." He tucked
the cigarettes into her shirt pocket, touching, exploring.

She shrank back, tried to cry out, and gagged.

Burnsey was gone with a wink, out the door.

Ruth stood, mouth wide open, her lips groping for air as if
she'd been hit in the solar plexus. She slid down the cabinet
to the floor and hung her head between her knees. Her breath
returned in convulsive gasps.

He couldn't get away with it. He couldn't get away with
it.

She hugged her knees and sucked in lungfuls of medicinal
air. Yes, he could get away with it. He already had.

Ruth couldn't tell Lieutenant Shepard, or she'd lose her
job. Burnsey knew that.

She couldn't tell May, or her friend would worry. And what
if May intervened with the chief? Ruth would still lose her
job, and May would be in trouble as well.

Worst of all, she couldn't tell Jack. When she leaned on him, she fed his fantasy. What she wouldn't give for Ma's comfort and Pa's wisdom.

Her quarter tinkled to the ground, and silver coin blurred with gray concrete. Ruth blinked back her tears, but they left dark spots on her blue wool trousers.

"Oh Lord, you're all I have."

45

Sunday, May 7, 1944

Early afternoon sun glinted off silver as P-51 Mustangs cut S-patterns a thousand feet above the bomber formation. Jack would never take the Little Friends for granted.

He massaged the four throttles in his grip to get the right rpm out of each engine. As the lead Pathfinder for Third Division, he had to keep his course and speed steady and true. Two of his ships headed each group in Fourth Wing on the way to Berlin, the ideal maiden run for his newly trained squadron. A cottony blanket obscured the ground, so if they hit the target, the H2X "Mickey" radar would be solely responsible.

Jack studied the fuel gauges. All looked good for *My Macaroon.* Charlie teased him about the name for the H2X-equipped B-17G since Babcock almost got a black eye for calling Ruth "one hot cookie." But Jack's nickname for Ruth was affectionate. She liked it.

Or did she?

Her letters had grown sporadic, short, and impersonal, with no mention of Burns or the chief, and no arguments to his watertight reasons they should get married. She just ignored them.

Jack hardened his abdominal muscles to stop the queasy feeling. Why was he thinking about Ruth? He had a mission to fly.

"Navigator to pilot. We should be near the IP," Pete Gustafson said from down in the nose.

"Mickey operator to pilot. Wow, you should see the images I'm getting. Beautiful, beautiful."

Jack smiled under his oxygen mask. He could almost see Nick Panapoulos's bright, doughy face leaning over the radar scope in the radio room. "Do you agree with Gus?"

"You should see this, the crook in the Havel River clear as can be."

"The IP?"

"Oh yeah. IP coming up."

Jack chuckled at Nick's enthusiasm for his toy. A round plastic radome protruded from *Macaroon*'s belly where the ball turret used to be. H2X radio waves flowed from the radome and bounced off the terrain back to the scope, where a practiced eye could distinguish water from land and built-up areas from earth.

"Mickey operator to pilot. We're at the IP."

"Navigator to pilot. I concur."

"Roger. Fire two yellow flares," Jack said to Marvin Cox, the radio operator, who would fire the flares through the roof hatch of the radio room to signal the rest of the squadron.

"Bomb bay doors open," Oggie Drake said from the bombardier's chair.

Jack put *My Macaroon* into a thirty-degree turn. The H2X was almost unnecessary, because flak marked Berlin's boundaries. Instead of looking down at the largest sheep in the world, Jack now felt as if he hovered over a giant Dalmatian, except this dog's spots leaped up and nipped at him.

"Down, boy," he said, but the flak gunners aimed low.

Shells rumbled like thunder and added to the ship's vibrations. Today the Germans had plenty of targets. For the first time, the Eighth dispatched over one thousand bombers. In addition, 750 fighters performed escort duty.

So far flak hadn't claimed any victims, and the Luftwaffe hadn't come up. The relentless growth of the Eighth Air Force had tipped the scales of air superiority, and now the Luftwaffe picked their fights. Some days they didn't show, and others they mounted savage attacks.

A flak burst waggled the Fort's wings.

"Steady, girl." Jack's control of the wheel soothed the trembles. If only he could soothe Ruth as easily. The woman was skittish, he knew that the day he met her. But now it didn't make sense. He'd dealt with all her concerns, yet he had the uneasy feeling she was slipping away.

Why? The night of the party shimmered in his memory. That night he was certain she loved him. But now?

Jack gave his head a shake. He was on a mission over Berlin with the whole blasted Third Division behind him, and he needed to focus.

He swept the instrument panel. "How's the formation, Al?"

"A-OK." Capt. Albert Feldman rode in the tail gunner's seat to keep the formation in line.

Jack nodded. A milk run over Berlin would look good on his record. While Jack was at Alconbury, Colonel Castle had been promoted to command the Fourth Wing, also based at Bury, and Col. Charles Dougher had been brought in to head the 94th. Jack didn't know how the change in leadership would affect his future.

Was it wrong to want a promotion? Even in prayer, he couldn't tease out his motivations. He had to admit he liked recognition, which was pure pride, but he also knew he'd do the job well and enjoy it. No matter what, he didn't doubt his decision to stay in the Army Air Forces. Next he had to work up the nerve to tell his father.

"Mickey operator to crew. We're at the target, and she's a beauty. Ready, Oggie? And now."

"Bombs away."

"Double red flares fired," Marvin said from the radio room.

The plane climbed, relieved of her load. The flares would signal the other planes to drop, and two Skymarker bombs would leave trails of smoke to guide groups further to the rear.

Jack turned the Fort for the Rally Point. "Okay, boys. Who wants to go home?"

Home in Antioch, Walt was now a married man. Yesterday was his wedding, and Jack missed it. Home in Antioch, Ray visited every weekend after his transfer to the Sacramento Air Depot, and he saw a lot of Helen Carlisle.

Ray and Helen? There had to be ten years between them, and Helen was a widow with a little boy. Could be tough.

As tough as Ruth? Jack squinted against the sun coming through the windscreen. Since when had a challenge ever stopped a Novak?

He tapped his thumb on the control wheel. He had to get up to Prestwick and soon. Could he get a pass? He had a new CO, a new squadron, and the invasion could come any day. Most of April, the Eighth had bombed installations in the Pas de Calais area, the obvious invasion site, as well as rail yards to impede German reinforcements.

And Jack wanted a forty-eight-hour pass to see his girl? Fat chance.

His stomach churned. Time was running out. He felt it draining away. After all they'd been through, he could not, he would not let Ruth slip away.

46

Prestwick

Sunday, May 14, 1944

"Come on, Ruth. We can't wait all day."

Her head jerked up, and she sloshed coffee onto her metal tray. She couldn't believe she'd fallen asleep in the breakfast line. For two weeks straight, she'd flown patients to New York. Finally she had a day off for church and laundry, if she could stay awake.

She apologized to Dottie La Rue in line behind her, who replied with a lash-fluttering eye roll.

Ruth sighed and stepped forward in line. While never a confidante, Dottie had been a friend, and Ruth missed the days at Bowman when the nurses liked her. A year ago she'd taken defiant pleasure in keeping people away, but now loneliness carved into her soul.

A year ago.

A year ago today she'd met Jack. She camouflaged another sigh as a yawn. How painful to write bland letters when she longed to empty her heart to him. For his own sake, she had to cut him off, but that didn't reduce her wretchedness.

The private behind the counter handed her a plate with one pancake.

And sausage.

She held up the plate. "Please take back the sausage, and may I have another pancake?"

The private's heavy lids suggested he needed sleep as much as Ruth did. "Only two sausages each. Move on."

"No, I don't want sausage. I don't like sausage."

"This ain't a restaurant, lady. Move on."

Dottie nudged her from behind. "For heaven's sake, take it and move on."

Norma Carpenter leaned toward the private, with a sly look at Ruth. "Ignore her, Private. We all do. All she does is whine, whine, whine."

Ruth glared at Norma and walked away with the unwanted plate. She couldn't afford to make a scene. Despite Norma's remark, Ruth hadn't made a complaint for over two months, although Burnsey gave her plenty of reason.

She scanned the nurses' mess, glad May was away on a flight. Schedule conflicts and fatigue provided excuses, but sometimes May couldn't be avoided, and conversation was strained. How Ruth ached for the former openness of their friendship.

Off to the side, Ruth found an unoccupied table and sat with her back to the room. She couldn't get through the morning on a single pancake.

That left the sausage.

She stared down the enemy. Tendrils of steam wafted into her nose.

Ruth could almost see Pa stride through the apartment door with a rope of sausage held high, could almost feel the joy as she jumped up and down with Ellen and Harold. Rich German sausages, succulent Polish sausages, Italian sausages full of garlic and spice—they made any meal savory. Ruth would sop up every bit of grease with her bread or boiled potatoes.

Since that day in the alley, even the smell nauseated her.

Yet today her stomach lay tranquil. Hungry, but tranquil.

Ruth poked a link with her fork. It didn't bite back. She pressed in the tines, tension released with a pop, and four rivulets of juice trickled to her plate.

She glanced around. Some women talked and laughed, some chewed in silence. No one looked her way. No one knew what a victory it would be.

Ruth took a deep sniff, and her mouth watered. She missed the taste, longed for the taste. Quickly she sliced, shoveled a piece into her mouth, and chewed.

Yes, she was still in Prestwick, not a Chicago alley. She swallowed. No nausea, no white spots before her eyes, only her tongue slipping around the inside of her mouth, begging for more.

She took another bite, another, and finished both sausages with strange euphoria. One more area of her life healed. *Thank you, Lord. I never even asked you to take this away.*

No, she'd prayed for God to take away her aversion to kissing. She never said one word about sausage. Maybe he got her prayers mixed up.

Or maybe . . .

Ruth swallowed the lump of pancake in her mouth and took a swig of coffee. "Breathe in, breathe out," she whispered. "In, out. In, out. Keep it slow. Don't think."

★

Jack stood outside the Nissen hut chapel and burrowed his hands in the pockets of his flight jacket. Prestwick served as the trans-Atlantic hub because it had the lowest incidence of fog in the United Kingdom.

Except today. He walked in a circle to keep warm. Perhaps he should have slipped into the pew beside Ruth to surprise her, but the closing hymn already played.

> Under His wings, oh, what precious enjoyment!
> There will I hide till life's trials are o'er;
> Sheltered, protected, no evil can harm me,
> Resting in Jesus, I'm safe evermore.
>
> Under His wings, under His wings,
> Who from His love can sever?
> Under His wings my soul shall abide,
> Safely abide forever.

Jack stood back from the door. Ruth came out first in her olive drab dress uniform, her Bible in hand. When she saw him, joy flashed on her face. Then she abruptly glanced away.

In that moment, Jack heard the roaring of tempestuous waters, yet he had to go on, had to walk to the brink of that dark river, up to the woman he loved. "Hi there."

Ruth's gaze darted up to him, then away. "I'm surprised to see you."

"It's been a long time. Six weeks."

"Oh? That long?"

Slapped Jack's breath away, like falling into ice water. "Talked the new CO into a forty-eight-hour pass."

Ruth frowned. "Oh dear. You wasted all your time on travel."

"Visiting you is never a waste of time." He gave her a tender smile, but she looked past his right shoulder.

"Today it is. I haven't had a day off in weeks, and I have chores. Can't spare any time."

That ice water seeped in and made his voice as cool as hers. "Half an hour."

Her frown deepened. "I guess so."

"We'll go for a walk. No more than half an hour, I promise."

Ruth nodded, still with a frown, and walked several feet from his side. "I'm sorry you came all the way up here."

"I was worried about you. Your letters—"

"I've been busy. Evac flights every day. I haven't had time to do laundry, much less write letters."

Jack had been busy too, busier than ever with preinvasion missions and a new squadron to organize, but he wrote her daily. "You haven't mentioned—well, I know what things are like and—"

"Don't worry about me. I can take care of myself."

A wave crashed over his head. Ruth hadn't talked like that in ages. Groping for reeds along the shore, Jack pulled a narrow box from his pocket. "I brought you an anniversary present."

"Anniversary?" Despite her detached tone, her rapid blinking showed she remembered.

"We met a year ago today. The best year of my life."

For one second her eyes agreed, but then her gaze skittered away.

"Here." Jack held out the box.

Ruth hesitated. Then she took the box and opened it.

Now he saw how stupid the gift was. Although his lungs filled with water, he forced a smile. "The scissors reminded me of my time in the hospital. As soon as I heard you snipping tape, I knew you were done, and we could talk. These scissors—they're antique."

Ruth traced one finger over the mother-of-pearl on the handles. Her lips parted, and furrows divided her forehead. "I can't—I can't take these."

"Yeah, I know they're not for work, but you can use them for mending or something." He strained for the surface, for air.

"No." She thrust the box back into his hands. "I can't take these. You need to stop. Stop trying to fill the holes in my life."

Lungs full, aching, bursting. "Ruth . . ."

She shook her head and glanced every which way. "You don't know when to quit. You're trying to do God's job. I need to rely on him, not you. You're pulling me away from him."

"I'm not. Don't you see? I want to help in his work."

Ruth huffed. "I don't think the Almighty needs the help of Jack Novak."

He grimaced. "That's not what I meant. Sometimes God uses people to do his work and—"

"So now you're on a mission from God? Would you stop it? Stop it. Stop trying to love me, and stop buying me gifts, and stop visiting, and stop—stop writing me. Stop it. Stop all of it."

The last reed broke in his hand. "Ruth," he said in one final gasp.

"No. Stop it. Go home. Leave me alone." She turned and hurried away, her hand pressed to her forehead.

He could keep kicking and fighting, but it wouldn't do any good. His hands drooped to his sides, and the little box almost fell.

Jack opened it. Antique scissors? Stupid, stupid, stupid. He stuck his fingers through the inlaid brass handles.

Ruth was only an olive drab blur in the fog. She wanted to sever all ties, and for the first time since he'd met her, he'd do as she wished.

Jack held the scissors in the gray between them and cut with a cold, metallic snip.

47

Monday, June 5, 1944

Sergeant Whitman clawed at the bandages on his charred face. "No! Put it out! Ah! It burns."

Ruth struggled to grasp his hands. "Wake up, Sergeant. Wake up."

"It's just a dream, pal." Burnsey held down the flailing legs.

"Where is it? Where's the fire extinguisher? Ah!" A loose fist clocked Ruth in the chin.

She winced and wrestled his arm to the litter. "Please wake up. Everything's all right." They weren't supposed to take psych cases on evacuation flights, but Sergeant Whitman had never been diagnosed with shell shock. No one realized the motion and sounds of flight would awaken memories of the fire in the waist of his B-17 that killed his fellow gunner and left him blinded and scorched over 20 percent of his body.

On the flight from Prestwick to Meeks, his anxiety had increased. After they left Meeks, he'd fallen into fitful sleep, but his nightmare started when they were still two hours from Stephenville.

"Danny! No! The extinguisher's empty. Lord God, help me."

Poor Sergeant Whitman. Sgt. Robert Whitman, a hurting little boy. Ruth stroked the curly brown hair protruding from the bandages around his face. "Robert, it's all right. Bob, Bobby, wake up. You're having a nightmare. It's all right, Bobby. It's all right."

"No . . ." he moaned. His body twitched under her weight.

"Ssh. It's all right, Bobby. It's only a dream, a bad dream. Please wake up."

His head turned from side to side. "Mama? Oh no, I'm dead. I'm dead."

"No, you're alive. I'm a nurse. We're flying you home, remember? You're going home."

"Oh, the plane. I've gotta get off. I can't stand this. Please, nurse, get me off this plane."

Ruth kept stroking his hair. "We'll land in two hours. Did your mama call you Bobby?"

He nodded, then groaned. "Two hours? I can't make it. Can't make it."

"Yes, you can. May I call you Bobby?"

"Please," he said, his voice choked.

"All right, Bobby. I'm going to go get some medication to relax you, help you sleep."

His free hand clutched her arm. "No! Don't leave me."

She looked over her shoulder. Burnsey still lay across Sergeant Whitman's legs. "Sergeant Burns, would you mind?"

"Not at all. I'll be right back." He made his way down the aisle past all the patients' craned heads. Burnsey wasn't all bad. She could count on him in an emergency.

Ruth sat back on her heels, glad she'd placed this patient in the lowest tier. She kept her hand on his head to reassure him. He wasn't fighting anymore, but his muscles remained taut.

"Where are you from, Bobby?"

"Michigan, ma'am. A farm outside Grand Rapids."

"Hmm. How nice. I always thought I'd like to live on a farm."

"A city girl? I'm sorry, ma'am. I forgot your name. Lieutenant . . . ?"

Ruth smiled down at his bandaged face. Sergeant Whitman couldn't see what she looked like. "Lieutenant Doherty," she said, but her heart warmed to this polite and tortured young man, and she leaned forward to whisper in his ear. "If you promise to keep it quiet, you can call me Ruth."

"That's a pretty name. My sister's name. From the Bible, you know."

"I know."

"Here you go." Burnsey handed her a syringe and a vial.

She frowned and read the turquoise label on the vial. "Pentothal?"

"That'll take care of him."

Ruth's presence had calmed Sergeant Whitman, but she had too many duties to stay by his side for the rest of the flight. Still, Pentothal wasn't indicated. While it would knock him out in ten seconds flat, it only lasted half an hour. Besides, he needed sedation, not unconsciousness.

"Bobby, do you think you could swallow a pill for me?"

His bandages shifted. The poor man was trying to smile. "For you, I would."

She returned the syringe to Burnsey. "Why don't you put this back and bring me some phenobarbital, please? Half a grain."

Ruth gazed down at her patient. Yes, she liked her men helpless—horizontal, bandaged, and sedated so they couldn't hurt her. Jack had figured it out so long ago. She fought off a crush of grief and patted Sergeant Whitman's arm. "Newfoundland. Have you ever been to Newfoundland, Bobby?"

48

Bury St. Edmunds Airfield

Tuesday, June 6, 1944

Today Jack wouldn't have to cheer the men up. In fact, he'd have to calm them down.

Most of the thirty-nine crews in the briefing room chattered and fidgeted like kids on the last day of school. No one complained about the powdered eggs for breakfast, about the briefing at 0100, or about flying two missions in a single day.

Even Charlie would fly—and with Jack. In the seat beside him, Charlie grinned at Jack with cheeks as pink as ever. He wouldn't be smiling when May found out he'd flown a combat mission. But how could Charlie miss it? How could any man in the Eighth Air Force?

Today was D-Day. Someday they'd tell their kids how they'd flown over the Normandy landing beaches.

Normandy. Still made Jack smile. All that bombing in the Pas de Calais area was sure to fool Hitler. It had fooled Jack. He'd had a few days' advance notice since his crews required specialized briefing. H2X bombing through a solid undercast with landing forces less than a mile offshore was bold, brilliant, and a potential disaster.

"All right, men. Calm down." At the front of the room, Colonel Dougher held up one hand. "Every detail is vital. Your lives and the lives of thousands of your brothers on the ground depend on your attention."

"Ah, it's a milk run," the rookie in front of Jack whispered.

Jack tapped him on the back of the head and gave him a stern but humorous look. The rookie smiled sheepishly and turned back.

Sure, the men would think it was a milk run. The map on the slide projector showed Allied fighter coverage in a semicircle around Normandy and up to the English coast extending from the deck to thirty thousand feet.

Dougher showed a slide of a P-51. "Our aircraft have been painted with black and white invasion stripes around the fuselage and wings. Gunners, keep your eyes open. Do not shoot at any plane unless fired upon first."

Jack settled back and took it all in. Today he'd fly his last two missions with the Eighth Air Force, and tomorrow he'd put in for a transfer. The day before, the Twentieth Bomber Command in India had flown the first mission ever in B-29 Superfortresses. New groups would head to China and to Pacific islands once they were secured. Just what Jack needed—a new plane, a new outfit, and a new locale.

England held nothing for him anymore, not a promotion or love or even friendship—Charlie was busy with May and his job. Besides, the action would shift to the Pacific. Germany would be defeated soon, now that the Allies had air superiority and, later today, a foothold on French soil.

"Men, your attention please." Dougher tapped the pointer on the wall, where a slide showed the flight route.

Jack's gaze followed the rectangular path he had committed to memory. Assembly over Bury St. Edmunds, south over Gravesend, cross the English coast near Beachy Head, hit the target at Caen, head straight west over Normandy, swing around the Channel Islands, then back over England at Weymouth.

Dougher's pointer traced the route. "Any deviation will draw friendly fire. Our ships and fighters have been ordered to shoot down any planes flying outside the corridor or against the stream. All aborts must be made before we leave England. If you experience problems after that, you must continue with the bomber stream."

Jack crossed his arms. Even if the Luftwaffe failed to show and flak was light, this would be no milk run. The assembly of masses of bombers in the dark, the strict route, the novel flight formation, and the rigor of radar-guided bombing so close to ground troops would make for a demanding mission.

49

Harmon Field, Stephenville, Newfoundland

Ruth's shoes crunched over the tarmac in the still darkness.

On the rare occasions she had a Remain Overnight at Stephenville, she enjoyed seeing the fishing boats on St. George's Bay, the whitewashed homes on the rocky slopes, and the giant bounding dogs unique to the island.

Tonight she had only a few hours before the return to Prestwick. A shuttle system had started recently. The squadrons based at Prestwick brought patients to Newfoundland, and then the 822nd MAETS based at Harmon Field took them to La Guardia. While Ruth would have preferred to accompany Sergeant Whitman to New York, the 822nd promised to send an extra nurse on the flight.

Ruth wandered about the airfield. It was 2300, or two-thirty in the morning in Scotland, since Newfoundland's time zone was three and a half hours behind Greenwich Mean Time. The other nurses napped, but Ruth couldn't sleep. How could she when the only thing she could see was Jack's devastated, resigned face?

From the moment she'd seen him after church and wanted to smother him with kisses and knew she wouldn't flinch, she realized she had to shove him out of her life forever.

SARAH SUNDIN

Why? Wasn't that what she'd prayed for? She should have been elated, but she was terrified. Her secret and her aversion had stood in twin guard over her heart. Now both had been dismissed, and her heart lay unguarded. If Jack knew, he'd take possession, and she couldn't let him do that.

"Why?" Ruth whispered as she meandered around the planes. "I trust him."

With searing pain in her chest, she knew it was a lie. She only trusted him partway, not with her heart and not with her family. She didn't want to. She could take care of her family. She could take care of herself.

"That's an even bigger lie." Ruth ground gravel beneath her foot. In the past year she'd learned how much she needed both God and friends.

A chill gust of wind made her wrap her arms around her middle. Maybe she could inventory her medical chest, which had been transferred to a cargo-laden C-54 from La Guardia.

A faint light glowed from the open cargo door. Ruth frowned. The base slumbered. Had someone left on a flashlight?

She climbed the stairs. No one was inside, but a lantern sat on a stack of boxes about halfway forward. Ruth went to investigate. Below the lantern, Burnsey's typewriter sat on the floor with an invoice sheet rolled in and flopping down the back. Another invoice lay next to the typewriter—an Air Transport Command form, signed and dated June 5, listing the cargo loaded on the plane. Why did Burnsey have that? It had nothing to do with his business. She lifted the paper in the typewriter, also an ATC invoice. "What on earth?"

Ruth knelt and compared the two forms. They were identical in every way, except the one in the typewriter listed three fewer items—two cases Camel cigarettes, one case Wrigley's spearmint gum, and one case Hershey's chocolate bars.

"What?" She glanced at the boxes around her—Camels,

Wrigley's, Hershey's, all with shipping labels from Samuel Burns to Staff Sgt. William Burns. Burnsey's cargo? But the invoices . . .

Ruth looked closer. The lowercase *e*'s on the labels were set too high, and so were the *e*'s on the invoice in the typewriter, but not the invoice in her hand, the real invoice.

"Oh my goodness." Burnsey had taken blank invoices and blank labels, and routed the supplies to himself. All this time, all those goods he said he got from his uncle—he did get them from his uncle, his Uncle Sam. He claimed he sold them at cost, with no profit whatsoever. What a lie. He made 100 percent profit.

"Can't sleep?" Burnsey stood behind her with his elbow on a stack of crates.

Ruth jumped to her feet. The invoice fluttered to the floor. "I just—I came to inventory the—the medical chest."

He studied the scene. Fear flickered on his face and drove all fear from Ruth's heart. For months, he'd had the power to destroy her, but now she had the power to destroy him. Triumph lifted her smile. "Now don't you wish you'd treated me with respect?"

All his usual charm returned. "It's not too late. You want me to pretend you're an ugly old hag like Lieutenant Shepard? Sure, I can do that. Just pretend you didn't see this. After all, it's only a little entrepreneurial enterprise."

She met his amused eyes in the yellow lantern light. "Entrepreneurial?"

"Sure. This is what we're fighting for. Capitalism. The American way."

"It's stealing."

Burnsey shook his head. "This is government property—government of the people, remember? My tax dollars."

"And mine, and—"

He laughed and crossed his ankles. "You have no idea how much money I made before the war. I'm a first-rate salesman. First-rate. My brother's a lousy salesman, but he's making a fortune in this war. Got out of the draft on a 4-F because of a bum knee. Now me, I serve my country. Very noble, very patriotic, very unprofitable. Why should I lose out because my knees work?"

Ruth gestured at the boxes. "But—"

"But what?" He patted a case of cigarettes. "I only sell luxury items, not necessities, and I charge no more than the PX. I run a fair business."

She stared at the typewriter. This wasn't a business. It was—

"Listen, I'm willing to cut you a deal. You're always short on cash, right?"

Ruth raised her chin at him. "I do fine."

Burnsey huffed. "I've heard you talk. All those kids to support, and no money for yourself. Wouldn't you like a treat for a change? A reward for your hard work?"

"I don't need that." But her voice came out soft.

"You could have it. Buy yourself a book, a record, maybe a record player."

"I don't—"

"What about your family? You could provide for them in style."

College. Aunt Pauline. Her chin lowered a bit. "I do fine."

"Sure, but you can do better, and I can help." He leaned forward, his eyes bright in the lantern light, but not leering. Perhaps he could treat her with respect. She didn't dare turn him in. Wouldn't Lieutenant Shepard love it if Ruth lodged one last complaint? And they probably didn't trust Ruth enough to investigate her claim. No, turning him in was too risky.

"Listen, this is what I'm willing to do for you. I'm looking to take on a partner. Now, this requires no work on your part whatsoever. None. All you have to do is distract Quartermasters if they get nosy. For that you get the deal of a lifetime. I'll give you two hundred bucks in advance, then 20 percent of the profits. If we keep running flights this often, you could clear a hundred bucks a month."

Ruth gasped. A hundred divided four ways—no, three ways. Chuck graduated this month.

Burnsey grinned. "Yeah. Think what you could do with that."

"That's a whole lot of money," she whispered.

"Sure is. Solve all your problems. Let you have a little fun for once. More important, you'll be independent. That's important to you, isn't it?"

Ruth nodded. She could meet Aunt Pauline's demands, start a college fund for Bert and Maggie, and buy a few things for herself. Not many, just a few.

For the first time.

50

Jack took one hand off the control wheel and worked his gloved fingers as if playing piano scales. He had to keep his fingers relaxed so he wouldn't lose his feel for the plane.

He checked the clock on the instrument panel and put the plane into a left-hand turn, peering into the black murk for the Aldis lamps in the tail of each B-17. Every once in a while, a "dot-dash" flashed in the clouds, the letter A for the 94th.

Two minutes later, he pulled out of the 180-degree turn. In six minutes, he'd turn again. Each rectangular loop assembled the elements, then the squadrons, and then the group into formation.

"Radio to pilot," Marvin Cox called on the interphone. "Adjust heading one degree south."

"Roger." Jack nudged the wheel right. Back in the radio room, Cox had his ear tuned to Buncher Twelve, the radio beacon over Bury, which guided the 94th in assembly.

Jack adjusted the throttles to keep his airspeed at 150 and tilted the wheel to keep his rate of climb at three hundred feet per minute. Assembly in the clouds, especially before dawn, required precise instrument flying.

Ralph Purcell, the newest pilot riding as copilot for training, let out a sigh. "About time."

Jack looked up from the panel. *My Macaroon* had finally broken through the clouds. Moonlight spilled silver on the clouds below. As far as he could see, blinking lights and arcs of flares marked the assembly of the largest air force ever. Between the fighters and bombers of the Eighth Air Force, Ninth Air Force, and RAF, and cargo planes returning from delivering paratroops, eleven thousand planes were expected over southern England in the morning.

Every precaution was being used to prevent collision, from Bunchers and Aldis lamps and flares to searchlight beacons marking the boundaries of each division's assembly area.

The clock read 0429, an hour since takeoff and at least another half hour in assembly.

"Zimmerman's too close again," Bob Ecklund said from the tail.

Jack groaned and flipped on his command radio. "Cedar lead to Agmer three. Adjust your position." Ted Zimmerman was on his second mission and flew a tight formation. Too tight. The formations the kids learned over the plains of Kansas didn't work in the tumultuous weather of northern Europe.

"Novak, pull up!" Ecklund cried.

Jack pulled back on the wheel.

"That was close," Ecklund said. "He banked her, almost clipped us."

Stupid rookie. Jack readjusted his wheel. "Cedar lead to Agmer three. Do not make sudden moves in formation. Never."

"Ro—roger. I was—I was—"

"I know. Radio silence." By now German radar had probably picked up the mass of planes approaching altitude over England, but the policy allowed him to cut off excuses. He'd placed Zimmerman in his three-plane element to keep an eye on him and avoid a repeat of May 19, when the 94th's *Miss Donna Mae* strayed under another Fort at bomb release and went down when a bomb from above sheared off her horizontal stabilizer.

Thousands of flashing lights spiraled upward. When Jack arrived in England, only four bomb groups operated. As of today, there were forty. Jack was flying his fifty-fourth mission with the Eighth, and he'd also flown thirty-three from Hawaii and Australia.

He should have been dead many times over.

Jack wasn't dead, although he had to burrow under the collar of his flight jacket to prove it. Yeah, he still had a pulse. In the last few weeks, he had to remind himself occasionally.

Jack made a turn in the continuing ring-around-the-Buncher until the 94th would be in formation.

Nope, God wouldn't let him die yet, because he was still teaching him. Trust God, not Jack. Pride, pride, pride. When he proposed to Ruth, he thought he was so noble, so selfless, so concerned with her needs.

Baloney. Charlie was right again. How could it be for her if she didn't want it?

If he hadn't pushed for marriage, he could have kept her friendship, and that's what hurt most, as if his heart had been carved up and splayed open.

To make it worse, worry for Ruth drilled like acid on the raw parts. He didn't trust this Burns fellow one bit. Did Burns know Ruth would lose her position if she complained? Would he take advantage of that?

Powdered eggs and bacon and toast turned into chill slime in Jack's stomach. If Burns forced himself on Ruth, would she report him? Could she?

51

In the back of the C-54, with a flashlight in hand, Ruth knelt before the medical chest to tidy it up. "'I'll think about it?' What kind of response was that?" The drone of the four engines masked her groan.

Although it was almost five in the morning back in England, she still couldn't sleep. She found a bottle of aspirin, popped a tablet in her mouth, and shuddered it down.

As bitter as the memory of telling Burnsey she'd think about it. What was there to think about? His business was illegal. She had to take the risk and report him. Even Lieutenant Shepard couldn't deny those invoices, but neither that thought nor the aspirin stopped the throb in her temples.

Burnsey typed away, most likely adding items to his shipment now that he thought he had a partner. Of course, he thought he had a partner. She told him she'd think about it.

Ruth fumbled with the ampules, the vials, and the stupid syringe of Pentothal Burnsey had drawn up. What a shame to waste it. She set the syringe in the top tray. Maybe Surgery could use it.

She massaged her pounding forehead. An hour had passed since takeoff, but guilt would keep her awake more than the headache would. *Forgive me, Lord, for even considering it. You always provide. Shouldn't I know that by now? I can't believe I was tempted. Please forgive me.*

The Lord would take care of her family. Fifty-seven dollars a month was plenty for Chuck, Bert, and Anne, and plenty for Maggie too. In a few weeks Chuck would join the Navy, and Ruth would put his portion in a college fund. If Aunt Pauline threatened to send Maggie away, Ruth had other options. Perhaps Uncle Nolan would take Maggie in Chuck's place, or perhaps Aunt Peggy would let her share Anne's room now that her daughter had joined the WACs.

God always provided. Why, oh why did she consider Burnsey's deal?

If she hadn't let temptation worm a slimy tunnel into her head, she could have reported him at Harmon Field. Now she had to wait until they landed at Prestwick in the evening.

"Hi there." In the fuzzy glow of the flashlight, Burnsey sat on the floor beside the chest and propped his forearms on his bent knees. "Figured out how to spend that two hundred?"

Ruth straightened a pile of bandages. "I'm thinking about it." She despised the lie but she didn't dare tell the truth.

"What are you thinking about? Jewelry? Perfume? The London theater?"

"I'm thinking about my decision." Yeah, thinking how stupid she was to consider it.

"What's there to think about? You said it yourself—that's a whole lot of money."

So was ten cents for ten minutes. Ruth shivered and pushed aside a coil of IV tubing. Compromising morals for money? "Never again."

"What was that?"

Ruth sucked in her breath. The flashlight clunked to the floor.

The beam of light pointed at her knees. She reached for the flashlight, but it drew away. Burnsey pointed it at her, not in her eyes, but she could no longer see his face.

"What exactly are you thinking about, Ruth?"

Now was not the time to remind him of military courtesy. She glanced into the medical chest, away from the revealing light. "I'm thinking about whether I should take your offer."

She rearranged piles, although she couldn't see past the beam of light. She tried to relax her face, but every nerve jittered.

"Might as well," he said in a slow, cool voice. "You should get some reward for not snitching."

Her face twitched. She couldn't help it.

Clothing rustled. The beam rose and angled down at her. "You won't snitch."

Ruth wrapped her hands around the open edge of the chest and pushed herself to standing. She had to keep her voice as cool as his, although her breath came too fast. "I never said I would. Now, may I please have my flashlight back?"

"You never said you wouldn't, either." He aimed the beam right at her.

She shielded her eyes and walked down the aisle. "It's late and I'm tired."

"You're not sleeping until I know you won't snitch."

Ruth whirled around and let all the past months' frustration show on her face. "Who on earth would believe me if I did? Tell me. Would any single person believe me?"

Burnsey's chuckle bounced down the beam of light. "Remember that. Remember that when you think you can play Little Orphan Annie, girl detective."

She turned down the dark canyon of crates and boxes toward the seats at the front of the cabin, past the lantern and typewriter. Little Orphan Ruthie only had to convince the authorities to compare the phony invoice with the carbon copy of the original at La Guardia.

Then they'd see she'd told the truth all along.

52

"Say, Skipper, if you get a chance, look down."

In the dawn light, Jack made a quick sweep of the instrument panel and glanced out the window. Through a ragged hole in the cloud blanket, the English Channel glinted steely gray eighteen thousand feet below, studded with hundreds of ships.

He whistled. "Say a prayer for your brothers down there, boys. They've got a rugged day ahead. Let's do our job and make theirs a little easier."

The clock read 0534. They had to bomb by 0555 and clear out before British Commonwealth soldiers landed at 0700.

"Mickey operator to crew," Nick Panapoulos called. "I'm getting beautiful pictures of the coast, the Orne River."

"Good," Jack said. "Close to the IP?"

"About five minutes."

Jack had flown historic missions before, but the sight of all those planes and ships bearing down on the Normandy coast made his chest swell under the layers of flight gear.

Instead of flying in trail as usual, the groups flew line abreast so they could bomb simultaneously. Jack felt as if he marched to the fife and drum with his trusty musket over his shoulder, except he marched to the beat of Wright-Cyclone engines and carried 500-pound general purpose bombs. Still he found himself whistling "Yankee Doodle."

"Novak, we've got a problem." From back in the tail, Bob Ecklund's voice sounded strained. "Zimmerman—he's drifting underneath us. He's not responding to the radio. I don't know if the problem's with my set or his."

In the copilot's seat, Purcell cussed and not like a rookie.

Zimmerman was supposed to fly behind, below, and to the right of *My Macaroon*, but the noses were lined up, with Zimmerman's left wing directly under Jack's right wing. Jack flipped the overhead radio switch to command. "Cedar lead to Agmer three."

No response.

More cussing. "His wingtip's under our fuselage."

Jack edged the wheel back, but the rookie followed. "Cedar lead to Agmer three."

"He's not even looking our way," Purcell said. "He's playing with the radio overhead."

"You'd better be turning it on, you fool." Jack gave the Fort a little left rudder to slip to the side.

"Ah! He saw us! Watch—"

The plane bucked. Metal screeched on metal, and men yelled.

A collision! The B-17 pitched left. Jack fought the wheel and pulled into a slight climbing turn to get away from the formation and avoid further collisions.

"He turned," Purcell said. "The idiot plowed his wing through our undercarriage."

"Call through the stations, Purcell. Damage report." Jack looked out the window. Engine four's propellers were bent so badly they could never be feathered, and manifold pressure was falling. "Swell. Shut down four."

Purcell moved the mixture control to "off."

Jack leveled the plane, then turned off the ignition to number four and closed the throttle, while Purcell called through the stations. Thank God, no one was injured except *My Macaroon*.

"Agmer three to Cedar lead." Panic scrambled Zimmerman's voice. "Oh no. I've lost number one. My wing's chewed up."

"What on earth were you doing?" Jack eased the plane back into formation.

"The radio. Command wasn't working. Morrie and I were switching to liaison."

"Swell. Next time watch where you're going." He couldn't keep the anger out of his voice, even though he kept a gentle hand on the aileron trim wheel beside his seat.

Purcell tapped Jack's arm. "Nick says the Mickey's working. The collision missed the radome. He says we're at the IP, and Gus agrees."

"Good." The formation consisted of six-plane flights, with a Pathfinder plane in every third flight. If his H2X failed, eighteen B-17s would return with their bombs. "Tell Cox to fire flares and tell Charlie to open bomb bay doors."

Purcell relayed the messages. Underneath the plane, metal ground on metal. A motor whined and strained.

Jack moaned. Zimmerman's wing must have mangled the bomb bay doors. "Mel, better check on that. See if you can crank them open manually."

The flight engineer hadn't waited for Jack's order. He stepped out of the top turret with a portable oxygen bottle in hand.

"What do I do? What do I do?" Zimmerman again.

Jack didn't have time to hold the kid's hand and teach him how to fly. "Shut down number one, transfer fuel, keep that

wing up, stick with the flight plan as briefed, and watch—
where—you're—going."

He switched to command radio and told his group to bomb
when he fired flares. Whether or not *My Macaroon* could
drop, the target was too important to be missed.

The 94th aimed for machine gun installations and an-
titank emplacements in the crucial communication center
of Caen behind Sword beach, the easternmost site. H2X
didn't produce pinpoint bombing, but that didn't matter.
The objective was to demoralize the Germans and disrupt
communication.

A heavy hand on his shoulder. "Can't get those doors
open," Mel yelled over the engines. "They're buckled up.
Won't budge."

Jack sighed. "Thanks for trying. Now I need you to transfer
fuel from engine four to one."

Mel tipped his big hand to his flak helmet and squatted in
the back of the cockpit.

Jack wiped his forehead, surprised by the chill coating of
sweat. As the Eighth Air Force mushroomed, so did collisions.
Thank goodness no one had been killed.

"There she is," Nick said on the interphone. "Target 16C2
confirmed, clear as can be."

"Good job," Jack said. "Marvin, wait thirty seconds,
then fire those flares." The delay was required to prevent
short-bombing. Better to miss the target than to hit friendly
troops.

"Double red flares fired."

"They got the signal," Bob said from the tail. "All seventeen
are dropping."

"Great." Jack put the plane in a sharp left-hand turn to
loop away from the target area before shooting west over
Normandy.

"I wish you all could have been back here," Nick said. "Beautiful pictures on the scope, clear as can be, just like the briefing pictures."

"Thanks," Charlie said. "Took those pictures myself."

Jack shook his head and whistled. "I don't want to be around when May finds out you've been flying over enemy territory again."

Charlie laughed. "I'll deal with May. Just get me home, Skipper."

Jack didn't like the looks of engine three, but he'd flown planes in far worse condition. Even if he lost number three, he could still bring her home. It would be close, but he could do it. "I plan on it, buddy. You can trust—no, don't trust me. Trust God."

53

"Wake up, gorgeous." A rough hand shook Ruth's shoulder.

She looked up from her canvas seat along the side of the plane.

At the front of the cabin, Burnsey leaned back against a high stack of crates. "Decision time."

Oh no. Ruth rubbed her eyes to conceal a glance at her watch—9:45 in England, and they wouldn't land at Meeks until 11:30. She'd avoided Burnsey for over four hours by sleeping. She'd slept fitfully, but she'd slept. What good did it do now? How could she avoid this conversation? She drew a deep yawn. "Later. I'm still tired."

Burnsey laughed, cool and humorless. "You want to wait until Prestwick."

"Well, yes."

"Where you'll rat on me."

Clammy fingers coiled around her heart. "I didn't say that."

"You don't have to say it." A bottle of scotch dangled from his hand. Although the cabin temperature hovered around freezing, he wore his wool jacket. He'd taken off his sheepskins.

Those clammy fingers dug in. Burnsey had drunk enough liquor to warm up—enough to affect his judgment? Ruth nodded to the bottle. "Let's wait until you sleep that off."

He took a swig. "You think you've got this figured out. Wait till Prestwick, show them the invoices, and you'll get what you've always wanted—to get rid of me."

She took a measured breath. Although he had her motive wrong, he knew her strategy. "I don't want to get rid of you. I just want to be treated—"

"Your plan won't work. I retyped the labels, switched back the invoices. You have no evidence, gorgeous. None." He rested his head back against the crates in front of the cabin door.

The cabin door? He'd blocked the way to the cockpit. The clamminess raced down to her fingertips.

"I've got a bit of a problem." Burnsey swung the bottle like a pendulum and thumped it into his palm. "See, I like my business. I really like it. You've made me lose this shipment, but I can't afford to do that again. Now, everything will be fine if you accept my offer."

And if not . . . ? Ruth studied his wry smile and narrowed eyes. The smart thing would be to accept his offer, then report him when safely on the ground. Was it wrong to lie to a thief? To betray a swindler?

"I knew I couldn't trust you."

A band constricted around her chest. She'd waited too long to answer, and even if she said she'd cooperate, he wouldn't believe her.

Burnsey took one more swig and set down the liquor bottle. "Too bad. You could have had everything. Now you lose everything."

"Lose?" Her gaze skittered around. Could she get past him? Could she move the crates in time? Or reach the interphone jack? If she screamed, no one would hear her over the engines.

Burnsey sauntered over, right in front of her, and Ruth pressed back in her seat. He wasn't a big man, but he was big enough.

"See, I need a new nurse, someone more compliant, so you're out of a job." He cocked his head in mock sympathy.

"I won't lose my job." Ruth wrapped her arms around her stomach to quell the nausea and to unfasten her seatbelt.

"I heard old lady Shepard. One more complaint and you're out." He leaned forward and planted his hands on the fuselage on either side of Ruth's head.

She recoiled. Burnsey's breath was flammable, but she didn't have a match. "I won't complain. I won't."

"Today you will. I'll make sure of it." His gaze fell to her chest and her legs. "You see, if you were my partner, I'd behave. But now, well, I can do anything I want."

Never—never had her hands been so uncooperative. Her seatbelt, why wouldn't it open?

"And guess what I want." He lifted his eyes to hers.

Oh no, Ruth knew that look, the lethal mixture of power and contempt and lust. This time she wasn't trapped by brick walls and locked doors and bulky men, but by crates and aluminum and five thousand feet of air.

"Finally." He smashed his mouth over hers.

No, no, no. She pressed her hands to Burnsey's chest and kicked at him.

He laughed putrid fumes over her face. "Don't fight me. Don't even bother."

When he swooped down again, Ruth twisted to the side and let his mouth crawl over her cheek. She had to get her seatbelt unfastened, get to the cockpit somehow.

Burnsey slobbered all over her neck, and Ruth's stomach contracted. *Lord, please don't let me get sick. Don't let me hyperventilate.*

He grabbed the collar of her sheepskin flight jacket, ripped open the zipper.

"No!" The buckle came loose, and Ruth jerked up her knee.

He cried out, clutched one hand to his stomach.

Ruth shoved him aside, dashed from her seat, and slammed into the stack of crates. They didn't budge. Oh no, she'd have to move them one at a time. She wrapped her arms around the top crate.

Burnsey hurled expletives, charged at her, grasped the back of her collar in both fists, and with a guttural, triumphal cry, yanked the jacket down and off, scraping Ruth's hands over the raw wood.

She moaned. Red lines scratched the truth across her palms. She couldn't stop him. She couldn't escape.

54

The propeller blades on engine three rotated into the feathered position. Boy, did Jack hate to lose that engine.

Charlie hummed on the interphone, then broke into song. "'With our full crew aboard and our trust in the Lord, we're comin' in on a wing and a prayer.'"

A wing and a lot of prayers would be better. Jack kept solid left pressure on the rudder to compensate for the loss of both engines on the right wing.

The rest of the 94th had passed him when they rounded the Channel Islands. The Allied fighters scared off the Luftwaffe, so solitude didn't present the usual danger, but Jack had plenty of concerns with falling fuel levels and the muscle required to keep the wings level. At least they'd descended below ten thousand feet and didn't need oxygen anymore.

"Okay, Mel," he said. "Let's transfer fuel from three to two." The transfer from engine four had failed, probably due to a ruptured fuel line, and Jack needed every drop.

Mel flipped the lever on the bulkhead below the door to the bomb bay, and Purcell switched the fuel gauge to monitor number two.

"Come on, baby." Jack willed the gauge to rise, but it didn't. "Oh, swell."

"I was afraid of that." Mel sat on the platform of the top turret. "Zimmerman sure ripped up that wing, didn't he? What about—"

"Landing gear. I know." The right wheel nestled in the nacelle of damaged engine three. "Okay, crew, let's test the landing gear. Purcell?"

The copilot flipped the switch in the center of the panel.

Jack looked out the side window. "Down left."

"Tail wheel down," Fred Garrett called on the interphone from the waist.

Jack glanced at Purcell, but the kid shook his head. Jack rapped his fist on his knee. "Mel, try to crank it down."

If Mel couldn't lower the right wheel manually, Jack had a dilemma. A belly landing would be suicidal with a full bomb load. A one-wheeled landing was safer, but tough without power on the same wing he needed to keep high on the landing. What else? Ditching in the Channel? Never. Abandoning ship would be the best option.

Mel leaned through the door to the cockpit. "Something's disconnected. It cranks too easily. The wheel's not coming down."

"Gear up." Jack couldn't afford the drag. "Gus, how long to Weymouth?"

"About six minutes."

"Hallelujah." He wasn't going in the drink today. "Okay, crew, listen up. Prepare to bail out in a few minutes. Then I'll put this bird on autopilot and point her out to sea."

If the men were scared about making a jump, they were smart enough to keep it to themselves, or smart enough to know it was safer than landing or ditching.

Charlie crawled up from the passageway between the pilots' seats. "Got a minute?"

One look told Jack that Charlie questioned his judgment.

Fair enough—he'd earned the right to be heard. "Sure do. Here, take my spot."

Charlie raised his eyebrows but switched positions with Jack while Purcell held the plane steady.

"Thanks, buddy." Jack kicked out a cramp in his left leg. "I could use a rest. What's up?"

"The autopilot?"

Jack pulled the release tabs on his flak vest and laid it aside. At least Charlie didn't voice his concern over the interphone. "I know. I don't think it'll hold her true."

"So . . ."

"So I'll land her."

"Jack . . ."

"I can do it. Remember that time in Townsville? Only had one engine then."

"But no bombs."

Jack smiled. "Doesn't change the landing, just the results if I fail. I won't fail."

Charlie narrowed his eyes, then rolled them. "Why not ditch her?"

"You've heard the latest statistics—43 percent chance of survival. I stand a higher chance on land, you know that. Besides, I'd hate to lose this plane. She's a beauty."

"All right. I'll take Purcell's spot."

Jack laughed. "Absolutely not. I'd rather ditch than earn the wrath of Little Miss Jensen."

"Jack . . ."

He stretched his arm down between the seat and the wall and flipped the alarm switch for six seconds to signal the crew to stand by for bailing out, and to silence his friend. Then he motioned Charlie out of the seat and resumed his wrestling match with the rudder and wheel. "Go on, buddy. Get out of here. I'll see you at Bury."

Charlie laid a hand on Jack's shoulder and looked down at him with staggering finality.

Jack swallowed hard. "Pray. And—and give May my love."

"And Ruth?"

Jack turned to the altimeter, which fell rapidly. Give his love to Ruth? If only he could. "Tell—tell her I'm sorry. Now, go. Watch how you land on that leg."

Charlie squeezed Jack's shoulder. "I'll be praying."

"Thanks. So will I." He looked out the window to solid green land. "Gus, are we far enough inland to bail?"

"Yes, sir."

Jack gave the bell three short rings. "Bail out, boys. Bob, count chutes for me before you go."

Over the next minute, Bob counted off parachutes from his seat in the tail. Good, Charlie didn't play stowaway. After Bob bailed, Jack relaxed his grip and let *My Macaroon* turn to the right as she wanted to. When she pointed south toward the sea, Jack activated the autopilot.

"Okay, Purcell. Thanks for the help. Out you go." He didn't have to ask twice. The kid scrambled down to the nose.

Jack marked two minutes to make sure Purcell was clear, then released the controls. The Fort banked to the right. As he suspected, the autopilot didn't hold. If he bailed, the plane would spiral down and explode on English soil. "Okay, Lord, give me a nice big landing field."

A one-wheeled landing. Jack could do it. He knew how to handle a plane.

What a story that would be. Jack would get his name in the papers, another Distinguished Flying Cross, maybe a Silver Star, and a good position when he transferred.

Ditching, on the other hand, would result in the loss of the plane and probably his life.

Jack shuddered and searched the ground, where a village tapered off to small farms. Fear didn't influence him this time, and neither did pride.

Or did it? "Lord, am I counting on my abilities again?"

Jack shook it off and turned the plane away from the main road out of town. In this case counting on his abilities was warranted. Logic, not fear, said land offered a greater chance of survival than water. Still, he sent up a prayer. "Lord, guide me. And help me listen."

There it was, a nice green field at eleven o'clock. Jack grinned and turned the plane to approach the field from the side. He extended the landing gear and swung over the tail wheel lock on the floor. Then he tested the brakes. The hydraulic pressure stayed above six hundred pounds per square inch. Good, something worked.

What a great field. Jack visualized his course—a right turn into the downwind leg, a left turn for the base leg, and a left turn into the final approach. He'd have plenty of room before the thatched farmhouse at the end of the field.

Jack chuckled. Wouldn't those people be surprised? A cocky Yank landing a B-17 in their field with one pilot, two engines, two out of three wheels, and—

Then his blood froze in his veins.

And a full bomb load.

What if he couldn't keep the wing up? He risked not only his life, but the lives of anyone in that house.

Nonsense. He could keep that wing up. He'd be the hero.

Jack groaned at the ugly tentacle of pride. But what was the alternative? Ditching. Drowning.

"Trust God, you idiot."

The stretch of warm, green, grassy life sang out its temptation, but Jack gritted his teeth and wheeled the Fort toward cold, gray, watery death.

55

Burnsey tossed aside Ruth's leather flight jacket. "That's better. Now for the rest."

She backed against the crates and raised her trembling chin. "Don't touch me."

"I'll do what I want." He seized her shoulders and pressed his mouth over hers.

"No!" She stomped on his foot. He cursed and drew up his leg, and Ruth planted her hands on his chest to push him away.

Burnsey shackled her wrists in his hands. "You little—" His mouth twisted with fury, with vile words.

Ruth stared him hard in the eye and with all her strength, drove her knee into his groin. He gasped, doubled over, and Ruth broke free, down the aisle, down the valley of crates, down the valley of the shadow of death. "'I will fear no evil: for thou art with me.'"

But where was she going? She didn't have time to plug headphones into the rear interphone jack and call the crew, and the only exit led to Arctic waters five thousand feet below.

Cuss words pummeled her, nearer and nearer. Burnsey grabbed her left arm, and she stumbled. He yanked her around to face him. "Let's get this straight. You hurt me and I'll hurt you worse."

With his eyes spewing hateful fire, he took her left wrist in one hand, her elbow in the other, and cracked her arm over the edge of a crate.

White heat blazed through her arm. Screaming, she crumpled to the floor and pulled her shattered arm to her belly.

"Why do you always make things hard, gorgeous? If you'll be nice, we'll both have fun. Either way, I will."

Ruth opened one pain-scrunched eye to see Burnsey shrug off his jacket and loosen his tie. She crawled down the aisle. *Please, Lord. I trust you to stop him.*

"Think you're so high-and-mighty with those lieutenant's bars, do you? Think you can boss me around? Well, look at you. Who's in charge now, huh? Who?"

"God is." She staggered to her feet and cried out from the pain.

"I'm in charge. I am." He threw his arms around her waist.

A great wet bubble of a sob rose in her throat, but she swallowed it, even as Burnsey's hands clawed at her chest, the buttons of her uniform jacket.

Ruth shivered from his touch. Not ten feet in front of her stood the medical chest, the lid open from her inventory. If only she could fit inside, could curl up inside and shut the lid.

"You need this. Put you in your place." He spun her around, engulfed her in the dark cavern of his mouth.

She hated his kiss, despised it, not because of past memories, but because it was Burns, so rough and contemptuous. Why couldn't she have given herself to Jack, to dear Jack, so tender and loving? She could have. She could have. But now it was too late. Now there was only Burnsey, his sickening hands up her shirt in the back.

"No . . ." She shoved him off and rolled away.

He clutched her jacket. Ruth tugged free, lost her balance, and reached for the edge of the medical chest. It tipped over with a crash of metal on metal, shattering glass. She screamed, banged her head on the chest, and landed—on her broken arm.

Pain curled her body, shards of ampules pierced her shoulder and side, medications seeped liquid ice through her clothes.

"Finally." Burnsey threw himself on top of her and slammed her shoulders flat against the cold metal floor. "About time you get what you deserve. 'Bout time I get what I deserve."

His weight crushed the breath and the hope right out of her. She couldn't stop him. He was bigger and stronger. She was injured and trapped.

Trust me.

A glimmer of hope gave her strength to turn away from the slobber. *I do, Lord. I trust you to stop him.*

No, trust me.

God would give her the strength. Ruth pushed against Burnsey's chest, but he wrestled her arm down, continued grabbing and kissing and pulling.

Wet grief tightened across her chin and up her jaw. She swept away a vial under her elbow. Burnsey would hardly hold still and let her draw up a syringe, one-handed nonetheless. Maybe she could cut him, distract him.

No, the last time she hurt him, he broke her arm. Tears rolled across the bridge of her nose and down her temple.

Trust me no matter what.

No matter what? Even if Burnsey raped her? How could she bear it?

Trust me.

A sob burst out. *Oh Lord, that's it, isn't it? That's trust.*

I have to trust you even if he rapes me. You'll be with me. You'll help me through somehow.

Tears flowed freely, not from the knowledge of what was to come, not from Burnsey's loathsome touch, not from her wretched memories, but from a strange place of detached comfort.

Ruth squeezed her eyes shut. *I do, Lord. I do trust you. "They that dwell in the land of the shadow of death, upon them hath the light shined."* The other day she'd read that in Isaiah, and now God brought it to mind when she needed his light most.

The storm would rage in torrential tears, thunderous humiliation, and lightning pain, but God had lifted her above the gray.

Burnsey shifted forward and ground his mouth into her neck. "That's right, gorgeous. Relax. We'll both have more fun."

56

"Mayday. Mayday. Mayday. Cedar four nine. One, two, three, four, five. Five, four, three, two, one." Jack repeated the distress call on Channel B of his VHF radio. The more he talked, the better fix Air-Sea Rescue could get on his position.

If they could get a fix at all. Jack didn't think he'd drifted west of the temporary fixer station at Exeter, but he had little idea of his bearings.

He guided the Fort parallel to the ugly swells below. In a ditching, each crewmember had designated tasks, but since Jack was alone, he couldn't transmit his exact coordinates or jettison the roof hatch in the radio room.

Jack hated to lose *My Macaroon*, but somehow it was appropriate to lose the plane named after the girl he'd already lost. But why did it have to be in water? He wanted to think the sweat tickling his neck and sides came from his struggle with the controls, but his choppy breath and quivering muscles betrayed him.

It was fear. Pure, cold fear.

Landing gear stowed, flaps to medium. Jack picked a trough to land in, only a few feet below. "Lord, please." He'd never prayed with more fervency.

Airspeed ninety miles per hour. He let the plane settle about a foot from the water, cut the ignition switches, and lost the reassuring throb of engines in his ear. He muscled the rudder and wheel to keep level. If the tail hit first, the fuselage would snap in half. If one wing hit first, he'd cartwheel.

He grimaced as the valley of water rose before him.

A hard jolt. The plane jostled down the trough. Jack bounced off the control wheel, coughed to get his breath, bumped his shoulder. The Fort shuddered to a halt.

Now the plane rose and fell, rose and fell. Sickening.

Jack whipped off his seatbelt. The side window of the cockpit was the fastest way out, but he wanted a life raft, which had to be released from the radio room.

He bolted from his seat, tripped over the platform of the top turret, rammed his knee. He cried out in annoyance more than pain. At most he had thirty seconds, and he couldn't afford mistakes.

He yanked open the door to the bomb bay and slipped as water lapped over the aluminum catwalk. With a full bomb load and warped doors, she'd sink fast.

Jack pushed on the door to the radio room, but it was jammed. Cold water soaked his ankles, down into his shoes and into his soul.

"Oh Lord, no." He whipped around. If he hurried, he could make it back to the cockpit and out the window.

Without a life raft.

With a furious cry, Jack drove his shoulder against the door like a defensive lineman. Again. He fell through, landed on hands and knees in a foot of water, and recoiled from the icy splash in his face.

Up to his feet. He sloshed forward, gripped the life raft release handles in the ceiling and pulled down hard. The water covered his knees. "Why water? Why does it have to be water?"

The plane creaked and shifted under his feet. He grabbed the radio desk. His heartbeat boomed in his ears.

Now to open the roof hatch. Stupid, double-crossing hands wouldn't cooperate. Took too long to pull the first two red handles, then the last two. The hatch was heavy and awkward, designed to fly off in the slipstream during flight, and Jack lost leverage as freezing water rose to his belt.

With a giant heave, he shoved it aside. It scraped down the side and splashed into the ocean.

The next splash would be Jack. He wrapped his fingers around the rim of the hatch, but his arms shook so hard he couldn't hoist himself up.

The plane pitched forward. Jack slipped, yelled, fell underwater. He shut his eyes against the sting of salt water and shut his mind against the terror of drowning, trapped in a sinking plane.

No! He had to get out. Jack planted his feet, pushed off, and banged his head on the ceiling. The Fort was submerged.

Lord, no! Panic swelled like the breath in his lungs. Jack groped along the ceiling until his hand plunged through the hatch. He hauled himself out, kicked upward. He broke the surface and gasped for air. Only the tail fin of the plane was still visible, coming straight at him like a giant silver shark.

Jack cried out and dived to the side. Sharp, hot pain exploded in his right foot. He grabbed his ankle, screamed, swallowed seawater, spat it out. When he kicked to tread water, pain ripped through his foot. He must have broken something.

He had to get to a life raft. A swell lifted him. Two yellow patches bobbed over a hundred feet away. "Oh, great."

Jack reached for the tab to inflate his life vest. Where was it? He tore off his gloves and felt under the straps of his parachute harness.

Parachute harness? Oh no. He was supposed to take it off before ditching, but he'd been occupied with the controls.

Jack dropped under the icy water, weighted down by sodden sheepskin. He kicked for the surface, wincing at the pain in his foot. He couldn't survive long in the water, but without the life vest, he'd drown before hypothermia overtook him.

He had to get the harness off. If he inflated the life vest now, it would expand inward and crush his chest.

Jack worked at the clip, but tremors of fear and cold rattled his hands. Water sloshed over his head. He flung out his arms, pulled himself up, and sputtered out a salty mouthful of water.

With all the flight gear dragging him down, he needed all four limbs to tread water. But he had to get the harness off, and that would require both hands—which meant submersion. He needed to work fast. The cold numbed the pain in his foot, but it also numbed his fingers and wanted to numb his brain.

"Lord, help me." Jack drew a deep breath. His fingers jerked, unfeeling, over the harness, and he slipped under the waves, cold and gray and impersonal.

So this was it. This was how he would die. Somehow it seemed right.

57

Burnsey fumbled with Ruth's belt buckle, cursed at it, cursed at Ruth every time she squirmed.

Soon it would be over. He'd want her put together before they landed, but how would he explain away her injuries? This would strain even Burnsey's skill at dissembling.

"Wanted you first time I saw you. Thought you were too good for me, huh? Well, I got you now."

No, God had her. In her mind, a hymn played its unusual melody and comforting words. *"Under His wings my soul shall abide, safely abide forever."*

Still, the pain would come—flaming, ripping, pounding pain.

Ruth felt around in the sharp wet mess from the medical chest. Maybe she could find something to grip to take her mind off the pain. Off to the side she found a glass cylinder, a syringe. She rolled her fingers around its coolness, and then frowned.

The plunger of the syringe was halfway out, as if . . .

She craned her neck to see around Burnsey's shoulders. The syringe was full. Pentothal—the Pentothal drawn up for poor Sergeant Whitman.

Ruth eased her head down, her lips tingling with incredulous hope even as Burnsey flopped her belt open.

Pentothal. The facts raced through her head. Onset of unconsciousness in ten to twenty seconds, duration of action thirty minutes—the perfect drug, but how could she administer it? An intramuscular shot would be easy, but the onset would be delayed and the required dose might be higher. No, she had to give it intravenously.

How can I, Lord? You gave me this syringe. Please show me how to use it.

Burnsey's shirtsleeves covered the antecubital vein in the crook of his elbow. The only good-sized vein in view was the jugular, but that was crazy. She'd never heard of anyone administering a medication in the jugular.

Burnsey unzipped her trousers.

The jugular would have to do. Ruth clenched the syringe in her hand with her thumb on the plunger. She would have only one chance, one stick.

Burnsey raised himself on his knees, grabbed her waistband, and sneered at her. "Now you'll have something to complain about."

He was too far away. Ruth bucked her hips and rolled to her right side as if she were trying to get away.

He slapped her hard across the face and threw himself down on top of her.

She gasped from the pain but kept her hand steady on the syringe. Burnsey's jugular lay only inches from her face. She wriggled her torso to keep him in position and raised her right arm above his shoulder.

Lord, this is my only chance. Guide me. In one smooth move, she swung the syringe down, inserted the needle, and depressed the plunger.

Burnsey cried out and grabbed his neck. Droplets arched from the needle tip. "What the—? What'd you do?"

"Pentothal. Your Pentothal."

He rose to his knees, a spout of expletives.

Ruth covered herself. "Count to ten, Sergeant."

His face convulsed. He lifted one hand high and coiled it into a fist. Then he yawned, gave Ruth a look of furious disbelief, and collapsed to the side.

She kicked herself free, rolled to her side, and clutched her throbbing, swelling arm to her chest. She shuddered with cold and laughter and sobs.

"It worked. Oh my goodness, it actually worked. Thank you, Lord. Thank you." Burnsey was out. He was unconscious. He wouldn't rape her. The Lord would have seen her through no matter what, she knew it, she trusted him, but he had spared her. She lay soaking in God's light, praising him until the shudders died down.

Then a thought seized her. Burnsey would wake in half an hour, maybe less, madder than ever.

She pushed herself up on wobbly legs. She couldn't get help like this, couldn't let anyone see her in such a state. After she made herself decent, she plugged the headset into the interphone jack in the rear of the plane. "Flight nurse to crew."

Nothing.

The jack box stood at an odd angle. At her touch, it slipped to the side and exposed snipped wires. Burnsey had planned everything.

Ruth stumbled down the aisle to the stack of crates in front of the cabin door. She tried to move the top crate. Why did he have to pick such heavy ones? She couldn't move them. Weak from spent adrenaline and shaking from the cold, she couldn't get enough force with her good arm.

Ruth glanced down the aisle to Burnsey's unconscious form. How much time did she have left? She tried to look at

A MEMORY BETWEEN US

her watch, but she couldn't twist her arm or slide the watch around her swollen wrist. Wincing from pain, she unbuckled the strap and held up the watch.

Ten minutes before ten? The whole ordeal took place in only five minutes? Impossible. Then she noticed the second hand lay still. Dead. Her throat constricted. Why did Burnsey have to do that? Why did he have to break her watch?

Ruth pressed the cool glass to her lips and squeezed her eyes shut. She was as trapped as ever, and time was running out.

58

Wasn't his life supposed to flash before his eyes?

All Jack saw was gray sky and gray water alternating as he drifted below and struggled above, gray to gray, merging together.

Mom and Dad would be devastated, but of the three boys, Jack was the most expendable. Walt, the married man, would fulfill Mom's dreams of grandchildren. Ray, the gifted pastor, fulfilled Dad's dreams. Maybe it was best Jack had never told Dad his career plans.

He tried to unclasp the harness again, but his fingers could no longer distinguish metal from fabric. Water slobbered out of his mouth. He was almost too tired to push it out.

Jack knew what would come. He remembered too well falling unconscious, waking up, and spitting out water in panic. Last time a fishing boat saved him from repeating the cycle, but today no boats were in sight. How many times would he go under before he died?

Please make it fast, Lord. Then he'd be with Jesus. No more sorrow, no more pain.

Would Ruth mourn? In his mind he saw her thrust the scissors into his hands and into his heart. But then he saw her upturned, worry-creased face. "Please be careful, Jack."

She didn't love him, couldn't love him, but she cared and she'd mourn and she'd find some way to blame herself, to punish herself, to cut off anyone who might care.

No! He couldn't let that happen. Jack opened his eyes underwater, accustomed to the salt, and looked down at the clasp. His fingers clenched like granite, but he pressed the clip against his chest and squeezed his wrists together.

Pop.

Hallelujah! He flung his arms over his head, down in a giant arc. Up, around, down. Air! He filled his lungs, then scrubbed his face to wake himself up. He shrugged the harness off his shoulders, wriggled it over his hips, and kicked it off.

Then he pulled the tab on his life vest, which inflated and lifted his chest. Jack smiled, tugged off his flight helmet, and let his head droop back. The water played with his hair as he gazed at the clouds. He could rest now. He wouldn't drown.

When the next swell elevated him, he searched for the rafts in vain. The shore lay close enough to taunt him, yet out of reach.

No, he wouldn't drown. He'd die of hypothermia. How long had he been in the water? Half an hour? An hour? He'd stopped shivering, which meant his body had given up.

All his striving, all his life, for nothing. Promotions, prestige, positions—all meant nothing. *Lord, did I do what you wanted? That's all that matters.*

At least he'd followed God into the ocean. He was supposed to. He was supposed to face his fear, swallow his pride, and die here.

Why did he resist the gray? It was softness. It was comfort. It was peace. Waves pulsed on his cheeks, the pulse of engines vibrating through the controls, through his arms, through his soul. Water roared in his ears, the roar of cylinders and propellers and air on the windscreen. A shadow slipped over him and closed his eyes.

Seeing planes in the clouds. All his life. How fitting that his last thoughts were about planes.

59

Would God rescue her to leave her in greater danger? Ruth groaned her answer. No, of course not.

She returned to the back of the plane, passing Burnsey's sprawled form, and rummaged in the pile from the medical chest. After she fashioned a crude sling from gauze and cradled her tender arm inside, she shook out two lengths of rubber IV tubing. "Please, Lord. Please give me strength."

With her good hand and her knee, she knotted the tubing around Burnsey's right wrist, and then around his left, as close to the first knot as possible. She doubled it, tripled it.

Burnsey's fingers curled. Ruth gasped. He was still unconscious, but how long did she have? Her hand shook as she tied up his ankles.

From a canvas bag on the ceiling, she released some web strapping. She threaded it under Burnsey's arm and buckled it to the anchoring pole on the floor, and repeated the process at his feet. She'd clamped the sergeant in position like a litter.

After she threw a blanket over Burnsey, Ruth returned to the front of the cabin, found her flight jacket, and draped it over her shoulders. She sank to the floor and pulled her knees as close as her broken arm allowed. Every muscle in her body shook in jolting unison, shook out great, soundless sobs. God had spared her, but more importantly, he had been with her in her darkest moment and was with her still, faithful and good and trustworthy.

A moan rose from the tail of the plane. The blanket rippled. Ruth clenched her hand around her shin and prayed her knots would hold.

Burnsey vomited. Buckles clanged. He cussed. "Ruth! Get me out of here."

A laugh burst from her throat. "I'm not stupid, Sergeant."

He fell still. Ruth kept a sharp eye on him. Her shivers kept rhythm with the engine vibrations.

"Come on, Lieutenant," he said in honeyed tones. "You can't leave me like this. I'm cold."

"You have a blanket."

"At least let me clean up this mess."

"Thank you so much for your helpfulness, but I'll manage just fine when we land."

More silence. When they landed at Meeks, Burnsey would be locked up, and everyone would see the truth. Lieutenant Shepard would realize she had been wrong, but could she ever treat Ruth with respect? What about the other nurses? Would they accept her again, or would they avoid her, embarrassed at how they'd acted?

And May? Despite the pain, cold, and trauma, Ruth smiled. How sweet it would be to enjoy the fullness of May's friendship once more.

If only . . .

She frowned. No, it was too late with Jack, too much. Too much what? Too much trust?

Trust me.

Ruth shook her head. Now she was imagining things. It was one thing to trust God, another thing entirely to trust a man.

★ 396 ★

The plane angled downward for the descent to Meeks Field.

"All right, Lieutenant, I'm ready to cut a deal."

"A deal?" Her laugh jarred her arm and made her wince. "You're in no position to cut a deal."

"Listen, I've got it all figured out. You cut me free and we'll get everything cleaned up before we land. I promise I won't touch you. No time for that anyway. I'll talk to Shepard, get her to switch crews. She'll listen to me. You keep your job, I keep my business, and everyone wins."

"And let you get away with fraud and theft and attempted rape? Never. Besides, I'm in no danger of losing my job."

"I'm afraid you are if I tell them about your morals violation."

Ruth gasped. "Mine? You're the one—"

"Really, officer, I don't know what happened. I was minding my own business, having a little drink—I know, but I couldn't sleep. She must have spiked it with something. Next thing I know, I wake up like this—clothes messed up, tied up like a hog. That woman's crazy. She's always had it out for me. Bet you anything she'll say I tried to rape her. Look over there—I saw her knock over the medical chest, waste those meds, just to make it look as if we'd struggled. Her arm? Yeah, that's too bad. She slipped in that mess she made, fell over the chest, right on top of her arm. She said I broke it? I'm not surprised. She's been lying about me for months. Everyone knows she hates me. Ask Lieutenant Shepard."

Ruth's jaw dangled.

Burnsey's eyes glinted down the aisle. "Your word against mine, gorgeous. Who will they believe?"

They would believe him. Of course they would. They always did. And Burnsey had covered every detail. He'd probably say she cut the interphone wires and blocked the door to frame him.

"Here's the deal. Cut me loose, and you keep your job. Remember, you need the money."

She didn't need his reminder. If they believed his charges, she'd be kicked out of the Army Nurse Corps and the nursing profession.

The truth brought enormous shakes throughout her body. God would provide. Even if she lost everything—everything, even if she were imprisoned, God would provide for her family. She had to trust him. She had to tell the truth.

60

Jack always imagined heaven would be blindingly white and gold. Not gray.

He blinked and focused on the gray stripes before his eyes. Soft voices spoke. The book of Revelation said they'd be "of all nations, and kindreds, and people, and tongues."

Nope, only English.

Jack squinted, and a framework of bars emerged from the gray. So cold. Heaven shouldn't be cold. So tired. He groaned, and his eyes flapped shut.

"Jack?"

He hiked up his eyelids and turned to the voice. Gray eyes and black hair. Jesus had gray eyes? But where was the beard? No, it was Ray. Oh swell. How did Ray get killed working at a supply depot?

"Jack?" Ray smiled and rubbed Jack's upper arm. "Hi there. Think you can stay awake?"

"Awake?" he croaked, and broke into a ripping, wet cough.

"Look who woke up just in time for bed."

Jack wiped his mouth. A curly-haired brunette stood over him. At least she wore white, not gray.

"I can't give you anything for that cough, Major," she said

in a chirpy voice. "You need to clear out that seawater, but would you like some more morphine?"

Why would he need morphine in heaven? "But I'm—didn't I?—I didn't die?"

Ray laughed softly. "You came mighty close. You were unconscious when Air-Sea Rescue plucked you out of the water. You had a bad case of hypothermia."

He was alive. The gray stripes—the corrugated ceiling of a Nissen hut. The brunette—a nurse. The framework of bars—Jack followed them to where his right foot hung suspended, wrapped in white.

A heavy weight crushed him, crushed out spasms of briny coughs. Jack had been in the hospital when Walt woke up to find his arm had been amputated, and now Ray was here when Jack woke up to find his foot—

"My foot?"

"Oh, you broke several bones." The nurse had a perky laugh to go with her voice. "You'll be in a cast about six weeks, young man."

Young man? The girl couldn't be older than twenty-one. Jack scanned the hut, like countless others in England, the windows dark already. "What day is it?"

"The seventh," Ray said. "The invasion was a success. We're making progress."

"My crew—did they make it?"

"All safe. Startled a flock of sheep, but they're fine."

"Good." But Jack frowned. Ray was in California, and Jack was in England. Or was he? "Where am I?"

The brunette stuck a thermometer in Jack's mouth and wrapped hot fingers around his wrist. "You're at the 65th General Hospital. We just came to Redgrave Park in Botesdale in Suffolk. You wouldn't believe the quaint little villages we have around here. The nearest town of any size is Bury St. Edmunds, which is about—"

"I been 'ere b'fore," he mumbled around the thermometer. This gal better be the night nurse so he could sleep through her shifts.

"Jack's based at Bury St. Edmunds," Ray said, always the peacemaker.

Then Jack stared hard at his older brother. "What're you doin' 'ere?"

Ray managed to look amused and grim at the same time. "Took you long enough to notice."

"But what—where?"

"The Combat Crew Replacement Center in Bovingdon—training, waiting for assignment to a bomb group."

"Com'at . . ." Jack hitched himself up in bed, winced at the pain in his foot, and spat out the thermometer over the nurse's protest. "But—but you're an instructor. No, you're in that supply job. What happened?"

"I volunteered."

"You what?"

"Major, I need your temperature." The nurse poked the thermometer at his lips.

He set his mouth hard and stared her down. "Later."

She skittered away, chattering like a squirrel that lost an acorn.

Jack searched his brother's solemn, determined face. Ray? Volunteering for combat? What on earth? When they were boys, Ray played with blocks while Jack played with tin soldiers. Ray read books while Jack wrestled Walt into submission. Not that Ray was a sissy—the man played a mean game of baseball, and he'd stood up to more bullies than Jack ever had—he just never got a black eye doing it.

"You volunteered?"

"Yes. I need to be here." Ray had a set to his eyes and chin Jack had never seen before.

"But why? And why now? I thought you and Helen . . ."

The firm set to Ray's eyes collapsed. "Long story. I'll tell you later."

"Women always make for long stories."

Ray gave him a sympathetic frown. "Didn't work out with Ruth?"

"Nope. Category E, damaged beyond repair." He slid down under the heavy blankets, tired and cold, inside and out. "Remember those balsa wood planes Grandpa always put in our Christmas stockings?"

Ray leaned forward on his knees. "Sure do. Never lasted long, did they?"

"Kind of like macaroons." Jack nestled his head into the thin pillow. "Remember? You'd get one or two flights out of them, then crack the horizontal stabilizer, glue it together. Next flight you'd snap the wing in half, glue it together. Chip the nose, more glue. Eventually the glue weighed it down so much it couldn't fly."

Ray murmured.

"That's what it's like with Ruth. Too many crashes, too many cracks, too much glue. Can't fly."

★

Sunday, June 11, 1944

Jack propped the box of stationery against his thighs. This letter was tough enough to write, even tougher with his leg in traction.

He wrote "Dear Dad" and paused. Over two months of procrastination, and he still didn't know how to say he'd dashed his father's dreams.

Jack puffed his cheeks full of air and set pen to paper.

After much thought and prayer, as well as consideration of your feelings, I have decided

to stay in the military. God gave me abilities
as a leader, which I assumed he intended to use
in the ministry, as he has used your abilities.
However, being a pastor requires God's calling
and spiritual gifts, which he has not given me.

   This is not a matter of obedience or
perseverance or maturity, but of God's will, and
he has made it clear he never meant for me to
be a pastor. All my striving, all my work can
never lead to success without God's blessing.
As Psalm 127 says, "Except the Lord build the
house, they labour in vain that build it." This
year I learned the hard way that when I aim for
a goal the Lord never intended me to achieve, it
leads to disaster.

Jack rested his head on the metal headboard. The ministry,
a promotion, Ruth Doherty's heart—all goals he was never
meant to achieve. How much damage had he caused with
his prideful striving?

"Fear not, oh Skipper, for I come to release you from your
cruel bondage."

Charlie. Jack smiled up at his friend.

"Time for a walk." Charlie pushed a wheelchair to the
bedside, while the nurse, Lieutenant Taylor, twittered away
and unfastened straps on his leg.

"Thanks, buddy." When he went to the Pacific, he'd sure
miss Charlie. Ray's arrival complicated his transfer as well.
Not only would he enjoy his brother's company, but Jack
could find Ray a noncombat position. Sending Ray into battle
would be detrimental, not just for Ray but for the Eighth
Air Force.

"There you go, young man. Snug as a bug in a rug." Lieutenant Perky tucked too many blankets over Jack's lap.

He sent a tortured look over her shoulder to Charlie, who turned away with the back of his hand pressed to his mouth. "Fresh air, Charlie. And fast."

"Sure thing." He grasped the handles of the wheelchair and raced off, while the nurse prattled on about safe driving.

"Boy, oh boy, oh boy," Jack said when they got outside. "She's like a happy little chipmunk nibbling away at me all day."

Charlie laughed. "Makes you appreciate . . ."

Jack sighed. "Yeah, it does."

They reached the main road and a dilemma. Redgrave Hall lay to the right, the park and lake straight ahead. Memories drenched every spot. Jack pointed to a grassy ridge. "Let's go up there."

Charlie wheeled him up and sat beside him in the grass. "This place has grown."

"Yeah. The 12th Evac is preparing to go to France. The 65th General is a lot bigger."

Charlie nodded and stared ahead. "Sure you want to go to the Pacific?"

"Positive." He'd told Charlie the balsa wood analogy the other day. Would he have to repeat it?

"Too bad." Charlie plucked a blade of grass and set it between his teeth. "Heard there'll be some changes at Bury."

"I know. Colonel Dougher came by yesterday. He offered me air exec."

"Offered? You—you turned him down?"

Jack looked down into his friend's eyes, as blue as that sky and as big as those clouds. "I told him I'd consider it, but only to be polite."

"But that's what you've always wanted."

"That's why I can't take it."

Charlie's round cheeks twitched. "Listen, I know I've given you a tough time about pride and ambition, but you'd make a great air exec. The best."

"How was your trip to Prestwick?"

Charlie sighed, then sighed again, deeper and heavier. "That's why I came today."

"Hmm? How's May?"

Charlie chewed on the grass between his lips and studied Jack's face. "Concerned."

Jack held his breath. Concerned? Why?

"Ruth's okay, more or less, but they're still sorting out what happened."

"What happened? What do you mean, what happened?"

Charlie plucked more grass. "A few days ago, D-Day, actually, she flew back from Newfoundland with her technician. No witnesses. Her word against his."

Jack gripped the armrests of his wheelchair. If that man laid one finger on her . . .

"Her story." Charlie spoke slowly, as if weighing each word. "She says she discovered Burns was stealing government supplies and selling them. She says he offered her money to keep quiet, and when she refused . . ."

"He what? What, Charlie? Tell me."

"He—she says he attacked her, broke her arm, and then he tried to—to have his way with her."

Kicked Jack in the chest. She couldn't survive that. She couldn't.

"She says she knocked him out with some medicine and tied him up."

"She can't—she can't survive this."

"She's okay, Jack. I saw her. She really is. She's calm, rational, composed."

"On the outside," he whispered. On the outside she was strong. She always was. But on the inside she was dying, shutting everyone out, shutting God out.

"The problem is . . ." Charlie stared at the grass between his knees. "Burns says she framed him, drugged him, set the scene to fit her story."

"Baloney." He whacked the armrest. "They know he's lying, don't they?"

"They're investigating, but it doesn't look good. Burns is well respected at Prestwick, but Ruth . . . ?"

"Only 'cause of him, 'cause of his lies." If only, if only . . .

If only what? What could Jack have done to stop this?

He leaned forward and ran his hands into his hair. Ruth's family took advantage of her, her CO didn't believe her, her partner tried to violate her, and Jack—he showed love by putting his needs above hers.

He gathered his hair in his fists. *Lord, please don't let her down.*

61

Prestwick

Monday, June 19, 1944

Ruth clutched May's arm. "Don't they say orphans always turn out badly?"

"Only those who don't know us."

White-capped MPs flanked Ruth as she walked down the road to Headquarters, and everyone she passed gave her the same look—she'd turned out badly. Who could blame them? She faced serious charges, and rumors flew thicker than the fleets of planes coming into Prestwick.

Everyone believed Burnsey. They believed him as soon as she opened the cargo door at Meeks and he cried for help—Burnsey! They took his testimony first, and then hers sounded ludicrous. Perhaps she was too cool and peaceful, but who was she to fake hysteria and tears?

Ruth stopped and stared at the brick building.

"I'll be right outside waiting for you," May said. "Praying."

"Thank you." Her vision blurred. May was the only person who believed her. Of course, May wished Ruth had confided in her the last few months, but she held no grudges.

"Don't worry, honey. The truth will prevail."

Ruth's chin quivered. The truth might not prevail, but God would. Even if she were discharged or imprisoned, somehow the Lord would take care of her family.

One of the MPs held the door open, and the other led Ruth inside and into an office. Colonel Farley, commanding officer at Prestwick, stood behind his desk, and Ruth snapped him a salute. Beside the desk stood Major Young, CO of the 815th MAETS, and a civilian police officer Ruth hadn't seen before. Why was a civilian present?

"Lieutenant Doherty, this is Captain Murdoch of the Prestwick police."

He bowed his bald head with such a kind, fatherly smile that Ruth's chin trembled again. Why was he there? Maybe because the Lord knew she needed a friendly face.

"At ease." Colonel Farley gestured to a chair. "Please take a seat."

"Thank you, sir." She sat across from the desk and rested her cast on her good arm to relieve the pressure of the sling on her shoulder.

Colonel Farley pointed his eagle gaze at her.

Ruth was not a mouse. She refused to lower her eyes. Her testimony was accurate and complete. She would not playact. She would not plead.

The colonel laid his hands on two stacks of papers on his desk. "I have before me two contradictory sets of charges— the charges preferred against Staff Sgt. William Burns and those preferred against you."

"Yes, sir." Her throat tightened. She'd already seen the charges she faced—assault with intent to do bodily harm, willful damage of military property, and conduct unbecoming an officer.

"Under Article 70 of the Articles of War, I can conduct

a hearing to determine whether to refer these charges for court martial."

Court martial. The words prickled behind Ruth's eyes.

Colonel Farley tapped a pen on the smaller of the two stacks. "One of you is lying."

"Sir, I would never—"

He held up one hand. "I've examined the evidence and depositions. The physical evidence is inconclusive. Signs of a struggle, both sets of fingerprints on the interphone jack, a puncture wound in Sergeant Burns's jugular vein, cuts and bruises consistent with both accounts." A tic formed in his eye. The man was probably more comfortable with theft, insubordination, and drunken brawls.

"We have numerous recorded complaints from you regarding Sergeant Burns, which support either story. However, Lt. Agnes MacKinnon of the 12th Evacuation Hospital and Lt. Vera Benson of the 2nd Evac testified that you registered no complaints and worked well with the men in your wards."

A tiny light of truth, but it warmed her.

Colonel Farley lifted his salt-and-pepper head and looked her in the eye. "Only one set of charges yielded conclusive evidence—the charges against Sergeant Burns for unlawful disposition of military property and for fraud. A comparison of the invoices at La Guardia, with what should be carbon copies here at Prestwick, showed significant discrepancies."

Ruth wrapped her hand around the elbow of her cast. The light grew. At least Burnsey could be convicted of something. And maybe they would take that into consideration in the court-martial. Didn't it call his testimony into question? Didn't it prove he had motive?

Colonel Farley turned to the civilian. "This brings us to Captain Murdoch's investigation."

"Aye, that it does." Captain Murdoch nodded his smooth

head to Ruth. "I want to thank you. Your brave testimony allowed us to solve a case of assault on a lass in town."

Ruth struggled with his brogue. "Assault?"

"Aye." His lips twisted.

No one could say it. No one could say the loathsome word. Ruth understood. It had taken her eight years to even form the word in her head.

"Colonel Farley and I worked together on this investigation, so when he notified me of your case, we brought the victim up to the base. She identified Sergeant Burns as her assailant."

"Another?" Ruth pressed her good arm over her stomach. The poor woman—the pain and humiliation and helplessness she went through.

"Aye, but thanks to you there will be no more." Captain Murdoch smiled at Ruth.

She held her breath. Colonel Farley smiled as well. At her. "Does this—does this mean—"

"We will investigate multiple charges against Staff Sgt. William Burns and will dismiss all charges against you."

"Dismiss? Against me? I'm clear? Thank you." Ruth pressed her hand over her mouth, and wet droplets formed on her eyelashes. "I'm free? I'm really free?"

"Aye, that you are, lass." The brogue came from Colonel Farley this time, and not a bad imitation.

Ruth gave a strange hiccup of a laugh. "Thank you. Oh, thank you." She wouldn't go to prison. She wouldn't lose her job. Bert could be a doctor, Anne could stay under firm but loving hands, and Maggie—oh, Maggie could be anything she wanted to be.

Tonight Ruth would write Aunt Pauline and lay down the law. Ruth would start a college fund, and if her aunt protested, Ruth would look for another home for Maggie—and Maggie's fifty-seven dollars a month.

Oh, but her job. Lieutenant Shepard had taken Burnsey's side. How could Ruth work with someone who didn't trust her?

She turned to her commanding officer. "Major Young, I'd like to request a transfer to another squadron."

The major twisted a pen in his hands. "That won't be necessary. Lieutenant Shepard's being sent back to Bowman."

Ruth's jaw hung slack. Never once had she hoped the chief would be disciplined. Enlightened, yes, but not disciplined. And what shame she would face. If her wounded pride ever surrendered to the truth, she'd see she had failed to protect a nurse in her charge because a charming criminal duped her.

Soon the colonel dismissed Ruth without MP guard. She rushed out of the building to surprise May with a grin and a hug. "It's over. It's over. I'm free."

"Oh my goodness. I knew it. I knew they'd believe you."

Ruth laughed and squeezed her friend. "Not really, but I don't care. They believed the evidence, and I'm free, and Burnsey isn't. That's all that matters."

May pulled back and held Ruth by the shoulders. "This is wonderful news. I'll send Charlie a telegram. He'll be so relieved and so will . . ."

Ruth's grin collapsed. "Charlie told him?"

"Well, yes."

Ruth groaned. "Just what he needs. Doesn't he have enough concerns of his own?" A near drowning? What a terrible thing for Jack to endure. Not only had he almost died, but in the way he feared most.

"Funny. He didn't want you to know about his ordeal either. He didn't want to add to your troubles." One corner of May's mouth elevated somewhere between sympathy and amusement. It settled back down to sympathy. "He's worried about you."

Ruth screwed her eyes shut. She didn't deserve his concern, not after how she'd treated him. "Tell him I'm okay. I am."

"I know. Charlie keeps telling him, but he doesn't believe it."

Ruth fixed her gaze on May. "Make him believe."

"I can't. Charlie can't. He won't believe unless he sees."

"Oh no." She whirled away and aimed for the barracks. "Oh no, no, no. That's the worst thing—"

"It's the best thing for both—"

"Oh no. You don't know."

"I know you still care about him."

Ruth slammed into the wall of truth.

May took her arm. "What's the matter?"

The force of the collision made Ruth's eyes water. "I don't—I don't just care for him. I love him."

May's face turned soft and fuzzy. "Oh, honey, that's wonderful. So, go to him."

"Oh no." Her head wagged from side to side. Go to him? If she went to him, she'd have to do what she should have done months before—offer him her heart and her life. "Oh, May, didn't Charlie say he kept talking about toy planes and glue? He knows it's too late, and so do I."

Furrows divided May's pale forehead. "Still . . . maybe . . ." The furrows deepened. She was giving up, as Jack had already done.

Ruth headed back to the barracks with May. Go to him? Over the last few days, she couldn't shake this prodding. Go to him. Like Ruth in the Bible, she was being called to the threshing floor to present herself to a godly, respected man, to uncover his feet and lay herself down.

Go to him.

Ruth looked west, where dark clouds marred the horizon. *Oh Lord, was that Ruth terrified at the idea? Because I am.*

How could I do that? Jack doesn't love me anymore. I can't imagine what he'd think.

Trust me, trust me, trust me, God kept saying, and she had obeyed so far. But this? *Lord, if only I knew what Jack . . .*

Her sigh joined the wind from the sea. If she knew the results, it wouldn't be trust.

62

65th General Hospital

Saturday, June 24, 1944

Jack gave his lunch tray to the medic, appropriately named Sergeant Sauer, and stared at the clock. Only 1309? He couldn't make it move faster with the dry books Ray had loaned him nor with conversation. Richards to his left slept, and Henderson to his right had his jaws wired.

A letter? No, he'd sent long letters to everyone he knew within the past week, and he couldn't write the letter on his heart. Ruth told him to leave her alone, not to write whenever he got news. But what good news—Burns in jail, and Ruth free and cleared and vindicated.

Jack picked up the *Stars and Stripes*. He'd read it this morning, but maybe he missed an article or two. He flipped through. Nope, he'd read every stinking word.

He gazed out the window, where blue skies taunted him. He would gladly put up with Lieutenant Taylor or Sergeant Sauer or a bittersweet memory of Ruth to feel wind and sun on his face, but both Perky and Sauer were busier than ever with D-Day casualties.

The door swung open. Every man in the ward looked up,

but only Jack smiled. Good old Charlie held the door open for May, and Jack's smile grew. He hadn't seen her for weeks, and she would have news about—

Ruth? His heart stopped as if bogged in one of Ray's books.

Her eyes were wide and dark, her mouth formed a tiny knot, and the sling cut a stark white triangle across her gray blue uniform. The thought of what Burns did to her smacked Jack in the face and started his heart again. Now if he could only close his jaw.

What brought her here? Did Charlie and May trick her with some ruse about looking around Redgrave Park for old time's sake?

"Hi there, Skipper."

Jack maneuvered his mouth into a smile. "Hi, everyone. What a surprise."

One look at Ruth's pale, drawn face told him Charlie had been lying. She was not all right. Far from it. Now Charlie brought her here? What was he thinking? Jack had to keep the visit as short as possible to show respect for Ruth. However, Charlie and May pulled up chairs, and Ruth sat right on the cot.

May looped her arm through Charlie's and leaned forward. "How do you feel?"

Jack shrugged. "Can't wait to get out of traction, out of this cast, out of the hospital. What about you? Got a forty-eight-hour pass from Prestwick?" He looked at May only.

"No." She chuckled and glanced at Ruth, but Jack didn't follow her gaze. "We were called back from Temporary Duty the other day, and were immediately sent on another TDY to Membury over in Berkshire."

"Membury? Say, Charlie, that's good for you."

"Sure is. Still a long train ride, but we can see each other more often."

"Will you fly into Normandy?" Jack asked May.

Her face lit up. "Yes. We'll really get to put our training to use."

May kept talking and Jack kept nodding, but all he noticed was the warmth of Ruth's hip seeping through his blanket to his good leg. Swell. She'd think he was making advances, just what she needed in her present condition. He eased his foot away from her.

Ruth glanced at his leg, then up to him.

Jack cut his gaze back to May. "Sounds great. Bet you can't wait to get started."

"Oh, we can't, but poor Ruth has to wait a few more weeks."

Now he had to give Ruth an acknowledging nod. The directness of her gaze threw him. Her expression held fear, but it held something else, something unfamiliar and undecipherable that flung his heart into a spiral. He whipped back to May. "So—"

"This ward sure brings back memories." May snuggled up to Charlie. "Wouldn't it be fun to see our favorite spots again?"

The perfect opportunity to cut the visit short. Real short. "Yeah, wouldn't you—"

"Lieutenant?" Charlie hailed the nurse. "Could I get a wheelchair for my friend, please?"

Oh boy. As much as he wanted a walk and some company, he didn't want to prolong Ruth's agony. "You don't have to drag me along. I'm kind of tired anyway."

"Exactly." May stood and started to unhook the traction apparatus. "You're tired because you're cooped up all day."

Lieutenant Perky got Jack into his bathrobe, into the wheelchair, and bundled in enough blankets to stay warm in the Arctic. Jack mouthed along when she chirped, "Snug as a bug in a rug."

Charlie wheeled him outside, and Jack's face rose to the sun's warmth. What a shame to ruin a beautiful day with an awkward situation. The ladies fell several paces behind, probably so Ruth could give May a heated piece of her mind. Jack wanted to do the same to Charlie, but his voice would carry.

Yes, his voice would carry. He could use that.

"Nice day for a change." He settled back in the wheelchair as Charlie guided him across the road toward the park. "Won't miss this weather. I'll think of you as I bask in the balmy Pacific. Our troops are on Saipan now, right in range for the B-29s."

Charlie laughed. "Have you forgotten the bugs and humidity? Balmy comes at a price."

"It'll be worth it to be behind the controls of a Superfort—8,800 horsepower, 3,000-mile range, 20,000-pound bomb load, and don't forget the pressurized cabins—no more oxygen masks."

"You're serious about this?"

"Absolutely." Jack raised his voice a notch for Ruth's benefit, to prove he no longer harbored notions of winning her over. "Yesterday I put in my transfer request."

"Hmm." Charlie pushed the chair through the grass and among the trees. "I thought you might change your mind with your brother here."

"Nope. Got that straightened out." The bumps in the grass made him glad his injury was in his foot this time and not his backside. "We got Ray assigned to the 94th, and Dougher promised to find him a noncombat position, much better suited to his abilities."

Charlie came to a stop. "Which way, Ruth?"

"Over there. That big tree by the lake."

Jack turned and stared at her. What was going on?

Charlie pushed Jack to the sturdy oak. May took one of the blankets from his lap, and she and Ruth spread it on the ground. Why would Ruth pick the spot where they'd had their first picnic and many others?

"A picnic?" Jack asked.

"Do you see any food?" Charlie laughed and helped him to stand. Jack leaned on his friend to hop over to the blanket. If they were settling down, this visit would drag on for some time.

When he was seated on the blanket with his back against the tree trunk, the women piled blankets on his lap and tucked them around his outstretched legs. "Comfortable?" May asked.

Jack gave her a stiff smile. "Snug as a bug in a rug." Or a caterpillar encased in a cocoon.

"Wonderful." May turned to Charlie. "Ready for our walk?"

"Yeah, let's go."

Jack gaped at them. Why would they bring him outside only to leave him stranded alone under a tree?

May sent a series of strange expressions over to Ruth, who stood at the edge of the blanket to Jack's right.

"All right then." Ruth's voice sounded high and tinny. "Off you go. We'll see you later."

63

Ruth's stomach contorted so its shape no longer resembled the lake in front of her. Why on earth was she here? This was a disaster. From the moment she'd entered the ward, every look, every word, every action showed Jack wanted nothing to do with her. Even Charlie and May's presence hadn't eased the tension.

Still, she had to trust God and do what she'd come to do. She coiled her fingers around her purse strap and turned to Jack propped against the oak. His expression sent spasms through her stomach. He definitely didn't want to be alone with her.

"You don't have to," he said. "You don't have to stay on my account."

A polite stab, and well deserved. She was the one who told him to go away. "Um, yes, I do. I do have to stay. On your account."

His forehead bunched up.

"Charlie and May said you were worried about me. That's why I'm here," she said to remind herself as much as to explain to Jack. "Well, one of the reasons. So you'd see I'm all right. So you wouldn't worry." She tried to give him an assuring smile.

Concern joined the confusion in his expression.

Ruth groaned and tilted her face to the sky. "I know I don't look all right, but it's not because of Burns. It isn't. I'm just nervous, incredibly nervous, but I really am all right."

"Okay." He didn't sound convinced.

She drew a deep breath and lowered her gaze to Jack. "I *am* all right. Not because of my strength but because of God's. He was with me that day. Last time I pushed him away, but this time I trusted him—not to get me out of the situation, but to get me through. And he did. Even if the worst had happened, the Lord would have seen me through. I know it."

Jack's face relaxed somewhat.

She stepped closer. "I'm not broken, Jack. Not this time. Last time my watch was shattered, and so was I. This time my watch had a few gears knocked loose—it's already been fixed—but it wasn't shattered, and neither was I. In fact, I've never felt more whole. Even if I'd gone to prison, I know the Lord would have kept me under his wings. Do you see? Do you see I'm all right?"

For a long moment, Jack studied her. "Yeah. Yeah, I see."

"Thank goodness. I didn't want you to worry about me, not after what you've been through."

He shrugged and glanced toward the lake. "Ah, that was nothing."

"Nothing?" Her laugh drew back his attention. "Nothing? You faced your worst fear that day."

"So did you."

"Yes, but you chose to. You chose to trust God and face that fear, even though I know you could have landed that plane."

A smile twitched on his lips, and he turned back to the lake. "Most likely. I couldn't take that risk, but I hated to ditch."

It was time, but Ruth's feet balked on every step, and only strength of will bent her knees so she could sit on the blanket beside Jack. Although overpowered by his presence, she forced a smile. "Watching that plane sink probably bothered you as much as facing death."

His face folded into amused crinkles. "She was a swell plane."

Ruth could raise her hand and trace those sweet crinkles and say all those words she needed to say, the words she'd rehearsed that felt foreign but right. So why couldn't she move her hand or her tongue?

"My last B-17," he said. "Next bird will be a B-29 Superfortress."

"In the Pacific." The words tasted foul—she had pushed him away, half a world away.

"If they accept my transfer, but Dougher's sure they will."

She could congratulate him and bid him farewell, and he'd never be the wiser, but no, she had to do this. She had to. "Would you—would you like my opinion?"

A flicker of surprise, and then he shrugged. "Sure."

"I think . . ." She slid her hand inside the sling and rubbed the rough plaster. "I think you should stay. Your brother's here, and Charlie, and—and I think you should take the promotion and the position at Bury. You've earned it and you'd make a good air executive. I think you should. I really think you should."

Now for the hardest part. She was on the threshing floor, and in front of her lay the blanketed feet of the man she loved. Jack deserved this. Even though it was too late, he deserved to know he had won her heart and her trust.

"I think . . ." She forced out a trapped breath. "I think . . ."

Ruth leaned forward, grabbed the edge of the blanket, and pulled it back to reveal one foot in a black sock and the other in a white cast with five bare toes peeking out. There, she did it. In one gesture she told him everything on her heart.

Jack stared at his feet, at Ruth, at his feet again. "You think—my feet are too warm?"

"No." She groaned and tossed the blanket back in place. How on earth could he understand when she hadn't explained?

"Are you okay?"

"I'm fine. I just—I'm on the threshing floor. The Bible and Ruth and Boaz and—and the threshing floor." She blew out a breath and uncovered Jack's feet again.

"Threshing floor?" His face worked through several emotions, none of them good.

Oh no, he thought she'd lost her mind. Ruth moaned and pressed her forehead to check. Maybe she did have a few gears knocked loose.

"What's all this—"

Ruth let out an exasperated cry and pushed herself to standing. "Of all the stupid—of all the speeches I practiced in my head, I picked this one."

She turned to the lake and pounded her fist up and down as if shaking out a rug, as if she could shake out her mind. "Why couldn't I just say it? Say I love you? Oh no, I couldn't do that. That's something a normal person would do. No. It took me months to admit to myself, even longer to admit to you, then I don't even say it. No, I pick some—some obscure biblical reference and give you frostbite." She spun around and flung her hand toward his poor little bare toes.

"Ruth . . . ?" His voice sounded scraggly.

"I know it's too late." She shook her fist by her ear and

squeezed her eyes shut. "Charlie told me—wood and glue, and I know it's too late, and I know I should have told you I wanted to marry you when you still wanted to marry me, and not today, not like this, not when it's too—too—"

"Ruth?"

"I know it's too late." She couldn't bear to see his anger or regret or pity, so she hurried off and scanned the banks of the lake. "I'll—I'll get Charlie and May. They'll help you get back."

"Don't you dare. Don't you dare say you love me and run away."

Ruth smashed her good hand over her ear and picked up her pace. If only she could cover both ears. And where were Charlie and May?

"Don't make me chase you," Jack called. "I will, you know. I'll hobble along on this stupid cast, and Nurse Chipmunk will skitter after me, and I don't want her around right now."

Why? Why would he chase her? Ruth glanced over her shoulder.

He struggled to stand up. "I will chase you. I'll swim that blasted lake if I have to, and you know how I feel about swimming." He took a step.

"Jack, no! You'll fall. You'll crack your cast."

"So, don't make me. Get back over here, would you?" Determination burned in his eyes across the hundred feet between them.

"Why?" What did he have to say, and did she really want to hear it?

"What was it—what did Boaz do? Didn't he spread his garment over her?"

She gave a slow, bewildered nod. Yes, that's what Ruth asked Boaz to do, to accept her.

Jack picked up a blanket. "You're too far away, darling.

Either you come here, or I'll drag this blanket and come after you."

Her lips parted, her mind parted from everything she knew. It was too late. He no longer loved her. Right? "But—but the wood—the glue."

"Boy, was I wrong, and for the second time in a year I am glad to be wrong. Now, would you please, please get over here?"

The blanket dangled from his hand, and Ruth's jaw dangled too. He couldn't. Impossible. She'd shoved him away too hard, too many times, too long ago. This couldn't be happening. This wasn't one of the responses she'd imagined when she'd rehearsed her lines.

"Please, Ruth? These are things I should whisper in your ear, not shout across a park, but I'll shout if I have to." Then he laughed—a deep, surprised, joyful sound. "I love you! Do you hear me, Ruth Doherty? I still love you. I never stopped loving you, and I never will."

She stared at the man with the striped pajamas and the blue bathrobe knotted around his waist and the smile overflowing with wonder. Oh goodness, he was telling the truth. He still loved her. Now what was she going to do?

"All right, but you forced me to do this." He shifted his weight onto his cast.

"No!" She ran toward him. "If you split your cast, you'll never get out of here."

"Don't want that now, do we?" He leaned back against the tree and opened his arms to welcome and protect her, while he beamed his love and acceptance.

Ruth inhaled sharply and stopped two feet short, struck by his nearness and power. Could she do this? Did she want to?

"Do I have to create another medical emergency to get you into my arms?" He smiled that great smile, the one that always made her forget her reservations.

What good were those stupid reservations anyway? She could do this, she should do this, and oh, she wanted to do this. "You did say I like my men helpless—horizontal, bandaged, and sedated."

Jack chuckled. "I'll see what I can do to accommodate you."

Ruth raised a shaky hand and rolled her fingers around the collar of his bathrobe. "Please don't. I trust you, and I prefer you vertical and healthy and—and dressed."

He wrapped his hand around hers. "I sure missed you."

"I missed you too, so much." She hadn't stood this close to him for months, felt his warmth and seen the bright lines in the blue of his eyes. She could have if she'd let herself trust. "Oh, Jack, I'm so sorry."

"Oh no. No, you don't." He gathered her in his arms and laughed over her shoulder. "I know—you're sorry, I'm sorry. You forgive me, I forgive you. The explanations can wait. We can do that later, but not now. I want to enjoy this."

She smiled and relaxed into his warm, sheltering embrace to enjoy the moment, the man she loved, the man who loved her.

"Did you mean it?" Jack's voice became throaty and hesitant. He pulled back and looked at her with his eyes full, as vulnerable as the night after Charlie disappeared. "Did you mean it? About loving me and wanting to—to marry me? 'Cause you don't have to. I won't push—"

"Ssh." Ruth pressed her fingers over his lips, his soft lips. She could, but not yet. First she wanted to give him her heart and her hand. "I do love you. I have for a long time. And yes, I do—I do want to marry you."

His mouth twisted, and he blinked too many times. "Oh, darling, I can't believe it. I can't. I don't deserve this."

"No, I'm the one—"

"Don't say it. Don't even think it. Not about the woman I love." Jack's gaze caressed her, gentle and yet fiercely protective.

"Oh my." Ruth swayed forward against his chest and tilted her face into the warmth of his breath, of his love.

He lifted the blanket up around her shoulders. "This might have been good enough for Boaz, but it's not much of an engagement ring." He glanced down to the cast sandwiched between them. "Guess you can't wear a ring yet anyway."

Never had a scratchy brown Army blanket felt so soft and warm and wonderful. "I don't need a ring. This is—"

"Yes, you need a ring. Don't argue." Then mischief spread all over his face. "Here, give me your cast."

"What?"

He motioned with his fingers. "Come on. Out of the sling."

Ruth frowned but slid her arm out. "You sure are bossy."

"You don't give me a choice sometimes, my fiery friend." Jack pulled a pen from the breast pocket of his pajamas and tucked her cast under his arm with his back to her.

"What are you writing?" She tried to look around the wall of his broad shoulders.

"Uh-uh. No peeking. Hold your horses." The pen scratched on the surface of the cast. If only it could scratch the itching under the cast.

Jack released her arm. "Here you go."

Over her ring finger, Jack had drawn a ring with sparkle lines radiating out. Below, in his loose, confident script, he had written, "Engagement ring on requisition, by the order of Maj. Jack Novak."

Ruth looked up into the eyes of her major, her darling major.

He took her in his arms again, under his imperfect but capable wings, and leaned his forehead against hers. "I love you so much."

Her throat tightened at the joy and tenderness mingled on his face. Such joy over a woman he thought he would never kiss. If she left it on his terms, he'd be content and she'd be unthreatened, but she had to, she wanted to press on, to show her trust in God by trusting Jack, by giving this dear man the love he deserved, not just the love he was willing to settle for.

Ruth ran her fingers into his hair, the soft waves she hoped their children would have. "I love you too."

Then she gave him the last bit of herself that she had withheld, and the giving was easier and sweeter and more thrilling than she thought possible.

64

A second passed before Jack realized Ruth was kissing him, then another second while he enjoyed it, and then the third second it hit him hard.

He broke away and clutched her to his chest. "What are you—what are you doing? Darling, you don't have to—"

"Oh, but it was wonderful." Her voice purred into his neck.

What on earth? He grasped her shoulders. The look on her face jolted him. Her eyes formed dreamy half-moons, and her lips curved in a way he'd never seen before, without guarding or distance or fear.

"Did you notice?" she said. "I didn't flinch. Oh, I knew I wouldn't."

Jack shook his head and shook it hard. "That wasn't part of the deal, remember? I promised. And I meant it this time. I don't need that, don't even want it."

Somehow she got closer and trailed her hand over his shoulder. "I know. That's one of the reasons I love you. But I want a normal marriage. I want to have children, yours and mine."

"No. Absolutely not." He held her shoulders tight and leveled his gaze at her. "I would never—never ask you to do that. Never. I want you to be happy and protected and loved. That's my goal for the rest of my life."

"But, Jack—"

"No, Lieutenant. I won't pull rank on you often, but on this I will. No negotiating."

"But didn't you notice? I didn't flinch. I liked it. Oh goodness, I liked it. Do you understand?"

His mind turned slowly at first, a propeller building up speed until it spun into a blur. If she didn't flinch, that meant . . . "But—but . . ."

"I saw your face, darling. Only yours. I knew I would." She leaned in, and those smiling, inviting lips threatened to steal his resolve.

"No, you don't." Jack pressed back against the tree until the bark scratched the back of his head. "Keep those lips away from me."

Ruth laughed. "I said the same thing the night you proposed." She nuzzled her warm face into his neck and pressed a kiss under his jaw.

"Oh, wow." His eyes slid shut. If she kept this up, he'd never be able to keep his promise. He rolled around the tree trunk and stepped to the side.

He couldn't get the cast underneath him. Jack cried out, landed on his rear end, and flopped onto his back. Ruth tumbled down beside him. "Ruth! Are you okay?"

She laid her head on his chest and she laughed and laughed and laughed.

Jack rested in the cool grass, gazed up through the branches to the blue sky, and joined in her laughter. All those months trying to kiss her, and now he was the one running away.

"Oh, Jack. My dear, sweet Jack." She lifted herself so her face hovered over his, and her hair swung down and swept his cheeks.

He brushed grass from her chin. She loved him. He saw it in every curve of her face, and Jack loved her too, so much it twisted things up inside him. He needed to protect her and never let anything or anyone hurt her, especially him. He caressed her smooth cheek. "Darling, I don't want to hurt you."

"You won't." She ran her hand into his hair. "Besides, I'd tell you if anything bothered me."

He chuckled. "Yeah, you would. Anything and everything."

Ruth smiled and nodded, which made her hair stroke his cheek in a tantalizing way.

He couldn't resist her. Why was he resisting anyway? This was her idea, not his. Jack traced the contours of her lips. "You'd take advantage of a turtle trapped on his back, wouldn't you?"

"I'm planning on it."

"Let's sit up."

She looked surprised but pushed back onto her knees.

Jack sat up and scooted over to rest against the tree. He wanted this to be respectful, not the least bit cheap or tawdry. "Come here, my little macaroon."

Ruth came to him, into his arms, with her intoxicating mix of fire and virtue.

"Are you sure?" he asked.

"Absolutely sure, my big baboon."

Oh boy, did he love this woman. He cupped her face in his hand and searched for hesitation or fear or shame but found none. Instead her eyes glowed. Even though the runway looked clear, he made a slow approach and a cautious landing. A sweet, sweet landing. Then he pulled up. He had to stop and gauge her reaction, although every part of him cried out for more of her sweetness.

Her eyelids fluttered open. "Oh darling, see? I didn't flinch."

Jack mumbled something, too bowled over to speak.

This time Ruth didn't push him away. She tipped her face to him, and he molded his mouth around hers, a perfect fit, and he buried his hand in that gorgeous hair. He kept his eyes open to watch her, but she didn't crumble. She melted.

So did Jack.

"I'm getting vertigo," he murmured against her lips.

"Me too," she said with a light laugh. "I like vertigo. Vertigo's fun."

He leaned his forehead against hers. "Too much of this, and they won't put either of us back on flying duty."

Something flattened her smile—something like bravery. Of course, the transfer, his stupid transfer.

Jack adjusted his arms around his—yes, his fiancée. "You know, I made a mistake on that inscription on your cast. It should read Lieutenant Colonel, not Major."

Her gaze darted back and forth between his eyes.

He kissed the tip of her nose. "I think you're right. I think, I think, I think I should stay."

"But—"

"The problem with the Pacific . . ." He lifted one hand and spread his fingers wide. "Bugs as big as this, and the mosquitoes suck you dry. Then you have to take Atabrine to prevent malaria, turns your skin yellow."

"You don't have to stay for—"

"Never liked yellow much. Red—that's what I like." Jack fingered a strand of Ruth's hair and winked at her. "Besides, I want to stay so I can spoon with my girl."

"Jack Novak!"

He grinned, warmed and kindled by the flame in her eyes. God had softened her up, but he hadn't quenched that fire.

Ruth clutched his arm and dissolved into a laugh. "Oh, darling, it's June. It's still June."

"The moon's not out, but you're awfully loony."

She smiled, open and trusting and loony through and through. "People in love get like that, don't they?"

"They sure do." Jack gazed into those beautiful blue eyes, the pupils ringed by gold. Ruth had given him the ring of gold around her heart, and, Lord willing, someday soon he'd put a ring of gold around her finger. "Ain't it swell?"

Acknowledgments

Writing an acknowledgments page can be more difficult than writing a novel. I am indebted to many people who have taught me, encouraged me, and prayed for me, and I'd hate to forget a single name.

Thanks must go first to my Lord, who forgave my sins and taught me to shove off shame. It's only by his hand that this story ever came to be.

Thanks also to my husband, Dave, and our children, Stephen, Anna, and Matthew, for enduring the craziness of having a writer in the house. My parents, Ronald and Nancy Stewart, and my sister, Martha Groeber, have been a source of loving support and careful editing. Mom and Martha, you are not responsible for any missing commas.

Thanks also to the faculty at the Mount Hermon Christian Writers Conference, the members of American Christian Fiction Writers, and most of all, Diablo Valley Christian Writers Group—Kathleen Casey, Ron Clelland, Carol Green, Cynthia Herrmann, Susan Lawson, Marilynn Lindahl, Debbie Maselli, Georgia Sue Massie, Paula Nunley, Evelyn Sanders, and Linda Wright. And deepest thanks to my critique partners, Marcy Weydemuller and Marci Seither. See? No prologue!

Writing is a bizarre, solitary profession, and I couldn't do it without the prayerful support of my church, my small group, and my book club. Thanks also to my friends who read this story in a massive three-ring binder when I'd given up hope of publication—Andrea Balderrama, Joy Benson, Twilla Bordley, MaryAnn Buchanan, Jill Combs, Tami Fanucchi, Laquetta Franz, Cindi and Sonja Grovhoug, Rosanna Hunter, Laura Juranek, Sue Lautz, Sue Matt, Don and Nancy McDaniels, Janice Moore, Lisa Prevost, Laurie Ratterree, Karen Spangler, Susan Stuteville, Linda Templeton, and Sandy Wall. And thanks to Suzanne Russo for printing a portable version for my poor readers.

I owe special thanks to the staff at the Antioch Public Library for their enthusiastic help with obscure research questions, and to Rick Acker and Nicklas Akers for guiding me through the baffling world of military law. And my story would have been flat without the opportunity to walk through the restored B-17s of the Collings Foundation and the Experimental Aircraft Association.

Still more blessings! My agent, Rachel Zurakowski at Books & Such Literary Agency, keeps me grounded with her calm and wise spirit, and my editor, Vicki Crumpton, not only took a chance on me but pushes me as a writer. Plus they laugh at my jokes. Many thanks to the entire team at Revell, from editing to marketing to cover art to sales. I tell everyone I know, "Revell rocks!"

And I'm so thankful for you, dear reader. I hope you enjoyed Ruth and Jack's story, and I pray your trust in the Lord will continue to grow. Please visit me at www.sarahsundin. com to send me a message or sign up for my quarterly newsletter. You'll also find a diagram of a B-17, historical information, and tips on starting a book club. I'd be thrilled to hear from you!

Discussion Questions

1. Deep inside, most women wish they were beautiful. How is Ruth's beauty a blessing and how is it a curse?
2. Jack is a natural leader. Is his desire for a promotion good or bad? How does his ambition change throughout the story? How are Jack Novak and Jeff Babcock alike and different?
3. The Eighth Air Force took heavy losses before long-range fighter escort was available. On Aug. 17, 1943, they lost 60 of 376 bombers, and on "Black Thursday," October 14, 1943, they lost 60 of 320 over Schweinfurt, with ten men on each plane. How did those young men deal with such staggering losses? How do you think Americans of today would deal with the same circumstances?
4. Although Jack has no desire to be a pastor, he pushes for that goal. Why do you think he does so? Have you ever tried to fill a role you weren't cut out for?
5. Ruth feels a great responsibility for her family. What circumstances in her life factor into this? How does Aunt

Pauline manage to manipulate Ruth? What does Ruth have to learn before she can stand up to her aunt?

6. Five hundred women served as flight nurses during World War II, and seventeen were killed in action. Considering the role of women at the time, flight nurses were pioneers in many ways. What ways do you see?

7. Ruth encounters behavior that would lead to sexual harassment lawsuits nowadays. How does she deal with this? Does it work? How does Burnsey get away with it?

8. Are Jack's plans to romance Ruth clever, loving, manipulative, selfish? Is his proposal any different than his earlier plans?

9. Why do you think Jack reacts the way he does when he discovers Ruth's secret? Why does May react so differently? What was your gut reaction to Ruth's secret?

10. At the beginning of the story, Ruth says she doesn't need friends. Is she telling the truth? Why does she reject female friends? Ruth also deals with cattiness and gossip among her fellow nurses. Why do you think female relationships, which can be so close and supportive, can veer in the opposite direction?

11. What is it about May Jensen that gets through Ruth's defenses? How does their friendship change over the year?

12. At the beginning of the story, Jack and Charlie are content in their roles as hero and sidekick. What changes in their lives cause friction? How does their friendship change?

13. Ruth doesn't trust God because of the bad things that have happened to her. Have you ever felt like that? Do you tend to pray for God to take you out of "the val-

ley of the shadow of death," or to be with you in the valley? How does Ruth learn to trust God?

14. Jack sees Ruth as wearing a "cloak of shame." How does shame weigh Ruth down? How does she learn to throw off her shame, and how does this change her life? Have you ever felt the burden of shame? Have you thrown it off?

15. Charlie tells Jack, "You're too good . . . You've never let yourself down, and you trust in yourself." How do you see this in Jack's life? How does Jack learn to trust God?

16. Jack comes to see pride as his root problem. How is this manifested in Jack's life? Do you struggle with pride? In general, what role does pride play in sin?

17. Ruth identifies with her biblical namesake. What parallels do you see? Is there a Bible character you identify with?

18. Jack's fear of drowning leads to a tragic decision. Have fears ever gotten in your way or affected your judgment?

19. Discuss the symbolism of the wristwatch to Ruth—the one she lost, the scar, and the one Jack gives her. What lessons does God teach her through this?

20. If you read A Distant Melody, did you enjoy the update on Walt and Allie? The third book focuses on Jack's brother Ray and Helen Carlisle, a widowed mother. From what you've seen of these characters, what might you expect?

Sarah Sundin is the author of *A Distant Melody*. She lives in northern California with her husband, three children, a cat, and a yellow lab prone to eating pens and manuscripts. She works on-call as a hospital pharmacist and teaches Sunday school and women's Bible studies. Her great-uncle flew with the U.S. Eighth Air Force in England. Please visit her online at www.sarahsundin.com, www.facebook.com/SarahSundin Author, or www.twitter.com/sarahsundin.

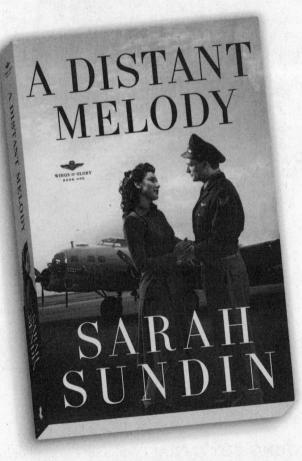

"Make sure you have a tissue nearby, because you are going to need it!"
—TERRI BLACKSTOCK, bestselling author

A YOUNG BOY'S PRAYERS, a shoebox full of love letters, and an old wooden soldier make a memory that will not be forgotten. Can a gift from the past mend a broken heart?

Revell
a division of Baker Publishing Group
www.RevellBooks.com

Available Wherever Books Are Sold